6/2011
ACPL, Laramie, WY   01/2017
39092079234193
Dekker, Ted,
Black
The circle ;bk. 1
Pieces: 1

WITHDRAWN

P9-DVV-640

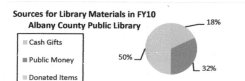

Sources for Library Materials in FY10
Albany County Public Library

- Cash Gifts
- Public Money
- Donated Items

18%
50%
32%

BLACK

Also by Ted Dekker
in Large Print:

Thunder of Heaven

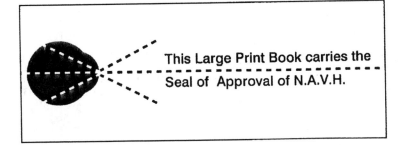

This Large Print Book carries the
Seal of Approval of N.A.V.H.

BLACK

TED DEKkER

Albany County
Public Library
Laramie, Wyoming

Thorndike Press • Waterville, Maine

Copyright © 2004 Ted Dekker.
The Circle: Book One: The Birth of Evil #1.

All rights reserved.

Published in 2005 by arrangement with Thomas Nelson, Inc.

Thorndike Press® Large Print Christian Fiction.

The tree indicium is a trademark of Thorndike Press.

The text of this Large Print edition is unabridged.
Other aspects of the book may vary from the original edition.

Set in 16 pt. Plantin by Minnie B. Raven.

Printed in the United States on permanent paper.

Library of Congress Cataloging-in-Publication Data

Dekker, Ted, 1962–
    Black / by Ted Dekker. — Large print ed.
      p. cm. — (The circle ; bk. 1) (Thorndike Press
large print Christian fiction)
    Originally published: WestBow/T. Nelson, 2004.
    ISBN 0-7862-8135-9 (lg. print : hc : alk. paper)
    1. Title.   II. Thorndike Press large print
Christian fiction series.
PS3554.E43B57 2005
  813′.6—dc22   2005022108

For my children.
May they always remember what
lies behind the veil.

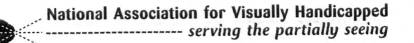

As the Founder/CEO of NAVH, the only national health agency solely devoted to those who, although not totally blind, have an eye disease which could lead to serious visual impairment, I am pleased to recognize Thorndike Press* as one of the leading publishers in the large print field.

Founded in 1954 in San Francisco to prepare large print textbooks for partially seeing children, NAVH became the pioneer and standard setting agency in the preparation of large type.

Today, those publishers who meet our standards carry the prestigious "Seal of Approval" indicating high quality large print. We are delighted that Thorndike Press is one of the publishers whose titles meet these standards. We are also pleased to recognize the significant contribution Thorndike Press is making in this important and growing field.

Lorraine H. Marchi, L.H.D.
Founder/CEO
NAVH

* Thorndike Press encompasses the following imprints: Thorndike, Wheeler, Walker and Large Print Press

Switzerland

Carlos Missirian was his name. One of his many names.

Born in Cyprus.

The man who sat at the opposite end of the long dining table, slowly cutting into a thick red steak, was Valborg Svensson. One of his many, many names.

Born in hell.

They ate in near-perfect silence thirty feet from each other in a dark hall hewn from granite deep in the Swiss Alps. Black iron lamps along the walls cast a dim amber light through the room. No servants, no other furniture, no music, no one except Carlos Missirian and Valborg Svensson seated at the exquisite dining table.

Carlos sliced the thick slab of beef with a razor-sharp blade and watched the flesh separate. *Like the parting of the Red Sea.* He cut again, aware that the only sound in this room was of two serrated knives cutting through meat into china, severing fibers. Strange sounds if you knew what to listen for.

Carlos placed a slice in his mouth and bit firmly. He didn't look up at Svensson, although the man was undoubtedly staring at him, at his face — at the long scar on his right cheek — with those dead black eyes of his. Carlos breathed deep, taking time to enjoy the coppery taste of the fillet.

Very few men had ever unnerved Carlos. The Israelis had taken care of that early in his life. Hate, not fear, ruled him, a disposition he found useful as a killer. But Svensson could unnerve a rock with a glance. To say that this beast put fear in Carlos would be an overstatement, but he certainly kept Carlos awake. Not because Svensson presented any physical threat to him; no man really did. In fact, Carlos could, at this very moment, send the steak knife in his hands into the man's eye with a quick flip of his wrist. Then what prompted his caution? Carlos wasn't sure.

The man wasn't really a beast from hell, of course. He was a Swiss-born businessman who owned half the banks in Switzerland and half the pharmaceutical companies outside the United States. True, he had spent more than half his life here, below the Swiss Alps, stalking around like a caged animal, but he was as human as any other man who walked on two legs. And, at least to Carlos, as vulnerable.

Carlos washed the meat down with a sip

of dry Chardonnay and let his eyes rest on Svensson for the first time since sitting to eat. The man ignored him, as he almost always did. His face was badly pitted, and his nose looked too large for his head — not fat and bulbous, but sharp and narrow. His hair, like his eyes, was black, dyed.

Svensson stopped cutting midslice, but he did not look up. The room fell silent. Like statues, they both sat still. Carlos watched him, unwilling to break off his stare. The one mitigating factor in this uncommon relationship was the fact that Svensson also respected Carlos.

Svensson suddenly set down his knife and fork, dabbed at his mustache and lips with a serviette, stood, and walked toward the door. He moved slowly, like a sloth, favoring his right leg. Dragging it. He'd never offered an explanation for the leg. Svensson left the room without casting a single glance Carlos's way.

Carlos waited a full minute in silence, knowing it would take Svensson all of that to walk down the hall. Finally he stood and followed, exiting into a long hall that led to the library, where he assumed Svensson had retired.

He'd met the Swiss three years ago while working with underground Russian factions determined to equalize the world's military powers through the threat of biological weapons. It was an old doctrine: What did it matter if the United States had two hundred thousand nuclear weapons trained on the rest of the world if their enemies had the right biological weapons? A highly infectious airborne virus on the wind was virtually indefensible in open cities.

One weapon to bring the world to its knees.

Carlos paused at the library door, then pushed it open. Svensson stood by the glass wall overlooking the white laboratory one floor below. He'd lit a cigar and was engulfed in a cloud of hazy smoke.

Carlos walked past a wall filled with leather-bound books, lifted a decanter of Scotch, poured himself a drink, and sat on a tall stool. The threat of biological weapons could easily equal the threat of nuclear weapons. They could be easier to use, could be far more devastating. *Could.* In traditional contempt of any treaty, the U.S.S.R. had employed thousands of scientists to develop biological weapons, even after signing the Biological and Toxin Weapons Convention in 1972. All supposedly for defense purposes, of course. Both Svensson and Carlos were intimately familiar with the successes and failures of former Soviet research. In the final analysis, the so-called "superbugs" they had developed weren't super enough, not even close. They were far too messy, too unpredictable, and too easy to neutralize.

Svensson's objective was simple: to develop a highly virulent and stable airborne virus with a three- to six-week incubation period that responded immediately to an antivirus he alone controlled. The point wasn't to kill off whole populations of people. The point was to infect whole regions of the earth within a few short weeks and then control the only treatment.

This was how Svensson planned to wield unthinkable power without the help of a single soldier. This was how Carlos Missirian would rid the world of Israel without firing a single shot. Assuming, of course, such a virus could be developed and then secured.

But then, all scientists knew it was only a matter of time.

Svensson stared at the lab below. The Swiss wore his hair parted down the middle so that black locks flopped either way. In his black jacket he looked like a bat. He was a man married to a dark religious code that required long trips in the deepest of nights. Carlos was certain his god dressed in a black cloak and fed on misery, and at times he questioned his own allegiance to Svensson. The man was driven by an insatiable thirst for power, and the men he worked for even more so.

11

This was their food. Their drug. Carlos didn't care to understand the depths of their madness; he only knew they were the kind of people who would get what they wanted, and in the process he would get what he wanted: the restoration of Islam.

He took a sip of the Scotch. *You would think that one, just one, of the thousands of scientists working in the defensive bio-technological sector would have stumbled onto something meaningful after all these years.* They had over three hundred paid informants in every major pharmaceutical company. Carlos had interviewed fifty-seven scientists from the former Soviet bioweapons program, quite persuasively. And in the end, nothing. At least nothing they were looking for.

The telephone on a large black sandal-wood desk to their right rang shrilly.

Neither made a move for the phone. It stopped ringing.

"We need you in Bangkok," Svensson said. His voice sounded like the rumble of an engine churning against a cylinder full of gravel.

"Bangkok."

"Yes, Bangkok. Raison Pharmaceutical."

"The Raison Vaccine?" Carlos said. They had been following the development of the vaccine for over a year with the help of an informant in the Raison labs. He'd

12

always thought it would be ironic if the French company Raison — pronounced ray-ZONE, meaning "reason" — might one day produce a virus that would bring the world to its knees.

"I wasn't aware their vaccine held any promise for us," he said.

Svensson limped slowly, so slowly, to his desk, picked up a piece of white paper and scanned it. "You do remember a report three months ago about unsustainable mutations of the vaccine."

"Our contact said the mutations were unsustainable and died out in minutes." Carlos wasn't a scientist, but he knew more than the average man about bioweapons, naturally.

"Those were the conclusions of Monique de Raison. Now we have another report. Our man at the CDC received a nervous visitor today who claimed that the mutations of the Raison Vaccine held together under prolonged, specific heat. The result, the visitor claimed, would be a lethal airborne virus with an incubation of three weeks. One that could infect the entire world's population in less than three weeks."

"And how did this visitor happen to come across this information?"

Svensson hesitated.

"A dream," he said. "A very unusual

dream. A very, very convincing dream of another world populated by people who think his dreams of this world are only dreams. And by bats who talk."

Now it was Carlos's turn to hesitate.

"Bats."

"We have our reasons for paying attention. I want you to fly to Bangkok and interview Monique de Raison. If the situation warrants, I will want the Raison Vaccine itself, by whatever means."

"Now we're resorting to mystics?"

Svensson had covered the CDC well, with four on the payroll, if Carlos remembered correctly. Even the most innocuous-sounding reports of infectious diseases quickly made their way to the headquarters in Atlanta. Svensson was understandably interested in any report of any new outbreak and the plans to deal with it.

But a dream? Thoroughly out of character for the stoic, black-hearted Swiss. This alone gave the suggestion its only credence.

Svensson glared at him with dark eyes. "As I said, we have other reasons to believe this man may know things he has no business knowing, regardless of how he attained that information."

"Such as?"

"It's beyond you. Suffice it to say there is no way Thomas Hunter could have

14

known that the Raison Vaccine was subject to unsustainable mutations."

Carlos frowned. "A coincidence."

"I'm not willing to take that chance. The fate of the world rests on one elusive virus and its cure. We may have just found that virus."

"I'm not sure Monique de Raison will offer an . . . interview."

"Then take her by force."

"And what about Hunter?"

"You will learn by whatever means necessary everything Thomas Hunter knows, and then you will kill him."

1

It all started one day earlier with a single silenced bullet out of nowhere.

Thomas Hunter was walking down the same dimly lit alley he always took on his way home after locking up the small Java Hut on Colfax and Ninth, when a *smack!* punctuated the hum of distant traffic. Red brick dribbled from a one-inch hole two feet away from his face. He stopped mid-stride.

Smack!

This time he saw the bullet plow into the brick. This time he felt a sting on his cheek as tiny bits of shattered brick burst from the impact. This time every muscle in his body ceased.

Someone had just shot at him!

Was shooting at him.

Tom recoiled to a crouch and instinctively spread his arms. He couldn't seem to tear his eyes off those two holes in the brick, dead ahead. They had to be some mistake. Figments of his overactive imagination. His aspirations to write novels had finally ruptured the line between fantasy and reality with these two empty eye sockets staring at him from the red brick.

"Thomas Hunter!"

That wasn't his imagination, was it? No, that was his name, and it was echoing down the alley. A third bullet crashed into the brick wall.

He bolted to his left, still crouching. One long step, drop the right shoulder, roll. Again the air split above his head. This bullet clanged into a steel ladder and rang down the alley.

Tom came to his feet and chased the sound in a full sprint, pushed by instinct as much as by terror. He'd been here before, in the back alleys of Manila. He'd been a teenager then, and the Filipino gangs were armed with knives and machetes rather than guns, but at the moment, tearing down the alley behind Ninth and Colfax, Tom's mind wasn't drawing any distinction.

"You're a dead man!" the voice yelled.

Now he knew who they were. They were from New York.

This alley led to another thirty yards ahead, on his left. A mere shadow in the dim light, but he knew the cutaway.

Two more bullets whipped by, one so close he could feel its wind on his left ear. Feet pounded the concrete behind him.

Two, maybe three pairs.

Tom dived into the shadow.

"Cut him off in the back. Radio."

Tom rolled to the balls of his feet then sprinted, mind spinning.

Radio?

The problem with adrenaline, Makatsu's thin voice whispered, *is that it makes your head weak.* His karate instructor would point to his head and wink. *You have plenty of muscle to fight, but no muscle to think.*

If they had radios and could cut off the street ahead, he would have a very serious problem.

He looked frantically for cover. One access to the roof halfway down the alley. One large garbage bin too far away. Scattered boxes to his left. No real cover. He had to make his move before they entered the alley.

Fingers of panic stabbed into his mind. *Adrenaline dulls reason; panic kills it.* Makatsu again. Tom had once been beaten to a pulp by a gang of Filipinos who'd taken a pledge to kill any Americano brat who entered their turf. They made the streets around the army base their turf. His instructor had scolded him, insisting that he was good enough to have escaped their attack that afternoon. His panic had cost him dearly. His brain had been turned to

18

rice pudding, and he deserved the bruises that swelled his eyes shut.

This time it was bullets, not feet and clubs, and bullets would leave more than bruises. Time was out.

Short on ideas and long on desperation, Tom dived for the gutter. Rough concrete tore at his skin. He rolled quickly to his left, bumped into the brick wall, and lay facedown in the deep shadow.

Feet pounded around the corner and ran straight toward him. One man. How they had found him in Denver, four years after the fact, he had no clue. But if they'd gone to this trouble, they wouldn't just walk away.

The man ran on light feet, hardly winded. Tom's nose was buried in the musty corner. Noisy blasts of air from his nostrils buffeted his face. He clamped down on his breathing; immediately his lungs began to burn.

The slapping feet approached, ran past. Stopped.

A slight tremor lit through his bones. He fought another round of panic. It had been six years since his last fight. He didn't stand a chance against a man with a gun. He desperately willed the feet to move on. *Walk. Just walk!*

But the feet didn't walk.

They scraped quietly.

Tom nearly cried out in his hopelessness. He had to move now, while he still had the advantage of surprise.

He threw himself to his left, rolled once to gain momentum. Then twice, rising first to his knees then to his feet. His attacker was facing him, gun extended, frozen.

Tom's momentum carried him laterally, directly toward the opposite wall. The gun's muzzle-flash momentarily lit the dark alley and spit a bullet past him. But now instinct had replaced panic.

What shoes am I wearing?

The question flashed through Tom's mind as he hurdled for the brick wall, left foot leading. A critical question.

His answer came when his foot planted on the wall. Rubber soles. One more step up the wall with traction to spare. He threw his head back, arched hard, pushed himself off the brick, then twisted to his right halfway through his rotation. The move was simply an inverted bicycle kick, but he hadn't executed it in half a dozen years, and this time his eyes weren't on a soccer ball tossed up by one of his Filipino friends in Manila.

This time it was a gun.

The man managed one shot before Tom's left foot smashed into his hand, sending the pistol clattering down the alley. The bullet tugged at his collar.

Tom didn't land lightly on his feet as he'd hoped. He sprawled to his hands, rolled once, and sprang into the seventh fighting position opposite a well-muscled man with short-cropped black hair. Not exactly a perfectly executed maneuver. Not terrible for someone who hadn't fought in six years.

The man's eyes were round with shock. His experience in the martial arts obviously didn't extend beyond *The Matrix*. Tom was briefly tempted to shout for joy, but, if anything, he had to shut this man up before *he* could call out.

The man's astonishment suddenly changed to a snarl, and Tom saw the knife in his right hand. Okay, so maybe the man knew more about street-fighting than was at first apparent.

He charged Tom.

The fury that flooded Tom's veins felt all too welcome. How dare this man shoot at him! How dare he not fall to his knees after such a brilliant kick!

Tom ducked the knife's first swipe. Came up with his palm to the man's chin. Bone cracked.

It wasn't enough. This man was twice his weight, with twice his muscle, and ten times his bad blood.

Tom launched himself vertically and spun into a full roundhouse kick, screaming despite his better judgment. His foot had to be doing a good eighty miles an hour when it struck the man's jaw.

They both hit the concrete at precisely the same time — Tom on his feet, ready to deliver another blow; his assailant on his back, breathing hard, ready for the grave. Figuratively speaking.

The man's silver pistol lay near the wall. Tom took a step for it, then rejected the notion. What was he going to do? Shoot back? Kill the guy? Incriminate himself? Not smart. He turned and ran back in the direction they'd come.

The main alley was empty. He ducked into it, edged along the wall, grabbed the rails to a steel fire escape, and quickly ascended. The building's roof was flat and shouldered another taller building to the south. He swung up to the second building, ran in a crouch, and halted by a large vent, nearly a full block from the alley where he'd laid out the New Yorker.

He dropped to his knees, pressed back into the shadows, and listened past the thumping of his heart.

The hum of a million tires rolling over asphalt. The distant roar of a jet overhead. The faint sound of idle talk. The sizzling of food frying in a pan, or of water being poured from a window. The former, considering they were in Denver, not the Philippines. No sounds from New York.

He leaned back and closed his eyes, catching his breath.

Crazy! Fights in Manila as a teenager were one thing, but here in the States at the ripe age of twenty-five? The whole sequence struck him as surreal. It was hard to believe this had just happened to him.

Or, more accurately, *was* happening to him. He still had to figure a way out of this mess. Did they know where he lived? No one had followed him to the roof.

Tom crept to the ledge. Another alley ran directly below, adjoining busy streets on either side. Denver's brilliant skyline glimmered on the horizon directly ahead. An odd odor met his nose, sweet like cotton candy but mixed with rubber or something burning.

Déjà vu. He'd been here before, hadn't he? No, of course not. Lights shimmered in the hot summer air, reds and yellows and blues, like jewels sprinkled from heaven. He could swear he'd been —

Tom's head suddenly snapped to the left. He threw out his arms, but his world spun impossibly and he knew that he was in trouble.

Something had hit him. Something like a sledgehammer. Something like a bullet.

He felt himself topple, but he wasn't sure if he was really falling or if he was losing consciousness. Something was horribly wrong with his head.

He landed hard on his back, in a pillow of black that swallowed his mind whole.

2

The man's eyes snapped open. A pitch-black sky above. No lights, no stars, no buildings. Only black. And a small moon.

He blinked and tried to remember where he was. Who he was. But all he could remember was that he'd just had a vivid dream.

He closed his eyes and fought to wake. He'd dreamed that he was running from some men who wanted to hurt him. He'd escaped like a spider up a wall after leveling one of the men. Then he'd stared out at the lights. Such beautiful, brilliant lights. Now he was awake. And he still didn't know where he was.

He sat up, disoriented. The shadows of tall, dark trees surrounded a rocky clearing in which he'd been sleeping. His eyes began to adjust to the darkness, and he saw a field of some kind ahead.

He clambered to his feet and steadied himself. On his feet, leather moccasins. On his body, dark pants, tan suede shirt with two pockets. He instinctively felt for his left temple, where a sharp ache throbbed. Warm. Wet. His fingers came away bloody.

He'd been struck in his dream. Something had plowed into his head. He turned and saw a dark patch glistening on the rock where he'd fallen. He must have struck his head against the rock and been knocked unconscious. But he couldn't remember anything but the dream. He wasn't in a city. He wasn't anywhere near a dark alley or traffic or guns.

Instead he was here, in a rocky clearing, surrounded by large trees. But where? Maybe the knock to his head had given him amnesia.

What was his name? *Thomas.* The man in his dream had called him Thomas Hunter. Tom Hunter.

Tom felt the bleeding bump on his head again. The surface wound above his ear had matted his hair with blood. It had knocked him senseless, but thankfully no more.

The night was actually quite bright now. In fact, he could make the trees out clearly.

He lowered his hand and stared at a tree without full comprehension. Square branches jutted off from the trunk at a harsh angle before squaring and turning skyward, like claws grasping at the heavens. The smooth bark looked as though it might be made of metal or a carbon fiber rather than organic material.

Did he know these trees? Why did this sight disturb him?

"It looks perfectly good."

Tom jumped and spun to the male voice. "Huh?"

A man, a redhead dressed like him, stood looking down at a cluster of rocks ten feet away. Did . . . did he know this man?

"The water looks clean to me," the man said.

Tom swallowed. "What's . . . what happened?"

He followed the man's eyes and saw that he was staring at a small puddle of water nestled in a boulder at the edge of the clearing. There was something strange about the water, but he couldn't put his finger on it.

"I think we should try it. Looks good," the man said.

"Where are we?" Tom asked.

"Good question." The man looked at him, then tilted his head and grinned. "You really don't remember? What, you get knocked in the head or something?"

"I guess I must have. I honestly can't remember a thing."

"What's your name?"

"Tom. I think."

"Well, you know that much. Now all we have to do is find a way out of here."

"And what's your name?" Tom asked.

"Seriously? You don't remember?" The man was staring at the water again.

"No."

"Bill," the man said absently. He reached down and touched the water. Brought it to his nose and sniffed. His eyes closed as he savored the scent.

Tom glanced around the clearing, willing his mind to remember. Odd how he could remember some things but not others. He knew that these tall black things were called trees, that the material on his body was called clothing, that the organ pumping in his chest was a heart. He even knew that this kind of selective memory loss was consistent with amnesia. But he couldn't remember any history. Couldn't remember how he got here. Didn't know why Bill was so mesmerized by the water. Didn't even know who Bill was.

"I had a dream about being chased down an alley," Tom said. "Is that how we got here?"

"If only it were that simple. I dreamed of Lucy Lane last night — if only she really did have an obsession over me." He grinned.

Tom closed his eyes, rubbed his temples, paced, and then faced Bill again, desperate for some sense of familiarity. "So where *are* we?"

"This water smells absolutely delicious. We need to drink, Tom. How long has it been since we had water?" Bill was looking at the liquid on his finger. That was another thing Tom knew: They shouldn't drink the water. But Bill seemed to be considering it very seriously.

"I don't think —"

A snicker sounded in the night. Tom scanned the trees.

"You hear that?"

"Are we *hearing* things now?" Bill asked.

"No. Yes! That was a snicker. Something's out there!"

"Nope. You're hearing things."

Bill dipped three fingers into the water. This time he lifted them above his mouth and let a drop fall on his tongue.

The effects were immediate. He gasped and stared at his wet finger with a look of horror. Slowly his mouth twisted into a smile. He stuffed his fingers into his mouth and sucked with such relief, such rapture, that Tom thought he'd lost his mind on the spot.

Bill suddenly dropped to his knees and plopped his face into the small pool of water. He drank, like a horse from a trough, sucking down the water in long, noisy pulls.

Then he stood, trembling, licking his lips.

"Bill?"

"What?"

"What are you doing?"

"I'm drinking the water, you idiot. What does it look like I'm doing, backflips? Are you that —" He caught himself mid-sentence and turned away. His fingers crept across the rock into the water, and he sampled the liquid again in a way that made Tom think he was intentionally being sneaky. This man named Bill, whom he supposedly knew, had flipped his lid completely.

"You have to try the water, Tom. You absolutely have to try the water."

Then, without another word, Bill hopped over the rock, walked into the black forest, and was gone.

"Bill?" Tom peered into the night where Bill had disappeared. Should he follow? He ran forward and pulled up by the boulder.

"Bill!"

Nothing.

Tom took three long steps forward, planted his left hand on the rock, and vaulted in pursuit. A chill flashed up his arm. He glanced down, midvault, and saw that his index finger rested in the puddle of water.

The world slowed.

Something like an electrical current ran up his arm, over his shoulder, straight to his spine. The base of his skull buzzed with intense pleasure, pulling him to the water, begging him to plunge his head into this pool.

Then his foot landed beyond the rock and another reality jerked him from the water. Pain. The intense searing pain of a blade slicing through his leather moccasins and into his heel.

Tom gasped and dived headlong into the field past the boulder. The instant his outstretched hands made contact with the ground, pain shot up his arms and he knew he had made a dreadful mistake. Nausea swept through his body. Razor-sharp shale sliced through his flesh as though it were butter. He recoiled, shuddering as the shale pulled free from deep cuts in his forearms.

Tom groaned and fought to retain consciousness. Pinpricks of light swam in his clenched eyes. High above, a million leaves rustled in the night breeze. The snickers of a thousand —

Tom's eyes snapped open. *Snickers?* His mind wrestled between throbbing pain and the terrible fear that he wasn't alone.

From a branch not five feet above him hung a large, lumpy growth the length of his arm. Next to the growth hung another, like a cluster of black grapes. If he hadn't fallen, he might have hit his head on the clumps.

The growth nearest him suddenly moved.

Tom blinked. Two wings unfolded from the growth. A triangular face tilted toward him, exposing pupil-less eyes. Large, red, pupil-less eyes. A thin pink tongue snaked out of black lips and tested the air.

Tom's heart crashed into his throat. He jerked his eyes to the other growths. A thousand black creatures clung to the branches surrounding him, peering at him with red eyes too large for their angular faces.

The bat closest to him curled its lips to expose dirty yellow fangs.

Tom screamed. His world washed with blackness.

3

His mind crawled out of darkness slowly, beating back images of large black bats with red eyes. He was breathing in quick, short gasps, sure that at any moment one of the growths would drop off its branch and latch onto his neck.

Something smelled putrid. Rotten meat. He couldn't breathe properly past the stuff in his face, this bat guano or this rotten meat or —

Tom opened his eyes. Something was sitting on his face. It was clogging his nostrils and had worked its way into his mouth.

He jerked up, spitting. No bats. There were big black bags and there were swollen boxes and some of them had broken open. Lettuce and tomatoes and rotten meat. Garbage.

High above, the building's roof drew a line across the night sky. That's right, he'd been hit on the head and he'd fallen into the alley, into a large garbage bin.

Tom sat in slimy vegetables swamped with a moment of intense relief. The bats had just been a dream.

And the men from New York?

He hauled himself up by the lip, glanced down a vacant alley. Pain throbbed over his temple and he winced. His hair was matted with blood, but the bullet must have only grazed him.

There were two possibilities here, depending on how much time had elapsed since he'd fallen. Either the shooter was still making his way toward Tom, or the shooter had already come and gone without digging through the garbage bin.

Either way, Tom had to move now, while the alley was empty. His apartment was only a few blocks away. He had to reach it.

Then again, if they knew where he lived, wouldn't they just wait for him there?

He crawled out of the bin and hurried down the alley, glancing both ways. If they knew where he lived, they would have waited for him there in the first place, rather than risk confronting him in the open as they had.

He had to get to the apartment and warn Kara. His sister's nursing shift ended at one in the morning. It was now about midnight, unless he'd been out a long time. What if he'd been out for several hours? Or a whole day?

His head ached, and his new white Banana Republic T-shirt was soaked with blood. Ninth Street still roared with traffic. He would have to cross it to get to his apartment, but he didn't fancy the idea of scurrying down the sidewalk to the next intersection for all to see.

Still no sign of his attackers. He crouched in the alley and waited for traffic to clear. He could vault the hedge, cross the park, and get to the complex over the concrete wall in the back.

Tom closed his eyes, took a deep breath, and let it out slowly. How much trouble could one person possibly get into in the span of twenty-five years? Never mind that he'd been born an army brat in the Philippines, son of Chaplain Hunter, who'd preached love for twenty years and then abandoned his wife for a Filipino woman half his age. Never mind that he'd grown up in a neighborhood that made the Bronx look like a preschool. Never mind that he'd been exposed to more of the world by the age of ten than most Americans were exposed to in a lifetime.

If it wasn't Dad leaving, it was Mom going ballistic and then sinking into bottomless depression. That's why these men were here now. Because Dad had left Mom, and Mom had gone ballistic, and Tom, good old Thomas, had been forced to bail Mom out.

Admittedly, what he'd done to bail her out was a bit extreme, but he'd done it, hadn't he?

A fifty-yard gap opened in the traffic, and he bolted for the street. One horn blast from some conscientious citizen, whose idea of a desperate situation was probably a dirty Mercedes, and Tom was across. He vaulted the hedge and sprinted across the park under the shadows of lamp-lit aspens.

Amazing how real the bat dream had felt.

Three minutes later, Tom rounded the exterior stairs to his third-floor apartment. He took the stairs two at a time, eyes still peeled for any sign of the New Yorkers. None. But it would only be a matter of time.

He slipped into his flat, eased the door closed, twisted the deadbolt home, and dropped his head on the door, breathing hard. This was good. He'd actually made it.

He glanced at the clock on the wall. Eleven p.m. Half an hour since that first bullet had plowed into the brick wall. He'd made it for all of one half-hour. How many more half-hours would he have to make it?

Tom turned and walked to the chest under the window. The flat was a simple two-bedroom apartment, but one glance and even the most jaded traveler would know its inhabitants were not your average, simple people.

The north side of the room looked like it could be a set piece of one of Cirque du Soleil's extravagant acts. A large ring of masquerade masks circled a huge globe, six feet in diameter, cut in half and hung to give the appearance it protruded from the wall. A chaise lounge rested below amid at least twenty silk throw pillows of various designs and colors. Spoils of Tom's travels and episodic seasons of success.

On the south wall, two dozen spears and blowguns from Southeast Asia surrounded four large, ceremonial shields. Below them stood no fewer than twenty large carvings, including a life-sized lion carved out of ironwood. These were the remnants of a failed attempt at importing exotic artifacts from Asia to sell in art houses and at swap meets. If Kara knew that the real purpose of the venture had been to smuggle crocodile skins and bird of paradise feathers in the carvings' carefully hollowed torsos, she would have undoubtedly thrown him out by the ear. The streets of Manila had taught her a few lessons as well, and his older sister could handle herself surprisingly well. Maybe too well. Fortunately, he'd come to his senses without the need for such persuasion.

Tom dropped to his knees and threw open the lid of an old chest. He twisted around, saw that the door was indeed firmly locked, and began rummaging through the musty wood box.

He grabbed handfuls of papers and dumped them on the floor. The receipt was yellow; he was sure of that. He'd buried it here four years ago when he'd first come to Denver to live with his sister.

A thick ream of paper came out in his hands. He grunted at the manuscript, struck by its weight. Heavy. Like a stone. Dead on arrival. This wasn't the receipt, but it arrested his attention anyway. His latest failed endeavor. An important novel entitled *To Kill with Reason.* Actually it was his second novel. He reached into the box and pulled out the first. *Superheroes in Super Fog.* The title was admittedly confusing, but that was no reason for the self-appointed literary wizards scouring the earth for the next Stephen King to turn it down. Both novels were either brilliant or complete trash, and he wasn't yet sure which. Kara had liked them both.

Kara was a god.

Now he had two novels in his hands. Enough dead weight to pull him to the bottom of any lake. He stared at the top title, *Superheroes in Super Fog,* and considered the matter yet again. He'd given three years of his life to these stacks of paper before entombing them in this grave with a thousand rejection slips to keep them company.

The whole business made his stomach crawl. As it turned out, dishing out coffees at Java Hut actually paid more than writing brilliant novels. Or, for that matter, importing exotic carvings from Southeast Asia.

He dropped the manuscripts with a loud thump and shuffled through the chest. Yellow. He was looking for a yellow slip of paper, a carbon-copy sales receipt. The kind written by hand, not tape from a machine. The receipt had a contact name on it. He couldn't even remember who had loaned him the money. Some loan shark. Without that receipt, Tom didn't even know where to start.

Suddenly it was there, in his hand.

Tom stared at the slip of paper. Real, definitely real. The amount, the name, the date. Like a death sentence. His head swam. Very, very, very real. Of course, he already knew it was real, but now, with this tangible evidence in his hand, it all felt doubly real.

He lowered his hand and swallowed. At the bottom of the chest lay an old blackened machete he'd bought in one of Manila's back alleys. He impulsively grabbed it, jumped to his feet, and ran for the light switch by the door. The place was lit up like a bonfire. It was these kinds of stupid mistakes that got people killed. So says the aspiring fiction writer.

He slapped off the lights, pulled back the curtains, and peered out. Clear. He released the drape and turned around. Faces peered at him. Kara's masquerade masks, laughing and frowning.

His knees felt weak. From loss of blood, from the trauma of a bullet to the head, from a growing certainty that this fiasco was only just beginning and it would take more than a whole lot of luck and a few karate kicks to keep it from ending badly.

Tom hurried to the kitchen, set the machete on the counter, and called his mother in New York. She answered on the tenth ring.

"Hello?"

"Mom?"

"Tommy."

He released a silent breath of relief. "It's Tommy. Um . . . you're okay, huh?"

"What time is it? It's after one in the morning."

"Sorry. Okay, I just wanted to check on you."

His mother was silent.

"You sure you're okay?"

"Yes, Tommy. I'm fine." Pause.

"Thanks for checking though."

"Sure."

"You kids doing okay?"

"Yes. Sure, of course."

"I talked to Kara on Saturday. She seems to be doing well."

"Yeah. You sound good." He could always tell when she was struggling. Depression was difficult to hide. Her last serious bout had been over two years ago. With any luck the beast was gone for good.

More to the point, it didn't sound like there were any gunmen in her apartment, holding her hostage.

"I have to run," he said. "You need anything, you call, okay?"

"Sure, Tommy. Thanks for calling."

He dropped the receiver in its cradle and steadied himself on the counter. He was really in a pickle this time, wasn't he? And no quick solutions were coming to mind.

He had to get off his feet.

Tom grabbed the machete and hurried to his bathroom, head swimming. He stood in front of the mirror and ran his fingers along his head wound again. No more bleeding, that was good. But his whole head throbbed. For all he knew, he had a concussion.

It took him less than five minutes to clean up, change his clothes, and don a baseball cap. He walked back out to the living room and collapsed on the couch. Kara could dress the cut properly when she got home.

He lay back and thought about calling her at work but decided an explanation over the phone would be too difficult. The room began to spin, so he closed his eyes.

He had an hour to think of something. Anything.

But nothing came.

Except sleep.

4

Tom wasn't sure if it was the heat or the buzzing that woke him, but he woke with a start, snapped his eyes open, and squinted.

Impressions registered in his mind like falling dominoes. The blue sky. The sun. The black trees. A lone bat perched high above him, like a deformed vulture. Thomas held perfectly still and stared up through slits, determined to make sense of what was happening.

He'd just had another incredibly lifelike dream of a place called Denver.

For a fleeting moment he felt relieved that his dream was only that, a dream. That he really hadn't been shot in the head and that his life really wasn't in danger.

But then he remembered that he really *was* in danger. He had banged his head on a rock and cut his foot on the shale and passed out under the red gaze of a hungry bat. He wasn't sure what he should fear more, the horrors in his dream or the horrors here.

Bill.

Tom opened his eyes wide and ran them in circles to view as much as he could without having to move. He couldn't see where the buzzing came from. Stark, square branches jutted from the leafless trees. Lifeless, charred trees.

Tom concentrated, grasping for memories. None that preceded his fall came to mind. The amnesia had locked them out. His surroundings looked oddly familiar, as if he'd been here before, but he felt disconnected from the scene.

His head ached.

His right foot throbbed.

The bat didn't look as threatening as it had last night.

Tom slowly pushed himself up to his elbow and glanced around the black forest. To his left, a large black field of ash lay between him and a small pond. Fruit that he hadn't seen last night hung on the trees in a stunning variety of colors. Red and blue and yellow, all hanging in an impossible contrast to the stark black trees. Something seemed very wrong here. More than the strange surroundings, more than the fact that Bill had disappeared. Tom couldn't put his finger on it.

Except for the one high above, the bats were gone. He knew about the bats, didn't he? Somewhere back in his lost memories, he was completely familiar with bats. He knew that they were dangerous and evil and had very sharp teeth, but he couldn't remember other details, like how to avoid them. Or how to wring their necks.

A blanket of black rose from the field. The buzzing swelled.

Tom scrambled to his feet. What he'd thought was black soot on the field was actually a blanket of flies. They buzzed a few feet off the ground and then settled again. As far as the clearing extended, the squirming, black-winged insects crawled over one another, forming a thick, living carpet.

He backed up, fighting a sudden panic. He had to get out of here. He had to find someone who could tell him what was going on. He didn't even know what he was running from.

But he *was* running, wasn't he?

That's why he was having those crazy dreams of Denver. He was dreaming of running in Denver because he really *was* running. Here, in this black forest.

He glanced back in the direction he assumed he'd come from, then quickly realized he had no idea which direction he'd truly come from. Behind him, the sharp shale that had sliced into his feet and arms. Beyond the shale, more black forest. Ahead, the field of flies and then more black forest. Everywhere, the black, angular trees.

45

A cackle rasped through the air to his right. Tom turned slowly. A second bat within spitting distance stared at him from its perch on a branch. It looked like someone had stuffed two cherries into the flier's eye sockets and then pinned its eyelids back.

Movement in the sky. He glanced up. More bats. Streams of them, filling the bare branches high above. The bat nearby did not flinch. Did not blink. The treetops turned black with bats.

Eyes fixed on the lone creature, Tom backed into a rock and reached out his hand to steady himself. His hand touched water.

A chill surged through his fingers, up his arm. A cool pleasure. Yes, of course, the water. Something was up with the water; that was another thing he remembered. He knew he should jerk his hand out, but he was off balance and his eyes were fixed on the black bat, who stared at him with those bulging red eyes, and he let his hand linger.

He dropped to his elbow and pulled his hand out of the water, turning to it as he did.

The small pool of water pulsed with emerald hues. Immediately he felt himself drawn in. His face was eighteen inches from this shimmering liquid, and he desperately wanted to thrust his head into the puddle, but he knew, he just knew . . .

Actually, he wasn't sure what he knew.

He knew he couldn't break his stare and look off somewhere else, like at the buzzing meadow or at the canopy still filling with black bats.

The bats screeched in delight somewhere in the back of his mind.

He slowly dipped a finger into the puddle. Another shot of pleasure surged through his veins, a tingling sensation that he liked. More than liked. It was like Novocain. And then he felt another sensation joining the first. Pain. But the pleasure was greater. No wonder Bill had —

A shriek pierced the sky.

Tom's eyes sprang open and he stared numbly at his hand. Red juice dripped from his fingers. Red juice or blood.

Blood?

He stepped back.

Another shriek high above him. He looked at the sky and saw that a lone white bat was streaking through the ranks of black beasts, scattering them from their perches.

The black creatures gave chase, obviously opposing the presence of the white flier. With a piercing cry, the white intruder looped over and dived through the squawking throngs again. *If the black bats are my enemies, the white one might be my ally.* But were the black bats his enemies?

He looked back at the water. Pulsing, wonderful. It occurred to Tom that he wasn't thinking clearly.

A shrill call like a trumpet sounded from the white bat's direction. Tom turned again and saw that the white bat had circled and was streaking over the meadow, trumpeting as it blasted through the horde of black flies. And then Tom caught a single, brief glimpse of the white bat's green eyes as it swooped by.

He knew those eyes!

If he wanted to live out this day, he had to follow that white flier. He was sure of it. Tom tore his feet from the ground and lurched toward the meadow. His flesh throbbed from the cuts of yesterday's fall and his bones felt like they were on fire, but everything was suddenly quite clear. He had to follow the white creature or he would die.

He forced his legs forward and ran into the meadow despite the pain. He'd made it this far into the black forest by running, hadn't he? And now it was time to run again.

At first the flies let him pass. An unbroken swarm lifted from the pond and buzzed in chaotic circles, as if confused by

48

the sudden turn of events. Tom was midfield, racing toward the black trees on the far side, when they began attacking. They came in from his left, swarming, slammed into his body and face like dive bombers on suicide runs.

He cried out in panic, raised his arms to cover his eyes, and nearly beat a hasty retreat. But he had come too far already.

His shoulders suddenly felt like they were on fire, and with a single terrified glance Tom realized the flies were already through his shirt, eating his flesh. He slapped madly at his skin and sprinted for the trees. The flies blanketed his body, chewing.

Fifty yards.

He swatted at his face to clear his vision, but the little beasts refused to budge. They were getting in his ears and his nose. They furiously attacked his eyes. He screamed, but the flies bit at his tongue and he clamped his mouth shut. He wasn't going to make it.

A chorus of screeches filled the air behind him. The black bats.

Fangs sank into his left calf. Pain shot up his spine, and the last threads of reason fell from his mind. Time and space ceased to exist. Only reaction remained. The only messages that managed to get through the buzz in his brain were to his muscles, and they said run or die, kill or be killed.

He smashed at his calf. The black bat fell away but took a chunk of flesh with it.

Twenty yards.

Another bat attached itself to his thigh. Tom clamped his mouth to keep from screaming and pumped his arms with every ounce of strength remaining in his strained muscles.

He plunged into the forest, and immediately the flies cleared.

The bats did not.

His shirt was tattered and his skin was red. Covered in blood. He stumbled through the trees, nauseated, legs numb from the loss of blood.

A black bat landed on his shoulder, but each nerve cut by the beast's sharp teeth was already inflamed with pain, and Tom barely noticed the black lump on his shoulder now. Another attached itself to his buttocks. He ignored the bats and lurched drunkenly through the trees.

Where was the white bat? There. Left. Tom swerved, hit a tree head-on, and dropped to the ground. He tried to catch his fall with his right arm, but his forearm broke with a tremendous snap. White-hot pain flashed up his neck.

The bats lodged on his body lost their places and screeched in protest, beating their wings furiously. He struggled to his feet and lurched forward, right arm dangling uselessly at his side. The bats landed on Tom's jerking body, struggled for footing, and began chewing again.

He stumbled on, vaguely aware that his moccasins and most of his clothes were now gone, leaving only a loincloth. He could feel fangs working on his thigh.

A voice, slippery and deep, echoed quietly through the trees. "You will find your destiny with me, Tom Hunter."

The voice had come from one of the bats behind him, he could swear it. But then he broke from the forest onto the bank of a river and the thought was lost.

A white bridge spanned the flowing water. A towering, multicolored forest lined the far bank, dazzling like a box of crayons topped with a bright green canopy. The sight stopped him.

Green. A mirage or heaven.

Tom limped toward the bridge, hardly aware of the bats squawking on his back. His breathing came in great gasps. His flesh quivered. The black bats fell from his back. The lone white bat flapped eagerly on a low branch across the river. His ally was large, maybe as high as Tom's knees with a wingspan three times that. Its kind green eyes fixed on him.

He knew this bat as well, didn't he? At

least he knew that his hope rested in this creature now.

In his peripheral vision, Tom saw that thousands of the black creatures were lining the stark trees behind him. He wobbled onto the bridge and gripped its rail tightly for support. His mind began to drift with the water below. Slowly but steadily he hauled himself across the bridge, over the rushing waters, all the way to the other side. He collapsed into a thick bed of emerald green grass.

He was dying. That was the last thing he thought before the pain shoved him into the world of unconsciousness.

5

Something woke him. A noise or a breeze — something had pulled him from his dreams.

Tom blinked in the darkness. Breathed hard, tried to clear his mind. The bats weren't simply figments of his imagination. Nothing was. His name was Tom Hunter. He'd fallen on a rock and lost his memory, and he'd just escaped the black forest. Barely. Now he'd just passed out and he was dreaming.

Dreaming that he was Tom Hunter, being chased by loan sharks he'd stiffed for $100,000 four years ago in New York.

Problem was, this dream of Denver felt as real as the black forest had. There had to be a way to tell if he really was, at this very moment, physically lying on a bed of green grass or staring at the ceiling of an apartment in Denver, Colorado. He could test the reality of this environment by standing up and walking around, but that wouldn't help if his dreams felt like reality. He would be able to see if his skin was stripped off or if his arm was broken, but since when did dreams reflect reality? He'd broken his arm in the black forest, but here in this dream of Denver, he could be totally healthy. In dreams, the condition of one's body didn't necessarily correlate.

Tom moved his arm. No broken bone. He had to find a way to push past this dream and wake up on the riverbank before he died there, lying on the grass.

The door opened and Tom reacted without thinking. He grabbed the machete, rolled to the ground, and came up in position one, blade extended toward the door.

"Tom?"

Kara stood at the door, facing him with wide eyes. She certainly looked real enough. Standing right there, still wearing her white nurse's outfit, long blonde hair pulled up off her neck, blue eyes as bright and feisty as ever. He straightened.

"Expecting someone?" She flipped the switch.

Light flooded the apartment. If this was real and not a dream, light could attract the night crawlers. The New Yorkers.

"Does it look like I'm expecting someone?" Tom asked.

"What's the machete for?" She nodded at his right hand.

He lowered the blade. This couldn't be a dream, could it? He was here in their apartment, not lying unconscious by some river.

"I had a crazy dream."

"Yeah, how so?"

"It felt real. I mean *really* real."

Kara tossed her purse on the end table. "Nightmare, huh? Don't they all?"

"This wasn't like just any dream that feels real. I keep falling asleep in my dream, and then waking up here."

She stared at him, uncomprehending.

"What I'm saying is that I only wake up here if and when I fall asleep there."

A blank stare. "And?"

"And how do I know I'm not dreaming here, right now?"

"Because I'm standing here, and I can tell you that you're not dreaming right now."

" 'Course you would. You'd be in the dream, wouldn't you? That's why you'd think you're real. That's why I think you're —"

"You've written one too many novels, Thomas. It's late, and I need to get some sleep."

She was right. And if she was right, their problems weren't as simple as a case of the delusional novelist being chased by black bats.

Kara turned and started for her room.

"Uh, Kara?"

"Please. I don't have the energy for another crisis right now."

"What makes you think this is a crisis?"

She turned. "You know I love you, brother, but trust me, when you wake up with a machete in your hand, telling me I'm just part of your dream, I think to myself, *Tommy's going off the deep end.*"

She made a good point. Tom glanced at the window. No signs of anything.

"Have I gone off the deep end before?" he asked. "I don't remember doing that."

"You *live* off the deep end." She paused. "I'm sorry, that's not fair. Apart from buying $20,000 worth of statues you can't sell and trying to smuggle crocodile skins in them and —"

"You knew about that?"

"Please." She smiled. "Good night, Thomas."

"I was shot in the head tonight." His urgency suddenly returned. He ran to the window and peered past the curtain. "If this isn't a dream, then we have a very big problem."

"Now you *are* dreaming," she said.

He yanked off his hat. The cut must have been obvious, because her eyes went wide.

"I kid you not. I was chased by some guys from New York and got shot in the head. I passed out in a garbage can but escaped before they could find me. And you're right, I'm not dead."

Kara hurried over, incredulous. "You got shot in the head?" She touched his scalp gently, as a nurse would.

"It's fine. But we may not be."

"It's a head wound! You need a dressing on this."

"It's just a surface wound."

"I'm so sorry, Tommy. I had no idea."

He closed his eyes and took a deep breath. "If you only knew. I'm the one who should be sorry." Then under his breath, "I can't believe this is happening."

"You can't believe *what's* happening?"

"We have a problem, Kara," he said, pacing. She was going to kill him, but he was beyond that now. "Remember when Mom lost it after the divorce?"

"And?"

"I was there with her in New York. She couldn't work, she got into some serious debt, and they were going to take everything away from her."

"You helped her out," Kara said. "You sold out your end of the tour company and bailed her out."

"Well, I helped her out. And then I came to help you out."

She tilted her head. "But you *didn't* sell your end of the tour company. Is that what you're going to say?"

"No, I didn't sell out. It was already a bust."

"Don't tell me you borrowed money from those crooks you used to talk about."

He didn't answer.

"Thomas? No!" She lifted her hands in exasperation and turned away. "No." She spun back. "How much?"

"Too much to pay back right away. I'm working on it."

"How *much?*"

He dug out the receipt, handed it to her, and walked back to the curtain, as much now to avoid her eyes as to check the perimeter again.

"One hundred dollars?"

"Thousand," he said.

She gasped. "One hundred thousand? That's insane!"

"Well, unless I'm dreaming, it's real. Mom needed sixty to come clean, you needed a new car, and I needed twenty-five for my new business. The carvings."

"And you just took off from New York, hoping they would be fine with that?"

"I didn't just take off. I left a trail to South America and then split with full intention to pay them back in time. I have a buyer in Los Angeles who's interested in the carvings — should bring in fifty, and that's without the contraband. Just took a little longer than I expected."

"A *little* longer? What about Mom? You're endangering her?"

"No. No connection they ever knew about. As far as the records go, she got her money from the divorce settlement. But that's not important. What is important is that they found me, and I doubt they're interested in anything other than cash. Now."

The full meaning of what he was saying settled over Kara. Any sympathy she'd felt for his bullet wound vanished. "Of course they found you, you idiot! What do you think this is — Manila? You can't just walk away with $100,000 of the mob's money and expect to live happily ever after. They let one person get away with it, and every Tom, Dick, and Harriet will be robbing them blind!"

"I know! I just got shot, for crying out loud!"

"We'll be lucky if we *both* don't get shot! What were you thinking, moving here?"

Her statement hit him broadside. He took a deep breath and closed his eyes. The whole business suddenly felt impossibly heavy to him. He'd risked more than she could ever know to help out their mother. He'd left a life behind in New York to protect her, to make a clean break, to get back on his feet with the import business. That he would endanger Kara by bringing this debt to Denver had never oc-curred to him.

What was he thinking moving here, she wanted to know? He was thinking that they'd both been abandoned by their par-ents. That they didn't have any real friends. Or any real home. That they were suspended between countries and societies and left wondering where they fit in. He wanted to be Kara's brother — to help her and to be helped by her.

"I was twenty-one," he said.

"So?"

"So I wasn't thinking. You were having a tough time."

Her hands dropped to her thighs with a slap. "I know. And you've always been there for me. But this . . . I just can't be-lieve you were so stupid."

"I'm sorry. Really, I'm sorry."

Kara looked at him and began to pace. She was steaming all right, but she couldn't bring herself to take his head off. They'd been through too much together. Being raised as outcasts in a foreign land had woven an inseverable bond between them.

"You can be an idiot, Thomas."

Then again, the bond wasn't beyond being stretched now and then.

"Look," he said, "I know this isn't good, but it's not all bad."

"Of course not. We're still alive, right? We should be eternally grateful. We're walking and breathing. You have a cut on your head, but it could have been much worse. We should be toasting our good fortune!"

"They don't know where we live."

"See, that's the problem here," she said. "It's already gone from *I* to *we*. And there's nothing *we* can do about it."

The pain in Tom's head was making a strong comeback. A wave of dizziness swept over him, and he walked unsteadily for the chaise lounge. He sat hard and groaned.

Kara sighed and disappeared into her room. She came out a few seconds later with some gauze, a bottle of peroxide, and a tube of Neosporin and sat by him.

"Let me see that."

He faced the wall and let her dab the wound with peroxide.

"If they knew where we lived, they would be here already," he said.

"Hold still."

"I don't know how long we have."

"I'm not going anywhere," she said emphatically.

"We can't stay here, and you know that. They found me in Denver, probably through the dinner theater. I should've thought about that — the theater advertises all over the country. My name's in the credits."

She wound the gauze around his head and taped it. "Seems appropriate that a production of *Alice in Wonderland* would end up being your demise, don't you think?"

"Please. This isn't funny anymore."

"Never was funny."

"You've made your point, okay? I was a fool, I'm sorry, but the fact is, we *are* still alive, and some pretty bad people *are* trying to kill me."

"Have you called the police yet?"

"That won't stop these guys." He ran his fingers along the bandage and stood. His world tipped crazily.

"Sit down," Kara ordered.

She was being bossy, but he deserved to be bossed at the moment. Besides, allowing her to boss him would help repair any breach in their relationship.

He sat.

"Take these." She handed him two pills. He threw them into his mouth and swallowed without water.

Kara sighed again. "Okay, from the top. You have some mob thugs after you for stiffing them out of $100,000. After four years your sins have finally caught up with you, presumably through the Magic Circle dinner theater or the Java Hut. They shot at you and you escaped. But you were on foot, so they know you live close by, and it's only a matter of time before they find you again. Right?"

"That's about it."

"To top it all off, the blow to your head is tempting you to think that you live in another world. Still right?"

He nodded. "Maybe. Sort of."

She closed her eyes. "This is insane."

"Maybe. But we still have to get out of here."

"And exactly where are we supposed to go? I have a job. I can't just pick up and take off."

"I'm not saying we can't come back. But we can't just wait here for them." He stood and began to pace, ignoring a sudden whirl of disorientation. "Maybe we should go back to the Philippines for a while. We have passports. We have friends who —"

"Forget it. It's taken me ten years to make the break from Manila. I'm not going back. Not now."

"Please, you have more Filipino in you than American. You can't run forever."

"Who's got the bullet wound in his head? *I'm* not running anymore. I'm here. I'm an American, I live in Denver, Colorado, and I like who I've become."

"So do I. But if they came this far to

settle a debt, they'll hound me for the rest of my life!"

"You should have thought about that earlier."

"Like I said, you made your point. Don't beat me into the ground with it." He took a deep breath. "Maybe I can fake my death."

"How on earth did you manage to talk them out of $100,000 to start with?"

He shrugged. "I convinced them I was an arms dealer."

"Oh, that's just great."

The pain pills were starting to make him woozy. Tom sat again, leaned back, closed his eyes. "We have to do something."

They sat quietly for a long minute. Kara had always insisted she was happy here in Denver, but she was twenty-six and she was beautiful and she hadn't dated in three years despite her talk of getting married. What did that mean? It meant she was a stranger in a strange land, just like him. Try as they may, they couldn't escape their past.

"I'm sure you'll think of something," Kara said. "I don't think I can leave."

"I'm not going to leave you alone here. Not a chance." His head was spinning. "What did you give me?"

"Demerol." She stood and walked to the window. "This is completely insane."

Tom said something. Something about leaving immediately. Something about needing money. But his voice sounded distant. Maybe it was the Demerol. Maybe it was the knock on the head. Maybe it was because he was really lying on the bank of a river, stripped of his skin, dying.

Kara was saying something.

"What?" he asked.

". . . in the morning. Until then . . ."

That's all he got.

6

At the foot of the arching bridge, on thick green grass, the bloodied man lay face-down as though he had been dead for days. The black beasts on the opposite shore had deserted the charred trees. Two white creatures leaned over the prone body, their wings folded around their furry torsos, their short, spindly legs shifting so that their bodies swayed like penguins.

"Hurry, into the forest," Michal said.

"Can we drag him?" asked Gabil.

"Of course we can. Grab his other hand."

They bent, though not so far — they stood only about three feet if they stretched — and hauled the man from the bank. Michal led them over the grass, through the trees, into a small clearing surrounded by fruit trees. The ground was clear of debris and rocks, but they couldn't be doing the man's belly any favors. Soon it wouldn't matter.

"Here." He dropped the man's arm. "I assume he can't hear us."

"Of course he can't understand us. No sir," Gabil said, kneeling beside the man. "How can he understand us when he's unconscious?"

Michal nudged the man in the shoulder with a frail foot resembling a bird's. "You say you *led* him out from the black forest?" Not that he should doubt his friend, but Gabil did have a way of milking a story. It was more of a comment than a question.

Gabil nodded and scrunched his lightly furred forehead. The expression looked out of place on his round, soft face.

"He's lucky to have lived." Gabil stretched one wing in the direction they'd come. "He barely made it through the black trees. You should have seen the Shataiki that had him. Ten at least." Gabil hopped around the fallen body. "You should have seen, Michal. You really should have. He must be from the far side — I don't recognize him."

"How could you possibly recognize him? His skin is missing."

"I saw him before they took his skin. I'm telling you, this one's never been in these parts before." Gabil stood over the prostrate body again, swaying.

"Well, he didn't drink the water; that's what really matters," Michal said.

"But he may have if I hadn't flown in," Gabil said enthusiastically.

"And you flew in because . . . ?" They rarely confronted the black bats anymore. There was a time, long ago, when heroic battles had been fought, but not for a millennium now.

"Because I saw the sky black with Shataiki about a mile in, that's why. I went in high, but when I saw him, I couldn't leave him. There were a thousand of the beasts flying mad circles around me, I'm telling you. It was nothing short of spectacular."

"And how did you manage to escape a thousand Shataiki?"

"Michal, please! It's I! The *conqueror* of Shataiki." He raised his wing in a mock salute. "Flies or beasts, black or red, urge them on. I'll dispatch them to darkness." He waited for a response from Michal and continued when he received none.

"Actually, I took them by surprise. Out of the sun. And did I tell you about the flies? I blasted through a horde of flies like they were the air itself."

"Of course you did." And then after a moment of thought, "Well done."

Michal tilted his head and studied the man's rising back. Fresh blood still oozed from three gaping holes at the man's neck, his buttocks, and his right thigh where the Shataiki had eaten him to the bone. His flesh quivered under the hot sun. There was something strange about the man. It was strange enough that someone from one of the distant villages had entered the black forest at all. It had happened only once before. But the strangeness was more than that. He could smell the stench that came from the man's ragged breathing — like the breath of the Shataiki bats.

"Well, let's get on with it then. You have the water?"

"Hello?"

They both turned as one. A young woman stood at the edge of the clearing, eyes wide. Rachelle.

Rachelle stared at the bloodied body, stunned by the gruesome sight. Had she ever seen anything so terrible? Never! She hurried forward, red tunic swishing below her knees.

"What . . . what is it?" A man, of course. She could see that by the muscles in his back and legs. He lay on his belly, head turned toward her, a bloody mess. "Who is he?"

The Roush, Michal and Gabil, exchanged a glance. "We don't know," Michal said.

"He's no one we know," Gabil blurted. "No sir, this one's from one of the other villages."

Rachelle stopped, mesmerized. One arm

lay at an odd angle, cleanly broken below the elbow. Empathy swelled in her chest. "Dear. Oh dear, oh dear." She dropped to her knees by his shoulder. "How could anything like this possibly have happened?"

"The bats. I led him from the black forest," Gabil said.

Alarm flashed. "The bats? He's been *in* the black forest?"

"Yes, but he didn't drink the water," Michal said.

Silence settled over them. This was the work of the Shataiki! She'd never actually seen one, much less encountered their fangs, but here on the grass was evidence enough of the terrible beasts' brutality. So much blood. Why hadn't the Roush healed him immediately? They knew as much as she how blood defiled a man. It defiled man, woman, child, grass, water, anything that it touched. It wasn't meant to be spilled. And on the rare occasions that it was, there were accommodations.

Rage displaced her alarm. What kind of thinking could influence any creature to do this to a man?

"This is why Tanis has talked about an expedition to destroy the bats!" she said. "It's horrible!"

"And any expedition would put Tanis in the same condition!" Michal snapped impatiently. "Don't be ridiculous."

70

Rachelle returned her gaze to the bloodied body. He was breathing steadily, lost to this world. Such a poor, innocent soul.

Yet an air of mystery and intrigue seemed to rise from the man. He had entered the black forest without succumbing to the water. What kind of man could do such a thing? Only a very strong man.

"The water, Gabil," Michal said.

The smaller Roush withdrew a gourd of water from under his wing.

Rachelle wanted to reach out. To touch the man's skin. The thought surprised her.

Could *he* be the man? This thought surprised her even more. How could she dare think of choosing a man she didn't know for marriage?

Michal had taken the pouch from Gabil. He pulled the cork from its neck.

How absurd that she should think of this brutalized man as anything more than someone who desperately needed the water and Elyon's love. But the thought swelled in her mind. She felt herself irrevocably drawn to it, like blood to the heart. Since when did men and women qualify the ones they chose? All men were good, all women were good, all marriages perfect. So then why not this man if she felt so suddenly drawn by compassion for him? He was the first she'd ever seen in such desperate need of Elyon's water.

Michal waddled forward. He tilted the flask.

Rachelle lifted her hand. "Wait."

"Wait?"

She wasn't sure what had come over her, but emotion tugged at her heart in a way she'd never quite felt before. She looked at Michal. "Is . . . do you think he's marked?"

The two Roush exchanged another glance.

"What do you mean?" Michal asked.

The man's forehead, which would bear the mark of union, was covered in blood. She was suddenly desperate to wipe the blood and see if he bore the telltale one-inch circle that signified his union to another woman. Or the half circle that meant he was promised. But she hesitated; spilled blood was the undoing of Elyon's creation and should be avoided or immediately restored.

Michal lowered the water pouch. "Please, you can't seriously be thinking —"

"It's a wonderful idea!" Gabil said, hopping up and down. "How wonderfully romantic."

"Why not?" Rachelle asked Michal.

"You don't even know him!"

"Since when has that made any difference to any woman? Does Elyon exercise such discrimination? And I *did* find him."

"What you're feeling is empathy, certainly not —"

"Don't be so quick to decide what I'm feeling," Rachelle said. "I'm telling you I have a very strong feeling for this man. The poor soul has been through the most awful ordeal imaginable."

"No, it's not the worst imaginable," Michal said. "Trust me."

"But that's not the point. The point is, I feel very strongly for this man, and I think I may be meant to choose him. Is that so unreasonable?"

"No, I don't think it's unreasonable at all," the smaller Roush said. "It's very, very, very romantic! Don't be so cautious, Michal; it's a delicious thought!"

"I have no idea if he's marked," Michal said, but he seemed to have softened.

Rachelle was twenty-one, and she'd never once felt such a strong desire to choose a man. Most women her age had already chosen and been chosen. She certainly was eligible. And it really didn't matter whom she chose, more that she did choose. That was the custom.

She snatched up a handful of grass and brought it to the man's forehead. Careful not to let it make any contact with her skin, she wiped the blood away.

No mark!

Her heart pounded. The custom was rare but clear. Any eligible woman who brought wholeness to an eligible man showed her invitation. She was choosing him. The man would then accept her invitation and choose her by pursuing her.

Rachelle stood slowly. "There's no mark."

Gabil hopped. "It's perfect, perfect!"

Michal looked at her, then at the man. "It seems highly unusual, not even knowing which village he comes from. But I suppose you're right. It's your choice. Would you like to bring him wholeness?"

Her bones trembled. It seemed so daring. So audacious. But she knew, staring down at the man, that the reason she hadn't made her choice until this day was because she was more adventurous than most. Was he a good man? Of course. *All* men were good. Would he pursue her? What man would not romance a woman who had invited him? And what woman would not romance a man who had chosen her? It was the nature of the Great Romance. They all knew it. Thrived on it.

In this most unusual and daring situation, she was ready to choose this man. She was suddenly more ready to choose and be chosen by this man than she could express to any Roush, even the wisest, like Michal. How could they understand?

They weren't human.

"I would," Rachelle said. "Yes, I would." She reached a trembling hand for the pouch. "Give me the water."

A smile tugged at Michal's mouth. His left brow arched. "You are sure?"

"Give me the pouch. I am very sure!"

"So you are." He handed her the water.

Rachelle took the gourd. She impulsively brought the pouch to her lips and sipped the sweet green water. A surge of power washed through her belly and she shuddered.

"Well, come on, Gabil," Michal said. "Roll him over."

Gabil stopped his pacing, clasped the man's arm, and hauled him over onto his back. "Oh dear," he said. "Yes sir. He *is* bad off, isn't he? Yes sir. Oh, may Elyon have mercy on this poor being." His broken arm now lay doubled over on itself.

The emotion that had compelled Rachelle swallowed her. She could hardly wait another second to bring wholeness to this man. She sank to her knees, tilted the pouch over his face, and let the clear green water trickle onto his lips.

The water seemed to glow a little and then spread over the man's face, as though searching for the right kind of healing for this pulp. Immediately red lumps of flesh began to recede and blend in with pink skin. The skin rippled. Shapes of a nose and lips and eyelids rose from the face.

She poured the water over the rest of the man's body now, and as quickly as the liquid spread over his skin, the blood dissipated, the redness faded, the cuts filled in with new flesh. The bruises beneath his skin lost their purple color. The man's broken forearm suddenly jerked from where it lay and began straightening. Gabil yelped and stepped back from the flailing appendage. With a loud pop the arm snapped true.

Rachelle gazed at the transformed man before her, amazed at his beauty. Golden skin, strong face, muscles that rippled, veins running up his arms. Elyon's water had healed him completely.

She'd just chosen this man as her mate, hadn't she? The thought was almost more than she could comprehend. She had actually just chosen a man! There was still his choosing of her, naturally, but —

The man heaved a tremendous breath. Gabil uttered a small cry, which alarmed Rachelle even more than the man's sudden movement. She scrambled back and jumped to her feet.

The man's eyes flickered open.

Bright light filtered into Tom's eyes and slowly brought him to his senses. His mind scrambled for orientation. A blue sky above. Brilliant green canopy shimmering in the breeze.

This wasn't Denver.

He wasn't lying on the couch after consuming Demerol after all. Denver had all been a dream. Thank heavens. Which meant . . .

The black bats.

Tom jerked himself to a sitting position and faced a forest of trees that shone with amber- and topaz- and ruby-colored trunks. He twisted to his left. Two white creatures gazed at him with curious emerald eyes. Like white cousins to the black bats, with rounded features.

The smaller of the two looked behind him. Tom followed his stare. A woman with long brown hair, wearing a red satin dress, stood ten feet from him, eyes wide with wonder.

He rose to his feet, immediately aware that his body wasn't brutalized. It wasn't even bloody.

The woman watched him without moving. The small furry creatures looked up quizzically. He heard rushing water nearby. Where was he? Did he know this woman? These creatures?

"Is there a problem?" the larger of the two white furries asked.

Tom stared. He had just heard speech

come from the lips of an animal. But that was nothing unusual, was it? Not at all. He shook his head to clear his thoughts, but they remained muddled.

"You came from the black forest," the creature said. "Don't worry, you didn't drink the water. I am Michal, this is Gabil, and that" — he pointed his wing at the woman — "is Rachelle." He said her name as if it should mean something to him. "How do you feel?"

"Yes, how do you feel?" the other one, Gabil, repeated.

Details of his sprint through the black forest strung through his mind. Everything felt vaguely familiar, but his memory didn't extend beyond last night, when he'd awakened after knocking his head on the rock. He felt for the wound on his skull. Gone.

He looked down at his body and slowly ran a hand over his bare chest. No cuts, no bruises, not even a hint of the carnage he remembered from the chase.

Tom looked at the woman. "I feel fine."

She arched a brow and smiled. "Fine?" She stepped forward on bare feet and stopped at arm's length. "What is your name?"

He hesitated. "Thomas Hunter?"

"So nice to make your acquaintance, Thomas Hunter."

She reached out her hand and he tried to

take it, but instead she slid her fingers over his palm. That was the greeting. He'd forgotten even that much.

"You are a beautiful man, Thomas Hunter," she said. "I have chosen you." She said it softly, her eyes bright as stars. Clearly this information implied something significant, but Tom didn't have the foggiest notion what it could be. He said nothing.

She dipped her head, stepped back, and drilled him with a positively infectious stare, as if she'd just shared a deep, delightful secret.

Without another word, she turned and ran into the forest.

7

Kara awoke at three o'clock in the morning with a splitting headache. She tried to ignore the pain and slip back into sleep before waking completely, but the moment she remembered the predicament Tom had brought home, her mind resisted.

She finally climbed from the covers, entered her bathroom, and washed down two Advil with a long drink of cool water. If the apartment had any shortcoming, it was the absence of air conditioning.

She headed out to the living room and stopped by the chaise. Tom lay under the batik quilt she'd thrown over him, his position virtually unchanged from when she'd left him a couple of hours ago. Dead to the world.

Tangled brown hair curled over his eyebrows. Mouth shut, breathing steadily and deeply. A square, clean-shaven jaw. Lean, strong body. Mind as wide as the oceans.

She'd been unfair to question his decision to bring his troubles to Denver. He'd come for her sake; they both knew that. He was the baby of the family, but he'd always been the one to take care of them all. The only reason he hadn't responded to Harvard's acceptance as initially planned was because Mother needed him after the divorce. And the only reason he hadn't resumed his education after he'd settled Mother in was because his older sister needed him. He'd put his own life on hold for them. She might play tough with him, but she could hardly blame him for his alternative exploits. He'd never been one to sit back and let the world pass him by. If it wasn't going to be Harvard, it would be something else as extravagant.

Something like borrowing $100,000 from a loan shark to pay off Mother's debt and start a new business. Given enough time, he would pay it back, but time wasn't on their side.

Yes, the problem belonged to both of them now, didn't it? What on earth would they do?

She considered waking him to make sure he was sound. Despite her dismissal earlier, this business of his vivid dream was unlike him. Tom never did anything without careful consideration. He wasn't given to fancy. His consideration might be quick and creative — even spontaneous — but he didn't walk around speaking of hallucinations. The blow to his head had clearly affected his thinking.

What was he dreaming now?

She recalled their short transfer stateside when she was in tenth grade and he in eighth. He'd wandered around school like a lost puppy for the first two weeks, trying to fit in and failing. He was different and they all knew it. One of the football players — a junior linebacker with biceps larger than Tom's thighs — had called him a spineless-gook-Chinese-lover one afternoon, and Tom had finally lost his cool. He'd put the boy in the hospital with a single kick. They left him alone after that, but he never made many friends.

He was so very strong during the days, but she could hear his soft cries late at night in the room next to hers. She'd come to his rescue then. In the years since, she'd thought maybe her dissociation with the all-American male had started then. She'd take her brother over a steroid-stuffed football player any day of the week.

Kara stepped forward, leaned over, and kissed his forehead. "Don't worry, Thomas," she whispered. "We'll get out of this. We always have."

Tom stood in the clearing and looked at the two white creatures. They were odd to be sure, with their furry white bodies and thin legs. The wings weren't made of feathers, but of skin, like a bat's wings, white like the rest of their bodies.

All familiar, but only oddly so.

"The black bats," he said. "I dreamed black bats chased me from the forest."

"That was no dream," Gabil replied in an excited tone. "No sir! You were lucky I came along when I did."

"I'm sorry, I don't . . . I can't quite remember what's going on."

The two creatures studied him with blank stares. "You don't remember anything?" Michal asked.

"No. I mean, yes, I remember being chased. But I hit my head on a rock last night and I was knocked out." He paused and tried to think of the best way to explain his disorientation. "I can't remember anything before I hit my head."

"Then you've lost your memory," Michal said. He waddled forward. "You do realize where you are?"

Tom stepped back instinctively and the creature stopped. "Well . . . actually not entirely. Sort of, but not really." He rubbed his head. "I must have really bumped my head."

"Well then. What *do* you know?" Michal asked.

"I know that my name is Tom Hunter. I somehow got into the black forest with someone named Bill, but I fell and smashed my head on a rock. Bill drank the water and just wandered —"

"You saw him drink the water?" Michal demanded.

"Yes, he definitely drank the water."

"Hmm."

Tom waited for him to explain his reaction, but the creature just waved him on. "Go ahead. What then?"

"Then I saw you" — he looked at Gabil — "and I ran."

"That's all? Nothing more?"

"No. Except my dreams. I remember my dreams."

They waited expectantly.

"You want to know my dreams?"

"Yes," Michal said.

"Well, they make no sense. Completely different from this. Crazy stuff."

"Well then. Tell us this crazy stuff."

Denver. His sister, Kara. The mob. A fully formed world with amazing detail. He told the creatures the gist of it all in a long run-on sentence, but he felt self-conscious telling them his dreams, no matter how vivid they had seemed. Why would they want to know his dreams anyway? The creatures looked at him, unblinking, absorbing his brief tale without reacting.

They and the colored forest behind them were perfectly normal. He just couldn't remember them.

"That's all?" Michal asked when he'd finished.

"Mostly."

"I didn't think anyone but the wise ones knew the histories so vividly," Gabil said.

"What histories?"

"You don't know what the histories are?" Michal asked. "You're speaking about them as if you know them well enough."

"You mean my dreams of Denver are real?"

"Heavens no." Michal waddled in the direction the woman had run, then turned back. "Not your running about with men in hot pursuit anyway. That's certainly not real, at least. But the histories of ancient Earth are real. Yes, of course they are. Everyone knows about them." He paused and looked at Thomas with skepticism. "You honestly don't know what I'm talking about?"

Tom blinked and looked at the colored forest. The tree trunks glowed. So very foreign, yet so familiar.

"No," he said, rubbing his temples. "I just can't seem to think straight."

"Well, you seem to be thinking quite straight when it comes to the histories. They're an oral tradition, passed on in each of the villages by the storytellers. Denver, New York — everything you dreamed about is taken from the histories."

Gabil hopped sideways like a bird. "The histories!"

Michal cast a side glance at the other as if impatient. "My dear friend, I do believe you have a classic case of amnesia, though I can't understand why the water didn't heal that as well. The black forest has sent you into a state of shock — no surprise there. Now you're dreaming that you live in a world you've fabricated and are being chased by men with ill intent. Your mind has created a detailed dream using what you know about the histories. Fascinating."

"Fascinating!" Gabil said.

Another glance from Michal.

"But if I lost my memory, why would I remember the histories?" Thomas objected. "It's almost as if I know more about my dreams than I do about . . . you."

"As I said, amnesia," Michal explained. "The mind is an amazing thing, isn't it? Selective memory loss. It seems you can remember only certain things, like the histories. You're hallucinating. You're dreaming of the histories. Reasonable enough. I'm sure the condition will pass. As I said, you've been through quite a shock, not to mention the knock to your head."

Made sense. "Just a dream. Hallucinations because I've knocked my head senseless."

"In my estimation," Michal said.

"That means there was an ancient Earth? One that no longer exists? The one I'm dreaming about?"

The Roush frowned. "Not quite, but close enough. Some call it ancient Earth, but it could also be called other Earth. Either way, this is Earth."

"And what's the difference between this Earth and the one I dream about?"

"If I were to characterize it in a few words? In the other place, the forces of good and evil could not be seen. Only their effects. But here, both good and evil are more . . . intimate. As you experienced with the black bats. An incomplete differentiation, but simple enough, wouldn't you say, Gabil?"

"I would say, simple enough."

"Well then, there you have it."

The explanation didn't seem quite so simple to Tom, but he let it suffice. "And what happened to ancient Earth?" he asked.

"Oh dear, now you ask too much," Michal said, turning. "That story is not so simple. We would have to start with the great virus at the beginning of the twenty-first century —"

"The French," Gabil cut in. "The Raison Strain. In the year 2010. Or was it 2012?"

"Ten," Michal said. "And not really the

French. A Frenchman, yes, but you can't say it was . . . never mind. They thought it was a good thing, a vaccine, but it mutated under intense heat and became a virus. The whole business ravaged the entire population of Earth in a matter of three short weeks —"

"Less than three," Gabil inserted. "Less than three weeks."

"— and opened the door to the Deception."

"The *Great* Deception," Gabil said.

"Yes, the Great Deception." Michal gave his friend a let-me-tell-the-story look. "From there we would have to move on to the time of the tribulations and wars. It would take a full day to tell you how other Earth — ancient Earth — saw the end. Clearly you don't know all of the histories, do you?"

"Obviously not."

"Perhaps your mind has inserted itself at a particular point and is stuck there. The mind, a wonderfully tricky thing, you know?"

Tom nodded.

"But how do I know *this* isn't the dream?" he asked.

They both blinked.

"I mean, isn't it possible? In the Denver place I have a sister and a history, and things are really happening. Here I can't remember a thing."

"Clearly you have amnesia," Michal said. "You don't think my easily excited friend here and I are real? That isn't grass under your feet, or oxygen passing through your lungs?"

"I'm not saying that . . ."

"You've lost your memory, Thomas Hunter, if that's indeed your real name. I would guess it's the name from your dreams — they used double names in ancient Earth. But it'll do until we can figure out who you really are."

"We can see you," chirped Gabil. "You're no dream, Thomas!"

"So you really can't remember *anything* about this place?" Michal asked. "The lake, the Shataiki? Us?"

"No, I can't. I really can't."

Michal sighed. "Well, then I suppose we'll have to fill you in. But where to start?"

"With us," Gabil, the shorter one, said. "We are mighty warriors with frightening strength." He strutted to Tom's right on his short, spindly legs, like a furry Easter egg with wings. A huge white baby chick. Tweety on steroids. "You saw how I sent the black bats flying for cover! I have a thousand stories that I could —"

"We are Roush," Michal interrupted.

"Yes, of course," Gabil said. "Roush. Mighty warriors."

"Some of us are evidently mightier warriors than others," Michal said with a wink.

"Mighty, mighty warriors," said Gabil.

"Servants of Elyon. And you, of course, are a man. We are on Earth. You know *none* of this? It seems quite elementary."

"What about the man who drank the water?" Tom asked. "Bill."

"Bill was no man. If he was a man and he drank the forbidden water, we would probably all be dead by now. He was a figment of your imagination, formed by the Shataiki to lure *you* to the water. Surely you remember the forbidden water."

Tom paced and shook his head. "I'm telling you, I don't know anything! I don't know what water is forbidden, or what water is drinkable, or who these Shataiki bats are, or who the woman was." He stopped. "Or what she meant when she said she's chosen me."

"Forgive me. It's not that I doubt you can't remember anything; it's just very strange to talk to someone who's lost his memory. I am what they call a wise one — the only wise one in this part of the forest. I have perfect memory. Dear, dear. This is going to be interesting, isn't it? Rachelle has chosen a man with no memory."

Gabil smiled wide. "How romantic!"

Romantic?

"Gabil finds nearly everything romantic.

He secretly wants to be a man. Or perhaps a woman, I think."

The smaller Roush didn't argue.

"At any rate, I suppose we should start with the very basics then. Follow me." Michal headed toward the sound of the rushing water. "Come, come."

Tom followed. The thick carpet of grass silenced his footfalls. It didn't thin out under the trees but ran heavy and lush right through. Violet and lavender flowers with petals the size of his hand stood knee-high, scattered about the forest floor. No debris or dead branches littered the ground, making walking surprisingly easy for the two Roush hopping ahead of him.

Tom lifted his eyes to the tall trees shining their soft colors about him. Most seemed to glow with one predominant color, like cyan or magenta or yellow, accented by the other colors of the rainbow. How could the trees glow? It was as if they were powered by some massive underground generator that powered fluorescent chemicals in large tubes made to look like trees. No, that was technology from ancient Earth.

He ran his hand gently across the surface of a large ruby tree with a purple hue, surprised at how smooth it was, as if it had no bark at all. He took in the tree's full height. Breathtaking.

Michal cleared his throat and Tom jerked his hand from the tree.

"Just ahead," the Roush said.

"Just a moment more," Gabil piped in.

They exited the forest less than fifty yards from the meadow, on the banks of the river. The white bridge he'd stumbled over spanned flowing water. On the far side, the black forest. Tall trees lined the bank as far as he could see in either direction. Behind the trees, deep, dark shadows. The memory of them sent a wave of nausea through Tom's gut.

Not a black bat in sight.

Michal stopped and faced him. He might not be the more excitable of the two Roush, but at the moment he was eager enough to take on the role of teacher. He stretched one wing toward the black forest and spoke with authority.

"That is the black forest. Do you remember it?"

"Of course. I was in it, remember?"

"Yes, I do remember that you were in it. I'm not the one with the memory problem. I was just double-checking so as to give us a common point of reference."

"The black forest is the place where the Shataiki live!" Gabil said.

"If you don't mind, I'm telling the story here," Michal said.

"Of course I don't mind."

"Now. This river you see runs around the whole planet. It separates the green forest from the black forest." He absently flipped his wing in the direction of the far bank. "That's the black forest. The only way into the black forest from this side is over one of three Crossings." He pointed to the white bridge. "The river runs too fast to swim, you see? No one would dare attempt to cross except over one of the bridges. Do you follow?"

"Yes."

"Good. And you can remember what I just told you, correct?"

"Yes."

"Good. Your memory was wiped clean, but it seems to be working with any new data. Now." He paced and stroked his chin with delicate fingers on the underside of his right wing. "There are many other men, women, and children in many villages throughout the green forest. Over a million now live on Earth. You likely stumbled into the black forest over one of the other two Crossings on the far side and then were chased here by the Shataiki."

"How do you know I don't come from nearby?"

"Because, as the wise one given charge over this section of the forest, I would know you. I don't."

"And I am the mighty warrior who led

you from the black forest," Gabil said.

"Yes, and Gabil is the mighty warrior who cavorts with Tanis in all kinds of imagined battles."

"Tanis? Who's Tanis?" Tom asked.

Michal sighed. "Tanis is the firstborn of all men. You will meet him. He lives in the village. Now, Elyon, who created everything you see and all creatures, has touched all of the water. You see the green color of the river? That is the color of Elyon. It's why your eyes are green. It's also why your body was healed the moment the water touched it."

"You poured water on me?"

"No, not I —"

"Rachelle!" Gabil blurted out.

"Rachelle poured the water over you. Trust me, it's not the first time you've touched his water." Michal's cheeks bunched into a soft smile. "But we'll get —"

"Rachelle has chosen you —"

"Gabil! Please!"

"Yes, of course." The smaller Roush didn't seem at all put off by Michal's chiding.

Michal went on. "As I was saying, we'll get to the Great Romance later. Now, the black forest is where evil is confined. You see, good" — he pointed to the green forest — "and evil." He pointed to the black forest. "No one is permitted to drink the water in the black forest. If they do, the Shataiki will be released to have their way with the colored forest. It would be a slaughter."

"The water in the black forest is evil?" Thomas asked. "I touched it —"

"Not evil. Not any more evil than the colored trees are good. Evil and good reside in the heart, not in trees and water. But by custom, water is given as an invitation. Elyon invites with water. The black Shataiki invite with their water."

"And Rachelle invited you with water," Gabil said.

"Yes. In a moment, Gabil," Michal said. But the more stately Roush couldn't hide a slight smile. "For many years, the people have agreed not to cross the river as a matter of precaution. Very wise, if you ask me." The Roush paused and looked about. "That is the heart of it. There are a thousand other details, but hopefully they will return to you in short order."

"Except for the Great Romance," Gabil said. "And Rachelle."

"Except for the Great Romance, which I will let Gabil tell you about, since he's so eager."

Gabil didn't miss a beat. "She's chosen you, Thomas! Rachelle has. It is her choice and now it's yours. You will pursue her and woo her and win her as only you can." He grinned delightedly.

Tom waited for Gabil to continue. The creature just kept grinning.

"I'm sorry," Tom said. "I don't see the significance. I don't even know her."

"Even more delicious! It's a wonderful twist! The point is, you don't bear the mark on your forehead, so you are eligible for any woman. You will fall madly in love and be united!"

"This is crazy! I hardly know who I am — romance is the farthest thing from my mind. For all I know, I'm in love with another woman in my own village."

"No, that wouldn't be the case. You would bear another mark."

Surely they didn't expect him to pursue this woman out of obligation. "I still have to choose her, right? But I can't. Not in this condition. I don't even know if I'll like her."

The two Roush stared, stupefied.

"I'm afraid you don't understand," Michal said. "It's not a matter of liking. Of course you'll *like* her. It is your choice, otherwise it wouldn't be choosing. But — and you must trust me on this — your kind abound in love. He made you that way. Like himself. You would love any woman who chooses you. And any woman you choose would choose you. It's the way it is."

"What if I don't feel that way?"

"She's perfect!" Gabil said. "They all are. You *will* feel that way, Thomas. You will!"

"We're from different villages. She would just go away with me?"

Michal raised his eyebrow. "Minor details. I can see this memory loss could be a problem. Now we really should be leaving. It will be slow on foot, and we have quite a road before us." He turned to his friend. "Gabil, you may fly, and I will stay with Thomas Hunter."

"We must go," Gabil said. He unfurled his wings and leaped into the air. Tom watched in amazement as the white furry's body lifted gracefully from the earth. A puff of air from the Roush's thin wings lifted the hair from his forehead.

Tom stared at the magnificent forest and hesitated. Michal looked back at him patiently from the tree line. "Shall we go?" He turned back to the forest. Tom took a deep breath and stepped after the Roush without a word.

They proceeded through the colored forest for ten minutes in silence. The sum of it was that he lived here, somewhere, perhaps far away, but in this wonderful, surreal place. Surely when he saw his friends, his village, his . . . whatever else was his, his memory would be sparked.

"How long will it take to return me to my people?" Tom asked.

"These are all your people. What village you live in isn't terribly significant."

"Okay, but how long before I find my own family?"

"Depends," Michal said. "News is a bit slow and the distances are great. It could take a few days. Maybe even a week."

"A week! What will I do?"

The Roush pulled up and stopped. "What will you do? Are your ears not working as well? You've been chosen!" He shook his head and continued. "Dear, dear. I can see this memory loss is quite impossible. Let me give you some advice, Thomas Hunter. Until your memory returns, follow the others. This confusion of yours is disconcerting."

"I can't pretend. If I don't know what's happening, I can't —"

"If you follow the others, perhaps everything will come back to you. At the very least, follow Rachelle."

"You want me to pretend to be in love with her?"

"You *will* be in love with her! You just don't remember how it all works. If you were to meet your mother but didn't remember her, would you stop loving her? No! You would assume you loved her and thereby love her."

The Roush had a point.

Gabil suddenly swept down from the treetops and lit next to Tom, plump face grinning. "Are you hungry, Thomas Hunter?" He held up a blue fruit with his wing. Tom stopped and stared at the fruit.

"No need to be afraid, no sir. This is very good fruit. A blue peach. Look." Gabil took a small bite out of the fruit and showed it to Tom. The juice glistening in the bite mark had the same green, oily tinge he recognized from the river.

"Oh, yes," Michal said, turning back, "another small detail, in the event you don't remember. This is the food you eat. It's called fruit and it, too, along with the water, has been touched by Elyon."

Tom took the fruit gingerly in his hands and looked at Michal.

"Go ahead, eat it. Eat it."

He took a small bite and felt the cool, sweet juice fill his mouth. A flutter descended into his stomach, and warmth spread through his body. He smiled at Gabil.

"This is good," he said, taking another bite. "Very good."

"The food of warriors!" Gabil said. With that the short creature trot-waddled a few feet, leaped off the ground, and flew back into the sky.

Michal chuckled at his companion and

walked on. "Come. Come. We must not wait."

Tom had just finished the blue peach when Gabil brought another, a red one this time. With a swoop and a shrill laugh, he dropped the fruit into Tom's hands and took off again. The third time the fruit was green and required peeling, but its flesh was perhaps the tastiest yet.

Gabil's fourth appearance consisted of an aerobatics show. The Roush screamed in from high above, looping with an arched back then twisting into a dive, which he managed to pull out of just over Tom's head. Tom threw up his arms and ducked, sure the Roush had miscalculated. With a flurry of wings and a screech, Gabil buzzed his head.

"Gabil!" Michal called out after him. "Show some care there!"

Gabil flew on without a backward glance.

"Mighty warrior indeed," Michal said, stepping back along the path.

Less than a mile later, the Roush stopped on a crest. Tom stepped up beside the furry creature and looked down on a large green valley covered in flowers like daisies, but turquoise and orange, a rich carpet inviting a roll. Tom was so surprised at the sudden change in landscape that he didn't at first notice the village.

When he did, the sight took his breath away.

The circular village that nestled in the valley below sparkled with color. For a moment, Tom thought he must have stumbled onto Candyland, or possibly Hansel and Gretel lived here. But he knew that was a lost story from the histories. This village, on the other hand, was very, very real.

Several hundred square huts, each glowing with a different color, rested like children's playing blocks in concentric circles around a large pinnacled structure that towered above the others at the village's center. The sky above the dwellings was filled with Roush, who floated and dived and twisted in the afternoon sun.

As his eyes adjusted to the incredible scene, he saw a door open from a dwelling far below. Tom watched a tiny form step from the door. And then he saw that dozens of people dotted the village.

"Does it jog any memories?" Michal asked.

"Actually, I think it does."

"What do you remember?"

"Well, nothing in particular. It's just all vaguely familiar."

Michal sighed. "You know, I've been thinking. There may be some good that comes out of your little adventure in the

101

black forest. There's been talk of an expedition — an absurd idea that Tanis has somehow latched onto. He seems to think it's time to fight the Shataiki. He's always been inventive, a storyteller. But this latest talk of his has me in fits. Maybe you could talk him out of it."

"Does Tanis even know how to fight?"

"Like no other man I know. He's developed a method that is quite spectacular. More flips and twirls and kicks than I would know what to do with. It's based on certain stories from the histories. Tanis is fascinated with them — particularly the histories of conquests. He's determined to wipe out the Shataiki."

"And why shouldn't he?"

"The Shataiki may not be great warriors, but they can deceive. Their water is very inviting. You've seen. Maybe you could talk some sense into the man."

Thomas nodded. He was suddenly eager to meet this Tanis.

Michal sighed. "Okay, stay here. You must wait for me to return. Do you understand?"

"Sure, but . . ."

"No. Just wait. If you see them leaving for the Gathering, you may go with them, but otherwise, please stay here."

"What's the Gathering?"

"To the lake. Don't worry; you can't

miss it. There'll be an exodus just before dusk. Agreed?"

"Agreed."

Michal unfolded his wings for the first time in two hours and took to the air. Tom watched him disappear across the valley, feeling abandoned and unsure.

He could see now that the dwellings must have been made out of the forest's colored trees. These were his people — a strange thought. Maybe not his very own people, as in father, mother, brother, sister, but people just like him. He was lost but not so lost after all.

Was the woman Rachelle down there?

He sat cross-legged, leaned against a tree, and sighed. The houses were small and quaint — more like cottages than houses. Paths of grass separated them from one another, giving the town the appearance of a giant wheel with spokes converging on a large, circular building at the hub. The structure was at least three times as high and many times wider than any of the other dwellings. A meeting place, perhaps.

To his right, a wide path led from the village to the forest, where it vanished. The lake.

Thoughts ran circles around his mind. It occurred to him that Michal had been gone a long time. He was looking for an exodus and he was looking for Michal, but neither was coming fast. He leaned his head back on the tree and closed his eyes.

So strange.

So tired.

8

Tom opened his eyes and knew immediately that it had happened again.

He was lying on the beige chaise in the apartment in Denver, Colorado. Covered by a batik quilt. Light streamed through a gap in the drapes on his left. On his right, the back of the couch, and beyond it, the locked door. Above, the ceiling. Orange-peel texture covered by an off-white paint. Could be clouds in the sky, could be a thousand worlds hiding between those bumps. Tom lay perfectly still and drew a deep breath.

He was dreaming.

Yes, of course he was dreaming. This couldn't be real because now he knew the truth of the matter. He'd been knocked on the head while in the black forest. The blow had robbed his memories and kicked him into these strange dreams where he actually thought he was alive on ancient Earth, being chased by some men with *ill intent,* as Michal had put it.

He was, at this very moment, dreaming

of the histories of ancient Earth. Or other Earth.

Tom sat up. Amazing! It all looked so real. His fingertips could actually feel the texture of the quilt. Kara's mosaic of masquerade masks looked as real as real could be. He was breathing, and he could taste his musty morning mouth. He was engaging this dream with nearly as much realism as if he were actually awake, touching the trees of the colored forest, or biting into the sweet fruit brought to him by Gabil. This wasn't quite as real, but very convincing.

At least he knew what was happening now. And he knew why the dream felt so real. What an incredible trip.

He swung his feet to the floor and pushed the quilt aside. So, what could he do in his dreams that he couldn't do in real life? He stretched his fingers and curled them. Could he float?

He stood. As he expected, no ache in his head. 'Course not, this was only a dream. He bounced on the balls of his feet.

No floating.

Okay, so he couldn't float like in some of his dreams, but he was sure there were plenty of unusual things he could do. He couldn't get hurt, truly hurt, in his dreams, which gave him some interesting possibilities.

Tom took a few steps and then stopped. Interestingly enough, dream steps actually felt very similar to real steps, although he could tell the difference. His legs didn't feel totally real. In fact, if he closed his eyes — which he did — he couldn't really feel his legs. He could feel his feet, sure, but as far as he knew there could be air rather than flesh and bone connecting his feet to his hips.

Dream standing. Incredible.

He walked around the room in awe of how utterly real everything felt. Not quite as real as walking with Michal and Gabil, of course, but if he didn't know he was in a dream, he might actually think this room was real. Amazing how the mind worked.

He ran his hand over a black cassowary carving he'd imported from Indonesia. He could feel every bump and nick. It probably even — Tom bent to sniff the wood — yes, it did smell like smoke, exactly as he'd imagined. The wood had been hardened by burning. Had the carver been dreaming when he carved —

"Thomas?"

He wondered if that was Michal calling him. The Roush had returned from wherever he'd flown off to and was trying to wake him. Tom wasn't sure he wanted to be awakened quite yet. This dream —

"Tom."

Actually, the voice sounded higher, more like Gabil's voice.

"What are you doing?"

He turned around. Kara stood by the couch, dressed in a blue-flowered camisole and boxers. He should've known. He was still dreaming.

"Hi, sis."

She wasn't really his sister, of course, because she didn't really exist. Well, in this dream reality she did, but not in *real* reality.

"You okay?"

"Sure. Never been better. Don't I look okay?"

"So . . . so you're not freaking out over what happened last night, I take it?"

"Last night?" He paced to his right, wondering if Michal might wake him up at any moment. "Oh, you mean the chase through the alleys and the shot to the head and the way I handily dispatched the bad dudes? Actually, this may come as a shock to you, but none of that really happened."

"What do you mean? You made that all up?" Her face lightened a shade.

"Well, no, not really. I mean, it did happen here. But here isn't really real. The cow can't really jump over the moon, and when you dream that you're falling but you never actually land, it's because you're not really falling. This isn't real." He grinned. "Pretty cool, huh?"

"What on earth are you talking about?" Her eyes shifted to the end table where the bottle of pain pills sat. "Did you take any more medication?"

"Ah, yes. That would be the Demerol. No, I didn't, and no, I'm not hallucinating." He stretched out his arms and announced the truth of the matter. "This, dear sister, is a dream. We're actually *in* a dream!"

"Stop messing around. You're not funny."

"Say whatever you like. But this isn't really happening right now. You'll say I'm crazy because you don't know any better — how can you? You're part of the dream."

"What do you call the bandage on your head? A dream? This is insane!" She headed for the breakfast bar.

Tom felt the bandage around his head. "I'm dreaming about this cut because I fell on a stone in the black forest. Although not everything correlates exactly, because I don't have a broken arm here like I did there."

Kara faced him, incredulous. For a moment she said nothing, and he thought she might be coming to her senses. Maybe with the right persuasion, dream-people could be convinced that they lived only in your dreams.

"Have you given our situation with the New Yorkers any more thought?" she asked.

Nope. She was still in denial.

"You're not listening, Kara. There *was* no chase last night. This cut came from the black forest. This is a dre—"

"Thomas! Stop it! And stop smiling like that."

Her sincerity certainly sounded real. He flattened his mouth.

"You can't be serious about this nonsense," Kara said.

"Dead serious," he said. "Think about it. What if this really is a dream? At least consider the possibility. I mean what if all of this" — he swept his arms about — "what if it's all just in your mind? Michal told me this was happening, and it is, exactly like he said it was. Trust me, that was no dream. I was attacked by Shataiki. You wouldn't know about those, but they're big black bats with red eyes . . ."

He stopped. Maybe he should go light on the details. To Kara such realities would sound preposterous without having lived them firsthand.

"In reality, I live on the other Earth. I'm waiting for Michal, but he's taking forever, so I sat down and put my head back on a tree. I just fell asleep. Don't you see?" He grinned again.

"No, actually I don't."

"I just fell asleep, Kara. I'm sleeping! Right at this very minute, I'm asleep under a tree. So you tell me, how could I be standing here if I know I'm asleep under a tree waiting for Michal? Tell me that!"

"So you live in a world with big black bats and . . ." She sighed. "Listen to yourself, Thomas! This isn't good. I need you sane now. Are you sure you didn't take any more of those pills?"

Tom felt his frustration building, but he remained calm. It was, after all, just a dream. He could feel however he wanted to in a dream. If a great big ghost with fangs rushed him right now, he could just face it and laugh and it would vanish. No need to trounce all over Kara — she could hardly be blamed. If he couldn't convince her, he would just play along. Why not? Michal would wake him up at any moment.

"Fine, Kara. Fine. But what if I can prove it to you?"

"You can't. We have to figure out what we're going to do. I need to get dressed and then get you to the hospital. You have a concussion."

"But what if I can prove we're in a dream? I mean really? I mean, just move your hand around like this." He swept his hand through the air. "Can't you tell that it's not real? I can. Can't you feel that something's not quite right? The air feels thinner —"

"Please, Thomas, you're starting to scare me."

He lowered his hand. "Okay, but what if I could prove it logically?"

"That's impossible."

"What if I could tell you how the world is going to end?"

"Now you're a prophet? You live in a world with black bats, and you can read the future? None of that sounds stupid to you? Think, Thomas, think! Wake up."

"It's not stupid. I can tell you how the world is going to end because, in reality, it *has* ended, and it has been recorded in the histories."

"Of course it has."

"Exactly. It will begin with the Raison Strain — some kind of virus that comes from a French company. Everyone thinks it's a vaccine, but it mutates under intense heat and will ravage the world sometime in 2010. I'm not quite sure on that last detail."

"That's your proof? That the world is going to end sometime this year?"

She wasn't buying the argument.

Tom suddenly had another thought. Quite a fun thought, actually. He walked for the front door, twisted the deadbolt, and flung it open.

"Okay, I'll prove it to you," he said and stepped outside.

"What are you doing? What if they're out there?"

"They're not out here because they don't exist. Am I talking to a wall here?" The light stung his eyes. He stepped across the front walkway and gripped the railing. They were three floors up. The parking lot below was concrete.

Kara ran to the doorway. "Thomas! What are you doing?"

"I'm going to jump. In dreams you can't really get hurt, right? If I jump —"

"Are you crazy? You *will too* get hurt! What do you call the bullet wound on your head?"

"I told you, that was from a rock in the black forest."

"But what if you're wrong?"

"I'm not."

"What if you are? What if there's even a slight possibility that you are? What if it's the other way around?"

"What do you mean?"

"What if this is the real Earth, but you think the other one is because it feels so real?"

"The cut on my head from the fall, it's real. How can you —"

"Unless it really was a bullet that cut

your head, and so you dreamed something, like the rock. Step back, Thomas. You're not thinking clearly."

Tom looked down, suddenly struck with that possibility. Out here in the morning light, his confidence waned. What if she was right? He had hurt his head in both the black forest and in his dream here. What if there was a real connection? Or what if he had the dreams backward?

"Tom. Please."

He backed away from the railing, heart suddenly hammering. What was he thinking?

"You think that's possible?" he asked.

"Yes! Yes, I think. I know!"

He rubbed his fingers together, then looked at her. Actually, now that he thought about it, she was his sister. If he was only dreaming, did that mean Kara didn't really exist?

The morning newspaper lay by the front door. If she was right, then it meant they really *were* in trouble. He grabbed the paper.

"Okay, get inside."

She did, quickly, and he pulled the door closed.

"You have me worried," Kara said. She took the newspaper from him and led him into the kitchen. "This isn't good timing. That bullet obviously did more harm than we thought."

She dropped the paper on the counter,

114

turned the water on, and scanned the front page as she washed her hands.

"I'm sorry, honestly, I'm just . . ." Actually, Tom didn't know what he just was. Clearly, it was decision time. He had to assume that he was in Denver after all, and not as part of a dream, but in reality. What that said about the black forest and Michal made his head spin. He didn't have the brain capacity to figure it out at the moment. If he really had been chased down by New Yorkers last night, he and Kara had their hands full.

Panic rolled up his belly. They had to get out of town.

"Tom?"

He looked up. "We have to get out of here."

She wasn't listening. Her wet hands hung over the sink, unmoving. Her eyes were fixed on the newspaper to her left.

"What did you say that virus was called?"

"What virus? The Raison Strain?"

"A French company?"

He walked up to her and looked at the paper. A bold black headline ran across the top:

CHINA SAYS NO

"China says no?"

She lifted the paper, unconcerned with the dark water blotches her hands made on the page. He saw the smaller headline then, halfway down and on the left, the business-page headline:

FRENCH ASSETS:
RAISON PHARMACEUTICAL
TO ANNOUNCE NEW VACCINE,
SELLS U.S. INTERESTS

Tom took the paper, flipped to the business page, and found the article. The company's name suddenly seemed to fill the entire page. Raison Pharmaceutical. His pulse pounded.

"What —" Kara stopped, apparently confused by this new information. She leaned in and quickly read the short story with him.

Raison Pharmaceutical, a well-known French parent of several smaller companies, had been founded by Jacques de Raison in 1973. The company, which specialized in vaccines and genetic research, had plants in several countries but was headquartered in Bangkok, where it had operated without the restrictions often hampering domestic pharmaceutical companies. The company was best known for its handling of deadly viruses in the process of creating vaccines. Its contracts with the former Soviet Union were at one time quite controversial.

In the last few years, the firm had become better known for its release of several oral and nasal vaccines. The drugs, based on recombinant DNA research, weren't dose-restrictive — a fancy way of saying they could be taken in large quantities without side effects. Dibloxin 42, a smallpox vaccine, for example, could be deposited in a country's water supply, effectively administering the vaccine to the whole population without fear of overdosing any one person, regardless of how much water was consumed. A perfect solution for the Third World.

Several of the vaccines, however, would be subjected to a whole new gamut of rigorous testing procedures if Congress passed the new legislation introduced by Merton Gains before he became deputy secretary of state.

Raison advised this morning that in a matter of days it would announce a new multipurpose, airborne vaccine that would effectively eliminate the threat of several problematic diseases worldwide. Dubbed the Raison Vaccine —

Kara uttered a short gasp at the same time Tom read the sentence.

"Dubbed the Raison Vaccine, the vaccine promises to revolutionize preventive

medicine. Stocks are bound to react to the news, but the gains may be tempered by the announcement that the firm's Ohio plant will close in the interests of focusing on the Raison Vaccine, developed by the Bangkok facility."

The article went on, offering details about the stock market's anticipated reaction to the news. Tom's hand trembled slightly.

"How did you know about this?" Kara asked, looking up.

"I didn't. I swear I've never seen or heard this name until right now. Except . . ."

"Except in your dreams. No, that's impossible."

Tom laid the paper down and set his jaw. "Tell me how else I could have known about this."

"You must have heard about —"

"Even if I knew about the company, which I didn't before last night, there's no way I could have known about the Raison Vaccine — not without reading this paper. But I did!"

"Then you read the paper or heard it on the news last night."

"I didn't watch the news last night! And you saw the paper outside, exactly where it always is in the morning."

She crossed one arm and nibbled at her

fingernail, something she did only when she was beyond herself. Tom recalled his discussion about the Raison Strain with Michal as if it had occurred only a moment ago, which wasn't that far from the truth. For all he knew, he had been asleep under the tree for only a few minutes.

But this wasn't really a dream, was it?

"You're actually telling me that something's happening in your dreams that gives you this information?" she demanded. "What else did you learn about the future?"

He considered that. "Only that the Raison Vaccine has some problems and ends up as a virus called the Raison Strain, which infects most of the world population in a . . ."

"In a what?"

Tom scratched his head. "In a very short time."

"How short?" She exhaled sharply. "Listen to me, I can't believe I'm even asking these questions."

"In a few weeks, I think."

Kara paced the kitchen, still biting her fingernail. "This is just crazy. Yesterday the extent of my life's challenges consisted of whether I should cut my hair short, but that was before I came home to my crazy brother. Now the mob is breathing down our necks, and it just so happens that the whole world is about to be infected by a virus no one but my dreaming brother knows about. And how, pray tell, does he know about this virus? Simple: Some black bat with red eyes in the real world told him. Excuse me if I don't don my gas mask posthaste."

She was venting, but she was also troubled or she wouldn't *be* venting.

"Not a black bat," Tom said. "A white one. A Roush. And the Roush have green eyes."

"Yes, of course; how silly of me. Green eyes. The bat with green eyes told him. And did I mention the tidbit about this world all being a dream? Well, if it's a dream, we really don't have to worry, do we?"

She had a point there.

Tom walked into the living room and turned around to see she'd followed him. Her face was pale. She really was worried, wasn't she?

"But you don't believe for a second that you and I are in a dream right now," he said. "Which can only mean that the other stuff is a dream. Fine. That's worse. It means this is real. That a virus is about to threaten the world."

Kara walked to the window and eased back the drape. She still wasn't buying it, but her confidence had been shaken.

"Anyone?" he asked.

"No." She released the curtain. "But if I'm to believe you, a few killers from New York are the least of our problems, right?"

"Look, could you please lose the condescending tone here? I didn't ask for this. Okay, maybe I did set us up for the mob, but I've already begged your forgiveness for that. In the rest of this, I'm as innocent as you. Can I help what my dreams are?"

"It just sounds so stupid, Thomas. You at least see that, don't you? It sounds like something a kid would dream up. And frankly, the fact that you're so . . . youthful isn't playing in your favor here."

Tom said nothing.

Kara sighed and sat on the arm of the couch. "Okay. Okay, just say that there's something to your dreams. Exactly what are these dreams about?"

"For the record, I'm not agreeing that they are dreams," he said. "At the very least, I have to treat each scenario like it is real. I mean, you want me to treat this room like it's really here, right? You don't want me to jump off the balcony. Fine, but believe me, it's just as real there. I'm sleeping under a tree there right now. But the moment I wake up from my little nap under the tree, I'll have a whole set of new problems."

"Fine," she said, exasperated. "Fine,

let's pretend both are real. Tell me about this . . . other place."

"All of it?"

"Whatever you think makes sense."

"It *all* makes sense."

Tom took a deep breath and told her about waking up in the black forest and about the bats that chased him and the woman he'd met and about the Roush leading him to the village. He didn't think there was any evil in the colored forest. It seemed confined to the black forest. He told it all to her, and as he spoke, she listened with an intensity that undermined periodic scoffs until they stopped altogether.

"So every time you fall asleep in either place, you wake up in the other place?"

"Exactly."

"And there's no direct time correlation. I mean, you could spend a whole day there and wake up here to find out only a minute had passed."

"I think so. I've been there for a whole day but not here."

She suddenly stood and walked into the kitchen.

"What are you doing?" Tom asked.

"We're going to test these dreams of yours. And not by jumping over guardrails."

"You know how to test this?" He hurried after her.

She grabbed the newspaper and flipped through it. "Why not? You claim to have gained some knowledge from this place. We'll see if you can get some more."

"How?"

"Simple. You go back to sleep, get some more information, and then we wake you up to see if you have something we can verify."

He blinked. "You think that's possible?"

She shrugged. "That's the point — to find out. You said they have histories of Earth there. You think they would have the results of sporting events?"

"I . . . I don't know. Seems kind of trivial."

"History loves trivia. If there's history, it will include sporting events." She'd stopped on a sports section and glanced down the page. Her eyes stopped and then looked over the paper at him.

"You know anything about horse racing?" she asked.

"Uh, no."

"Name me a horse that's on the racing circuit."

"Any horse?"

"Any horse. Just one."

"I don't know any horse. Runner's Luck?"

"You're making that up."

"Yes."

"That's not the point. I'm just satisfying myself that you don't know any of the entries in today's race."

"Which race?"

"The Kentucky Derby."

"That's running today?" He reached for the paper and she pulled it back.

"Not a chance. You don't know the horses racing; let's not spoil that." She folded the paper. "The race is in" — she glanced at the clock on the wall — "six hours. No one on Earth knows the winner. You go and talk to your furry friends. If you come back with the name of the horse that wins, I will reconsider this little theory of yours." A slight smile lifted her small mouth.

"I don't know if I can get that kind of detail," Tom said.

"Why not? Fly over to the golden library in the sky and ask the attending fuzzball for a bit of history. What can be so hard about that?"

"What if it's not a dream? I can't just do whatever I want there any more than I can do whatever I want here. And the histories are oral. They won't know who won a race!"

"You said that some of them knew everything from the histories."

"The wise ones. Michal. You think Michal is going to tell me who won the

Kentucky Derby in 2010?"

"Why not?"

"It doesn't sound like something he'd tell me."

"Oh, stop it."

"I'm sleeping on a hill right now — I can't just go on some crazy search for something this trivial."

"As soon as you fall asleep here, you'll wake up there," she said. "You want to prove this to me — here's your chance."

"This is ridiculous. That's not how it works."

"So you're begging off?"

"The race is in six hours. What if I can't go back to sleep over there?"

"You said there wasn't necessarily any time correlation. I'll let you sleep for half an hour, and then I'll wake you. We can't afford to sit around here for much longer than that anyway."

Tom ran his fingers through his hair. The suggestion sounded absurd to him, yet his own demands that she believe him were as absurd to her. More so. Actually, he had no reason to believe that he *couldn't* get the information. Maybe Michal would understand and tell him right away. As long as Kara woke him up in time . . .

It just might work.

"Okay."

"Okay?"

"Okay. How do I fall asleep?"

She looked at him as if she hadn't really expected him to agree. "You sure you don't know any of the horses?"

"Positive. And even if I did, I wouldn't know who is going to win, would I?"

"No." Kara gave him one last suspicious glance and headed for her bedroom, taking the paper with her. She returned thirty seconds later shaking a bottle of pills.

"You're going to drug me?" he asked. "How will you wake me up if I'm conked out? I can't walk around drugged all day."

"I've got some pills that will wake you up in a hurry too. It's admittedly a bit extreme, but I think our situation is a bit extreme, don't you?"

She was a nurse, he reminded himself. He could trust her.

Ten minutes later he lay on the couch, having ingested three large white tablets. They were talking about where they would go. They had to get out of town. To his surprise, Kara was warming to the idea. At least until they figured this all out.

What . . . what about . . . what . . . the Raison Strain, he was asking her.

She still wasn't sold on the Raison Strain. That's why she'd fed him the pills. Big, monstrous, white pills that were big enough to be . . .

"Can you tell me which village he comes from?" Michal asked.

"Not as near as you might imagine. Not as far as you might think."

This meant: *No, I choose not to tell you at this time.*

"Rachelle has chosen him. I should just lead him into the village?"

"Why not?"

This meant: *Don't interfere with the ways of humans.*

Michal shifted on his spindly feet. He dipped his head in reverence. "He concerns me," he said. "I fear the worst."

His master's voice answered softly, unconcerned. "Don't waste your time on fear. It's unbecoming."

Two valleys to the east, the man who called himself Thomas Hunter was slumped against a tree, lost in sleep. Dreaming of the histories in vivid detail. Surely this couldn't be good.

Michal had left the man and flown to a nearby tree to consider his options. He had to think the situation through carefully. Nothing of the kind had ever happened, at least not in his section of the forest. He couldn't just usher Thomas into the village and present him to Rachelle with this complete memory loss of his. He didn't even seem to know Elyon, for heaven's sake!

When Hunter fell asleep, Michal decided he must seek higher guidance.

"He thinks that this might be a dream," Michal said, looking up. "He thinks that he lives in the histories in a place called Denver, and that he's dreaming of the colored forest, of all things! He's got it backward! I tried to tell him, but I'm not sure he believes me entirely."

"I'm sure he'll eventually figure it out. He's quite smart."

"But at this very moment he's lying against a tree above the village, dreaming that he lives before the Great Deception!" Michal swept his wings behind his back and paced. "He seems to know the histories in stunning detail — a family, a home, even memories. He's bound to engage Tanis!"

"Then let him engage Tanis."

"But Tanis . . ." Could he say it? Should he say it? "Tanis is teetering!" he blurted out. "I fear a small nudge might push him over the edge. If he and Hunter start talking, there's no telling how creative Tanis might get."

"He was created to create. Let him create."

How could he say it so easily, standing there with hardly an expression? Didn't he know what kind of devastation Tanis could bring them all?

128

"Of course I know," the boy said. Now his soft green eyes shifted. "I knew it from the beginning."

Michal felt a lump rise in his throat. "Forgive my fear. I just can't imagine it. May I at least discourage them? I beg you —"

"Sure. Discourage them. But let them find their own way."

The boy turned and walked to a large white lion. He ran his hand along the lion's mane, and the beast fell to its belly. He looked out to sea, shielding his eyes from Michal's sight.

The Roush wanted to cry. He couldn't explain the feeling. He had no right to feel such remorse. The boy knew what he was doing. He always had known.

Michal left the upper lake, circled high, and slowly winged his way to where Thomas Hunter slept under the tree above the village.

9

Tom heard the rush of wings and felt himself falling from his dream. Tumbling, tumbling into real light, breathing real air, smelling something that reminded him of gardenias. He opened his eyes.

Michal was just pulling his wings in, not ten feet away. They were back in the colored forest. He'd been sleeping against a tall amber tree, dreaming as if he lived in the histories of Earth again. This time he'd returned with a challenge from Kara. Something about —

"It's been a full day for you, I can see," Michal said, waddling over. Another rush of wings to Tom's left announced Gabil, who incorporated a roll into his landing.

Tom stood up, fully awake. The grass was green; the forest glowed in blues and yellows behind him; the village waited in all its brilliance. He stepped forward, suddenly eager to descend the hill and reconnect with his past.

"Are we going?"

"Absolutely going," Gabil said.

"Yes," Michal said. "Although I'm afraid you've missed the Gathering." He looked over his shoulder, and Tom saw the last of a huge group disappearing down a path that led into the trees several miles away. As far as he could see, the village had emptied.

"I'm terribly sorry, but it will take us too long to catch up. You'd best just wait in the village until they return."

"What took you so long?"

"Perhaps I should have taken you to the village first, but I wanted to make sure. This is quite unusual, I'm sure you must realize. You didn't drink the water in the black forest, but the Shataiki clearly had *some* effect on you. Your memory at least. I had to be sure I did the right thing."

They headed down the hill in the afternoon's waning light, Michal first, followed by Tom, and Gabil hopping along to bring up the rear.

The histories. He'd dreamed that Kara had insisted this colored forest was a dream and Denver was real. She'd sent him on a mission.

The winner of the Kentucky Derby.

Would the histories record something so insignificant as the winner of a horse race? If so, only someone with a perfect memory could possibly recall it. Someone like Michal.

But asking Michal to check something he'd dreamed of had a ring of insanity to it. Then again, it was no more absurd than insisting to Kara that *she* was a dream. So then, which was it?

Here in the colored forest, Michal had offered a perfectly reasonable explanation for his dreams of Denver: Tom had hit his head and was dreaming of ancient Earth. Logical.

There in Denver, however, he had no explanation for how he could be dreaming about the Raison Strain, especially since the related events hadn't happened yet. He was getting the information from Michal, from the histories. But that would only prove that this world in which he'd found the histories was real. If this was real, then the other had to be a dream. Unless they were both real.

"How many people live in this village?" Tom asked.

"Here? This is the smallest village. There are three tribes on the planet, each with many villages. But this is the first. Tanis is the firstborn."

"Over one thousand in this village," Gabil piped up.

"Fifteen hundred and twenty-two," Michal said. "There are seven villages in this tribe, and they all come to the same Gathering. The other two tribes, one of

132

which is yours, are very far away and much larger. We have over a million living now."

"Huh. How long do we live? I mean how long has —"

Michal had stopped, and Tom nearly tripped over him.

Gabil bumped into him from behind. "Sorry. Sorry."

Michal was staring at Tom as if he'd lost his mind.

Tom stepped back. "What's wrong?"

"There *is* no death here. Only in the black forest. You're confusing reality with ancient Earth. Losing your memory I can understand, but surely you can separate what is real from your dreams."

"Sure," Tom said, but he wasn't sure. Not at all. He would have to think through his questions more carefully.

Michal sighed. "In the event you're not so sure as you say, let me give you a quick refresher on your history. Tanis, the leader of this village, whom we've discussed, was the firstborn. He was united with Mirium, his wife, and they had eighteen sons and twenty-three daughters over the course of the first two hundred years. His first two sons left, one to the east and one to the west, a month's journey each, to form the three tribes. Each tribe is completely self-contained. There is no commerce or trading, but visitors are quite common and interunions aren't unusual. Three times a year the other two tribes make a journey here for a very, very large celebration, known as the Great Gathering, not to be confused with the Gathering each tribe experiences every night."

Michal looked longingly toward the path the villagers had taken. "You'll find a preoccupation with the Gathering. It's the focus of each day. By midday most of the people are preparing for it in one way or another. It's a very simple yet very extravagant life I would gladly exchange a year of torment for. You are exceedingly fortunate, Thomas Hunter."

The evening stood still.

"That makes me a descendant of Tanis?" Tom finally asked.

"Many generations removed, but yes."

"And my immediate family will be coming here for a celebration. When?"

"In . . . what, Gabil? Sixty days?"

"Fifty-three!" the smaller Roush said. "Only fifty-three."

"Gabil is the master of games at the celebrations. He knows them intimately. At any rate, there you have it."

Michal continued his duck-walk down the hill.

"I had another dream," Tom said.

"Yes?" Michal said. "Well, dreams are

quite common, or have you forgotten that as well?"

"It picked up where the one before left off. I was wondering if you could help me with something. Did the histories record sporting events?"

"The histories recorded everything."

"Really! Could I get, say . . . the winning horse from the Kentucky Derby for a particular year?"

"The histories are oral, as I mentioned. They were written . . . are written . . . in the Books of Histories, but these Books are" — he paused here — "no longer available. They are very powerful, these Books. At any rate, the oral traditions were given to Tanis and passed on."

"No one would know who won the Kentucky Derby?"

"Who would care about such trivia? Do you know what kind of mind it would require to hold such an insignificant detail?"

"So then no one knows it."

Michal hesitated. "I didn't say that. What Tanis knows of the histories is more than any other human. It's more than enough. Too much knowledge of some things can be worrisome. Tanis has tried many times to pry more information out of me. His thirst for knowledge is insatiable."

"But you have a perfect memory. You

don't know who won the Kentucky Derby in 2010?"

"And if I do?"

"Can you tell me?"

"I could. Should I?"

"Yes! My sister wants to know."

Again Michal stopped. "You remember your sister? You're beginning to remember?"

"No, the sister in my dreams," Tom said, feeling foolish.

"Now that's something, don't you say, Gabil?" Michal said. "His sister, in his dreams about the histories, wants to know something about the histories. Sounds quite circular."

"Round and round and round, for sure."

Tom diverted his eyes. "Yes, I guess you could say that."

"I'm not sure I *should* tell you," Michal said.

"Then is there anyone else who could tell me?"

"Teeleh," Gabil hissed. "He was a wise one."

Tom knew without having to ask who Teeleh must be.

"The leader of the Shataiki," Tom said.

"Yes," Michal said. Nothing more.

Tom directed the discussion back to the horse race. "Please, I just need to know if what you're saying ties directly into what

I'm dreaming. It might help me put the dreams aside."

"Perhaps. I'm not in the business of digging up the histories. We are making our own here, and it's enough. You already have enough of the histories running through your mind to distract you and confuse even me. I will tell you on one condition."

"I won't ask again. Agreed."

Michal frowned. "Exactly. You will not ask about the histories again."

"And as I said, I agree. Which horse?"

"The winner of the 2010 Kentucky Derby was Joy Flyer."

"Joy Flyer!" Gabil cried. "A perfect name!" He ran ahead and took flight. He gained altitude quickly, executed one loop, and winged in the direction of the Gathering.

Joy Flyer.

The village looked familiar to Tom, but not so much that his heart didn't begin to increase its pace as they approached.

They walked under a great blue-and-gold arch at the entrance and then down a wide brown path between rows of colored huts. Tom stopped at the first house, taken by the ruby glow of the wood. A lawn wrapped around the dwelling in a thick, uniform carpet of green, highlighted by flowers growing in symmetrical clusters.

What appeared to be carvings of brightly colored sapphire and golden wood accented the lawn, giving it a surreal beauty.

"Do you remember?" Michal asked.

"Sort of. But not really."

"It could take a while, I understand. You will stay with Rachelle's family."

"Rachelle! The woman who chose me?"

"Yes."

"I can't stay in her house! I don't have a clue about this Great Romance."

"Follow your instincts, Thomas. And if your instincts don't offer enough guidance, then pretend. Surely you can pretend to be in love."

"What if I don't want to be in love?"

"Stop that nonsense!" Michal ordered. "Of course you want to be in love. You're human." He turned up the path. "You're frightening me, young man."

Tom walked down the path, lost in thought at first, but then quickly distracted by the beauty around him. Both sides of the road were lined with beautifully landscaped lawns that bordered each colored cottage. The homes shone more like pearl than wood. Flowers like the daisies on the valley floor grew in wide swaths across the bright green lawns. Large cats and parrots meandered and fluttered about the village in harmony as though they, too, owned a part of this marvelous work of art.

The refined nature of the village kept Tom in awe as they made their way toward the large central structure. Although not necessarily symmetrical, every object, every carving, every flower, and every path was in exactly the right location, like a perfectly executed symphony. Move one path and the vision would crumble. Move one flower and chaos would ensue.

The Thrall, as Michal had called it, was huge compared to the other structures, and if the village was a work of refined art, then this was its crowning glory. Tom paused at the bottom of wide steps that ascended to the circular building. The jade-colored dome looked as though it had been made out of some flawless crystalline material that allowed light to pass through it.

He gingerly placed his foot on the first step and began the ascent. Ahead, Michal struggled up the steps one by one, ignoring him for the moment. Tom followed him and then turned at the top to view the village from this elevated vantage.

The village looked as if massive jewels — ruby and topaz and emeralds and opals and mother of pearl — had been transported here and then carved into solid structures over hundreds of years. What kind of technology could have possibly created this? So simple and elegant, yet so advanced.

"Who did this?"

Michal looked up at him. "You did this. Come."

Tom followed him into the Thrall.

The scope of the large auditorium was at once intimidating and spectacular. Four glowing pillars — ruby, emerald, jasper, and a golden yellow — rose from the floor to the iridescent domed ceiling. There was no furniture in the room. All of this Tom saw at the first glance.

But it was on the great circular floor, centered under the dome, that he rested his gaze.

He stepped past Michal and walked lightly to the floor's edge. The floor seemed to draw him into itself. He slowly knelt and reached out his hand. He couldn't see a single blemish on its hard, clear surface, like a pool of resin poured over a massive unflawed emerald. He stroked the floor, breathing steadily. A sudden, slight vibration shot up his arm and he quickly withdrew his hand.

"It's quite all right, my friend," Michal said behind him. "It's a sight that I never get used to myself. It was made from a thousand green trees. Not a blemish to be found. The creativity you humans display never ceases to amaze me."

Tom stood. "This is like the water?"

"No. The water is special. But Elyon is

the Maker of both. I will leave you here," he said, turning for the door. "Duty calls. Johan and Rachelle will come and collect you here as soon as they return from the Gathering. And remember, if in doubt, please play along." He waddled out of the building, and Tom thought he heard the Roush say, "Dear, dear. I hope Rachelle hasn't bitten off more than she can chew."

Tom started to protest. Waiting alone in this magnificent room struck him as a little terrifying. But he couldn't think of a reason why he should be terrified — beyond his memory loss, this was all very familiar to him. As Michal said, he had to play along.

10

Tom didn't have to wait long. A boy, maybe twelve, with light blond hair and dressed in a blue tunic, burst into the Thrall. A yellow bandanna wound about his head. He spun on his heel for a quick look around and then turned and ran backward, urging someone else to follow.

"Come on!"

He was followed by the woman Tom recognized as Rachelle. She wore the same red satin dress but now with a bright yellow sash draped over one shoulder.

The thrill of the sight was so unexpected, so sudden, that Tom found himself frozen in the corner shadows.

"Do you see him, Johan?" Rachelle asked, glancing around.

"No. But Michal said he would be here. Maybe . . ." Johan saw Tom and stopped.

Rachelle stood in the middle of the floor, staring into the corner where Tom stood watching.

Tom cleared his throat and stepped into the light. "Hi."

She looked at him, unabashed. For a few long seconds, all motion seemed to cease. Her eyes shone a rich jade, like a pool of water. She was fully grown and yet slender. Early twenties. Her skin was bronzed and milky smooth.

A soft, shy smile slowly replaced her thoughtful gaze.

"You are very pleasing to look at, Thomas," she said.

Tom swallowed. This sort of statement must be completely normal, but because of his amnesia, it felt . . . ambitious. Daring. Wonderful. He had to play along as Michal had demanded.

"Thank you. And so are you. You are very" — he had to stop for a breath — "pleasing to look at. Daring."

"Daring?" she asked.

"Yes, you look daringly beautiful." Tom felt his face blush.

"Daring!" Rachelle looked over at Johan. "Did you hear that, Johan? Thomas thinks I'm daring."

Johan glanced from one to the other and laughed. "I like you, Thomas."

Rachelle looked at him, amused, like a young, shy girl, but she wasn't bashful, not in the least. Was he supposed to do something here?

She offered him her hand. He reached for it, but, like before, she didn't shake it.

Without removing her eyes from his, she gently touched his fingers with hers.

He was so shocked by the touch that he didn't dare speak. If he did, surely idiotic mumbling rather than words would come from his mouth. Her caress lingered on his skin, sensuous yet completely innocent at once.

Tom's heart was pounding now, and for a brief moment he panicked. She was touching his hand, and he was frozen to the floor. This was the Great Romance?

He didn't even know this woman.

She suddenly took his hand in hers and pulled him toward the door. "Hurry, they are waiting."

"They are? Who are?"

"It's time to eat," Johan cried. He threw the door open, pulled up, and then rushed down the steps toward two men on the path below. "Father! We have Thomas Hunter. He is a very interesting man!"

Two thoughts struck Tom at the comment. One, Rachelle was still touching his hand. Two, these people seemed to have no shame. Which meant *he* had no shame, because he was one of these people.

Rachelle released his hand and ran down the steps. The man Johan had called Father embraced the boy and then turned to Tom. He wore a tunic that hung to his thighs, tan with a wide swath of blue running across his body from right shoulder to left hip. The hem was woven in intricate crossing patterns with the same colors. A belt of gold ran around his waist and held a small water pouch.

"So. You are the visitor from the other side." He clasped Tom's arm, pulled him into an embrace, and slapped his back. "Welcome. My name is Palus. You are most welcome to stay with my family." He drew back, frowning, eyes bright, delighted. "Welcome," he said again.

"Thank you. You are most kind." Tom dipped his head.

Palus jumped back and swept his arm toward the other man. "This is Miknas, the keeper of the Thrall," he said proudly. "He has overseen all the dances and celebrations on the green floor for well over a hundred years. Miknas!"

Miknas looked about forty. Maybe thirty. Hard to tell. How old was the firstborn, Tanis? Tom dismissed the question for the moment.

"It's an honor," Tom said.

Miknas stepped forward and embraced Tom in the same way Palus had. "The honor is mine. We rarely have such special visitors. You are most welcome. Most, most welcome."

"Come, walk to our house." Palus led them down the path.

They stopped at the arching sapphire entrance of a home close to the Thrall, and each took turns embracing Miknas farewell, bidding him a wonderful meal. Palus led them down several rows of homes to a cottage as brilliant green as its surrounding lawn, then up the walk and past a solid green door into his domed abode.

Tom entered the dwelling, hoping that here, in such intimate surroundings, the familiarity of his past would return. The wood here in the home had the appearance of being covered in a smooth, clear resin several inches thick. The furniture was carved from the same wood. Some pieces glowed a single color, and others radiated in rainbow moirés. Light emanated from all the wood. The light was not reflective as he had first guessed but came from the wood itself.

Incredible. But not familiar.

"This is Karyl, my wife," Palus said. Then to his wife, "Rachelle has touched his hand."

Tom smiled at Rachelle's mother awkwardly, eager to avoid any further discussion on the matter. "You have a beautiful home, madam."

"Madam? How quaint. What does it mean?"

"Hmm?"

"I've never heard this expression before.

What does 'madam' mean?"

"I think . . . I think it's an expression of respect. Like 'friend.' "

"You use this expression in your village?"

"Maybe. I think we might."

They all watched him in a moment of silence, during which he felt terribly conspicuous.

"Here," Karyl said finally, stepping toward a bowl into which she dipped a wooden cup, "we invite with a drink of water." She brought the cup to him, and he sipped. The water was cool at his lips but felt warm all the way to his belly, where its heat spread. He dipped his head and returned the cup.

"Thank you."

"Then you must eat with us. Come, come."

She took his arm and led him to the table. A large bowl of fruit sat in the center, and he recognized the colors and shapes. They were the same as those Gabil had given him earlier.

His sudden hunger for the fruit surprised him. Everyone had taken a seat at the round table now, and he was aware of their eyes on him. He forced himself to look away from the fruit, and he met Rachelle's eyes.

"You're most kind to have me in your

home. I must admit, I'm unsure of what I should do. Did they tell you that I'd lost my memory?"

"Michal mentioned that, yes," Palus said.

"Don't worry, I will teach you anything you need to know." Rachelle picked up a fruit topaz in color, looked him directly in the eye, and bit into it. She chewed and lifted the fruit to his lips. "You should eat the kirim," she said, holding his eyes with hers.

Tom hesitated. Was this like the touching of hands?

"Go ahead." Now Karyl urged him on.

They all waited, staring at him as though insistent on his tasting the fruit. Even Johan waited, anticipation painted in his bright, smiling eyes.

Tom leaned forward and bit into the fruit. Juice ran down his chin as his teeth broke the skin and exposed the flesh. The moment the nectar hit his tongue he felt its power ripple down his body like a narcotic, stronger than the fruit Gabil had given him earlier.

"Take it," Rachelle said.

He took the fruit, brushing her fingers as he did. She let her hand linger, then reached for another fruit. The others had reached into the bowl and eagerly ate the fruit. It wasn't a narcotic, of course, but a

148

gift from Elyon, as Michal had explained. Something that brought pleasure, like all of Elyon's gifts. Food, water, love. Flying and diving.

Flying and diving? There was something about flying and diving that struck a chord. What, he didn't know. Not yet.

Tom took another bite and beamed at his hosts. Johan was the first to begin laughing, a bite of yellow flesh still lodged in his mouth. Then Palus joined in the laughter, and within seconds they were joined by Rachelle and Karyl. Still chewing slowly, Tom shifted his gaze around the table, surprised at their odd behavior. His mouth formed a dumb grin, and he rested his eyes on Johan. He was one of them; he should be laughing as well. And now that he thought about it, he wanted to laugh.

Johan's shoulders shook uncontrollably. He had thrown his head back so his chin jutted out, his laughing mouth facing the ceiling. A nervous chuckle erupted from Tom's throat and quickly grew to laughter. And then Tom began to laugh uncontrollably, as though he had never laughed before, as though a hundred years of pent-up laughter had broken free.

Johan slipped out of his seat and rolled onto the floor, laughing hysterically. The laughter was so great that none of them could finish the fruit, and it was a good ten minutes before they gathered themselves enough to eat again.

Tom rubbed the tears from his eyes and took another bite of the fruit. He was struck by the obscure idea that he must be floating through a dream. That he was in Denver having an incredible dream. But the hard surface of the table told him this was no dream.

The scene was surreal to be sure: sitting in a room lit by drifting colors that emanated from resined wood, seeing the hues of turquoise and lavender and gold hang softly in the air, eating strange and delicious fruit that made him delirious, and laughing with his new friends for no apparent reason other than his simple delight at the moment.

And now, sitting in silence, except for the sound of slurping fruit, feeling totally content without uttering a word.

Surreal.

But very real. This was supper. This was the common eating of food.

Johan suddenly sprang up from his chair. "Father, may we start the song now?"

"The song. The dance." A grin formed on Palus's face.

Without clearing the table, Karyl rose and glided to the center of the room, where she was quickly joined by Johan, Rachelle, and Palus. Tom watched, feeling suddenly awkward, unsure whether he was expected to rise or stay seated. The family didn't seem concerned, so he remained seated.

He noticed the small pedestal in the center of the room for the first time. The four joined hands around a bowl perched on the pedestal. They raised their heads, began singing softly, stepped gingerly around the pedestal in a simple dance.

The moment the notes fell on his ears, Tom knew that he was hearing much more than just a tune. The plaintive melody, sung in low tones, spoke beyond its notes.

It quickened and broke out in long, flowing notes containing a kind of harmony Tom could not remember. Their dance picked up intensity — they seemed to have forgotten him completely. Tom sat, captivated by the great emotion of the moment, stunned by the sudden loss of understanding, surprised by the feeling of love and kindness that numbed his chest. Johan beamed at the ceiling, exhibiting sincerity that seemed to transport him well beyond his age. And yet Palus looked like a child.

Rachelle stepped with distinguished grace. Not a movement of her body was out of place. She danced as though she had choreographed the dance. As though it flowed from her first and then to the

151

others. She was lost in innocent abandon to the song.

He wanted to rush out and join them, but he could hardly move, much less twirl.

Then they each sang, but when young Johan finally lifted his head, smiled at the ceiling, and opened his mouth in a solo, Tom knew immediately that he was the true singer here.

The first tone flowed from his throat clear and pure and sharp and so very, very young. The tones rose through the octave, higher and higher until Tom thought the room might melt at his song.

But the boy sang higher, and still higher, bringing a chill to Tom's spine. No wasted breath escaped Johan's lips, no fluctuation in tone, no strain of muscles in his neck. Only effortless song spun at the boy's whim.

A moment's pause, and the tone began again, this time in a rich, low bass deserving of the best virtuoso. And yet sung by this *boy!* The tones filled the room, shaking the table to which Tom clung. He caught his breath and felt his jaw part. The entrancing melody swept through his body. Tom swallowed hard, trying to hold back the sentiment rising through his chest. Instead he felt his shoulders shake, and he began to weep.

Johan continued to smile and sing. His

tune reached into each chamber of Tom's heart and reverberated with truth.

The song and dance must have gone on late into the night, but Tom never knew, because he slipped into an exhausted sleep while they still sang.

11

"That's it, come on. Wake up."

Someone was squeezing his cheeks together and shaking his head. Tom forced lead-laden eyes open, surprised at how difficult the task was. He squinted in the light. His sister sat beside him, long blonde hair backlit by a halo of light.

He struggled to sit up and finally managed with a pull from Kara. He felt like he was moving in molasses, but that was to be expected — dreams often felt that way. Slogging instead of sprinting, floating instead of falling.

"You should wake up pretty quick," Kara said. "You feel okay?"

She was talking about the drugs. Sedatives followed by enough caffeine to wake a horse, if he remembered right.

"I gethh," he slurred. He swallowed a pool of saliva and said it again, concentrating on his pronunciation. "I guess." His head felt as though a rhino had stomped on it.

"Here, drink this." Kara handed him a

glass of water. He took a long slug and cleared his throat. The fog started to clear from his mind. This could be a dream, or that could be a dream, but at the moment he didn't want to think about it.

"So?" Kara asked, setting the glass aside.

"So what?"

"So, did you dream?"

"I don't know." He looked around the room, disoriented. "Am I dreaming now?" He reached out and bumped her forehead with his palm.

"What are you doing?" she demanded.

"Just checking. To see if my hand went through your head, like in a dream. Guess not."

"Please, indulge me. For all I've done for you over the years, do me this one favor: Pretend this isn't a dream. And that whatever went through your noodle while you were sleeping was a dream."

"I'm sleeping now."

"Thomas, stop it!"

"Okay!" He tried to stand, got halfway up, and settled back down. "But it's not easy, you know."

"I'm sure it's not." She stood, picked up the glass, and headed for the kitchen. "The fact is, you didn't learn anything from the white fuzzy creatures in the colored forest, right? I suggest we start giving some serious thought to getting out of this mess you got us into."

"The winner was Joy Flyer. Is. Will be . . . whatever."

Kara blinked once. Twice. Tom knew he'd hit a home run.

"You see?" he said. "I didn't have a clue who Joy Flyer was because you wouldn't even show me which horses were in the race. I'd never heard of the name before today. There's no way I could have guessed that. But the histories have recorded that a horse named Joy Flyer will win today's Kentucky Derby."

She snatched the newspaper off the counter and stared at the sports page. "How do you spell it?"

"How should I know? I didn't read it; Michal told me. Don't be —"

"Joy Flyer's a long shot." She stared at the paper. "How did you even know that name?"

"I told you, I didn't."

This time Kara didn't argue. "The race isn't for another five hours. We don't know that he will win."

"The race was run a long time ago, on ancient Earth, but I can understand your unease with that kind of thinking." Truth be told, even he felt plenty of unease with that kind of thinking.

"This is absolutely incredible! You're actually getting facts about the future in your dreams as if they're history?"

"Didn't I tell you that an hour ago?"

"How long were you there? What else can you tell me?"

"How long? Maybe, what? Four, five hours?"

"But you only slept for half an hour. What else did you learn?"

"Nothing. Except for what I said about the Raison Strain."

For a moment they faced each other in perfect stillness. Kara grabbed the rest of the paper and noisily crashed through it.

"What else did you find out about the Raison Strain?" she demanded, scanning the story on the French pharmaceutical company.

"Nothing. I didn't ask anything about —"

"Well, maybe you should have. You had the presence of mind to ask about a horse race. If this virus is about to wipe out a few billion people, you'd think you would have the presence of mind to ask about it."

"So now you're starting to listen," Tom said, standing successfully this time. He looked around and reached for the bandage above his right ear. He pulled it off and felt for the wound. Odd.

"Kara?"

"It says here that Raison Pharmaceutical operates almost exclusively just outside Bangkok where its founder, Jacques de

157

Raison, runs the company's new plant. His daughter, Monique de Raison, who is also in charge of new drug development, is expected to make the announcement in Bangkok on Wednesday."

"Kara!"

She looked up. "What?"

"Can you . . ." He walked toward her, still feeling the scar on his skull. "Is this normal?"

"Is what normal?"

"It feels . . . I don't know. I can't feel it."

Kara pushed his hand aside, spread his hair with her fingers, and stepped back, face white.

Tom faced her. "What is it?"

She stared, too stunned to answer.

"It's gone," Tom said. "I was right. This was an open wound eight hours ago, and now it's gone, isn't it?"

"This is impossible," Kara said.

Actually, it did sound a bit crazy.

"I'm telling you, Kara. This thing's real. I mean, real-real."

A tremble had come to Kara's fingers.

"Okay." He ran his fingers through his hair. The mob from New York City was still gunning for him, but the Raison Strain was the real threat here, wasn't it? For whatever reason, and through whatever device, he now possessed knowledge of the most damning proportions. Why him — third-culture vagabond from the Philippines, Java Hut extraordinaire, aspiring Magic Circle actor, unpublished novelist — he had no idea. But the significance of what he knew began to swell in his mind.

"Okay," he said, lowering his arm. "Maybe we can stop it."

"Stop it? I'm having trouble believing it, much less stopping it."

"Bangkok," Tom said.

"What, pray tell, are we going to do in Bangkok? Storm the Raison facilities?"

"No, but we can't just stay here." She broke off and walked for the kitchen desk. "We have to tell someone about this."

"Who?"

"CDC. Centers for Disease Control. The headquarters are in Atlanta."

"Tell them what?" Tom asked. "That a fuzzy creature told me the Raison Strain was going to wipe out half the world?"

"That's what you're saying, isn't it? This Raison Vaccine is going to mutate and kill us all like a bunch of rats? The whole thing's crazy!"

He rubbed the scar on his head. "So is this."

Her eyes lifted to where the bullet had grazed his head not ten hours ago. She stared at his temple for a long moment and then turned for the phone. "We have to tell someone."

He assured himself that her frustration wasn't directed so much at him as at the situation. "Okay, but you can't tell some pencil pusher at the CDC," Tom said. "You'll come off sounding like a kook."

"Then who? The local sheriff?" She scanned a list she'd placed in the front of the phone book, found the number, and dialed.

Tom brushed past her and began flipping through the phone book. The Roush had said that the Raison Strain led to the "Great Deception." His mind fully engaged the problem now.

"What if I know this because I'm supposed to stop it?" Tom asked. "But who really would have the power to stop it? The CDC? More like the FBI or the CIA or the State Department."

"Believe me, it'll sound just as crazy to the State Depar—" Kara turned, phone still plastered to her ear. "Yes, good morning, Melissa. This is Kara Hunter calling from Denver, Colorado. I'm a nurse. Who would I speak to about a . . . um, potential outbreak?" She paused. "No, actually I'm not calling on behalf of the hospital. I just need to report something I find suspicious." Another pause. "Infectious disease. Who would that be? Thanks, I'll hold."

Kara turned back to Tom. "What do I tell him?"

"I'm telling you, I really think —"

She held up her hand. "Yes, hello, Mark." Kara took a breath and told him her concerns about the Raison Strain, stumbling along as best she could. She met with immediate resistance.

"I can't really tell you precisely why I suspect this. All I want is for you to have the vaccine checked out. You've received a complaint from a credible source. Now you need to follow up . . ."

She blinked and pulled the receiver from her ear.

"What?" Tom demanded. "He hung up on you?"

"He said, 'Duly noted,' and just hung up."

"I told you. Here."

Tom took the receiver and punched in a number he'd found in Washington, D.C. Three calls and seven transfers finally landed him in the office of the Bureau for International Narcotics and Law Enforcement Affairs assistant secretary, who evidently reported to the under secretary for global affairs, who in turn reported to the deputy secretary of state. None of this mattered that much; what did matter was that

Gloria Stephenson seemed like a reasonable person. She at least listened to his claim that he, one, had information of utmost importance to U.S. interests, and, two, he had to get that information to the right party immediately.

"Okay, can you hold on a minute, Mr. Hunter? I'm going to try to put you through."

"Sure." See, now they were getting somewhere. The phone on the other end rang three times before being answered.

"Bob Macklroy."

"Yes, hi, Bob. Who are you?"

"This is the office of the Bureau for International Narcotics and Law Enforcement Affairs assistant secretary. I am the secretary."

The big gun himself. "Uh, morning, Mr. Macklroy. Thank you for taking my call. My name is Thomas Hunter, and I have information about a serious threat here that I'm trying to get to the right party."

"What's the nature of the threat?"

"A virus."

There was a moment of silence. "Do you have the number for the CDC?" Macklroy asked.

"Yes, but I really think this goes beyond them. Actually, we tried them, but they pretty much blew us off." It occurred to Tom that he may not have all day with someone as important as Macklroy, so he decided to give it to the man fast.

"I know this may sound strange, and I know you don't have a clue who I am, but you have to hear me out."

"I'm listening."

"Ever hear of the Raison Vaccine?"

"Can't say that I have."

"It's an airborne vaccine about to hit the market. But there's a problem with the drug." He told Macklroy about the mutation and ensuing devastation in one long run-on sentence.

Silence.

"Are you still there?" Tom asked.

"The earth's entire population is about to be decimated. Is that about it?"

Tom swallowed. "I know it sounds crazy, but that's . . . right."

"You do realize there are laws that prohibit defaming a company without —"

"I'm not trying to defame Raison Pharmaceutical! This is a serious threat and needs immediate attention."

"I'm sorry, but you have the wrong department. This is something the CDC would typically handle. Now, if you'll excuse me, I have a meeting I'm late for."

"Of course, you're late for a meeting. Everyone who wants to get off the phone is always late for a meeting!" Kara was motioning for him to calm down. "Look, Mr.

Macklroy, we don't have a lot of time here. France or Thailand or whoever it is that has jurisdiction over Raison Pharmaceutical has to check this out."

"Exactly what is your source for this information?"

"What do you mean?"

"I mean, how did you come across this information, Mr. Hunter? You're making some very serious allegations — surely you have a credible source."

The words slipped out before he could stop them. "I had a dream."

Kara put both palms to her forehead and rolled her eyes.

"I see. Very good, Tom. We're wasting tax dollars here."

"I can prove it to you!" Tom said.

"I'm sorry, but now I really *am* late for a meet—"

"I also know who's going to win the Kentucky Derby this afternoon," he yelled into the receiver. "Joy Flyer."

"Good day, sir."

The phone went dead.

Tom stared at Kara, who was pacing and shaking her head. He dropped the receiver into its cradle. "Idiots. No wonder the country's falling apart at the seams."

A car door slammed in the parking lot outside.

"Well," Kara said.

"Well what?"

"Well, at least we've reported it. You have to admit, it sounds a bit loopy."

"Reporting it isn't enough," Tom said, walking for the living room windows. He pulled aside one of the drapes.

"Why don't we make up some signs and stand on the corner; maybe that will get their attention," Kara said. "Armageddon cometh."

Tom dropped the drape and jumped back.

"What?"

"They're here!" Three of them that he had seen. Working their way, door to door, on their floor.

Tom sprang for his bedroom. "We have to get out of here. Grab your passport, money, whatever you have."

"I'm not dressed!"

"Then hurry!" He glanced at the door. "We have a minute. Maybe."

"Where are we going?"

He ran for his bedroom.

"Thomas!"

"Just go! Go, go!"

He grabbed his traveling papers and stuffed them in a black satchel he always used when he traveled. Money — two hundred bucks was all he had here. Hopefully Kara had some cash.

His toothbrush, a pair of khakis, three

T-shirts, boxers, one pair of socks. What else? Think. That was it; no more time.

Tom ran into the living room. "Kara!"

"Just hang on. I could *kill* you!"

Their yelling would wake the neighborhood. "Hurry!" he whispered hoarsely.

She mumbled something.

What else, what else? The bills? He grabbed the basket of bills, crammed them into his bag, and snatched up the machete from the coffee table.

Kara ran out, hastily dressed in black capris and a yellow tank top. Her hair was tied in a ponytail, a white bag under her arm. She looked like a canary ready for a cruise to the Bahamas.

"We're coming back, right?" she asked.

"Keep down and stay right behind me," Tom said, running for the rear sliding-glass door. He pulled back the drape — back lot looked clear. They slipped out, and he closed the door behind them.

"Okay, quick but not obvious. Stay behind me," he repeated. They hurried down metal stairs and angled for Kara's Celica. No sign of the men who were probably pounding on their front door at this very moment.

"Keys?"

She pulled them out and handed them to him. "How do you know it was them?" she asked.

"I know. One of them had a bandage on his head. Same guy I met last night. I put my foot in his mouth."

They climbed in and he fired the car. "Get down."

Kara slouched in the front seat for two blocks before sitting up and straining back for sight of any pursuit.

"Anything?" Tom asked.

"Not that I can see." She faced him. "Where are we going?"

Good question.

"Your passport is up-to-date, right?"

"Please, Tom, be serious. We can't just run off to Manila or Bangkok, or wherever!"

"You have a better idea? This is real! Those are *real* men with *real* guns back there! The Raison Vaccine is a *real* vaccine, and Joy Flyer is a *real* horse!"

She looked out her side window. "The Kentucky Derby hasn't been raced yet," she said quietly.

"How long did I say we had before the Raison Strain became a threat?" he asked.

"You weren't even sure what year it happened." She faced him. "If all these things really *are* real, then you need some better information. We can't just traipse all over the globe because Joy Flyer really is a horse."

"What do you suggest, finding out ex-

167

actly how to fix the problem in the Middle East in one fell swoop?"

She looked at him. "Could you do that?"

" 'Course not."

"Why not?"

Yes, why not?

"What was it the black bats said to you?" Kara asked. "Something about them being your destiny? Maybe you should talk to them instead of these white furry creatures. We need specifics here."

"I can't. They live in the black forest! It's forbidden."

"Forbidden? Listen to you. It's a *dream,* Tom! Granted, a dream with some pretty crazy ramifications, but just a dream."

"Then how do I know all this stuff? Why is my head wound gone?"

"I don't know. What I do know is that *this*" — she jabbed at the console — "isn't a dream. So your dreams are special. You're somehow learning things in there you shouldn't know; I give you that. I'm even *embracing* that. I'm saying, learn more! But I'm not going to go running off to Bangkok to save the world without the slightest idea of what to do once we get there. You need more information."

They entered the interchange between I-25 and I-70, headed for Denver International Airport.

"So at least you *are* admitting that this

168

information's important. And real."

She set her head back. "Yes. So it seems."

"Then we have to respond to it. You're right, I need more information. But I can't very well fall asleep at the wheel, can I? And you can't keep drugging me."

"Okay."

"MacIlroy seemed to think the CDC was the right place to go with this information."

"That's what I thought."

"Okay. So let's go to Atlanta. How much money do you have?"

She raised an eyebrow. "Just fly to Atlanta? I can't just leave my job without some notice."

"Then call them. But the phone obviously isn't the best way to get the attention of the CDC. They probably get a hundred kooks a day calling in crazy stories. So we go to the CDC headquarters in person."

"Not Bangkok?"

"No. Atlanta. You know we can't go back to the apartment — who knows how long they'll stake the place out?"

She considered the matter. Closed her eyes.

"Okay," she finally said. "Atlanta."

12

Try as he may at Kara's urging, Tom couldn't sleep on the flight to Atlanta. Not a wink.

Slowly but surely, Kara was laying aside her disbelief that something very significant was actually happening to Tom, although she still wasn't buying the notion that he'd actually stumbled onto the end of the world, so to speak. As she put it, just because he was admittedly experiencing some kind of precognition when he slept, didn't mean everything his highly active imagination latched onto was real. Who ever heard of fuzzy white bats anyway?

Tom desperately wanted to convince her that it could easily be the other way around. That there was no real evidence the Boeing 757 they were flying in wasn't actually part of some crazy dream. Who was to say which reality was more compelling?

"Think about what Dad used to say when we were kids," he said. "The whole Christian world-view is based on alternate realities. We fight not against flesh and blood but against principalities or whatever. Remember that? In fact, most of the world believes that most of what actually happens, happens without our being able to see it. That's a religious mainstay."

"So? I don't believe that. And neither do you."

"Well, maybe we *should* believe that. Not necessarily the Christianity part, but the whole principle. Why not?"

"Because I don't believe in ghosts," she said. "If there is a God and he made us with five senses, why wouldn't he show himself to us through those senses? A dream makes no sense."

"Maybe he does show himself to us, but we don't see. Maybe it's not our senses that are the problem, but our minds."

She twisted in her seat and looked at him. "Is this the same Thomas who used to tell Dad how crazy his silly faith was?"

"I'm not saying anything's changed. I'm just saying that it's something to consider. Like *The Matrix.* Remember that movie? Everyone thinks it's one way, when actually it's another way."

"Only the real world is a colored forest with fuzzy white bats, and all this is just a dream. I don't think so."

"The fuzzy white bats healed my head and told me who will win the Kentucky

Derby. And if I'm imagining one reality, it would be more likely that I'm imagining *this* one. In the other reality, both realities make sense — this one as a history and that one as the present. In this reality, the other reality makes no sense unless this reality isn't really a reality. Or unless it really is the future."

"Enough. You're giving me a headache. Go to sleep and find out how we solve the Middle East crisis."

"We don't. The Raison Strain hits us before then. Which is now."

"Unless the Raison Strain is stopped," she said. "Is it possible to change the future? Or better yet, change history?"

He didn't bother to respond.

They landed in Atlanta an hour later and spent thirty minutes on a run of errands. Kara owed the hospital in Denver an explanation and had some banking to do; Tom checked on the availability of flights to several overseas destinations, just in case. It was half past three before they met up in ground transportation.

"So," Tom said, holding the door open that led to the taxi line. "How much do we have?"

"We? About $5,000, and it's in my account. I don't recall you depositing any money in my account."

He'd found a 10:00 p.m. flight to

Bangkok through Los Angeles and Singapore, but the short-notice tickets would cost $2,000 a piece. Not good. He frowned.

"You expected more?" she asked.

"I thought you'd saved up over twenty thousand," he said.

"That was three months ago. I've made some purchases since. Five will hold us. As long as we don't go running off to Manila or Bangkok." She shut her door.

The yellow cab pulled up to the Centers for Disease Control headquarters on Clifton Road at 4:15, forty-five minutes before the government building presumably closed. Kara paid the driver and faced the front doors with Tom.

"Okay, exactly what is our primary goal here?" she asked.

"To wake the dead," Tom said.

"Let's be a little more precise."

"Someone in there has to take us seriously. We don't leave until someone with the power to do something agrees to look into the Raison Strain."

Kara glanced at her watch. "Okay."

They entered the building and approached a counter cordoned off with protective Plexiglas and identified by a black sign as "Reception." Tom explained their objective to a red-headed woman named Kathy and, when informed that they would have to see a caseworker, asked to see one immediately. He was handed a stack of forms containing a host of questions that seemed to have nothing to do with infectious diseases: birth date, Social Security number, grade school achievements, shoe size. They retreated to a row of cushioned waiting chairs, filled the forms out quickly, and returned them to Kathy.

"How long will we have to wait?" Tom asked.

Her phone buzzed and she answered it without offering a response to Tom. One of her coworkers was evidently having mice problems in her house. Tom tapped his fingers on the counter and waited patiently.

Kathy set her phone down, but it rang again.

Tom held up his finger. "Simple question: How long?"

"As soon as someone's available."

"It's already 4:35. When will someone be available?"

"We'll do our best to get you in today," she said and picked up the phone. Same party. Another critical question on tactics to hold back swarms of attacking mice. Something about wearing rubber gloves when removing the varmints from traps.

Tom sighed audibly and walked back to the waiting chairs. "Kathy was raised in an idiot factory," he said.

"Patience, Thomas. Maybe I should do the talking." Kara glanced at her watch again.

"I have a bad feeling we're wasting our time here," he said. "Even if we do report this, how long will it take for the bureaucracy to work? It takes months, sometimes years, to get FDA approval for a drug. How long does it take to reverse that? Probably months and years. I'm telling you, we have to go to Bangkok. They're making the announcement in two days. All we have to do is explain the problem to them — to this Monique de Raison. They'll check out our concerns, find the problem, and deal with it."

Kara looked at her watch and stood. "I doubt it would be that simple. I have to check something. Be right back."

Tom let his steam gather for another ten minutes before approaching Kathy for another round. This time she stopped him before he could ask the obvious question.

"Excuse me, sir, are you hard of hearing, or just stubborn? I thought I said I'd call you when a caseworker was available."

He stopped, shocked by her rudeness. No one else was within ear-shot — a fact obviously not lost on Kathy, or she wouldn't dare offer this verbal abuse.

"Excuse me?" he stammered.

"You heard me," she snapped. "I'll call

you if we have a caseworker available before we close."

Tom stepped up to the counter and glared through the Plexiglas. "This can't wait until tomorrow."

"You should've thought about that earlier."

"Listen, lady, we flew all the way from Denver to see you! What if something dead serious was wrong with me? How do you know I don't have a disease that could wipe out the world?"

She sat back, clearly smug in a certainty that she had won with this last absurdity of his. "This isn't a clinic. I don't think you have —"

"You don't know that! What if I had polio?" Wrong disease. "What if I had Ebola or something?"

"It says Raison something." She lazily pulled out his form. "Not Ebola. Sit down, Mr. Hunter."

Heat flared up his neck. "And what *is* the Raison Strain?" he demanded. "Do you even know? As a matter of fact, the Raison Strain makes the Ebola virus look like a common cold. Did you know that? The virus may just have broken out in —"

"Sit down!" Kathy rose to her feet, fists clenched by her hips. She pointed dramatically to the waiting chairs. "Sit down immediately."

Tom could never be sure if it was his martial arts instincts or his generous intelligence that took over in the next moment — either way, at least his courage couldn't be faulted.

He locked stares with the woman behind the Plexiglas for a full five seconds. The sight of her quivering jowls was the last straw. He suddenly grabbed his own neck with both hands and began to choke himself.

"Ahhhh! I think I might have been infected," he gasped. He stumbled forward and smashed his head into the Plexiglas. "Help!" he screamed. "Help, I'm infected with the Raison Strain!"

The woman stood rigid and shaking with fury, still pointing at the chairs. "Sit down!"

Tom smashed his cheek against the glass, tightened his choke hold, and stuck out his tongue. "I'm dying! Help, help!"

"Thomas!" Kara ran toward him from the hall.

He started to sag and rolled his eyes.

A half-dozen workers ran into the cubicles behind the receptionist.

"Stop it!" Kathy shrieked. "Stop it!"

"Thomas, what are you doing?" Kara demanded frantically.

He winked at her discretely and then banged his head against the glass, this time hard enough to give himself a headache.

"Excuse me!" A man dressed in a gray

suit had materialized behind the receptionist. "What seems to be the problem here?"

"He . . . he wants to see a caseworker," she said.

Tom lowered his hands and stood up. "Are you in charge here?"

"Can I help you?"

"Forgive me for the antics, but I'm a bit desperate and a junior-high fit was the only thing that came to mind," Tom said. "It's absolutely critical that we speak to someone from the infectious diseases department immediately."

The man glanced at Kathy's red face. "We have procedures for a reason, Mr. . . ."

"Hunter. Thomas Hunter. Trust me, you'll be very interested in what I have to say."

The man hesitated and then stepped through a door in the Plexiglas. "Why don't you come into my office?" He extended his hand. "My name is Aaron Olsen. Please excuse our delay. It gets a bit hectic around here at times."

Tom shook the man's hand and followed him, escorting Kara.

"Next time you're going to lose your hearing, warn me, will you?" Kara whispered.

"Sorry."

Kara couldn't hide a grin.

"What?" Tom asked.

"Nothing," she said. "I'll tell you later."

Aaron Olsen stared at Tom from behind a large cherry-wood desk, elbows propped on the surface, face stoic and impossible to read in the wake of Tom's detailed explanation of the fuzzy white bats.

Tom sat back and let out a long breath. A gold placard on Aaron's desk said he was the assistant director, and he explained that his department was indeed infectious diseases. And, although he'd started by explaining that the World Health Organization's rapid response unit was the right party to contact, he had agreed to listen to their story and had done so without emotion.

They were finally getting somewhere.

"So," Aaron said, and for the first time a slight grin nudged his lips.

"I know it sounds strange," Tom said. "But you have to consider the facts here."

"I am, Mr. Hunter, and that's what's troubling me. Am I missing something here, or are you actually telling me that this information came from a dream?"

Kara leaned forward. "You say that like it's preposterous." Her defensive tone was striking. "Did you hear a word of what he just told you? He knows about the Raison

Vaccine! He knew about it before it was made public."

"The Raison Vaccine has been touted in private circles for a few months now —"

"Not in *his* private circles."

Tom held up a hand. "It's okay, Kara." What had come over her? She was suddenly his ardent advocate. He faced Olsen. "Okay, let's go over this again. What exactly is confusing you?"

The man smiled, incredulous. "You're saying this came from a dream —"

"Not exactly," Tom said. "An alternate reality. But let's forget that for a minute. Regardless of how I know, I do have specific knowledge of things that haven't happened yet. I knew that a French company was going to announce a vaccine called the Raison Vaccine before it was public knowledge. I also know that the Raison Vaccine will mutate under extreme heat and become quite deadly. It will infect the world's population in less than three weeks. All we're asking you to do is check it out. What's so complicated about that?"

Olsen looked from Tom to Kara and back. "So let me summarize here. A man walks into the building, begins to scream for help while choking himself, and then claims some bats have visited him in a dream and told him that the world is about to end — in what, three weeks? — when a

180

vaccine overheats and turns into a deadly virus. Is that about it?"

"Three weeks *after* the virus is released," Thomas clarified. Olsen ignored him.

"Are you aware that intense heat kills things like viruses, Mr. Hunter? Your warning is flawed on the surface, regardless of the source."

Kara came to his defense again. "Maybe that's why Raison Pharmaceutical is ignorant of the problem, assuming they are. Maybe drugs aren't tested under extreme heat."

"You're a nurse," Olsen said. "You're buying all this dream nonsense?"

"Like Tom said, it's not necessarily dream nonsense. Just check it out, for goodness' sake!"

"How do you propose I do that? Send out a bulletin that announces the fuzzy white bats have issued a warning about the Raison Vaccine? Pretty clear case of defamation, don't you think?"

"Then explain to me how I knew that Joy Flyer was going to run in the Kentucky Derby," Tom said.

Olsen shrugged. "Public information."

"But it wasn't public that Joy Flyer was going to win," Kara said. "Not two hours ago when I placed my bet."

Tom faced her. "What bet?"

"Joy Flyer won?" Olsen said. He glanced

at his watch. "You're right, the results should be in. You sure Joy Flyer won? He was a long shot."

"You bet on Joy Flyer?" Tom demanded. "How much?"

"Yes, Tom, I did. And yes, he did win, long shot or not."

"Bummer." Olsen shook his head and looked out the window. "I had a thousand bucks on Winner's Circle."

"You're missing the point," Kara said. "Tom learned that Joy Flyer was going to win from the same source that gave him these details about the Raison Vaccine."

"How much?" Tom asked again.

Olsen sighed. "None of this can be substantiated. For all I know, you didn't even bet on Joy Flyer. And if you did, you could be claiming to have been tipped off by some angel to substantiate this other story. For all I know, you have stock in Raison Pharmaceutical's competitor and are looking to trash Raison. I can't do a thing with this information except put it through the normal channels."

"So you're dismissing it? Just like that?" Kara demanded.

"No, I said I'd report it." Olsen sat up and straightened some papers. "You've made your report — I suggest you go collect your winnings." He smiled condescendingly.

Kara stood abruptly. "You're a fool, Olsen. Don't you dare toss that report. If there's even a small chance that we're right, you could be messing with a very dangerous situation here. I just bet $15,000, most of my life savings, on a long shot named Joy Flyer because of what my brother knows. There's $345,000 sitting in an account with my name on it right now because I listened to him. I suggest you do the same."

She marched to the door.

"Exactly!" Tom said, standing. Three hundred forty-five thousand?

The cab had waited as instructed.

"That's true? You really won that much?"

"If we paid off your debt to the boys in New York, do you think they'd leave us alone?"

"With a little interest, sure. You're serious?"

"You've bailed me out more than once." She shrugged. "Now it's my turn. Besides, it's as much your money as mine."

"Where to?" the driver asked.

Tom searched his sister's eyes. "Airport," he said. Then to Kara, "Okay?"

"Where?" she asked.

"Bangkok. A flight leaves at ten. We no longer need visas, I checked."

She stared at the back of the driver's

seat. "Why not? Airport."

"Airport it is." The cab pulled out.

Tom nodded. "Okay, good. We don't have a choice, right?"

"Of course we don't," she said quietly. "We never have a choice with you, Thomas. Staying put isn't in your vocabulary."

"This is different. We can't pretend this isn't happening."

She looked out her window. "We need more information."

"We will. I promise. As soon as I can fall asleep."

"That should be when? Somewhere over the Pacific?"

13

Carlos Missirian walked through Bangkok International Airport eight hours after Valborg Svensson had given him the order to come. The company's jet served him well. His mind retraced the conversation with the Swiss.

"Our man at the CDC received a nervous visitor today who claimed that the mutations of the Raison Vaccine held together under prolonged, specific heat," Svensson had said. "The result, the visitor claimed, would be a lethal airborne virus with an incubation of three weeks. One that could infect the entire world's population in less than three weeks."

"And how did this visitor happen to come across this information?"

Svensson had hesitated. "A dream," he said. "A very unusual dream."

Carlos's shoes clacked on the concrete floor. Perhaps they had found the virus, although it was difficult to imagine they'd done so by this sort of means. He took a deep breath. The time would soon come when taking a long pull of air would bring death instead of life. An odorless virus borne on the wind, searching for human hosts. Not a simple disease as innocuous as Ebola that took weeks to spread properly, but a genetically engineered virus that traveled with the world's air currents and infected the entire world's population. An epidemic that could poison this very airport in a matter of minutes, incubate over a number of weeks, and then kill within twenty-four hours of its first symptom.

There was no defense for such a virus. Except an antivirus.

He rented a Mercedes and drove into the city. Monique de Raison was due to deliver an address at the Sheraton in twenty-four hours. He would wait until then. This gave him ample time to prepare. To plan for whatever contingencies might disrupt his primary course of action. To narrow any possible avenues of escape or disruptions to the kidnapping.

They'd chased down hundreds of leads over the last five years. A dozen times they'd been very hopeful of uncovering a virus with precisely the elusive characteristics they required. Once they were quite certain that they actually had it. But never had they acted on such an irregular report. Certainly not a dream. What had convinced Svensson to trust such a report,

Carlos didn't know. But the more he thought about it, the more he liked the idea.

Why not? Why couldn't the answer to his prayers be delivered through a dream? Was this beyond Allah? He'd never been a mystic, but this didn't mean that God hadn't spoken to Mohammed through visions in the cave. If this single weapon could deal such a blow to his enemies, wasn't it conceivable that Allah would open man's mind to it through something as mystical as a dream? The fact that this Thomas Hunter not only had such a dream but that he'd proceeded to the CDC with it seemed to suggest providence.

Furthermore, if any pharmaceutical research firm had the resources to develop such a virus, it would be Raison Pharmaceutical. He'd never met Monique de Raison, but her meticulous research in the field took what the Russians had accomplished to a whole new level. Carlos served death with force, not through the veins, but that didn't mean he was ignorant concerning the intricacies of bioweapons.

He could still hear Svensson's low, grinding voice that late night seven years earlier as they overlooked Cairo. "When you were six, in Cyprus, your father was a computer scientist who moonlighted as a strategic adviser to the PLO," Svensson said. "He was kidnapped by Israeli Mossad agents. He never came home."

"Okay, so you know your history," Carlos said, somewhat surprised that this man knew what few could possibly know.

"I would expect most young boys would turn bitter. Maybe one day act out deep-seated resentment. But these are pale words to describe you, yes?"

Carlos watched the tall Swiss draw deep on his cheroot. "Maybe."

"You left home at age twelve and spent the next fifteen years training with a long list of terrorists, including a two-year stint in an Al Qaeda training camp. You finally left this nonsense of petty terrorism. You're interested in bigger fish."

Carlos did not like this man.

"But your years of training have suited you well. Some say that there isn't a man alive who could live through five minutes of hand-to-hand combat with you. Is that true?" Another deep drag of smoke.

"I'll leave the business of judging me to others," Carlos said.

The man smiled. "Do you know what it would take to subdue the earth?"

"The right weapon," Carlos said.

"One virus."

"As I said, the right weapon."

"One virus and one antivirus."

Carlos dismissed the sudden urge to cut

the man's throat right there on the roof of the Hilton, not because Svensson presented any immediate threat, but because the man looked evil to him with his black eyes and twisted grin. He did not like this man.

"One virus, one vaccine, and one man with the will to use both," Svensson said, and then slowly turned to Carlos. "I am that man."

"Frankly, I don't care who you are," Carlos said. "I care about my people."

"Your people. Of course. The question is, What are you willing to do for your people?"

"No," Carlos said evenly, "the question is, What *will* I do? And the answer is, I will remove their enemies."

"Unless, of course, the Israelis remove you first."

Three months later they had struck a simple agreement. Svensson and his group would offer a base of operations in the Alps, an unprecedented level of intelligence, and the means to conduct a biological attack. In return, Carlos would provide whatever muscle Svensson required in his personal operations.

The broader plan involved nations and leaders of nations and was masterminded by the man Valborg Svensson answered to: Armand Fortier. Carlos had met Fortier on only two occasions, but after each, any doubts he'd harbored had been swept out to sea. Every conceivable detail had been excruciatingly planned and then planned again. Contingencies for a hundred possible reactions to the release of any virus that met their requirements. The primary nuclear powers were the greatest prize — each had been softened and judged in ways they could not begin to imagine. Not yet. One day the historians would look back and lament the missed signals, so many subtle signs of the coming day. No one would pay such a price as the United States. The final result would forever change history in a matter of a few short weeks. It was almost too much to hope for.

And yet it was a very real possibility. If a hundred million Americans woke up one morning and learned they had been infected with a virus that would kill them in a matter of weeks, and only one man had the cure and was demanding their cooperation in exchange for that cure . . .

This was true power.

All they needed was the right weapon. The one virus with its one cure.

Carlos took a deep breath and blew it out past pursed lips. The American was on his way. Thomas Hunter. According to his sources, Hunter would be arriving in Bangkok in a matter of hours. By this time tomorrow, Carlos would know the truth.

He breathed a prayer to Allah and eased the Mercedes toward the off-ramp.

14

Tom awoke with duplicitous images running circles in his head. He was in a soft bed, and light was streaming through a small window above him. This was Rachelle's home. Johan's home. In the colored forest where he lived.

He groaned, shook the dreams of the histories from his mind, rubbed his eyes, and struggled out of bed. The room was small and plain, but turquoise and golden hues from the wood gave it a rich beauty.

He slowly opened the door. Memories of the previous evening flooded his mind. He dipped his hands into a small basin of water by the bedroom door and splashed water over his face.

"Thomas!"

Tom whirled around, startled by the cry. Johan stood in the doorway, grinning. "Do you want to play, Thomas?"

"Play? Um, actually I have some things I have to do. I have to find my village." Not to mention figuring out what to do about the romance business.

"Then maybe Tanis and my father can help you find your village. He's waiting for you."

"Your father? With Rachelle?"

The boy grinned very wide. "You want to see Rachelle?"

"Uh, no, not necessarily. I just wondered if —"

"Well, I think she wants to see you. I think that's what my father wants to talk to you about. Yes, I do. And it's very exciting! Don't you think?"

"I . . ." Was he understanding this right? The whole village knew? "I'm not sure what you mean."

Johan beamed. "They said that you hit your head and lost your memory. Is that fun?"

"Not especially."

"But if you come with me, you will have fun. Come on! They're waiting." He ran off through the door.

Tom followed. His memory was still lost, even after a good sleep.

He stepped outside and allowed his eyes to adjust to the light. Everywhere, small groups of people busied themselves. He stared at a group of women to his right who sat on the ground working with leaves and flowers — they seemed to be making tunics. Some were quite thin, others fairly plump, their skin tone varied from dark to light. All watched him with knowing glints in their emerald eyes.

He turned to his left, where two men massaged a piece of red wood with their bare hands. Beside them a woman manned a fruit stand, ten or fifteen wood boxes filled with different fruits. Several others bordered the path farther down. A low note rang through Tom's ears, singing from a source he couldn't place. All of this he took in immediately, searching his memory for any recognition. His memory failed him completely.

Johan took his hand. "These are my friends," he said, pointing to two children who stared wide-eyed at Tom from the lawn. "This is Ishmael and Latfta. They are singers like me."

They both had blond hair and green eyes; both stood a tad taller than Johan. "Hello, Thomas."

"Hello, Ishmael and Laffta."

The one on the left lifted a hand to his mouth and giggled. "Latfta!" he blurted out. "My name is Latfta!"

"Oh, sorry. Latfta?"

"Yes. Latfta."

Tom braved another look at the women. One of them, a plump woman with beautiful eyes and long lashes, began to giggle. A glance across the path betrayed her.

There, under the eaves of a house twenty

feet away, leaning against the amber wall with arms crossed and head tilted, stood Rachelle. Bare feet. Simple blue dress. Tousled hair. Brilliant green eyes. Tempting smile.

She was stunning, and she was suddenly walking toward him. For an incredible moment the motion around Tom seemed to cease. Only her dress, flowing mid-thigh, and her hair swirling in her own breeze, and those emerald eyes swallowing him.

Rachelle winked.

His heart nearly ceased. Surely the whole village had seen it. Every eye was undoubtedly fixed on her seductive approach. This incredible display of . . .

Rachelle suddenly diverted her eyes, flattened her mouth, and veered to her right. She walked right past him and then past the other women without a single word. And if he wasn't mistaken, she had squared off her shoulders. A man chuckled. Tom felt his face flush.

"What did I tell you?" Johan whispered.

He and his little friend pulled Tom out onto the path. He followed, avoiding eye contact with anyone, looking instead directly ahead as if he were going somewhere important, stealing glances to take in the village. He wasn't sure what had just happened, but he wasn't about to reveal his ignorance of the matter.

There was no evil on this side of the black forest, Michal had told him. So then Rachelle couldn't dislike him, right? Wasn't dislike a form of evil? Yet a deity — such as his father's God in the histories — could dislike without being evil. So surely his creation could dislike without being evil. They would dislike evil. But would they love one person over another? Would they choose one man or woman over another? Evidently.

Johan stopped within twenty paces. "Marla! Good morning, Marla!"

A mature woman stepped into the path and ruffled Johan's hair. "Elyon is smiling, Johan. Like the sun in the sky, he's smiling over you." Her eyes darted over Tom. "Is this the stranger?"

"Yes."

"Then you must be Thomas Hunter. Most welcome to this side." She touched his cheek and studied him for a moment. "I am the daughter of Tanis. I would say that your mother came from my brother Theo's line. Yes, the same cheeks, the same eyes, the same mouth." She lowered her hand. "My brother always was a handsome one. Welcome."

"Thank you. So you think my father's name is Theo?"

She laughed. "Not likely. But a descen-

dant, more than likely. You don't remember?"

"I . . . no, I hit my head."

"Did you, now? How interesting. Take
care of him, Johan."

"Tanis and Palus are waiting for him,"
Johan said.

"Tanis, of course. Perhaps the four of
you could mount my father's famous expedition." She smiled and winked.

They passed by a woodworker who was
shaping a piece of red wood. Tom paused
to watch the man work. The wood moved
under the crafter's massaging fingers. He
shifted for a better perspective and
watched carefully. There could be little
doubt about what he saw. The wood was
actually moving under the woodworker's
bare hands, as if he were successfully
coaxing it to reshape itself.

"What's he doing?" Tom whispered.

"He's making a ladle. Maybe a gift for
someone. You don't remember?"

"That's incredible. No, I guess I don't."

Johan talked excitedly to Ishmael and
Latfta. "You see? He doesn't remember.
He's going to love the storytellers!" Then to
Tom. "Tanis is a storyteller." Johan pulled
a small piece of red wood formed to look
like a miniature lion from his pocket and
handed it to Tom. "Keep this," he said.
"Maybe it will help you remember." Johan

and Latfta grabbed his hands once again and pulled him along like a prized trophy.

They found Johan's father, Palus, talking to a man beyond the brilliant topaz arch that led into the village. The stranger's moccasins were strapped tight, and a dark brown tunic, made from something like leather that came from one of the trees, Michal had informed him yesterday, hung above his knees. His eyes were green, of course, set into a strong tanned face that looked not a day older than thirty. The man's legs were lean and well muscled. He looked born to run through the forest. A warrior by all appearances.

This must be Tanis. Firstborn. The oldest man on Earth.

"Ah, my dear young man, good morning to you," Tanis said. "So very, very glad that you've come into our village."

"That's very kind of you," Tom said. He scanned the forest at the crest of the hill beyond. "Have you seen Michal?"

"Michal? No. Have you seen Michal, Palus?"

"No, I haven't. I'm sure he'll be along."

Tanis looked at Tom, left eyebrow raised. "Well, there you have it then. Michal will be along."

"He was going to find my village for me," Tom said.

"Oh, yes, I'm sure he will. But I think it will take him some time. In the meantime, we have some wonderful ideas."

"Maybe I should try to help him. Won't my family be worried?"

"No, no, certainly not. You really have lost all of your memory, haven't you? What a thing, to experience everything as if it were the first time. It must be both exhausting and quite stimulating."

"Wouldn't my village worry about me?" Tom asked.

"Worry? Never! They will assume you are with Elyon, as you most definitely are. Do you think he hasn't allowed this?"

They all stared at Tom, waiting for an answer. Silence lingered.

"Of course he has," Tom said.

"There you go, then! Come, let us talk." Tanis led him up the hill. Palus walked abreast, followed by the three children. Overhead, several Roush winged through the air.

"Now, I would like to know a few things before we begin," Tanis said. "I would like to know if you've forgotten the Great Romance."

"Before we begin what?"

"Before we begin to help you."

"With what?"

"With the Great Romance, of course."

There it was. He couldn't escape this romance of theirs.

Tanis exchanged glances first with Palus, and then with the children. "So then you do forget. Wonderful!" He walked in a tight circle, thinking. Raised a hand. "Not wonderful that you've forgotten, mind you. Wonderful that you have so much to discover. As a storyteller, I must say the prospects we have here are incredible! Like an unmarked wood. Like a pond without a single ripple. Like a —"

"Well then, get on with it. Tell him!" Palus said.

Tanis stopped, hand raised. He dipped his head.

"Yes, of course. The Great Romance. Sit, sit, all of you."

The others quickly sat on the sloping grass, and Tom eased down beside them. Tanis walked back and forth, tan tunic flowing.

"The Great Romance," Tanis announced, one digit in the air. He spun to the children. "Tell him what the Great Romance is, Johan."

Johan leaped to his feet. "It is the game of Elyon!" He dropped to his seat.

"A game. Yes, it is a game, I suppose. As much as any story is a story. Exactly. Well, there you have it then. The *game* of Elyon. I'm going to assume, perhaps correctly, that you know nothing, Thomas. In either case, I want to tell you anyway. The Great Romance is the basis for all of the stories."

"You mean the histories?" Tom asked.

"Histories? No, I mean stories. The histories are fascinating, and I would love to talk to you about them. But the Great Romance is the root of our stories, stories that confront us with the eternal ideals. Love. Beauty. Hope. The greatest gifts. The very heart of Elyon. Do you understand?"

"Um . . . actually it sounds a bit abstract."

"Ha! The opposite, Thomas! Do you know why we love beautiful flowers? Because we love *beauty!*"

They all nodded. Tom looked at them blankly.

"The point is, we were created to love beauty. *We* love beauty because *Elyon* loves beauty. We love song because Elyon loves song. We love *love* because Elyon loves love. And we love to be loved because Elyon loves to be loved. In all these ways we are like Elyon. In one way or another, everything we do is tied to this unfolding story of love between us and Elyon."

Tom nodded, more because the response seemed appropriate than because he understood.

Tanis nodded with him. "Elyon's love for us and ours for him, the Great Romance, you see, is first." One index finger in the air. "And second" — his other index finger in the air — "that same love expressed between us." He paused, raised both fingers above his head like goalposts, and announced emphatically, "Between man and woman!"

Palus searched Tom's face expectantly. "Do you remember? Surely you remember."

"Love. Yes, of course I remember love."

"Between a man and a woman," Palus pressed.

"Sure. Yes, between a man and a woman. Romance."

Tanis clapped once, loudly enough to pass for a thunderclap. "Exactly! Romance!"

"Romance!" a voice cried behind them. Three Roush led by none other than Gabil drifted in for a landing. The other two quickly introduced themselves as Nublim and Serentus. When Tom asked if the names were male or female, Gabil laughed. "No, Roush are not like that. No romance, not like that at all."

"Unfortunately, not like that at all," Nublim said.

"Do you want to play?" Johan asked Gabil, jumping to his feet.

"Of course!"

As if on cue, all three children ran after the Roush, sending them hooting in flight down the hill.

The two village elders immediately put their arms around Tom's shoulders and turned him uphill.

"Now the question, my dear friend, is, of course" — Tanis looked across at Palus — "Rachelle."

It was all starting to make sense to Tom, but the implications were surprising. So bold. So unabashed. The village leader, this firstborn, and Palus were actually trying to set him up with Rachelle!

All he could manage was, "Rachelle."

Palus clapped again. "Exactly! You have it! My daughter, Rachelle! She's chosen you!"

"And that's why we are here to help you," Tanis said. "You've lost your memory, and we're going to help you remember. Or at least learn again. We think —"

"Perhaps I should say . . . ," Palus began, hand uplifted.

"Yes, of course, you should say it."

"We know there will be a wonderful romance between you and my daughter, Rachelle, but we realize you may not know how to proceed."

"Well . . ."

"It's perfect! I saw it in your eyes the

moment we met yesterday."

"You saw what?"

Tanis led him farther up the hill. "You find her beautiful, yes?"

"Yes."

"She must know this if you are to win her."

Tom wanted to ask the one question begging a voice here. Namely, what if he didn't want to win her? But he couldn't bring himself to betray his promise to Michal to play along or dampen the enthusiasm of Rachelle's father.

"I could write your story," Tanis continued. "A wonderful play of love and beauty, but then it would be mine, not yours. You must tell your own story. Or, in this case, live it. And to understand how love unfolds, you must understand how Elyon loves."

The sheer momentum of their zeal carried Tom. He asked the question he knew Tanis was demanding he ask. "And how does Elyon love?"

"Excellent question! He chooses."

"He chooses," Palus repeated.

"He pursues."

"He pursues," said Rachelle's father, fist clenched.

"He rescues."

"He rescues."

"He woos."

"He woos."

"He protects."

It was like a Ping-Pong match.

"He protects. Ha!"

"He lavishes," Tanis shouted.

Palus stopped. "Is that one of them?"

"Why not?"

"I mean, is that normally placed with the others?"

"It should be."

They looked at each other for a moment.

"He lavishes," cried Palus.

"This, my dear Thomas, is what you should do to win Rachelle's heart."

"Elyon does all this?"

"Yes, of course. You've forgotten him as well?" This seemed to astound both of them.

"No, not entirely. It's coming back, you know." He quickly diverted the discussion back to Rachelle. "Forgive my" — he tapped his head — "density here, but exactly what does a woman need rescuing from? There is no evil this side of the black forest. Right?"

Again, they stared at each other.

"My, my, it is strange, this memory loss of yours," Tanis said. "It's a game, man! A play! Something to take pleasure in. You give a flower to a maiden, why? Because she *needs* nourishment? No, because she *wants* it."

"What's that got to do with rescuing? What would she need rescuing from?"

"Because she wants to *feel* rescued, Thomas. And she wants to *feel* chosen. As much as you are desperate to be chosen. We all are. Elyon chooses us. He rescues us and protects us and woos us and, yes, lavishes love on us. This is the Great Romance. And this is how you will win Rachelle's heart."

Tom wasn't sure he wanted to ask again, but honestly he still didn't understand their concept of rescuing.

"Tell him, Palus," Tanis said. "I think maybe a story would be a good idea here. I could write it for you to read before you go into battle for this love."

"Battle?" Tom said. "Now it's a battle?"

"Figuratively," Palus said. "You know, you win a woman's heart as you would win a battle. Not as if you were fighting the Shataiki in flesh and blood, of course, because we never do that."

"Not yet we don't," Tanis said. "But there may come a time. Very soon, even. We've been thinking of an expedition to teach those terrible bats a lesson or two."

Michal's concern.

"They are confined to the black forest," Tom said. "Why not just leave them there to rot?"

"Because of what they have done!" Tanis

cried. "They are evil, despicable creatures who need a lesson teaching, I'm telling you! We know from the histories what they are capable of. Do you think I'm content to just sit back and let them plot their way across the river? Then you don't know me, Thomas Hunter. I have been working on a way to finish them for good!"

There was no lack of passion in his diatribe. Even Palus seemed slightly taken aback. There was something amiss in his reasoning, but Tom couldn't put his finger on it.

"Either way, we often pretend to fight with the same kind of passion and vigor we would in a real fight with the Shataiki," Palus said. "Show him, Tanis. Just show him."

Tanis made a stance similar to those of the martial arts from Tom's dreams of the histories. "Okay then —"

"You know martial arts?" Tom asked.

Tanis stood up. "That's what they called it in the histories. You know the histories?"

"Well, I'm dreaming of them. In my dreams I know the martial arts."

"You're dreaming of the histories, but you forget everything here because you hit your head," Palus said. "Now, that is something."

"That's what Michal thinks."

"And Michal is very wise." Tanis

glanced around, as if checking for the white furry. "How much detail do you dream about? How much do you know?"

"I don't know what happens after the great virus in 2010, but before then, I know quite a bit."

"You can tell me how Napoleon won his wars? What strategy he used?"

Thomas tried to think. "No, I don't know that I ever studied Napoleon. But I suppose I could find out. I could read a history book in my dreams."

The notion seemed to stun Tanis. "My, my. You can do that?"

"Actually, I've never tried. But I'm doing it the other way." He shifted on his feet. "What I mean is, it's occurred to me. Do you know anything about the Great Deception? The virus?"

"Not enough. Not nearly enough, but more than most. It happened before the great tribulations, I do know that. The only two around these parts who would know all the histories are the wise ones. Michal and Teeleh, though Teeleh is no longer a wise one. Michal is convinced the histories are a distraction that could lead us down the wrong path. And Teeleh . . . If I ever were so fortunate as to lay my eyes on Teeleh, I would tear him limb from limb and burn the parts!"

"Michal is right," Tom said. "An expedition would be pointless. I've been in the black forest and I can tell you, the Shataiki are wicked. They very nearly killed me."

This last admission proved to be nearly too much for Tanis. "You've been *in* the black forest? Over the Crossing?"

He was so excited that Tom wondered if he'd taken the wrong turn by telling him. But Michal had suggested it, hadn't he? How could he dissuade Tanis without this admission?

"Yes. But I barely survived."

"Tell us, man! Tell us everything! I've seen the black forest from a distance and seen the black bats flying overhead, but I've never worked up the nerve to approach the river."

"That's how I lost my memory. I fell in the black forest. Gabil led me out, but not before the bats had nearly chewed me to the bone."

"That's it? I need more detail, man. More!"

"That's about it."

Tanis eyed him in wonder. "I can see that you and I would make an excellent team," he said. "I could teach you how to fight, and you could teach me the histories!"

"Rachelle is waiting," Palus said patiently.

Although Tom wasn't altogether in sync

with the Great Romance, it suddenly sounded far better than delving into details of the black forest or the histories with Tanis. Either way, Tanis knew less than Tom did about the virus. He would be no help in uncovering more detail.

Unless the answers were in the black forest, and Tanis could help him get those answers from the black forest.

"Yes, the Great Romance," Tom said.

Tanis nodded. "Okay, but later we must talk. We must!" He spread his arms and looked up the hill. "Okay then, pretend that Palus is Rachelle. Just pretend now, it's only a story. There she is, and here you are." He pointed to the ground by his feet. "First, I will say that you have given her many flowers and wooed her with many words, telling her precisely how she makes your heart melt and why her hair reminds you of waterfalls and . . . well, you get the idea." He was still standing with arms spread, slightly crouched as if to receive an attack.

"You see, this will soften her heart. Whisper in her ear and keep your voice low so that she knows you are a strong man." He stopped and considered Tom for a moment. "Perhaps later I can give you some of the right things to say. Would you like that? I am very good at romance."

Tom was too far into their game to suggest anything but wholehearted endorsement now. "Yes," he said.

"Okay, that's wooing. You will become very good at this activity. We woo our women every day. But back to the rescue." He flexed his legs. "Now, as I was saying, Palus is Rachelle and you are here. Down the hill comes a flock of the black bats. The Shataiki. You can dispatch them easily enough, of course, because you're a man of great might. The object here, though, isn't only to dispatch the vermin, but to rescue your beauty while you do so. Are you following me?"

"Yes, I think so. Dispatch the vermin and rescue the beauty."

"Exactly. With your legs flexed as so, you throw one arm out to Rachelle and ready the other to beat back the bats. Then you cry in a loud voice, so that she knows everyone in the valley can hear your statement of valor." And here Tanis thundered to Palus, "Come, my love, throw yourself into my arm of iron, and I will strike the withering beasts from the air with my other, a fist of stone."

Tanis motioned to Palus with his hand.

"What?" Palus asked.

"Show him. Run and jump into my arm. You're Rachelle, remember? I won't drop you."

"Jump? How?"

"I don't know, just run and jump. Make it look real, as a woman might jump. Perhaps feetfirst."

"I don't think Rachelle would run and jump. She's quite a confident woman, you know. What do you think of sweeping me off my feet instead?" Palus asked. "You could strike a few of the bats that are diving in to eat me, then pluck me to safety while whispering wondrous words into my ear, then battle the beasts with your free arm."

Tanis arched an eyebrow. "Very clever. How many beasts would you say I should fell before I sweep you off your feet?"

"If you were to send a hundred back to hell, she would be very impressed."

"A hundred? Before I jump to her rescue? It seems over the top."

"Then fifty. Fifty is plenty."

Tanis seemed totally taken with the notion. "And what if we were to say that the big one, Teeleh himself, were leading the attack from two sides, leaving me no way for escape? I dispatch fifty easily enough, but then they are too many and all hope seems lost. At the last moment, Rachelle could direct my attack, and with a brilliant reversal I send the big one screeching for his life. The rest flee in disarray. Perfect!"

"Do you actually want to do it?" Palus asked.

In answer Tanis suddenly spun uphill. "Don't worry, my love! I will rescue you!" he thundered, looking at Palus.

He took three steps and then leaped into the air, executed a spectacular roundhouse, landed on his hands, rolled forward, and came up with two stunning kicks Tom wouldn't have thought possible in succession.

Tanis ended his first attack in a back handspring that placed him at Palus's side. He swept the man from his feet and struck out with another kick.

The momentum carried both off balance. They tumbled to the ground, rolled once, and came up laughing.

"Well, I suppose that one needs a bit of practice," Tanis said. "But you do get the idea. I wouldn't suggest anything so extravagant with Rachelle the first time you see her. But she will want to be surprised by your inventiveness. To what lengths would you go to choose her, to save her, to love her?"

Tom couldn't remotely imagine doing anything bold. Whispering lavish words of woo could prove challenging enough. Had he ever done anything like this before his amnesia? Evidently not, or he would bear the mark of union on his forehead.

"How did you do that kick?" Tom asked.

Tanis bounded to his feet. "Which one?"

Palus held up his hand. "Forgive me, but I must take my leave. Karyl waits." They bid him well and he headed for the village. The children were playing with several Roush on the other side of the valley, taking turns riding on a pair of the white creatures' backs as they locked wings and swooped down the hill.

"Which kick?" Tanis asked again.

"The first one. The one-two-back?"

"Show me what you mean," Tanis said.

"Me? I can't kick like that."

"Then I'll teach you. A woman loves a strong man. It was once the way men fought, you know. In the histories, I mean. I have created a whole system of hand-to-hand combat. Try the kick. Show me."

"Now?"

"Of course." Tanis clapped twice. "Show me."

"Well, it was something like . . ." Tom stepped forward and executed a round-house with a second kick, somewhat similar to the one he'd seen Tanis do. Surprisingly the roundhouse felt . . . simple. He could execute it with far more ease here than in his dreams of the histories. The atmosphere?

Unfortunately the second kick came up short. He landed on his side and grunted.

"Excellent! We'll make a warrior of you yet. I think Rachelle will be very impressed. Would you like to be my apprentice?"

"At fighting?"

"Yes, of course! I could teach what very few have learned, even here. We could talk of the histories and discuss ways to deliver a crushing blow to the putrid bats of the black forest."

"Well, I would like to learn from you —"

"Perfect! Come, let me show you the second kick."

Tanis was gifted and spared no passion in explaining precisely how to move so as to maximize the number of moves in the air. When he took off, he used his arms as a counterbalance, allowing for surprising maneuvers. Within an hour, Tom was able to execute some of the moves without landing on his head. Short of the movies, no living person could move like this in the histories, surely. There had to be a difference in the atmospheres. Or was it the water?

The hour wore Tom weak.

"Enough! Now we talk," Tanis finally announced, seeing Tom struggle for breath. "We will learn more fighting tomorrow. But now I want to know more about the histories. I would like to know, for example, what kind of weapons they had. I know some, devices that made large sounds and delivered terrible blows to hundreds at once. Have you ever heard of such a thing?"

"A gun?" Alarm rose through Tom's chest. Tanis really was seriously considering this expedition of his into the black forest. But he couldn't! It was far too dangerous.

"What is a gun?" Tanis asked. "I am considering an expedition, Thomas. Such weapons could be a great help. A very great help, indeed. You could go with me, since you've been there!"

He spoke with such enthusiasm and innocence.

"You don't know the black forest, Tanis. Entering would be the death of anyone who tried."

"But you! You're alive!"

"I was lucky. And trust me, no swift kicks would have helped me any. There's way too many of them. Millions!"

"Exactly. Which is why they must be defeated!"

"You have agreed with the others not to cross the river."

"A precaution. There are times to leave caution in the valley and strike out for the mountain."

"I don't think this is that time," Tom said. It occurred to him that he needed some water. He was desperately thirsty. Faint, in fact. They were walking up the hill, and he stopped to catch his breath. "Are you driven by anger against them, or curiosity?"

Tanis looked at the forest in thought. "Anger, I think. Perhaps it's not the right time. At the least, I could write a wonderful story about such a thing." He faced Tom. "Tell me what else you know."

This wasn't going as Michal intended.

Dizziness suddenly swamped him. He shook his head. "Please, Tanis, you don't understand."

"But I want to!"

Tom's world tipped and suddenly began to fade. He dropped to one knee. Felt himself falling. Reached out his hand.

Black.

15

"Excuse me, sir?" A hand touched Tom's shoulder.

He sat up, half awake. A stewardess leaned over him. "Please bring your seat up." Kara's seat was empty. Bathroom.

Tom tried to clear his mind. "We're landing?"

"We've begun our descent into Bangkok." She moved on.

They were in the cattle class of a Singapore Airlines 747. The yellow-and-blue upholstery that covered the seat directly in front of him was beginning to tear. On the seat-back monitor, a red line showed the flight's progress over the Pacific. This was the dream.

The plane smelled like home. Southeast Asia home. Soy soup, peanut sauces, noodles, herbal teas. His mind flashed back over the last eight hours. The flight to Singapore had been a long, sleepless affair during which Kara and Tom had flipped through channels on the small embedded screens and reminisced about their years in

Southeast Asia. Years of learning how to be a chameleon, switching skins between cultures.

Like switching mind-sets between his dreams now. He'd been bred for this.

"Scoot over, will you?" Kara bumped his knee, and he slid over to the center seat so she wouldn't have to climb over him.

"Welcome back to the land of the living." She fastened her seat belt. "Talk to me."

"About what?"

"About why ants build nests in the desert. What do you mean, about what?" she whispered. "What did you find out?"

He stared at her, struck by how much he loved his one and only sister. She came off tough, but her walls were paper thin.

"Tom?"

"Nothing."

Her left brow arched. "Excuse me? You just slept for five hours. We're flying across the ocean to Bangkok *because* of your dreams. Don't tell me they stopped working."

"I didn't say that. In fact, I think I am learning something. I think I may know why this is happening."

"Enlighten me."

"I think maybe these dreams of what happened in the histories are arming me with information that could stop something terrible in the future. I think maybe Elyon is allowing me to have these dreams. Maybe to stop Tanis from his expedition."

She just stared at him.

"Okay, so maybe it's the other way around. Maybe I'm supposed to stop something from happening here."

"I have $345,000 in my bank account that says it's the latter. Which is why you were going to find out what in the world we're supposed to do in Bangkok, remember? And you come back with nothing?"

"It's not like that. Believe me, when I'm there, I'm not exactly concerned about my dreams of this place. Trust me. I have bigger problems. Like who I am. Like how this Great Romance thing works."

"Great romance? Please don't tell me you're actually falling for this girl who healed you." He'd filled Kara in on the details of his dream before falling asleep.

The last meeting with Rachelle flooded Tom's mind. The way she had looked at him, smiled at him, walked by him without a word. His face must have shown something because Kara turned away.

Kara rolled her eyes. "Oh, please. You can't be serious."

"Actually, she's very interesting."

"Uh-huh. Of course she is. And built like a goddess, no doubt. Did she find you irresistible and smother you with kisses?"

"No. She walked away. But Tanis, the leader of the tribe, and Palus, her father, are showing me how to win the beauty."

"Okay, Tom. Win the beauty. Everyone is entitled to a fantasy now and then. In the meantime, we have a problem here."

The plane entered a turn and Kara looked across Tom at Bangkok's metropolitan skyline, not so different from New York's. The fairly modern and very exotic city packed nearly eight million people like sardines. Mid-day. To the east, Cambodia. To the south lay the Gulf of Thailand, and several hundred miles across it, Malaysia.

"I'm not pretending to know how this works, but you've got me scared, Thomas," she said quietly.

He nodded. "Me too."

She faced him. "No, I mean really. I mean, this isn't a dream here. For all I know, the other isn't a dream either, but I can't have you treating this reality like some dream. You hear me? You know things you shouldn't know — terrifying things. For all I know, you may be the only one alive to stop it."

She had a point. Not that he was treating this 747 like a dream no matter how much it felt like a dream. On the contrary, he was the one who'd convinced her they had to come in the first place. Would

221

he have done that if it were only a dream? No.

"And no offense," Kara said, "but you're starting to look pretty haggard. You have bags under your eyes, and your face is drooping."

"Drooping?"

"Tired. You haven't had a decent sleep since this whole thing started."

True enough. He felt like he hadn't slept at all. "Okay," he said. "I hear you. Any ideas?"

"As a matter of fact, yes. I think I can help you. I can keep you focused."

"I am focused. We wouldn't be here if I hadn't insisted."

"No, I mean really focused. As long as you keep tripping between these dreams and realities, you're bound to keep second-guessing yourself, right?"

"A little. Maybe."

"Trust me, a lot. Right now you probably still think you're in the colored forest, sleeping somewhere, and that Bangkok is some dream based on the histories of Earth. Well, you're both right and wrong, and I'm going to make sure you realize that."

"You lost me."

"I'm going to assume that both realities are real. After all, it is a possibility, isn't it? Alternate universes, divergent realities, time distortions, whatever. The point is, from here on we assume that both realities are absolutely real. The colored forest really does exist, and there really is a woman there named . . . what's her name?"

"Rachelle."

"Rachelle. There really is a beautiful babe over there named Rachelle who has the hots for you."

"I didn't say that."

She held up her hand. "Whatever. You get the idea. It's all real. You have to do whatever you're meant to do there, even if it's nothing more than falling madly in love. I'll help you with that. Give you ideas, advice. Maybe I can help you land this hot chick."

"Assuming I'm interested in landing the first hot chick who winks at me. What do you take me for?"

"Okay, I won't call her a hot chick. Does that help? You're missing the point. It's real. That's the point. The colored forest really exists. Everything that happens there is as real as real can be. And I won't let you forget that. Not one word about it being a dream anymore. We pretend it's another country or something. The furry bats are real."

This last sentence she said a bit loud, and a tall, dark-haired European with a gray mustache looked their way. Kara returned his stare.

"Can I help you?"

The man looked away without responding.

"You see, that's what we're going to get. That's why we have to stick together on this, because you know it, Thomas, this world is real too."

The huge plane bounced on the runway, and the overhead bins creaked with the strain of the landing.

"We really have landed in Bangkok and the Raison Vaccine really is going to be announced tomorrow and you really do know something about that."

"So we go a hundred percent in both realities," Tom said.

"Not me. You. I just help you do that."

It was the most sensible thing he'd heard in forty-eight hours. He wanted to hug her right there. "Agreed."

"Okay." She took a deep breath. "Now that we're in Bangkok, what do we do?"

"We find out everything we possibly can about Raison Pharmaceutical."

"Okay." Kara nodded. "How?"

"We go to their complex outside the city," Tom said.

"Okay. Then what?"

"Then we stop them from shipping any samples or product. Better yet, we stop them from making this announcement tomorrow."

"This is where the plan loses focus for me," Kara said. "I'm not exactly a stock-broker, but I've seen my share of new drugs released into the market, and I'll guarantee you, calling off an announcement would send their stock into a dive. It's up 100 percent in anticipation of this announcement already."

Tom nodded. "And we have to convince them to destroy any existing samples of the vaccine. And the means to make it."

"This whole thing is definitely out of focus. Who says we even get past the main gate? This is a high-security facility, right?"

"I guess we're going to find out."

She sighed and shook her head. "The next time you go back to the other place, you need more information. Period. In the meantime, is there anything you need here that will help you there?"

She looked at him, dead serious.

"I told you, Thomas, we treat both . . . what should we call them? Worlds? We treat both worlds, or whatever they are, as if they are real. And as a matter of fact, they have to be. So if we need information here, maybe you need information there too."

He shook his head. "No, not really. There's nothing happening there. I mean, I'm lost and I can't remember anything, but I don't see how anything here can help that."

"I wouldn't assume there's nothing happening there. How about this winning the beauty thing? Need some advice on how to land the chick?"

"Please —"

"Fine. On how to find true love then?"

"No."

"Just don't pass gas around her."

"You're not taking this seriously."

"That's exactly what I'm doing. You have enough idealism to fill a hundred novels. What you need is practical advice. Brush your teeth, wear deodorant, and change your underwear."

"Thanks, sis. Priceless advice." He twisted his mouth in a half-grin. "I think she's pretty religious."

"Then go to church with her. Just make sure it's not some cult. Stay away from the Kool-Aid."

"Actually, we're all quite religious. I'm pretty sure this Elyon is God."

She raised her eyebrow. "You don't believe in God, remember? Dad believed in God, and it about killed us all. God is where I'd draw the line with this chick. Girl. Keep religion and politics out of it. Better yet, find a different woman."

It took them an hour to make their way through Bangkok International Airport and negotiate the rental of a small green

Toyota Tercel from the Avis desk. Tom still had his international driver's permit from the Philippines, and he welcomed the thought of weaving his way through Third World traffic again. Kara spread the map on the dash and took the role of navigator, maybe the more difficult task of the two.

She traced a line on the map. "Okay, Raison Pharmaceutical is out by the Rama Royal Park, east of town. We go south on the Vibhavadi Rangsit to the Inthara cutoff, east to the Inthara Expressway, and then south all the way to the Phra Khanong district." She looked up as he pulled into traffic. "Just don't get us killed. This isn't Denver."

"Have faith."

A horn blared and he swerved.

"I'm not into faith, remember?" she said.

"Maybe now would be a good time to start."

He'd have to get used to the horns again — they were as ubiquitous as road markings here. The main roads were properly marked, but they acted as guides more than restrictions. The position of a car and the volume of its horn were nine-tenths of the law: The first and the loudest had the right of way. Period.

He hit his horn now, to warm up to the idea. Another horn went off nearby, like mating calls. No one seemed to mind. Except Kara.

"Yes?" Kara said.

"Yes. Sounds good, doesn't it?"

Tom drove into the city. A brown haze hung over towering midtown skyscrapers. In the distance, the sky train. Dilapidated taxis, held together with baling wire, and Mercedes crowded the same surface streets with motorcycle taxis and Tuk-Tuks — a three-wheeled cross between a car and a motorcycle.

And bicycles. Lots of bicycles.

Thais went about their daily business, some teetering along on bicycle carts that would unfold into frying stands, others piloting dump trucks, still others strolling in the orange garb of monks.

He cracked the window. It was early afternoon — the smells of the city were nearly overpowering. But to Tom they were intoxicating. There was exhaust, there was a touch of stale water, there was fried noodles, there was . . .

This could easily be the Philippines. Home. Ten years ago, one of the rascals on the street might have been him, mixing it up with the locals and then stopping by a stand for some satays with peanut sauce.

Tom felt a knot rise in his throat. It was the most beautiful sight he'd seen in years.

They drove in reflective silence for

twenty minutes. Kara stared out the windows, caught up in her own thoughts. A soupy nostalgia overtook them both.

"I miss this," Kara said. "It almost feels like a dream. Maybe we're both dreaming."

"Maybe. Exotic."

"Exotic."

They passed the Phra Khanong district midafternoon and headed out into the delta. The city sounds faded behind them. The concrete gave way to a carpet of trees and rice paddies known as the Mae Nam Chao Phraya delta — *the rice bowl of Asia* — a hot, steamy, fertile sea of vegetation infested with insects and creatures rarely seen.

Like a primordial soup from which would come the most deadly virus the earth had ever known.

"It's hard to believe we're actually here," Tom said.

"Halfway across the world in twelve hours. Nothing like the jet age. Turn left up here. It should be about a mile up the road."

Tom turned onto a private road that led into an area hidden by heavy jungle growth. The asphalt was black, freshly poured. There was no other traffic.

"You sure this is right?" Tom asked.

"No. Just following the clerk's directions.

It's kind of . . . spooky."

Good word.

The complex rose out of the delta like a wraith in the night. The jungle had been cleared directly ahead. There was a gate. Two or three guards. Manicured lawns. And a massive white building that stretched across several acres. Behind the building, the jungle reclaimed the land.

Tom stopped the car a hundred yards from the front gate. "This it?"

"Raison Pharmaceutical." She nodded at a sign he'd missed to their left.

He cracked his door, set one foot out, and stood. The jungle screeched around him — a billion cicadas screaming their warning. The humidity made breathing hard.

He plopped back down, eased the door closed, started the car moving again. They rolled up to the gate without speaking.

"This is it," Tom said. A guard dressed in a gray uniform complete with shiny pistol approached them. "Why are you so quiet?"

"What am I supposed to say, 'Let's go back. This doesn't feel right to me. Please don't do anything stupid'?"

"Please, this is me," he said, rolling down the window.

"Exactly."

The guard glanced at the license plate and stepped forward. "What is your business?"

"We're here to see Monique de Raison. Or Jacques de Raison. It's very important we see them."

The man scanned his clipboard. "I have no scheduled arrivals. What is your name?"

"Thomas Hunter."

He flipped one page and lowered the board. "You have an appointment?"

Kara leaned over. "Of course we do. We've just arrived from the United States. The Centers for Disease Control. Check again; we have to be there."

"And your name?"

"Kara Hunter."

"I have neither on my list. This is a secured facility. No one in without a name on the list."

Tom nodded patiently. "No problem. Just give them a call. Tell them that Thomas Hunter is here from the CDC. It's absolutely imperative that I see Monique de Raison. Today. We didn't fly all the way from Atlanta for nothing." He forced a grin. "I'm sure you understand."

The man hesitated, then walked into the booth.

"What if he doesn't let us in?" Tom asked.

"I knew this would happen."

"Maybe we'd be more convincing in a Mercedes."

"Here comes your answer."

The guard approached. "We have no record of a visit today. Tomorrow there will be an event at the Sheraton Grande Sukhumvit. You may see her then."

"I don't think you understand. I need to see her today, not tomorrow. It's critical, man. Do you hear me? Critical!"

The man hesitated, and for a moment Tom thought he might have made the right impression. He lifted a radio and spoke quietly. The door to the guardhouse opened and a second guard approached. Shorter than the other one, but his sleeves were rolled up over bulging muscles. Dark glasses. The kind who liked American T-shirts with Sylvester Stallone's Rambo persona stamped across the chest.

"Please leave," the first guard said.

Tom looked at him. At the other, who'd stopped by the hood. He rolled up the window.

"Any suggestions?"

Kara was biting one of her nails. But she wasn't demanding that they retreat.

The guard by the hood motioned him to turn the car around.

"How important is it that we stop this announcement of theirs?" Kara asked.

"Depends if you think we can really change history."

"We're past that," she said. "The answer is yes. Focus, remember? This is real. That's why we're here."

"Then it depends on whether stopping the announcement will change history." The guard was starting to get a tad animated. Tom reached over and locked the car. "Depends on whether they actually plan on shipping the vaccine tomorrow."

"Can we assume anything else? This isn't a game we can play over if we lose the first time."

A fist rapped on the window. The guards were both motioning vigorously now. The one with the bunched biceps put his hand on his holster.

"They wouldn't kill an American, would they?" Tom asked.

"I don't know, but I think this is getting out of hand, Thomas. We should leave."

Tom grunted and slammed the steering wheel. Maybe they were powerless to change history. Maybe they were the two martyrs who'd tried to change history but got gunned down at the gates to Raison Pharmaceutical. Or maybe changing history required extraordinary measures.

"Thomas . . ."

The guards were slamming his hood now. "Hold on."

He sprang the latch, shoved the door open, and rose from the car.

Both guards went for their guns.

"Whoa." Tom lifted his hands. "Easy. I just want to talk. Just one thing, I promise. I'm on official business with the United States government. Trust me, you don't want to hurt me."

"Get back in the car, sir!"

"I'm getting back in, but I want to say something first. The Centers for Disease Control has just learned that the vaccine this company is planning to announce tomorrow has a fatal flaw. It mutates under extreme heat and becomes a virus that we believe may have far-reaching implications."

He walked toward the short one with the big muscles. "You have to listen to me!" He spoke loudly and slowly. "We are here to stop a disaster. You two, Fong and Wong, will go down as the two imbeciles who didn't listen up when the Americans came to warn Monique de Raison. You have to tell her this!"

Both guards were stepping back, guns in hand, intent but clearly caught off guard by his audacity. Oddly enough, Tom wasn't terribly frightened by their guns. Yes, they had his stomach twisted in a knot, but he wasn't scrambling back in terror. The whole scene reminded him of the hillside lesson Tanis and Palus had given him. Taking on a hundred Shataiki with a few well-placed kicks.

He looked from one guard to the second and resisted a strong impulse to try the kick he'd learned from Tanis — the double-back kick that had at first looked impossible. He could do it too. They were perfectly placed. Saliva gathered in his mouth. He knew he could pull it off. Just like that: one, *whack,* twist; two, *whack.* Just like Tanis had taught him. Before they could react.

'Course, it was crazy. And what if, just what if, that had been only a dream? He would be doing flips in his mind but falling flat on the asphalt here in reality.

"You hear me?" he asked. "I have to talk to someone."

They stood their ground, crouched, ready for anything.

"Do you guys like Jet Li?"

"Back!" screamed the one with biceps. "Back, back!"

"Listen to me!" Tom yelled in a sudden fit of frustration.

"Back, back, back, or I shoot!" Biceps screeched.

Tom blinked at the man. And what would Tanis say to that?

"Okay. Relax." He turned to climb back in the car.

Perfect.

Right now, at this very moment, the situation was perfect for that particular kick. If they shot, they would hit each other. If he just . . .

Tom planted his left hand on the hood, scissored into the air. *Whack*, gun, *whack*, head. Continue the motion with the momentum, pirouette.

That was one. The other one stared with wide eyes.

A gun boomed.

Missed him.

Whack, gun. *Whack*, head.

Land. Perfect.

Tom stood by the hood, stunned by what he'd just done. Both guards lay on their backs. Biceps had shot harmlessly. He had done this? His heart pumped with adrenaline. He felt like he could take on the flock if he had to.

"Thomas!"

Kara. Yelling.

He ran for the guardhouse, found the button that opened the gate. Pushed it. Motors whirred, and the gate ground slowly open. He bolted for the car.

Kara stared at him with round eyes.

"Hold on!" he yelled and shoved the stick into drive. He pointed the car for the gap in the gate. They roared toward the white building.

Immediately another problem presented

itself. A round hole in the windshield. Bullet hole.

Kara slumped down. "They're firing!"

Four more guards had materialized from the main building. They had rifles and they were firing.

Reality crashed in on Tom. He whipped the wheel to his right and punched the accelerator. The car veered into gravel. Spun through a wide donut. Two more bullets cracked through the back window.

"Hold on!"

The moment the tires regained traction on the asphalt, the Toyota surged forward. Through the gate. By the time they passed the Raison sign, they were doing 120 kph.

Tom kept the accelerator pegged until they hit the intersection. Traffic on the main road limited his speed. It took another mile for his heart to match pace.

Kara blew out a long breath. "What was that?"

"Don't start. It was crazy, I know."

"No argument."

It appeared that they'd made a clean getaway.

"What exactly did you do back there?" Kara asked.

"I don't know. I really didn't plan on going after them like that. It just happened. We had to get in; they were in the way. You seemed to think we should —"

"No, I'm talking about that kick. I've never seen you do anything like that."

That fact had lingered in his own mind for the last five minutes.

"I haven't done anything like it. Not here."

"Not here, meaning . . . ?"

"Well, actually . . . it's something Tanis taught me."

"In the other reality?"

"It feels almost like instinct. Like my brain has learned a few new tricks and is using them automatically. They say we could walk through walls if we used all of our brainpower, right? Crazy, huh?"

She stared ahead, awed. "No, not crazy. It actually makes sense. In this wacky dream thing of yours. And we're treating them like they're both real, remember?"

"So what I learn there, I can use here. And what I learn here, I can use there."

"Evidently. Not just knowledge but skills." They drove in silence for a few seconds. "Now what?"

"Now we get a room at the Sheraton Grande Sukhumvit and hope we can make an impression on Monique de Raison tomorrow."

"Maybe you can woo her," Kara said.

"Woo her?"

"Never mind."

Tom sighed. "Don't be ridiculous."

"What we need is for you to sleep. And dream."

He nodded. "Sleep and dream."

16

"Thomas! Wake up. Open your mouth."

Thomas felt the cool juice run down his throat. He jerked up, sputtered, and spit a lump of something from his mouth.

"Easy, lad."

Tanis grinned beside him, yellow fruit in hand. Michal stood beside him.

"What happened?" Tom asked.

"You passed out," Tanis said. "But a bite of fruit and you came back quickly enough."

"You are weak; perhaps the effects of your fall in the black forest still linger," Michal said. "How do you feel now?"

"Fine."

He felt a bit disoriented, but otherwise well enough. He'd dreamed of Bangkok. Fighting two guards. Then retreating to a luxurious hotel called the Sheraton Grande Sukhumvit where he and Kara had taken a suite, walked the streets, and finally collapsed into bed, groggy with jet lag.

Tom shook his head.

"How long was I . . . out?"

"Only a few minutes," Tanis said.

Yet he'd dreamed of a whole day in Bangkok.

Two thoughts rang through his head. One, he had to treat both worlds as if they were real. Two, he had to get more information.

Which meant he might have to retrace his steps to the black forest after all. With Tanis's help. Unless he could persuade Michal to help him out.

What was he thinking? He could never go back to the black forest!

"Please," Tanis said, handing Tom the fruit, "have some more."

Tom bit deep into the fruit and immediately felt the nectar flow into his gut. He bit again and again and suddenly realized he'd lost himself in the process. He had already finished the fruit.

"Did . . . did you dream?" Tanis asked.

"Dream?" Tom stood.

"Just now, did you dream of the histories?"

Tom glanced at Michal, who arched a fuzzy eyebrow.

"I was only out for a few seconds," Tom said.

"Dreams do not keep time," Tanis said.

There was no hiding it from the leader.

"Yes, as a matter of fact, I believe I did dream."

"Did you go to the history books and read about Napoleon?"

What was Michal thinking of this exchange? Tanis wasn't hiding anything. No, of course not. He was purely innocent.

"No," Tom said. "Why would I do that?"

"Have you forgotten, man? I will teach you how to fight, and you will open my mind to the histories. It was our understanding!"

"It was?"

"It was my understanding. What do you think, Michal? Since Thomas Hunter seems to have unusual access to the histories and I am a very gifted fighter, I thought we would make a wonderful team, he and I. If we ever were to mount an expedition to the black forest, Thomas could be very helpful. Yes?"

The Roush frowned thoughtfully. "Hmm . . ."

Tom assumed that Michal would disapprove outright. But he didn't. He seemed in some way subservient to Tanis.

"It's an interesting idea, the two of you pairing up. But the expedition is a foolish notion on all counts. It would be like seeking a cliff to lean over. Are you so interested in seeing whether you will fall?"

"Then at the very least, Thomas could teach me more of the histories," Tanis said. "I understand why you won't. As you say, interfering with us is not your job, yes? The histories could interfere, you say. Understood. But Thomas Hunter is not a Roush. And the fact that he's here, having these dreams, must mean Elyon has willed it. Perhaps caused it! It's only natural that we form this bond. Wouldn't you agree?"

Innocence clearly didn't compromise the man's intelligence.

"The histories are oral for a reason," Michal said cautiously. "I would think very carefully before tempting that tradition."

Tom stepped forward. "Actually . . ." He stopped, remembering his promise to the Roush.

Michal eyed him. "Yes, Thomas? Actually what?"

"Well, to be perfectly honest, there were a few questions that I had about the histories too. I seem to be stuck in a certain time, just before the Great Deception. In my dreams, my sister and I seem to think we might be able to prevent the virus from being released. We think that may be our purpose. Maybe you could help me to do this. Make any sense?"

"No. Not really," Michal said. "How can you stop something that has already happened? You see, these dreams are not helpful. They are keeping you in a state of disorientation. They might actually be the

243

cause of your continued amnesia. You should be focusing on other things now, not trivia from the distant past. Does *that* make sense?"

"You're right, you're right. Perfect sense, but in my dreams it doesn't make perfect sense."

"And you want me to encourage these dreams? How about you, Tanis? Does this make sense to you?"

"Perfect. But if the dreams persist, they may have another purpose. How to make weapons, for example."

"Weapons! Why would you need weapons?" Michal demanded.

"To fight the Shataiki, of course!"

"You will fight them with your heart!" the Roush cried. "Forget the weapons! I will tell you something from the histories now, and then I will never speak to either of you of them again. There was a saying I want you to remember. It was used poorly then, but it will serve you both well now. Make love, not war, they said. Think of this, Tanis, when you consider making your weapons. Make love, not war."

Tanis looked stricken. He threw his hands wide, palms up. "You question my motives? Is there a man you know who is more versed in the Great Romance than I? No! I would rescue, as Elyon would rescue. If I would need a weapon to dispatch the black bats, is it even questionable? Is anything I suggest wrong?"

"No. And yes, you are a great lover of Elyon. I would never question your motives or your passions, Tanis. Do you hear me? Never!"

Tanis's eyes flashed desperately. He lifted a fist to the sky and cried out, "Elyon, oh, Elyon, I would never withhold my love from you! I would dive into your bosom and drink deep of your heart! I will never forsake you. Never!"

Tears wet Michal's eyes. It was the first time Tom had seen such emotion from the stoic Roush, and it surprised him.

Tanis paced back and forth quickly. "I must write a story for Elyon. I must speak of my love and the Great Romance and the rescuing of everything that is his! I have been inspired. Thank you, thank you both for this." He turned to Thomas. "We will talk later, my young apprentice. You are ready to win the beauty?"

His reference to the anticipated romance between him and Rachelle made Tom feel suddenly lightheaded. "Yes, I think so. I think it's all coming back." Slowly. Too slowly.

"That's my boy!" Tanis slapped him on the back. "Wonderful. Remember, he chooses."

Tom nodded. "Chooses. Got it."

"He pursues."

A pause. He was expected to repeat. "He pursues."

"He rescues."

"He rescues."

"He woos."

"He woos."

"He protects."

"He protects."

"He lavishes."

"That was the extra one."

Tanis pumped his fist. "He lavishes. It's a good one, and I'm going to include it in the story I will write now."

Tom mimicked Tanis with his fist. "He lavishes!"

"And so will you."

"And so will you."

"No, I. You say, 'So will *I.*'"

"And so will I," Tom said.

"And now I am off. A story is in the making!" Tanis dipped his head at both of them. "Until the Gathering." He ran a few yards and whirled around.

"Should I tell her you are waiting?"

"Who?"

"The beauty! Rachelle, lad! Rachelle, the beauty!"

Now? He wasn't even sure how to win a beauty. But especially now, in front of Michal, he had to follow the Roush's advice. Pretend.

"Sure," Tom said.

"Ha!" Off he ran.

Michal watched Tanis run. "Stunning, wonderful, magnificent."

"You can't seem to make up your mind about him," Tom said.

"He is human! I can't help but admire any human."

"Right. Yes, of course."

Tanis was already a tiny figure, running up the main street, probably telling the whole world that the dashing visitor from the other side was on the hill now, prepared to woo and win his beauty. Rachelle.

Michal turned from the valley. "The Great Romance. The Gathering. You have no idea what I would give to have what you have." He hopped a few yards and gazed longingly at the horizon. "It's all a bit much at times. I can hardly stand to sit by and watch."

That was it. There was no way Tom could question Michal's decision on withholding the histories after a spiel like that. It was all a bunch of nonsense any—

From the corner of his eye he saw a figure racing through the village below, and his heart bolted in his chest. It was Rachelle. He couldn't see her face from this distance, but he saw her blue dress. She was racing for the arching village entrance, like a child sprinting to catch the ice-cream truck.

Tanis had told her.

Panic swept through his bones. What had he gotten himself into? Wasn't this all going a bit fast? He'd been in the valley for less than a day. Love seemed to be a currency they were all swamped with. Naturally, without evil to rob their hearts, it would be.

Which meant he, too, was full of love. It would all come back. This was the way it worked.

Rachelle slowed at the entrance and started to meander up the hill. It was hard to imagine that anyone would be so eager to meet him, much less be romanced by him. Was he so appealing? Attractive?

"Michal!" He cleared his throat. "Michal."

The Roush was staring down the hill, swaying with anticipation.

"Michal, you have to help me."

"And take the fun out of it? It's in your heart, Thomas. Win her!"

"I don't know *how* to win her! I forget how!"

"No, you don't; no, you don't forget! Some things you can't forget."

"She's walking up here!" Tom paced quickly. "I don't know what she expects."

"You're nervous; that's good. That's a good sign."

"It is?"

"It betrays your true feelings!"

Tom stopped and stared at him. True enough. Why was he so nervous? Because he did want very much to impress the stunning woman sauntering up the hill toward him.

The realization only made it worse. Much worse.

"At least give me a pointer," he said. "Should I just stand here?"

"Didn't Tanis tell you? Okay." Michal lifted his wing and guided Tom up the hill, toward the forest. "Okay, not speaking from experience but from what I've seen, and I have seen a few to be sure, I would suggest you wait in the trees up there." His wings quivered. "Intrigue and mystery are what you're after, I think. Dear, dear. I should go. She's coming closer. I should go."

Michal waddled off, hopped twice, and took to the air.

"Michal!"

But Michal was gone.

Tom whirled back, saw that Rachelle was making good time up the hill, hands behind her back, looking nonchalantly away. He ducked down, despite his full knowledge that she'd seen him, and ran for the top.

He was beginning to think he'd gone too far into the trees. That the large amber tree behind which he'd hidden camouflaged him too well. She'd missed him. He wasn't even sure why he was hiding. Did rescuing the beauty look anything like hide-and-seek?

But he couldn't stand out in the open with his arms folded, pretending to be a mighty warrior. On the other hand, Tanis might do that. Maybe he should.

He poked his head around the tree.

No sign of her. The forest glowed in a dazzling display of color. Red and blue and amber in this section. Birds chirped overhead. A light breeze swept the rich scent of roses through his nostrils.

But no sign of Rachelle.

He stepped out, suddenly worried that he'd lost her. Should he call out? No, that would only make it clear that he'd lost her. She wanted to be chosen, which sounded more like seeking and finding than calling out like a frightened boy lost in the forest. And although it was true that part of his anxiousness was motivated by this unabashed approach to romance, in all honesty he was very much attracted to her. Perhaps meant for her.

A flash of blue caught the corner of his eye. He jerked to his right.

Gone! His heart pounded. But it had been her, about fifty yards that way, between two huge trees.

Rachelle suddenly walked into the open, stopped, stared directly at him, and then disappeared without so much as a smile.

Tom stood rooted for a full five count. *Go after her, you idiot! Run!*

He ran. Around a tree. Crashing through the underbrush like a stampeding rhino.

Stop! You're making too much noise!

He pulled up behind a tree and looked around it. Nothing. He walked forward in the direction she'd gone. But there was nothing. She'd vanished?

"Psst."

Tom spun around. Rachelle leaned against a tree, arms crossed. A provocative smile crossed her lips. She winked. Then she slipped around the tree and was gone.

He ran after her. But again she'd vanished. This time he sprinted from tree to tree, looking, winded now.

When she did appear, it was like the last time, suddenly and casually, leaning against another tree behind him. She raised her eyebrow and grinned. Then again she was gone.

It struck Tom then that he hadn't been paying any mind to the rescuing part of this romance. Maybe that's why she was leading him on. He'd chosen her by running after her, but she was waiting for him to show his strength. The time for subtlety had passed.

The show Tanis and Palus had put on raced through his mind.

He yelled the first thing that came to mind. "Hark, what see I? It is a streak of black in the trees!" He ran in the direction Rachelle had vanished. "Come hither, my dear!" He desperately hoped that wasn't too forward. "Come so that I mightest protectest thou!"

Mightest protectest thou? Was that the way Tanis had put it?

"Oh, dear!"

Rachelle!

She jumped out from behind a tree to his left, eyes round, one hand raised to her lips. "Where?"

Where? He shoved a finger in the opposite direction. "There!"

She cried out and ran toward him. The breeze whipped her blue dress around the leggings she wore. She grabbed his shoulder and hid behind him.

Tom was so stunned by his sudden success that he lost track of the black bats for a moment. He stared at her face, now only inches from his own. The forest fell silent. He could smell her breath. Like lilacs.

Her eyes shifted to meet his. They held for a moment.

"Are you going to stare at me or take on the bats?" she asked.

"Oh, yeah."

Tom jumped out ambitiously and cocked his arms to take on the phantom enemy with a few spectacular chops and kicks.

"They are coming in hoards. Don't worry, I can take them all. Ha, ya!" He sprang into the air, kicked with his right foot, then twirled through a full three-sixty before striking out again.

He'd gone for it impulsively, pushed by an inordinate desire to show his strength and skill. But the fact that he'd actually twisted through a full revolution in the air stopped him cold. Where had he learned that?

Just now he'd learned that.

In his self-admiration he lost track of his movements and crashed to the forest floor with a mighty thump.

"Ugh!"

Tom clawed his way to his knees, breath knocked clean out of his lungs. Rachelle ran up and dipped to one knee.

"Are you okay?" Her hand touched his shoulder.

He gasped. "Yeah."

"Yes?"

"Sure."

She quickly pulled him to his feet. A smile slowly twisted her lips. "I can see that you've forgotten some of your . . . mighty moves," she said. She glanced around. "The next time it might look something like this."

She leaped in the direction of the invisible Shataiki. "Ha!" She kicked. Not a simple forward kick, but a perfectly executed roundhouse that dropped her back to earth in the ideal position for a second move.

She looked back, winked. "Tanis taught me."

Then she went after the enemy in a long series of spectacular moves that stopped Tom's breath for a second time. He counted one, two, three backflips in the mix. At least a dozen combination moves, most of them in the air.

And she did it all with the grace of a dancer, careful to accommodate her dress as she flew.

This chick was good. Very good.

She landed on her toes, facing Tom at twenty feet, all business.

"Ha!" she said and winked again.

"Ha. Wow."

"Wow."

He swallowed.

She quickly lowered her guard and assumed a more feminine stance. "Don't worry, we'll just pretend you did that. I won't tell a soul."

He cleared his throat. "Okay."

She studied him for a moment. Her eyes twinkled. The game wasn't over. Of course not. It was probably just starting.

Or so he was beginning to hope.

Choose, pursue, protect, woo. The words echoed in his mind.

"You are very . . . strong," he said. "I mean graceful."

She started to walk toward him. "I know what you mean. And I like both strong and graceful."

"Well, you're also very kind."

"Am I?"

"Yes, I think so."

He wanted to tell her that she was beautiful. That she was intriguing and full of life and compelling. But suddenly he found the words too much. It was all too much, too fast. For a man with all of his senses properly engaged, this might be the natural way to romance a woman, but for him, having lost his memory . . .

Rachelle stopped at arm's length. Searched his eyes.

"I think it was a wonderful game. You are a mysterious man. I like that. Maybe we can pick this up later. Good-bye, Thomas Hunter."

She turned and walked away.

Just like that? She couldn't just walk away, not now.

"Wait!" He ran up to her. "Where are you going?"

"To the village."

Her interest seemed to have evaporated. Maybe this choosing and wooing business was more involved than he'd thought.

"Can I walk with you?"

"Sure. Maybe I can help you remember a few things along the way. Your memory certainly needs some prodding."

Before he could respond to her obvious needling, a large white beast stepped out of the trees toward them. A tiger, pure white with green eyes. Tom stopped abruptly.

Rachelle looked at him, then at the tiger. "That, for example, is a white tiger."

"A tiger. I remember that."

"Good."

She walked to the animal, hugged it around the neck, and ruffled its ears. The tiger licked her cheek with a large tongue and she nuzzled its nose. Apparently all in the course of a day. Then she insisted that he come over and scratch the tiger's neck with her. It would be easier for him to remember if he engaged the world actively.

Tom wasn't sure how to read her comments. She said them all with a smile and with apparent sincerity, but he couldn't help thinking that she was edging him on or chiding him for his lackluster romancing.

Or she could be playing hard to get. Could that be part of the Great Romance?

On the other hand, she may have already decided he wasn't quite what she'd hoped for. Maybe the game was at its end. Could you un-choose, once having chosen?

They walked a few steps with tiger in tow. Rachelle plucked a yellow fruit from a small leafed tree.

"What is this?" she asked.

"I . . . I don't know."

"A lemon."

"A lemon, yes, of course, I remember that too."

"And if you put the juice of this lemon on a cut, what happens?"

"It heals?"

She curtsied. "Very good." They walked on and Rachelle picked a cherry-sized purple fruit from a low tree with wide branches. "And this one?"

"I don't think I know that one."

She circled him as she held up the fruit. "Try to remember. I'll give you a hint. Its flesh is sour. No one likes them much."

He grinned and shook his head. "No. Doesn't ring any bells."

"If you eat it" — she imitated a small bite with perfectly formed white teeth — "your mind reacts."

"No, no. Still nothing."

"Rhambutan," she said. "It puts you to

sleep. You don't even dream." She tossed it back to the tiger, but the beast ignored it.

They'd come to the edge of the forest. The village sat peacefully in the valley, glimmering with the brightly colored homes leading concentrically to the great Thrall.

Rachelle gazed down the hill and spoke without looking at him. "You are even more mysterious and wonderful than I imagined when I chose you."

"I am?"

"You are."

He should respond in kind, but the words weren't coming.

"You might want to work on your memory, of course," she said.

"Actually, my memory works well in some areas."

She faced him. "Is that so? What areas are those?"

"In my dreams. I'm having vivid dreams that I live in the histories. And all of that I remember. It's almost as real as this place."

She searched his eyes. "And do you remember how to romance in these dreams?"

"Romance? Well, I don't have a girl-friend or anything, if that's what you mean, no. But maybe I do know some things." Kara's advice on romance came back to

258

him. Now would be a good time to turn up the wooing quotient. "But nothing like this. Nothing so wonderful and beautiful as you. No one who captures my heart so completely with a single touch or a passing smile."

The corner of her mouth tugged into a faint smile. "My, you are remembering. You may dream all you like, my dear."

"Only if I can dream about you," he said.

She reached up and touched his cheek. "Good-bye, Thomas Hunter. I will see you soon."

He swallowed. "Good-bye."

Then she was walking down the hill.

Tom walked back from the crest so that he wouldn't be visible from the valley. The last thing he wanted at the moment was for Tanis or Palus to come flying up for a report.

He knew he wouldn't be dreaming of Rachelle, despite his sentiments to do so. He'd be dreaming of Bangkok, where he was expected to deliver some critical information on the Raison Strain.

He stopped by a large green tree and looked east. The black forest was about an hour's walk. The answers to a dozen questions could be there. Questions about what had happened to him in the black forest. Where he'd come from. Questions about the histories. The Raison Strain.

What if he were to go? Just one quick visit, to satisfy himself. The others might not even know he was missing. Michal might. But he couldn't continue on with these impossible dreams or without knowing exactly how he'd come to be in the black forest in the first place. One way or the other, he had to know precisely what had happened, was happening, to him. He might find those answers only in the black forest, just as Tanis might find his satisfaction only in an expedition there.

But not now.

He leaned against the green trunk and crossed his arms. His legs had a rubbery feel to them, like noodles. He hadn't realized that romancing required so much energy.

17

"Of course she likes me," Tom said. He'd slept half the night, but felt as though he was running on fumes here.

Kara looked at him across the wrought-iron table. "I think wishful thinking is rearing its beautiful head, dear brother. For all you know, winking means, 'Take a hike.'"

They were seated in the café adjacent to the atrium where Raison Pharmaceutical would make its grand announcement as soon as the entourage arrived. The main courtyard milled with dozens of reporters and local officials awaiting this momentous occasion. You'd think they were receiving the president. In Southeast Asia — any excuse for a ceremony. Tom was surprised they didn't have a ribbon to cut. Any excuse to cut a ribbon.

Tom scanned the crowd for the hundredth time, considering yet again his options. Getting to Monique de Raison shouldn't be a problem. Convincing her to order additional testing of the drug didn't seem unreasonable either. The real challenge would be the timing. Getting to Monique before the announcement if possible; convincing her to do more testing *before* shipping.

"I have a bad feeling about this," he said. He felt like a worn leather sole. His eyes hurt and his temples throbbed.

"You sure you're okay?" Kara asked. "I know you've been insisting you're peachy all morning, but you really do look horrible."

"I'm tired is all. Soon as we deal with this thing, I'll sleep for a week."

"Maybe not."

"Meaning what?"

"Meaning the dreams. They're real, remember? Maybe the reason you're not getting any rest is because you're *not*."

"Because when I'm asleep there, I'm awake here and vice versa."

"Think about it," Kara said. "You're tired in both places. You just fell asleep on the hill overlooking the valley while contemplating the Great Romance."

"No, I was contemplating returning to the black forest at the urging of my sister."

Tom heard a commotion by the front doors. A guest's baggage had toppled from a cart, and several bellhops were frantically throwing it back on.

"You're right that I'm just as tired there.

I keep falling asleep. It's one of the only things that's similar. Everything else is different. I wear different clothes; I talk differently —"

"How do you talk?"

"More like them. You know, eloquent and romantic. Like a hundred years ago."

She grinned. "Charming."

"You'd be surprised."

"Oh, brother."

Tom felt the first of a blush warm his face. "I know it sounds sappy, but things are just different there."

"Clearly. The point is, you can't keep going like this. You're exhausted, you're nervous, you're sweating, and you're chewing on your fingernail. You have to get some rest."

Tom pulled his finger from his mouth. "Of course I'm sweating. It's hot."

"Not in here it's not."

For the first time Tom seriously considered his physical condition. What if she was right and he wasn't getting any real sleep at all? He instinctively ran his fingers through his dark curls in an attempt to put them in order. It helped that his hairstyle was a tad avant-garde, or "messy," as Kara put it. He wore a pair of Lucky jeans, featherweight black boots, and a black T-shirt, tucked in at Kara's insistence given the occasion. The shirt had an inscription in white schizoid letters:

I've gone to find myself.
If I get back before I return,
please keep me here.

"Maybe I'm sleeping, but my mind's so active that I'm not getting good rest," he said.

The loitering crowd suddenly surged toward the atrium.

Tom jumped to his feet, knocking over his chair. "She's here!"

"Did I mention edgy?" Kara asked. "Calm and collected, Thomas. Calm and collected."

He righted the chair and then strode toward the entrance with Kara hurrying to keep pace.

"Slow down."

He didn't slow down.

The door opened and two husky men dressed in black stepped into the reception area. Thai *sak* tattoos marked their forearms. There were basically two varieties of tattoos in Thailand: *khawm* designs meant to invoke the power to love, and *sak* designs meant to invoke the power against death. These were the latter, worn by men in dangerous lines of work. Clearly security. Not that Tom cared — he wasn't planning on jumping the woman. Their eyes made quick work of the room.

Two red cords draped through golden posts formed a temporary path toward the atrium. The men blocked the space between the last post and the entrance, pushed the doors open, and swept their arms to guide their employer.

The strong, confident face of the woman who stepped into the lobby of the Sheraton Grande Sukhumvit commanded attention. She wore expensive-looking navy heels without nylons. Sculpted calves. Navy blue skirt and blazer with a white silk blouse. Gold necklace with a nondescript gold pendant that looked vaguely like a dolphin. Flashing blue eyes. Dark, shoulder-length hair.

Monique de Raison.

"My, my," Kara said.

Flashbulbs popped. Most of the guests waited in the atrium, where a podium had been set up amid a virtual jungle of exotic flowering plants. Monique gave the room one glance and then walked briskly toward the atrium.

Tom angled for the ropes. "Excuse me!" They hadn't heard him. And she was a fast walker.

Tom hurried to intercept them. "Excuse me, Monique de Raison."

"Tom! You're yelling!" Kara whispered.

Monique and her security goons were ignoring him. Behind the lead three, an entourage of Raison Pharmaceutical employees were filing into the lobby.

"Excuse me, are you deaf?" he demanded. Yelled.

This time the security men swiveled in his direction. Monique turned her head and drilled him with a stare. The sight of an American strutting for her clad in a black T-shirt and jeans clearly didn't impress. She diverted her stare and walked on as if she'd passed nothing more than a curious-looking dog on the street.

Tom felt his pulse surge. "I'm here with the Centers for Disease Control. I lost my bags and don't have the right clothes. I have to talk to you before you make your announcement." He didn't yell now, but his voice carried loudly enough.

Monique stopped. The security stepped to either side, glaring like two Dobermans begging to pounce. She faced Tom at ten feet. Her eyes glanced at the inscription on his chest. Maybe he should have worn the shirt inside out. Kara bumped into his side.

"This is my assistant, Kara Hunter. My name is Thomas." He stepped forward, and the guard to her right immediately moved forward as a precaution.

"I just need a minute," Tom said.

"I don't have a minute," Monique said. Her voice was soft and low and carried a slight French accent.

"I don't think you understand. There's a problem with the vaccine."

Tom knew before the last word left his mouth that it was the wrong thing to say. Any such suggestion or any endorsement of any such suggestion would be poison to the value of Raison Pharmaceutical stock.

Monique's brow lifted slightly. "Is that so?"

No turning back now. "Yes. Unless you want me to spill the beans here, in front of them all, I suggest you take a moment, just one teeny-weeny moment, and talk to me." His confidence surged. What could she say to that?

"Afterward," she said and turned on her heels.

He took a long step in her direction. "Hey!"

The security man closest put up a hand. Tom had half a notion to take him on right here, right now. The man was twice his size, but he'd picked up a few new skills as of late.

Kara grabbed his arm. "Afterward will work."

The entourage came abreast with curious stares. Tom wondered if anyone would recognize him from the incident at the gates yesterday. Undoubtedly the whole thing had been caught by security cameras.

"Okay, afterward. Try to keep your head low. Someone might recognize us."

"My point exactly. We talked about this, remember? No scene. I didn't come to Bangkok to get thrown in jail."

The announcement was surprisingly short and to the point. Monique delivered it with all the poise of an experienced politician. Raison Pharmaceutical had completed the development of a new airborne super-vaccine engineered to vaccinate against nine primary viruses, including SARS and HIV. This was followed by a laundry list of details for the world health community. Not once did she look in Tom's direction.

She waited till the end to drop the bomb.

Although the company was waiting for FDA approval in the United States, the governments of seven countries in Africa and three in Asia had placed orders for the vaccine, and the World Health Organization had given its blessing after receiving assurances that the vaccine would not spontaneously spread beyond a specified geographical region, due to engineered limitations that shortened the vaccine's life. The first order would be delivered to South Africa within twenty-four hours.

"Now, I'll be happy to answer a few questions."

The mind works in strange ways. Tom's had worked in the strangest of ways over the last few days. In and out of realities, crossing the seas, waking and sleeping in starts and fits. But with Monique de Raison's final statement, everything came into simple focus.

There was a Raison Vaccine. It would mutate into a virus that would make SARS look like a case of the hiccups. It was now being shipped to South Africa. He, Thomas Hunter from Denver, Colorado, and Kara Hunter from the same were the only people on the face of the earth who knew this.

It had all seemed somewhat dreamlike until this moment. Now it was tangible. Now he was staring at Monique de Raison and hearing her tell the world that boxes of the drug that would kill millions was boxed and ready for shipment. Maybe shipped already. Maybe it was in the back of some transport plane now, being baked by the hot sun. Mutating.

The sum of his predicament shoved him out of his chair.

"Thomas."

"Did you hear that?"

"Sit."

She pulled at his arm. He sat. The reporters were asking her questions. Bulbs kept flashing.

"We have to stop that shipment."

"She said she'd talk to us *afterward,*" Kara insisted between clenched teeth. "A few more minutes."

"What if she won't listen?" Tom asked.

"Then we try the authorities again. Right?"

He'd considered the possibility that Monique was a brick upstairs and would scoff, but, listening to her, she seemed far too intelligent. He really hadn't considered anything other than her willingness to co-operate. That's the way it went in dreams. Ultimately, it all really does work out. Or you wake up.

Suddenly he wasn't sure of either.

"Right, Thomas?"

"Right."

"What does that mean?" she asked.

"It means *right.*"

"I don't like the way you said —"

A smattering of applause rippled through the courtyard. Tom stood. Monique was finished. Music swelled. This was it.

"Let's go." He headed to the front, eyes fixed on Monique, who was straightening papers at the podium. A rope lined with three security men now separated the platform from the dispersing audience. Several reporters were summarily turned away when they approached the platform.

Monique caught his eye, looked away as

if she hadn't noticed, and headed stage right.

"Monique de Raison!" Tom called. "A moment, if you don't mind."

Heads turned and the hubbub eased.

Here they went again. Tom walked straight for her. A guard moved to intercept.

"It's okay, Lawrence. I'll speak to them," she said quietly.

Tom stared the man off. They were wearing guns, this one on his waist. Tom stepped onto the stage, helped Kara up, and crossed to where Monique had stopped. He had no doubt that if he hadn't made a scene she would be in the limousine already. As his *sensei* was fond of saying, there was no better way to disarm an opponent than with an element of surprise. Not necessarily through timing as most assumed, but as often through method. Shock and awe.

Despite the fact that Monique looked neither shocked nor awed, he knew he'd gotten under her skin at least. More important, he was talking to her.

"Thank you for your time," Tom said. The time for shock and awe was now passed. Diplomacy. "It is most kind of you to —"

"I'm already late for an interview with the *TIME* magazine bureau chief. Make

271

your point, Mr. . . ."

"Hunter. You don't have to be rude."

She sighed. "You're right. I'm sorry, but it's been a very busy week. When a man walks up to me and lies to my face, my patience is the first to go."

"A simple test will easily demonstrate whether or not I'm lying."

"So then you are with the CDC?"

"Oh. That lie." He lifted a hand to his shoulder as if taking an oath. "You got me. I had to get your attention somehow. This is Kara, my sister."

"Hi, Kara." They shook hands. But she hadn't shaken his hand.

"I really do have to go," Monique said. "Please, to the point."

"Okay, to the point. You can't ship the vaccine. It mutates under intense heat and becomes a deadly virus that kills billions of people."

She stared at him, unmoved. "Oh. Is that all?"

"I can explain exactly how I know this, but you wanted the bottom line, so there it is. Have you submitted the vaccine to intense heat, Miss de Raison?"

"One of the things they teach in freshman biology is that intense heat kills things. The Raison Vaccine is no exception. Our vaccine begins to spoil at 35 degrees centigrade. One of our greatest challenges was keeping it stable for warmer regional climates. This is the most ludicrous thing I've ever heard."

Heat flared up Tom's back. "Then you haven't tested it at high heat?"

"Show a little respect, Monique," Kara bit off. "We didn't fly over the Pacific to be dismissed like beggars. The fact is, Thomas has a point here, and you'd be a fool not to listen."

Monique forced a smile. "I would love to. I really would. I have to go." She started to turn.

Something went off in Tom's head like a gong. She was dismissing them. "Wait."

She didn't wait, not a beat.

Tom eased back toward the guard called Lawrence and spoke quietly, in as menacing a tone as he could muster without raising the alarm.

"If you don't stop at this very moment, we'll go to the papers. My father-in-law owns the *Chicago Tribune*. They'll have to scrape your stock prices off the floor with razor blades."

A ridiculous claim. Monique didn't honor it with a single misstep. She was beyond the pale.

It occurred to Tom that what his mind was telling him to do now couldn't be justified in any sense of the word. Except in his world. The world in which a virus

called the Raison Strain was about to forever alter human history.

The two guards Tom had first encountered were making their way to assist
Monique's exit, but Lawrence still had his
back turned. Monique wasn't his primary
responsibility.

Tom was at the guard's back with a
single side step. In one quick move, he
slipped his hand under the man's jacket,
grabbed the gun, and whipped it out. He
bounced to his right, away from the man's
grabbing hands. The man hesitated, mouth
agape, probably appalled that he'd so easily
lost his weapon.

Tom ran forward on the balls of his feet,
reached Monique before an alarm could be
raised.

Shoved the gun in her back.

"I'm sorry, but you have to listen to
me."

She went rigid. Both guards saw the gun
at the same time. They crouched, weapons
immediately drawn. Shouts now, dozens of
them.

"Thomas!"

Including Kara's.

Tom had his left arm around Monique's
waist, pulling her close so that his chin was
over her left shoulder, breathing hard in
her ear. He kept the gun in her back and
stepped sideways, toward an exit sign.

"One move and she dies!" he cried. "You hear me? I'm not having a good day today! I'm very, very upset, and I don't want anyone to do anything stupid."

People were running for the door. Screaming. What were they screaming for? He wasn't pointing the gun at their backs.

"Please," Monique gasped. "Please get ahold of yourself."

"Don't worry," Tom whispered. "I won't kill you." The fire door was only ten feet away now. He stopped and glared at the two guards who had their pistols trained on him.

"Put the guns down, you idiots!" he yelled.

Monique flinched. He was yelling in her ear.

"Sorry."

The guards slowly lowered their guns to the floor.

"And you," he shouted in Kara's direction. "I want you as a hostage too. Get over here or I kill the girl!"

Kara looked frozen by shock.

"Move it!"

She hurried over.

"Get the door."

She complied and stepped into the hall beyond.

Tom pulled Monique through the door.

"Anyone follows us, any police or any authorities, and she's dead!"

He slammed the door closed with his foot.

18

The Paradise Hotel was a flea-infested joint frequented by street traders. Or the odd sucker who responded to the promise of exotic, all-inclusive Internet vacation specials. Or in this case, the kidnapper trying desperately to get his point across to a very stubborn French woman.

Monique had guided them under duress. Kara had appropriately and repeatedly expressed her horror over what Tom had done. Tom had insisted this was the only way. If the rich French snob refused to care about a few billion lives, then they had no choice but to persuade her to care. This was what persuasion looked like in the real world.

The old, rusted elevator doors in the underground parking garage screeched open. Kara walked to the rental car at a fast clip, newly acquired room keys in hand.

"Okay," Tom said, waving the 9-millimeter at Monique for show. "We go up, and we go quiet. I meant it when I said I would never kill you, but I might put a bullet in your pinkie toe if you get snobby. We clear? The gun will be in my belt, but that doesn't mean you can start hollering."

Monique glared at him, jaw muscles flexed.

"I'll take your silence as a chorus of agreement. Let's go."

He shoved the door open and waved her out.

"Top floor?" he asked Kara.

"Top floor. I don't know if I can do this, Tom."

"You're not doing this. I am. I'm the one having the dreams. I'm the one who knows what he shouldn't know. I'm the one who has no choice but to talk some sense into this spoiled brat."

"You don't have to yell."

A car nosed into the lot.

"Sorry. Okay, into the elevator." He pressed the button for the fifth floor and breathed some relief when the doors slid shut.

"What is it with you French, anyway? Is it always business before saving the world?"

"This from the man with the gun in my back?" Monique asked. "Besides, as you can see, I don't live in France. Their politics are disagreeable to my father and me."

"They are?" She didn't respond. Tom wasn't sure why he found the revelation surprising. Her perfume filled the small car quickly. A musky, flowery scent.

"If you cooperate, you'll be out of here in half an hour."

She didn't respond to that either.

No surprise, the rooms weren't as palatial as unsuspecting travelers might have been led to believe. Orange carpet turned brown. Flowered bedcovers on two double beds. A wicker dresser, crusted with enough dirt to wear out a power washer. The television worked, but only in green and without sound.

Tom directed Monique to take the room's only chair, a flimsy wood job, into the far corner and sit still. He put the gun on the dresser beside him and turned to his sister.

"Okay. I need you to sneak out of this dump, find the police, and demand to talk to Jacques de Raison. Tell the police that you escaped. Tell them I'm a wacko or something. I need you clear of this, you understand?"

"Smartest thing I've heard all morning." She looked at Monique. "What do I tell her father?"

"You tell him what we know. And if he doesn't agree to stop or recall the shipment, you tell him that I said I'm going to start shooting."

Tom faced Monique. "Only pinkies, of course. I don't like making threats, but you understand the situation."

"Yes. I understand perfectly. You've gone completely mad."

He nodded. "You see, that's why we need this backup plan, Kara. If she doesn't come around, maybe her father will. More important, it gets you off the hook. Make sure it's clear that I'm threatening his daughter, not you."

"And where do I tell them you are?"

"Tell them you jumped out of the car. You don't have a clue where we are."

"That's a lie."

"There's a lot at stake. Lies will be forgiven at this point."

"I hope you know what you're doing. How will I know what's going on?"

"Through Jacques. I'm sure he'll take a call from his daughter in the event we need to make contact. If you need to reach me, call, but make sure it's safe."

She walked over to the bedstand, lifted the phone receiver to her ear, and set it down, evidently satisfied that it had a dial tone. She'd lived in Southeast Asia too long to trust any such thing to chance.

Kara stepped forward and gave Tom a hug. "This is nuts."

"I love you, sis."

"Love you, too, brother." She pulled back, gave Monique a last look, and headed for the door.

"Good luck wooing that one," she said and closed the door softly behind her.

"Yes, good luck wooing this one," Monique said. "The unabashed American male flexing his muscles. Is that what this is?"

Tom picked up the gun, leaned on the dresser, and looked at his hostage. There was only one way to do this. He had to tell her everything. At least now she had to listen.

"Farthest thing from my mind, trust me. The fact of the matter is, I really did cross the ocean to talk to you, and I really am risking my neck to do so. Why would I risk so much to talk to a rude French woman, you ask? Because unless I'm sadly mistaken, you may be the only person alive who can work with me to stop a terrible thing from happening. Contrary to the overall impression I may have given you, I really am a very decent guy. And under all your fierce determination, I think you're probably a very decent girl. I just want to talk, and I just want you to listen. I'm very tired and I'm at my wit's end, so I hope you don't make this more difficult than it has to be. Is that too much to ask?"

"No. But if you expect me to burn the thousands of stockholders who've stuck out their necks for this company, you'll be disappointed. I won't spread a malicious rumor just because you say you'll shoot my pinkie toes off if I don't. If I were to guess, you've been hired by one of our competitors. This is some ridiculous plot to hurt Raison Pharmaceutical. What on earth would convince you that this makes any sense?"

Tom stood, walked to the window, peered out. The street bustled with thousands of Thailand's finest, oblivious to the drama unfolding five stories above their heads.

"A dream," he said. He faced her. "A dream that is real."

Carlos Missirian waited patiently in the Mercedes across the street from the Paradise Hotel. In a few hours it would be dark. He would make his move then.

A satay vendor wheeled his cart past the car. Carlos pressed a button on the door and watched the tinted window slide down. Hot air rolled into the cool car. He held out two five-baht coins. The vendor hurried over with a small tray of meat sticks, took the coins, and handed him the satays. Carlos rolled the window up and pulled a small slice of warm, spicy meat from the stick using his teeth. The taste was inspiring.

His father had often told him that good plans are useless without proper execution.

And proper execution depended on good timing more than any other factor. How many terrorists' plots had failed miserably because of bad timing? Most.

He'd been caught off guard by the appearance of the American at the press conference. Thomas Hunter, a desperate-looking maniac who had watched the proceedings from a seat two rows in front of his own. It had been his own intention to approach the Raison woman after the conference and suggest an interview using false credentials he'd scavenged from an Associated Press contact. Failing that, he would have taken more direct measures, but he'd long ago learned that the best plan is usually the most obvious one.

He'd taken several steps toward the podium when the American had barged up front and pulled off his incredible stunt. What more obvious way to deal with an adversary than to march up, steal a weapon, and kidnap her in broad daylight in front of half the world's press corps? Surprisingly, the plot had worked. Even more surprisingly, they had gotten away. If Carlos hadn't habitually positioned his own car for a quick exit, they might have escaped him as well.

The fact that the American had gone to such lengths carried its own meaning. It meant that the CDC hadn't paid him any attention. This was good. It meant that the American had a very, very high level of confidence in this so-called dream of his. This was also good. It meant that the American intended to force Raison Pharmaceutical into pulling the drug. This wasn't so good.

But that would soon change.

He'd followed the green Toyota here, to the Paradise Hotel. The news was turning the kidnapping into a major story. Word had already reached the American wires. The police scanners in Bangkok were busy coordinating a frenzied search, but no one had a clue where the crazed American had vanished to.

Except Carlos, of course.

He placed the satays between his teeth and slid another piece off the stick. The American was doing his job for him. He had nicely isolated Monique de Raison in a hotel room. Thomas's blonde cohort had left on foot an hour ago. This bothered Carlos some, but the other two were still inside. He was sure of it. From his position he had a full view of every exit except an emergency exit in the alley, which he'd found and subsequently disabled.

The situation had fallen perfectly into his hands. How convenient that he could deal with them both at the same time. It was now simply a matter of timing.

Carlos looked in the rearview mirror, brushed a speck of dirt from the scar on his cheek, and leaned back with a long, satisfied breath.

Timing.

Monique watched Thomas pace and wondered if there was any way, however unlikely, that the tale he'd spun over the past two hours was anything more than absolute nonsense. There always was that possibility, of course. She'd given herself to the pursuit of impossible new drugs precisely because she didn't believe in impossibilities unless they were proved mathematically. Technically speaking, his story could be true.

But then, technically speaking, his story was hogwash, as the Americans liked to say.

For the past five minutes he'd been silent, pacing with the gun dangling from his fingers. She wondered if he'd ever used a gun before. At first she had assumed so, judging by the way he handled it. But now, after listening to him, she wondered.

The air-conditioning unit rattled noisily but produced nothing more than hot air. They were both drenched in sweat. She had removed her jacket over an hour ago.

If she weren't so furious with the man for all this nonsense, she might pity him.

Honestly, she pitied him anyway. He was completely sincere, which meant he had to be wrong in the head. Maybe insane. Which meant that, although he gave no signal that he was capable of shooting her toes off, he might very well be the kind who suddenly snapped and decapitated his victim or some other such terrible thing.

She had to find a way to break through to whatever reason he might have.

Monique took a deep breath of the stuffy air. "Thomas, can we talk on my level for a moment?"

"What do you think I've been trying to do for the past two hours?"

"You've been talking on your level. It may all make perfect sense to you, but not to me. We're not accomplishing a thing, hidden away in this suffocating room. The vaccine is most likely in flight by now, and within forty-eight hours it will be in the hands of a hundred hospitals around the world. If you're right, we're only wasting time by sitting here."

"You're saying that you'll recall the shipments?"

She had considered lying to him a hundred times, but her indignation prevented her from doing so. He wouldn't believe her anyway.

"Would you believe me if I said yes?" she asked.

"I'd believe you if we made the call together. A call to the *New York Times* from Monique de Raison would go a long way."

She sighed. "You know I can't do that." They were getting nowhere. She had to earn his trust. Negotiate a settlement to this standoff.

"But if I truly did believe you, I would. You do understand my predicament, don't you?"

He didn't answer, which was answer enough. She pressed forward.

"You know, I grew up on a vineyard in the south of France. Much cooler than here, I'm glad to say." She smiled. For his sake. "We came from a poor family, my mother and I. She was a servant in our vineyards. Did you know that my family used to make wine, not drugs?"

He just stared at her.

She continued. "I never knew my biological father; he left when I was only three. Jacques was one of the Raison sons. He fell in love with my mother when I was ten. My mother died when I was twelve. That was fourteen years ago. We've come a long way since then, Father and I. Did you know that I studied at UCLA Medical School?"

"Why are you telling me all of this?"

"I'm making conversation."

"We don't have time for conversation,"

Tom said. "Haven't you been listening to me?"

She answered as calmly as possible. "Yes. I have. But you haven't been speaking on my level. Remember? I'm telling you who I am so that you can address me as a real, living person, a woman who is confused and a bit frightened by all your antics."

"I don't know how I can be clearer. Either you believe me, or you don't. You don't. So we have a problem." He held up his hand. "Don't get me wrong, I would love to sit and chat about how our fathers abandoned us. But not now, please. We have more pressing matters on our hands."

"Your father left you?"

He lowered his hand. "Yes."

"How sad." She was making progress. Not a lot, but some. "How old were you?"

"Sixteen. We lived in the Philippines. I grew up there. He was a chaplain."

The revelation cast Thomas in a completely new light. An army brat. Son of a chaplain, no less. Based in the Philippines. She spoke some Tagalog herself.

"Saan ka nakatira?" *Where did you live?*

"Nakatira ako sa Maynila." *I lived in Manila.*

They stared at each other for a long second. His face softened.

"This isn't going to work," he said.

She sat up. He was folding so quickly? "What do you mean?" she asked.

"I mean this psychobabble approach of yours. It isn't going to work."

"This . . ." He was forcing *her* to fold? "How dare you reduce my childhood to psychobabble! You want to talk to me? Then talk to me like a human, not some bargaining chip!"

"Of course. You're a frightened woman, trembling under the hand of her fearsome captor, right? You're the poor abandoned child in desperate need of a hero. If anything, *I'm* the poor abandoned loser who's worked his way into a pretty hopeless predicament. Look at me!" He shoved both arms out. "I'm a basket case. I have the gun, but it might as well be you. You know I wouldn't touch you, so what threat am I? None. This is crazy!"

"Well, you said it, not me. You talk about black bats and colored forests and ancient histories like you actually believe all that nonsense. I have a Ph.D. in chemistry. You really think some crazy dream would have me trembling on my knees?"

"Yes!" he shouted. "That's exactly what I expect! Those black bats know your name!"

Hearing him say it like that sent a chill through her gut. He glared at her, slapped the gun on the dresser, and yanked his shirt off over his head.

"It's hot in here!" He threw the shirt on the floor, snatched up the gun, and marched for the window.

His back was strong. Stronger than she would have guessed. It glistened with sweat. A long scar ran over his left shoulder blade. He wore plaid blue boxer shorts under his jeans — the tag on the elastic waistband read Old Navy.

Monique had considered rushing him before he'd told her that he was the blurred image in the security footage at the front gates yesterday. Looking at him now, even with his back turned, she was glad she'd rejected the idea.

Tom suddenly dropped the curtain and turned. "Tell me about the vaccine."

"I have."

He was suddenly very excited. "No, more. Tell me more."

"It wouldn't make any sense to you, unless you understand vaccines."

"Humor me."

She sighed. "Okay. We call it a DNA vaccine, but in reality it's actually an engineered virus. That's why —"

"Your vaccine is a virus?" he demanded.

"Technically, yes. A virus that immunizes the host by altering its DNA against certain other viruses. Think of a virus like a tiny robot that hijacks its host cell and modifies its DNA, usually in a way that ends with the rupturing of that cell. We've learned how to turn these germs into agents that work for us instead of against us. They are very small, very hardy, and can spread very quickly — in this case, through the air."

"But it's an actual virus."

He was reacting as so many reacted to this simple revelation. The idea that a virus could be used to humanity's benefit was a strange concept to most.

"Yes. But also a vaccine, though unlike traditional vaccines, which are usually based on weaker strains of an actual disease organism. At any rate, they are hardy enough, but they do die under adverse conditions. Like heat."

"But they can mutate."

"Any virus can mutate. But none of the mutations in our tests have survived beyond a generation or two. They immediately die. And that's in favorable conditions. Under intense heat —"

"Forget about the heat. Tell me something that no one could possibly know about —" He lifted his hand. "No, wait. Don't tell me." He paced to the bed and back. Faced her. The gun had become an extension of his arm; he waved it around like a conductor's baton.

"Would you mind watching where you

point that thing?" she said.

He looked at the gun then tossed it on the bed. Lifted his hands.

"New strategy," he said. "If I can prove to you that everything I've told you is true, that your vaccine really will mutate into something fatal, will you call it off?"

"How would you —"

"Just go with me. Would you call it off and destroy the vaccine?"

"Of course."

"You swear it?"

"There's no way to prove it."

"But *if? If,* Monique."

"Yes!" He was unnerving her. "I said I would. Unlike some people, I don't lie out of habit."

He ignored the jab, and she regretted her insinuation.

A smile twisted his mouth. "Okay. Here's what we're going to do. I'm going to go to sleep and get some information that I couldn't possibly know, and then I'm going to wake up and give it to you."

His eyes were bright, but the brilliance of his plan escaped her. "That's absurd."

"That's the point. You think it's absurd because you don't believe me. Which is why when I wake up and tell you something I can't know, you'll believe me! I can't believe I didn't think of this before."

He really believed that he could enter

this dream world of his, discover real information from the histories, and return to tell her about it. He really was mad.

On the other hand, if he was sleeping, she could . . .

"Okay. Fair enough. Go to sleep then."

"See? It makes sense, doesn't it? What kind of information should I look for?"

"What?"

"What could I bring back that would persuade you?"

She thought about it. Preposterous. "The number of nucleotide base pairs that deal specifically with HIV in my vaccine," she said.

"The number of nucleotide base pairs. Okay. Give me something else, in case I can't get that. The histories may not have recorded something that specific."

She couldn't hold back some amusement at his enthusiasm. It was like negotiating with one of the children right out of Narnia. "My father's birth date. They would have the year of his birth, right? Do you know what it is?"

"No, I don't. And I can come back with more than just his birth date if you want." He picked up the gun and walked to the window yet again.

"What do you keep looking at?"

"There's a white car that's been parked down the street for the last few hours. Just checking. It's getting dark."

He spun back. "Okay. How do we do this? I'll sleep on the bed."

"How long will this take?"

"Half an hour. You wake me up half an hour after I fall asleep. That's all I need. There's no correlation between time here and time there."

He walked to the bed and sat down, pulled off the cover, and ripped the sheet off.

"What are you doing?"

He tore the sheet in two. "I can't just let you wander around while I'm sleeping. I'm sorry, but I'm going to have to tie you up."

She stood up. "Don't you dare!"

"What do you mean, don't you dare? I'm the one with the gun here, and you're my prisoner, in case you forgot. I tie you up, and if you yell for help, I wake up and shoot off your pinkie toes."

He was impossible. "You're going to leave me sitting here while you fall asleep? How do I wake you up if I'm tied up?"

He grabbed one of the pillows and tossed it over by the air conditioner. "You throw this pillow at me. Move over to the air conditioner."

"You're going to tie me to the air conditioner?"

"Looks pretty solid to me. The anchor rod will hold you. You have a better idea?"

"And how will I throw the pillow if my hands are tied?"

He thought about that. "Good point. Okay, I'll tie you so that you can reach the bed with your foot. You kick the bed until I wake up. You don't yell."

She stared at him. Then the air conditioner.

"Didn't think so. Hurry up. The sooner I fall asleep, the sooner we can get this over with." He waved the gun. "Move."

It took him five minutes to rip up the sheet halves and form a short tether. He made her lie down on her back to measure the distance to the bed. Satisfied that she could reach it, he bound her hands behind her back. Not just her hands, but her fingers, so that she couldn't move them to untie anything. And her feet, so she couldn't stand.

He worked over her quickly, unconcerned that his sweaty torso was smudging her silk blouse. The whole thing was desperately absurd. But he clearly didn't think so. He was scurrying around like a rat on a mission.

When he'd finished, he stood back, admired his handiwork, carried the gun to the bed, and plopped down on his back, spread-eagle.

He closed his eyes.

"I can't believe this stupidity," she mumbled.

"Quiet. I'm trying to sleep here. Do I need to gag you?" He sat up, pulled off his boots.

Her teeth! She might be able to tear the cloth cords with her teeth.

"Do you really think you'll be able to fall asleep like this? I mean, I will be quiet, I promise, but isn't this just a bit ridiculous?"

"I think you've made yourself clear on that point. And actually I don't know if I can fall asleep or not. But I'm about ready to drop from exhaustion as it is, so I think there's a pretty good chance."

He plopped back down and closed his eyes.

"Maybe I could sing you a lullaby," Monique heard herself say. It was a surprising thing to say at a moment like this.

He turned his head and looked at her, sitting against the wall under the air conditioner. "Do you sing?"

She turned away and stared at the wall.

Five minutes passed before she braved a glance his way. He lay exactly as she'd last seen, bare chest rising and falling steadily, arms to either side. Very well built. Dark hair. A beautiful creature.

Totally mad.

Was he asleep? "Thomas?" she whispered.

He sat up, rolled out of bed, and picked

up a fragment of sheet.

"What is it?" she asked.

"I'm sorry, but I have to gag you."

"I wasn't talking!"

"No, but you might try to bite your way out. I'm sorry, I really am. I can't sleep unless I'm totally at ease, you understand, and I think a strong jaw might be able to tear this stuff." He wrapped the strip around her mouth and tied it behind her head. She didn't bother protesting.

"Not that I think you have a strong jaw. I didn't mean it like that. I actually like the sound of your voice."

He stood, crossed to the bed, and dropped onto his back once again.

19

Tom awoke with a start and jumped to his feet on the hill overlooking the village. He scrambled to the lip of the valley. Dusk. The people were already heading up the valley to the lake. The Gathering.

Two thoughts. One, he should join them. If he ran, he could catch them. Two, he had to get to the black forest. Now.

He'd dreamed how many times since waking in the black forest? Yet something had changed. For the first time, he'd awakened with a compulsion to treat this dream of Bangkok, this lucid fabrication in his mind, as real. It was no longer only a conscious choice that he was making, it was something in his heart. He really *did* have to treat the dreams as real. Both of them, in the event either or both *were* real.

If Bangkok was real, then he needed Monique's cooperation. The only way to get Monique's cooperation was to prove himself by retrieving information. Information he hoped he could find in the black forest.

Tom spun around and sprinted down the path that led to the Shataiki.

He had to learn the truth. The Great Deception, the Raison Strain, Monique de Raison — he had to know why he was having these dreams. He'd survived the black forest once; he would survive it again.

His feet slapped the earth as he jogged. The path soon faded, but he knew the direction. The river. It lay directly ahead. The slight glow from the trees lit the forest — even in the dead of night he would be able to find his way back.

He slowed to a walk and caught his breath. Then he fell back into a jog. This time he wouldn't actually enter the forest. He would call out. And if the black bats didn't respond? Then he would see. Either way, he couldn't return without some answers.

What had Monique suggested he learn? The number of nucleotide base pairs in the HIV vaccine.

The journey must have lasted an hour, but there was no way for Tom to know. When he finally broke into the clearing he recognized as the place he'd first been healed, he pulled up, panting hard. Just past the meadow lay a short stretch of forest, which ended at the river's edge. He stepped out into the meadow and jogged forward. A snapshot of the hotel room in Bangkok flashed through his mind and he plodded on, across the meadow and through the forest toward the rushing river.

The trees gave way to riverbank without warning. One second forest, the next only grass. And the river.

The scene took his breath away. He leaped back into the safety of the trees and flattened himself against a massive red tree. He waited for a moment and then carefully peered out onto the bank of the green river. The bridge the Roush had called the Crossing glimmered fifty yards upriver, white in the rising moonlight. The river glowed, translucent and sparkling with the colored light cast by the trees. Beyond the river lay the outline of ragged black trees in the darkness.

Tom stared into the black forest and began to shiver. There was no way he could enter that blackness again. He imagined red beady eyes lying in wait just beyond the black barrier. Or above. He slowly raised his eyes to the treetops across the river, but there was only darkness. He listened to the sound of the night, trying to filter out the river.

Was that a snicker?

Then he saw a lone dark shadow flee from the upper branches. He quickly pulled back into the colored forest's cover, his heart pounding in his ears. A Shataiki! But it had fled. Maybe it hadn't seen him.

He shut his eyes and took a deep breath. He should leave this place. He should turn and run.

But he didn't. Couldn't.

He stood by the red tree for ten minutes, slowly gathering his courage. The river bubbled on, undisturbed. The forest stood black, unmoving beyond. Nothing changed. Slowly his fear gave way to resolve again.

Tom stepped from the forest and stood on the bank, washed in moonlight. No bats. Just the bridge to his left, the river, and the dead trees beyond. He took a few more steps, angling for the bridge. Still nothing changed. The river still rushed on, the trees behind him still glowed in oblivion, and the blackness ahead remained pitch dark.

Tom took a deep breath and walked quickly toward the bridge. He gripped the rail of the white structure, and for the first time it dawned on him that the wood of the bridge, unlike any wood he had seen outside the black forest, did not glow. It had been constructed by the Shataiki, then? He paused and looked again at the black trees looming taller now. He should call out from here. What he should yell, he didn't know. Hello? Or maybe . . .

A speck of red suddenly flickered in the

corner of his right eye. Tom jerked his head toward the light. He saw them clearly now, the dancing red eyes just beyond the tree line across the river. He tightened his grip on the rail and caught his breath.

Another flicker of red off to his left made him turn his head, and he saw a dozen Shataiki step out of the forest and stop, facing the river. And then, as Tom watched with terror, a thousand sets of red gleaming eyes materialized, emerging from their hiding places.

Tom told himself to turn and run, but his feet felt rooted to the earth. He watched with dread as the Shataiki poured silently out of the forest, creating a line as far as he could see in either direction. The creatures squatted like sentinels along the tree line, gazing at him with blank red eyes set like jewels on either side of their long black snouts. And then the treetops began filling as well, as if a hundred thousand Shataiki had been called to witness a great spectacle, and the black trees were their bleachers.

Tom's legs began to shake. The pungent smell of sulfur filled his nostrils, and he checked his breathing. This whole thing was a terrible mistake. He had to get back to the colored forest.

The wall of Shataiki directly ahead of him suddenly parted. Tom watched as a single Shataiki walked toward the bridge, dragging brilliant blue wings on the barren earth behind him. This one stood taller than a man, much larger than the rest. Its torso was gold and pulsed with tinges of red. Stunning. Beautiful. The night air filled with the clucks and clicks of a hundred thousand bats as the huge Shataiki slogged toward the crossing. It moved slowly. Very slowly, favoring its right leg.

Tom watched without moving. The beast's green eyes were set deep into its triangular face, fixed on Tom. Pupil-less, glowing saucers of green. Frightening and yet oddly comforting. Luring. Tom could hear the scraping of its talons along aged planks, the whisper of its huge wings, as it slowly ascended the bridge. The Shataiki made its way to the center and stopped.

He raised one wing slightly and the throngs behind him fell silent.

Somewhere in the back of Tom's paralyzed mind, a voice began to reassure him that this Shataiki could certainly mean no harm. No creature so beautiful could harm him. He had come to talk. Why else would he have come out to the center of the bridge? According to the Roush, no Shataiki could cross the bridge.

"Come." The Shataiki sang as much as spoke. Hardly more than a whisper.

The leader was telling him to come. And

why should he give that suggestion any mind? He could speak from here just as easily as from up there.

"Come," the leader repeated.

This time, the Shataiki opened his mouth. Tom saw its pink tongue. As long as he stayed on this side of the bridge and out of the creature's reach, he would be safe. Right?

Tom stepped cautiously onto the bridge. The Shataiki made no move, so Tom stepped up the Crossing toward the beast. He stopped five meters from the Shataiki and looked directly into his eyes. They glistened like giant emeralds in the moonlight. A chill ran down Tom's spine. He had to be the one called Teeleh. But he wasn't what Tom had expected.

The creature let his shoulders droop and turned his head slightly. He retracted his talons and allowed a gentle smile to form on his snout.

"Welcome, my friend. I had hoped you would come." Now he spoke plainly, in a low voice without a hint of music. "I know this may all seem a little overpowering to you. But please, ignore them. They are imbeciles who have no mind."

"Who?" Tom said. But it came out like a grunt so he said it again. "Who?"

"The sick, demented creatures behind me." The beautiful bat withdrew a red fruit from behind his back and offered it to Tom. "Here, my friend, have a fruit."

Tom looked at the fruit, too terrified to move any closer to the beast, much less reach out to take something from it.

"But of course. You are still frightened, aren't you? Pity. It is one of our best." The Shataiki raised the fruit to his lips without removing his eyes from Tom and bit deeply into its flesh. A stream of juice dribbled through his furry chin and spotted the planks at his feet. "Possibly our very best. Certainly the most powerful." He smacked his lips. He lifted his chin to swallow the fruit and tucked the uneaten portion behind his back again.

He withdrew a small pouch. "Are you thirsty?"

"No, thanks."

"Not thirsty. I understand. We'll have plenty of time for eating and drinking later, won't we?"

Tom began to relax a little. "I didn't come to eat or drink." Was it possible Teeleh could be a friend to him? The creature certainly disapproved of the other black bats. "How did you know I was coming?"

"I have powers you can't imagine, my friend. To know you were coming was nothing. I have legions at my disposal. Do you think I don't know who comes and who goes? I think you underestimate me."

"If you have such power, then why do you live in the black trees instead of in the colored forest?" Tom asked, looking past the beast at the throngs milling in the trees across the river.

"The colored forest, you call it? And who in their right mind would want to live in the colored forest? You think their fruit can compare with my fruit? No. Is their water any sweeter than ours? Less. They are nothing but slaves."

Tom shifted on his feet. There was only one rule here. No matter what happened, he could never drink the water. As long as he followed that simple standard, he would be perfectly safe.

"What is that in your pocket?" the bat suddenly demanded.

Tom reached into his pocket and withdrew the small glowing carving that Johan had handed him in the village.

Teeleh recoiled. "Throw it over the side. Throw it over!"

Tom reacted without thought. He tossed the red lion over the edge of the bridge and gripped the rail to steady himself.

Slowly Teeleh lowered his arm and stared at Tom with his wide, green eyes.

"It is poison to us," the beast said.

"I didn't know."

"Of course not. They have deceived you."

Tom let the statement go. "What do they call you?" he asked.

"What does who call me?" the beast asked.

"Them." Tom nodded at the bats.

The Shataiki raised his chin. "I am called Teeleh."

"Teeleh." He'd expected nothing else. "You're the leader of the Shataiki."

"Foolish minds may call what they do not know whatever they wish. But I am the ruler of a thousand legions of subjects in a land full of mystery and power. This they call the black forest." The black bat swung a huge wing toward the forest behind him. "But I call it my kingdom. Which is why I've come to speak to you. To set your mind free. There are some things you should know."

Tom could hardly ignore the obvious fact that the creature wanted something from him. This show of power couldn't be arbitrary. But he had no intention of giving them anything. He'd come for one purpose only, to gather some information about the histories.

Despite his confusion over the true nature of this creature, Thomas couldn't allow Teeleh to gain the upper hand.

"And there are some things that you should know as well," Tom said. "It's forbidden for me to drink your water, and I have no intention of doing it. Please don't waste your time."

Teeleh's eyes brightened. "Forbidden, you say? Who can forbid another man to do anything? No, my friend. No one is forbidden unless he chooses to be forbidden." The Shataiki spoke fluidly, as though he'd argued the subject a thousand times. "What better way to keep someone from experiencing my power than to say he will suffer if he drinks the water? Lies. Surely you, more than the rest, should know that such small-minded talk only locks people in cages of stupidity. They follow a god who demands their allegiance and robs them of their freedom. Forbidden? Who has the right to forbid?"

The reasoning was compelling. But it had to be fast talk. Tom chose his next words carefully. "I also know that if even one of us drinks your water, the whole land will be turned over to those sick, demented creatures, as you call them, and we will become your slaves."

The air suddenly filled with angry snarls of outrage from the army of Shataiki in the trees. Startled by the outcry, Tom retreated a step.

"Silence!" Teeleh thundered. His voice echoed with such force that Tom instinctively ducked.

The beast dipped its head. "Forgive

them, my friend. I don't think you would blame them if you knew what they have been through. When you have lived through deception and tyranny and you survive, you tend to overreact to the slightest reminder of that tyranny. And believe me, those behind me have faced the greatest form of deception and abuse known to living souls." He paused and twitched his head as though he were trying to loosen a stiff neck.

In many ways the Shataiki's actions *were* consistent with creatures who'd been abused and imprisoned. Tom felt a sliver of pity run through his heart. For such a beautiful creature as Teeleh to be imprisoned in the black forest seemed unjust.

"Now come," Teeleh said. "You must surely know that the myths you speak of are designed to deceive the people of the colored forest — to control their allegiance. You think you know, but what you've been told is the greatest kind of deception. And I've come to make that clear to you."

Did Teeleh know that he'd lost his memory?

"Why did you try to kill me?" he asked.

"I would never do such a thing."

"I was in your forest and barely got out alive. If I hadn't made the Crossing when I did, I would be dead now."

"But you didn't have my protection," the

beast said. "They mistook you for one of them."

"Them?"

"Surely you don't actually believe that you're one of them, do you? How quaint. And clever, I might add. They're actually using your memory loss against you, aren't they? Typical. Always deceiving."

So he did know about the memory loss. What else did he know?

"How did you know about the memory loss?" Tom asked.

"Bill told me," the creature said. "You do remember Bill, don't you?"

"Bill?"

"Yes, Bill. The redhead who came here with you."

Tom took a step back. The creature before him shifted out of focus. "Bill is *real?*"

"Of course he's real. You're real. If you're real, then Bill's real. You both came from the same place."

Tom couldn't mistake the sense that he was standing at the edge of a whole new world of understanding. He'd come with a few questions about the histories, and yet before asking those questions, a hundred others had been deposited in his mind.

He glanced back at the colored forest. What did he really know? Only what the others had told him. Nothing more. Was it possible that he had it all wrong?

His heart thumped in his chest. The air suddenly felt too thick to breathe. Easy. Easy, Tom. He couldn't reveal his ignorance.

"Okay, so you know about Bill. Tell me about him. Tell me where we came from."

"You still don't remember?"

He eyed the bat circumspectly. "I remember some things. But I'll keep those to myself. You tell me what you know, and we'll see if that matches what I remember. Say the wrong thing, and I'll know you're lying."

The smile faded from Teeleh's lips. "You came from Earth."

"Earth. This is Earth. Be more specific."

Teeleh regarded him with a long stare. "You really don't know, do you? You're a sharp one, I'll give you that, but you just don't know."

"Don't be so sure," Tom said, careful to keep anxiety out of his voice.

"Don't be so sure that you're sharp? Or that you know?"

"Just tell me."

"You and your copilot, Bill, crashed less than a mile behind me," Teeleh said. "Which is why I'm here. I think I've found a way back."

It was all Tom could do to hide his incredulity. What a preposterous suggestion!

It actually eased his tension. If Teeleh was stupid enough to think he'd fall for such a ridiculous fabrication, he was much less an opponent than Michal had suggested. Hopefully the bat still knew the histories.

For now he would play along, see how far this creature would take the story.

"So. You know about Bill and the spaceship. What else do you know?"

"I know that you think the spaceship is preposterous because you really don't remember a thing."

Tom blinked. "Is that so?"

"The truth of it is this: You are stranded on a distant planet. Your ship, *Discovery III*, crashed three days ago. You lost your memory in the impact. You're standing on this bridge talking to me because you don't fit in with the simpletons in the colored forest, which is natural. You don't."

Tom's ears were burning. He wondered if this creature could see that as well.

He cleared his throat. "What else?"

"It's good to hear, isn't it? The truth. Unlike the pitifully deceived people of the colored forest, I will tell you only the truth."

"Fine. Tell me the truth then."

"My, my, we are hungry. The truth is, if you knew what I know about that colored forest and those who live in it, you would despise them."

The throngs of Shataiki had lost their respect for the silence. A sea of voices muttered and squealed under their collective breath. Somewhere in the darkness, Tom could just hear a dozen arguments raging in high pitch.

"We have been imprisoned in this forsaken forest," Teeleh said. "That is the truth. For a Shataiki to touch the land across this river means instant death. It is tyranny."

The throngs of bats screeched their outrage.

Teeleh lifted a wing.

Quiet fell over the forest like a blanket of fog.

"They make me ill," Teeleh muttered. He looked back to make sure his legions were in order.

"What about the histories?" Tom asked. The question he'd come to ask sounded out of balance in this new realm of truth.

"The histories. Yes, of course. I suppose you're dreaming of the histories, are you?"

"They're real? How can there be histories of Earth if this isn't Earth?"

The question seemed to set the big bat back. "Clever. Very clever. How can we have histories of Earth if we aren't on Earth?"

"And how do you know I'm dreaming of the histories?"

"I know you're dreaming because I've drunk the water in the black forest. Knowledge. The histories of Earth are really the future of Earth. To you, they're history, because you've tasted some fruit from the forest behind me. You're seeing into the future."

The revelation was stunning. Tom didn't remember eating any fruit. Perhaps before he hit his head on the rock? In its own way it made perfect sense. And there was a way to test this assertion.

"Fair enough," Tom said. "Then you should be able to tell me what happens in this future. Tell me about the Raison Strain."

"The Raison Strain. Of course. One of humanity's most telling periods. Before the Great Tribulation. Often called the Great Deception. I'll speak of it as history. It was a vaccine that mutated into a virus under extreme heat."

Teeleh licked his lips delectably. "Nobody would have ever known, you know. The vaccine never would have mutated because no natural cause would ever produce a heat high enough to trigger the mutation. But some unsuspecting fool stumbled upon the information. He told the wrong party. The vaccine fell into the hands of some very . . . disturbed people. These people heated the vaccine to precisely 179.47 de-

314

grees Fahrenheit for two hours, and so was born the world's deadliest airborne virus."

There was something very odd about what Teeleh was saying, but Tom couldn't put his finger on it. Regardless, the creature's information matched his dreams.

"Come closer," Teeleh said.

"Closer?"

"You want to know about the virus, don't you? Just a little closer."

Tom took a half step. Teeleh's claw flashed without warning. It barely touched his thumb, which was gripping the rail. A small shock rode up his arm, and he jerked the hand back. Blood seeped from a tiny cut in his thumb. It was smeared.

"What are you doing?" he demanded.

"You want to know; I'm helping you know."

"How does cutting me help me know?"

"Please, it's nothing but a scratch. I was merely testing you. Ask me a question."

The whole business was highly unusual. But then so was everything about Teeleh.

"Do you know the number of nucleotide base pairs for HIV?" he asked. "In the Raison Vaccine, that is."

"Base pairs: 375,200. But you know that it wasn't the actual Raison Strain that brought such destruction," Teeleh said. "It was the antivirus. Which conveniently also ended up in the hands of the same man who unleashed the virus. He blackmailed the world. Thus the name, the Great Deception."

Tom's head buzzed. "The antivirus?"

"Yes. Cutting the DNA at the fifth gene and the ninety-third gene and splicing the two remaining ends together." Teeleh suddenly grew very still. His voice softened. "Tell them that, Thomas. Tell them 179.47 degrees for two hours and tell them the fifth gene and the ninety-third gene, cut and spliced. Say that."

"Say the numbers?"

"Don't you want to know? Say them."

"One hundred and seventy-nine point four seven degrees for two hours."

"Yes, now the fifth gene."

"Fifth gene . . ."

"Yes, and the ninety-third gene."

"Ninety-third gene," Tom repeated.

"Cut and spliced."

"Cut and spliced."

"And you'll need her back door as well."

"The back door as well?"

"Yes. Now forget that I told you that."

"Forget?"

"Forget." Teeleh withdrew the same fruit he'd offered before. "Here. Have a bite of fruit. It'll help you."

"No, I can't."

"That's just not true. I've just proved

that those rules are a prison. How thick can you be?"

Teeleh stood, unmoving, the fruit perched lightly in his fingers. He spoke in a quieter voice now. "The fruit will open whole new worlds to you, Tom, my friend. And the water will show you worlds of knowledge you have only dreamed of. Worlds your friends in the colored forest know nothing about."

Tom looked at the fruit. Then up at the green eyes. What if there really was a spaceship behind those trees? It was as likely a scenario as anything else he'd considered.

"Assuming this is all true, where is Bill?"

"Would you like to see Bill? Maybe I can arrange that for you."

"You said you had a way to get us home."

"Yes. Yes, I can do that. We've found a way to fix your ship."

"Can you show it to me?" Tom's heart pounded as he asked the question. Seeing the ship would end the debate raging in his mind, but Tom had no guarantee the Shataiki wouldn't tear him to pieces. They'd tried once already.

"Yes. Yes, and I will. But first I need one thing from you. A simple thing that you could do easily, I think." Again the leader paused, as if tentative about actually asking what he had come to ask.

"What?"

"Bring Tanis here, to the bridge."

Silence engulfed them. Not a single Shataiki lining the forest seemed to move. All eyes glared with anticipation at Tom. His heart pounded. Other than the gurgling of the river below, it was the only sound he now heard.

"And if I do that, then you will guarantee me safe passage to my ship? Repaired?"

"Yes."

Tom reached a hand to the rail to steady himself.

"You just want me to bring him to the bridge, right? Not across the bridge."

"Yes. Just to the river here."

"And what guarantee do I have that you will lead me safely to the craft?"

"I will bring the craft here to the bridge as well. You may enter it with no Shataiki in sight, before I speak to Tanis."

If the Shataiki could actually show him this ship, the *Discovery III*, it would be proof enough. If not, he wouldn't cross the bridge. No harm.

"Makes sense," he said cautiously.

The living wall of black creatures lining the forest now hissed collectively like a great field of locusts. Teeleh stared at Tom, raised the fruit to his lips, and bit deeply again. He licked the juice that ran onto his fingers with a long, thin, pink tongue. All the while his unblinking eyes stared at Tom. Could he trust this creature? If what he said were true, then he had to find the spacecraft! It would be his only way home.

The leader stopped his licking. He stretched the fruit out to Tom. "Eat this fruit to seal our agreement," Teeleh said. "It's our very best."

He'd done this once already. According to the creature, it was why he was dreaming. Tom forced his fear back, reached out to the Shataiki, took the fruit from his claw, and stepped back.

He glanced up at the creature smiling before him. Raised the half-eaten fruit to his mouth. He was about to bite down when the scream shattered the night.

"Thomasssss!"

Tom jerked the fruit from his mouth and swung to his right. Bill? The voice sounded slurred and ragged.

Then he saw the redhead. Bill had emerged from the forest and was struggling weakly against the claws of a dozen Shataiki. His clothes had been stripped entirely, and his naked body looked shockingly white in the tangle of shrieking black Shataiki who now tore at him. Blood matted the redhead's hair and streaked his drawn face. Dozens of cuts and bruises covered the man's pale flesh. He looked like an abused corpse.

The blood drained from Tom's head. Nausea washed over him.

Teeleh swung around, his eyes blazing with an intensity that Tom had not yet seen. Tom's fingers went limp, and the fruit fell to the wooden deck with a deadening thump.

"Take your hands off him!" Teeleh screamed. He unfurled his wings and raised them above his head. "How dare you defy me!"

Tom watched, stunned. Immediately the Shataiki released Bill.

"Take him to safety. Now!"

Two bats pulled Bill by the hands. He stumbled into the trees.

Teeleh faced Tom. "As you can see, Bill is indeed real. I must keep him, you understand. It's the one assurance I have from you that you will return with Tanis. But I promise you, no more harm will come to him."

"Thomas!" Bill's voice cried from the trees. "Help me . . ." His voice was muted.

"Very real, my friend," Teeleh said. "He's been through a bit of turmoil lately and isn't thrilled with the way the others have treated him, but I can promise you my full protection."

Tom couldn't tear his eyes from the gap in the trees where Bill had vanished. It was real? Bill was real. Confusion clouded his mind.

A lone cry suddenly shrieked behind Tom. He spun his head and saw the white Roush swoop in from the treetops. Michal!

"Thomas! Run! Quickly!"

Tom whirled around and tore toward the forest. He slammed into a tree and spun around, gasping for air. Teeleh stood stoically on the bridge, drilling him with those large green eyes.

"Hurry," Michal called. "We must hurry!"

Tom turned from the scene and dived into the forest after Michal.

20

Finding the room had been a simple matter of handing the desk clerk a hundred U.S. dollars and asking which room the blonde American girl had taken several hours earlier. She was probably the only American who'd checked in all day.

Room 517, the clerk said.

Carlos stepped into the fifth-floor hall, saw that it was clear, and walked quickly to his left. 515. 517. He stepped to the door, tested the knob. Locked. Naturally.

He stood in the vacant hall for another three minutes, ear pressed to the door. Aside from the rattling air conditioner, the room was completely silent. They could be sleeping, although he doubted it. Or gone. Unlikely.

He reached into his pocket, withdrew a pick, and very carefully turned the tumblers in the lock. There was more than enough white noise to cover his entry. The American had a gun, but he wasn't a killer. One look at his face and Carlos had seen that. And guns weren't terribly familiar to him, by the way he'd gripped the 9-milli-meter in the hotel lobby.

No, what they had here was an American who was crazed and bold and perhaps even a worthy adversary, but not a killer.

If your enemy is strong, you must crush.

If your enemy is deaf, you must shout.

If your enemy fears death, you must slaughter.

Basic terror-camp doctrine.

Carlos rolled and cracked his neck. He was dressed in a black blazer, T-shirt, slacks, patent leather shoes. The clothes of a Mediterranean businessman. But the time for facades was at an end. The jacket would only encumber his movements. He eased the silenced gun from his breast pocket and slipped it under his belt. Shrugged off the jacket. Draped it over his left arm and handled the pistol. Twisted the knob with his left hand.

Carlos took a deep breath and leaned hard into the door, enough force to snap any safety device.

A chain popped and Carlos was through, gun extended.

Force and speed. Not only in execution but in understanding and judgment. He saw what he needed to see before his first full stride.

The woman bound to the air condi-tioner. Gagged. Cords made from sheets.

The American lying shirtless on the bed. Asleep.

Carlos was halfway across the room before the woman could respond, and then only with a muffled squeak. Her eyes flared wide. Powerless.

The American was his only concern then. He jerked the gun to his right, ready to put a bullet in the man's shoulder if he so much as flinched.

He was moving quickly, without wasted movement. But in his mind everything felt impossibly slow. It was the way he'd flawlessly executed a hundred missions. Break a simple movement into a dozen fragments and you can then influence each fragment, make corrections, changes. It was a supreme advantage he had over all but the very best.

Carlos reached the girl in four strides. He dropped to his right knee and slugged her with a quick chop to her temple, all the while keeping the gun trained on the American.

The woman moaned and sagged. Unconscious.

Carlos held his position for a count of three. The American's chest rose and fell. The 9-millimeter gun lay on the bed by his fingers.

Easy. Too easy. Almost disappointingly easy.

He rose, retrieved the American's gun, hurried to the door. Closed it quietly. He returned to the bed and studied the situation, gun hanging at his side. A windfall in any sense of the word. Two for the price of one, as the Americans would say. An unconscious woman and a sleeping man, helpless at his feet.

The man had several scars on his chest. Very well muscled. Lean fingers. The perfect body for a fighter. Perhaps he'd underestimated this one.

What was driving Thomas Hunter? Dreams? They would soon know, because he would take them both. The world would be looking for the crazed American who'd kidnapped Monique de Raison, never suspecting that they were both now in the hands of a third party. Svensson would wet himself over this one.

The air conditioner rattled steadily to his left. Outside, the street crawled with night business. The other woman could return at any moment.

Carlos walked to the Raison woman, removed her gag. Withdrew a marble-sized ball from his pocket. It was a product of his own making. Nine parts high explosive, one part remote detonator. He'd used it successfully on three occasions.

He pulled the woman to a sitting position, squeezed her cheeks to part her lips,

325

and slipped the ball into her mouth. Using his left hand, he squeezed her windpipe with enough sudden force to make her gasp involuntarily. At the same moment, while her mouth gaped, he shoved the ball down her throat with his forefinger.

She gagged. Swallowed. He clamped his hand over her mouth, and she struggled against him, regaining consciousness. When he was sure she'd swallowed the ball completely, he brought his fist across her temple.

She slumped to the floor.

Monique de Raison now carried enough explosive in her belly to disembowel her with the push of a single button. Undetonated, the explosive ball would pass out of her system in roughly twenty-four hours, but until then she was his prisoner to a range of fifty meters. It was the only way to get both her and the American to cooperate. She would comply with his instructions for obvious reasons. And if Carlos judged the American correctly, Hunter would comply to protect the girl.

"Wha—" The American's head jerked in his sleep. He was mumbling. "What?"

Carlos stepped to the base of the bed. He considered waking the man with a bullet through the shoulder. But they still had to descend to the basement and walk to the car. He could risk neither the mess nor the time of a bleeding shoulder.

"Say them?" Hunter mumbled. "Say them . . . 179.47 degrees for two hours . . . the fifth gene and the ninety-third gene, cut and spliced. The back door as well."

What was the idiot mumbling?

". . . Now forget . . ."

An interesting sight, this American jerking about, mumbling in his sleep. His dreams. Fifth gene, ninety-third gene, cut and spliced. You'll need the back door. Meaningless. Carlos stored the information out of habit.

He lifted the gun and trained it on the American's chest. One shot and the man would be dead. Truly tempting. But they needed him alive if possible. It reminded him of the time he'd assassinated another American. The owner of a pharmaceutical company whom Svensson wanted out of the way.

Carlos let the moment linger.

Michal flew below the treetops and glanced back wordlessly from time to time. Tom plunged ahead, mind numb. Something very significant had just happened. He'd snuck away from the village. He'd met with Teeleh, a thought that sent a chill down his spine every time he saw the creature in his mind's eye. He'd actually agreed to betray —

No, not betray. He could never do that. But he had!

And he'd seen a redhead named Bill, who was his copilot, barely alive. The horror of it all seeped into his mind, an indelible ink. He felt like a child stumbling through the streets of Manila.

Tom finally settled into a dumb hopelessness and lost himself in the drumming of his feet.

When they finally broke over the crest of the valley, Michal didn't turn down toward the lighted village as Tom expected. Instead, he turned up the valley where the wide road disappeared over the hill. Tom came to a panting halt and leaned over, hands on his knees, gulping the night air. The Roush flew on for a hundred yards before noticing Thomas had stopped. With a flurry of wings he turned and glided back down the hill.

"Would it be better if we walked now?" he asked.

Tom motioned toward the village. "Are we going?"

"Tonight you will meet Elyon," Michal answered.

"Elyon?" Tom stood up, alarmed.

The Roush turned and began walking toward the path.

"Michal! Please. Please, I have to know something."

"Oh, you will, Thomas. You will."

"Bill. You saw him? The Shataiki said he was my copilot. We crash-landed . . ."

Michal turned back and studied him. "This is what the deceiver told you?"

"Yes. And I saw him, Michal. *You* saw him!"

"I will tell you what I saw, and you must never forget it. Do you understand me? Never!"

"Of course!" Emotion swelled in Tom's chest. He placed his palms on his temples, desperate for clarity. "Please, just tell me something that makes sense."

"I saw nothing but lies. Teeleh is a deceiver. He will tell you anything to lure you into his trap. Anything! Knowing full well that you would quickly doubt what he told you, he showed you this redhead you call Bill."

"But if Bill is real —"

"Bill isn't real! What you saw was a figment of your imagination! A creation of that monster! From the beginning he was planted to deceive you."

"But . . . Bill warned me! He ran out of the forest and yelled at me!"

"What better way for Teeleh to convince you that he was real? He knew that you would likely break your agreement with him to betray the others." Michal shuddered with the last word. "But now that he has pulled this stunt and you're tempted to think Bill is real, you are more likely to return. It will haunt you until you finally return."

The Roush stared at him with eyes that made Tom want to cry.

"Never!" he said. "I would never return if that's true!"

Michal didn't reply right away. He turned and waddled down the hill.

"Even now you doubt," he said.

Tom let Michal walk on, suddenly sure that the Roush was both right and wrong. Right about the Shataiki's deception, wrong about him going back. How could he? He wasn't from the histories; he wasn't from some distant planet called Earth. He was from here, and here was Earth.

Unless Teeleh was right.

He followed the Roush at a respectable distance. They walked over the hill and into a second valley. Here a new landscape unfolded before his eyes. The gentle roll of the hills gave way to steep grades covered with trees much taller than those behind them.

Tom gazed at the landscape in wonder. The steep grades became cliffs and the trees grew massive, so the light they shed brightened the canyon to near daylight. Every branch seemed to carry fruit. It must have been from this forest that the huge columns of the Thrall had been harvested. Flawless pillars that shone in hues of ruby and sapphire and emerald and gold, lighting the path with an aura that Tom could almost feel.

This was his home. He'd lost his memory, but this incredible place was his home. He quickened his pace slightly.

Red and blue flowers with large petals covered a thick carpet of emerald grass. The cliffs looked as though they were cut from a single large, white pearl, which reflected light from the trees so that the entire valley glowed in the hues of the rainbow. Tom could hear the rushing of a river that occasionally wound its way close enough to the path that he could see the green, luminescent water as it rushed by.

Home. This was home, and Tom could hardly stand the fact that he'd ever doubted it. Rachelle should be here with him, walking up this very path.

They had walked no more than ten minutes when Tom first heard the distant thunder. At first he thought it must be the sound of the river. No, more than a river.

A tingle ran over his skin. The thunder grew. He picked up his pace again. Michal also moved faster, hopping along the ground and extending his wings to maintain balance. Whatever was drawing Tom also drew him.

The foliage to his left suddenly rustled and Tom stopped. A white beast the size of a small horse but resembling a lion sauntered into the path, eying him curiously. Tom took a step back. But the lion walked on, purring loudly. Tom ran to catch Michal, who hadn't stopped.

He saw other creatures now. Many looked like the first, others like horses. Tom watched a large white eagle land on a lion's back and fix its eyes on him as he stumbled down the path.

The thunder grew, a rumble low and deep and powerful enough to send a faint tremor through the ground. Michal had left his hopping and skipping and had taken back to the air.

Tom sprinted after the Roush. Vibrations rose through the earth. He ran around a sweeping bend in the road, heart pounding.

And then the path ended. Abruptly.

Tom slid to a halt.

Before him sprawled a great circular lake, glowing fluorescent with the same emerald water that contained the black forest. The lake was lined with huge, evenly spaced, gleaming trees, set back forty paces from a white sandy shore. Animals circled the lake, sleeping or drinking.

On the far side, a towering pearl cliff

shimmered with ruby and topaz hues. Over the cliff poured a huge waterfall, which throbbed with green and golden light and thundered into the water a hundred meters below. The rising mist captured light from the trees, giving the appearance that colors arose out of the lake itself. Here, there could hardly be a difference between day and night. To his right, the river he had seen along the path flowed from the lake. Michal had descended to the lake's shore and lapped thirstily at the water's edge.

All of this Tom registered before his first blink.

He took a few tentative steps down the shore, then stopped, feet planted in the sand. He wanted to run to the water's edge and drink as Michal drank, but he suddenly wasn't sure he could move.

Below, Michal continued drinking.

A chill descended Tom's spine, from the nape of his neck to the soles of his feet. An inexplicable fear smothered him. Sweat seeped from his pores despite a cool wind blowing across the lake.

Something was wrong. All wrong. He stepped back, mind grasping for a thread of reason. Instead, the fear gave way to terror. He spun and ran up the bank.

The moment he crested the bank, the fear fell from him like loosed shackles. He turned back. Michal drank. Insatiably.

In that moment, Tom knew he *had* to drink the water.

There on the beach, his feet spread and planted firmly in the soft white sand, his hands clenched at his sides, Tom's mind snapped.

He was vaguely aware of the low groan that broke from his lips, barely audible above the falling water. The animals loitered. Michal drank deeply below him. The trees stood stately. The waterfall gushed. The scene was frozen in time, with Tom mistakenly trapped in its folds.

The waterfall suddenly seemed to crash a little harder, and a large surge of spray rose from the lake. Mist drifted toward him. He could see it coming. It billowed over the shore. It hit him in the face, no more than a faint sprinkling of moisture, but it could have been the shock wave of a small nuclear weapon.

Tom gasped. His hands fell to the sand. Eyes wide. The terror was gone.

Only the desire remained. Raw, desperate desire, pulling at his aching heart with the power of absolute vacuum.

No one watching could have been prepared for what he did next. In that moment, knowing what he must do — what he wanted most desperately — Tom tore his feet from the sand and sprinted for the water's edge. He didn't stop at the shore and stoop to drink as the others did. Instead, he dived headlong over the bent posture of Michal and into the glowing waters. Screaming all the way.

The instant Tom hit the water, his body shook violently. A blue strobe exploded in his eyes, and he knew that he was going to die. That he had entered a forbidden pool, pulled by the wrong desire, and now he would pay with his life.

The warm water engulfed him. Flutters rippled through his body and erupted into a boiling heat that knocked the wind from his lungs. The shock alone might kill him.

But he didn't die. In fact, it was pleasure that racked his body, not death. Pleasure! The sensations coursed through his bones in great, unrelenting waves.

Elyon.

How he was certain he did not know. But he knew. Elyon was in this lake with him.

Tom opened his eyes and found they did not sting. Gold light drifted by. No part of the water seemed darker than another. He lost all sense of direction. Which way was up?

The water pressed in on every inch of his body, as intense as any acid, but one that burned with pleasure instead of pain. His violent shaking gave way to a gentle trembling as he sank into the water. He opened his mouth and laughed. He wanted more, much more. He wanted to suck the water in and drink it.

Without thinking, he did that. He took a great gulp and then inhaled unintentionally. The liquid hit his lungs.

Tom pulled up, panicked. Tried to clear his lungs, hacking. Instead, he inhaled more of the water. He flailed and clawed in a direction he thought might be the surface. Was he drowning?

No. He didn't feel short of breath.

He carefully sucked more water and breathed it out slowly. Then again, deep and hard. Out with a soft whoosh.

He was breathing the water! In great heaves he was breathing the lake's intoxicating water.

Tom shrieked with laughter. He tumbled through the water, pulling his legs in close so he would roll, and then stretching them out so he thrust forward, farther into the colors surrounding him. He swam into the lake, deeper and deeper, twisting and rolling as he plummeted toward the bottom. The power contained in this lake was far greater than anything he'd ever imagined. He could hardly contain himself.

In fact, he could not contain himself; he cried out with pleasure and swam deeper.

Then he heard them. Three words.

I made this.

Tom pulled himself up, frozen. No, not words. Music that spoke. Pure notes piercing his heart and mind with as much meaning as an entire book. He whipped his body around, searching for its source.

A giggle rippled through the water. Like a child now.

Tom grinned stupidly and spun around. "Elyon?" His voice was muffled, hardly a voice at all.

I made this.

The words reached into Tom's bones, and he began to tremble again. He wasn't sure if it was an actual voice, or whether he was somehow imagining it.

"What are you? Where are you?" Light floated by. Waves of pleasure continued to sweep through him. "Who are you?"

I am Elyon.
And I made you.

The words started in his mind and burned through his body like a spreading fire.

Do you like it?

Yes! Tom said. He might have spoken,

337

he might have shouted, he didn't know. He only knew that his whole body screamed it.

Tom looked around. "Elyon?"

The voice was different now. Spoken. The music was gone. A simple, innocent question.

Do you doubt me?

In that single moment, the full weight of his terrible foolishness crashed in on him like a sledgehammer. How could he have doubted this?

Tom curled into a fetal position within the bowels of the lake and began to moan.

I see you, Thomas.
I made you.
I love you.

The words washed over him, reaching into the deepest marrow of his bones, caressing each hidden synapse, flowing through every vein, as though he had been given a transfusion.

So then, why do you doubt?

It was the Thomas from his dreams — from his subconscious — that filled his mind now. He had more than just doubted. That was him, wasn't it?

"I'm sorry. I'm so sorry." He thought he might die after all. "I'm sorry. I am so sorry," he moaned. "Please . . ."

Sorry? Why are you sorry?

"For everything. For . . . doubting. For ignoring . . ." Tom stopped, not sure exactly how else he had offended, only knowing that he had.

For not loving?
I love you, Thomas.

The words filled the entire lake, as though the water itself had become these words. Tom sobbed uncontrollably.

The water around his feet suddenly began to boil, and he felt the lake suck him deeper into itself. He gasped, pulled by a powerful current. And then he was flipped over and pushed headfirst by the same current. He opened his eyes, resigned to whatever awaited him.

A dark tunnel opened directly ahead of him, like the eye of a whirlpool. He rushed into it and the light fell away.

Pain hit him like a battering ram, and he gasped for breath. He instinctively arched his back in blind panic and reached back toward the entrance of the tunnel, straining to see it, but it had closed.

He began to scream, flailing in the water, rushing deeper into the dark tunnel. Pain raged through his entire body. He felt as if his flesh had been neatly filleted and packed with salt; each organ stuffed with burning coals; his bones drilled open and filled with molten lead.

For the first time in his life, Tom wanted desperately to die.

Then he saw the images streaming by, and he recognized where he must be. Images from the Crossing, from his dreams, strung out here for him to see.

Images of him spitting in his father's face. His father the chaplain.

"Let me die!" he heard himself shrieking. *"Let me diiiieeee!"*

The water forced his eyes open and new images filled his mind. His mother, crying. The images came faster now. Pictures of his life. A dark, terrible nature. A red-faced man was spitting obscenities with a long tongue that kept flashing from his gaping mouth like a snake's. Each time the tongue touched another person, they crumpled to the floor in a pile of bones. It was his face he saw. Memories of lives dead and gone, but here now and dying still.

And he knew then that he had entered his own soul.

Tom's back arched so that his head neared his heels. His spine stressed to the snapping point. He couldn't stop screaming.

The tunnel suddenly gaped below and spewed him out into soupy red water. Blood red. He sucked at the red water, filling his spent lungs.

From deep in the pit of the lake a moan began to fill his ears, replacing his own screams. Tom spun about, searching for the sound, but he found only thick red blood. The moan gained volume and grew to a wail and then a scream.

Elyon was screaming! In pain.

Tom pressed his hands to his ears and began to scream with the other, thinking now that this was worse than the dark tunnel. His body crawled with fire, as though every last cell revolted at the sound. *And so they should,* a voice whispered in his skull. *Their Maker is screaming in pain!*

Then he was through. Out of the red, into the green of the lake, hands still pressed firmly against his ears. Tom heard the words as if they came from within his own mind.

I love you, Thomas.

Immediately the pain was gone. Tom pulled his hands from his head and straightened out slightly in the water. He floated, too stunned to respond. Then the lake was filled with a song. A song more wonderful than any song could possibly sound, a hundred thousand melodies woven into one.

I love you.
I choose you.
I rescue you.
I cherish you.

"I love you too!" Tom cried desperately. "I choose you; I cherish you." He was sobbing, but with love. The feeling was more intense than the pain that had racked him.

The current suddenly pulled at him again, tugging him up through the colors. His body again trembled with pleasure, and he hung limp as he sped through the water. He wanted to speak, to scream and to yell and to tell the whole world that he was the luckiest man in the universe. That he was loved by Elyon, Elyon himself, with his own voice, in a lake made by him.

But the words would not come.

How long he swam through the currents of the lake, he could never know. He dived into blue hues and found a deep pool of peace that numbed his body like Novocain. With the twist of his wrist, he altered his course into a gold stream and trembled with waves of absolute confidence that come only with great power and wealth. Then a turn of his head and he rushed into red water bubbling with pleasure so great he felt himself go limp once again. Elyon laughed. And Tom laughed and dived deeper, twisting and turning.

When Elyon spoke again, his voice was gentle and deep, like a purring lion.

Never leave me, Thomas.
Tell me that you'll never leave me.

"Never! Never, never, never! I will always stay with you."

Another current caught him from behind and pushed him through the water. He laughed as he rushed through the water for what seemed a very long time before breaking the surface not ten meters from the shore.

He stood on the sandy bottom and retched a quart of water from his lungs in front of a startled Michal. He coughed twice and waded from the water. "Boy, oh boy." He couldn't think of words that would describe the experience. "Wow!"

"Elyon," Michal said, his short snout split with a gaping grin. "Well, well. It *was* a bit unorthodox, diving in like that."

"How long was I under?"

Michal shrugged. "A minute. No more."

Tom slopped onto the shore and

dropped to his knees. "Incredible."

"Do you remember?"

He looked back at the waterfall. Did he remember?

"Remember what?"

"What village you come from. Who you are," Michal said.

Did he?

"No," Thomas said. "I remember everything since falling in the black forest. And I remember my dreams."

Where he was sleeping, he thought. Waiting to awake. But he knew that he wouldn't wake there until he fell asleep here. It could be two days here and one second there. That's the way it worked.

Assuming he ever dreamed again. He certainly didn't want to. The lake had revived him completely. He felt like he'd slept a week.

He dropped to his back and lay on the sandy beach, gazing up at the moon.

21

Monique blinked. Her head throbbed. She was lying on her side. Her vision was blurred. Her cheek was pressed into the carpet. She could see under the bed ten feet away. She'd fallen asleep?

Then she remembered. Her pulse spiked. Someone had broken in while Thomas was sleeping! He'd come in like a whirlwind and smashed her head before she could do anything. Something else had happened, but she couldn't remember what. Her throat was sore; her head felt like a balloon.

But she was alive, and she was still in the room.

She had to wake Tom!

Monique was about to lift her head when she saw the shoes under the end of the bed. They were connected to pants. Someone was standing at the end of the bed.

She caught her breath and froze. He was still here! Tom's breathing sounded ragged. He was hurt? Or sleeping.

Monique closed her eyes and tried to

think. The strips of bedsheet still bound her arms and feet. But her mouth. He'd taken the gag off. Why? Was this her rescuer? Had the police come to take her away? If so, then why had the man knocked her unconscious?

No, it couldn't be anyone who had her safety in mind. For all she knew, he was crossing the room at this very minute, knife in hand, intending to finish the job.

She opened her eyes wide. The shoes hadn't moved. She rolled her eyes upward as far as she could, desperate for a glimpse of her attacker.

Black shirt. There was a long scar on his cheek. His arm was extended. He had a gun in his hand. The gun was pointed at Thomas.

Monique panicked. She jerked up as hard as she could and screamed. "Thomas!"

The man spun to her, pistol leveled, eyes wide. Thomas bolted upright on the bed, like a puppet on strings. The man dropped to one knee and whipped the gun back toward Thomas.

"Don't move!"

But it was too late. Thomas was already moving.

He threw himself to his left. The gun spit. A pillow spewed feathers. Monique saw the American fall from the bed, hit the floor on the other side. He moved with lightning speed, as if he'd bounced off the carpet.

Then he was in the air, flying for the black-clad intruder.

Phewt! The gun spit again, ripping a hole in the headboard. Tom entered a scissors kick, like a soccer player lining up for a goal. His foot connected with the man's hand.

Crack!

The gun flew across the room and slammed into the wall above Monique's head. It fell to the floor at her side.

She was powerless to get it. But she swung her legs to cover it.

Thomas had rolled up onto the bed after his kick and now stood by the ruptured pillow, facing the attacker in a familiar ready stance.

The man glanced at her, then at Thomas. A smile twisted his lips. "Very good. I did underestimate you after all," he said. Mediterranean accent. Schooled. Not a thug. Monique pushed herself up, ignoring a splitting pain in her head.

"Who are you?" Thomas demanded. His eyes were wide, but otherwise he was surprisingly calm. "I don't want to hurt anyone."

"No? Then perhaps I did underestimate you."

"You're the one who wants the vaccine," Thomas said.

The man's left eye narrowed barely. Enough for Monique to know that Thomas had struck a chord.

"How did you know?" Thomas asked.

"I have no interest in a vaccine." The man's eyes darted to a jacket lying by the door. Tom saw it as well.

"I tipped you off, didn't I?" Thomas demanded. "If I hadn't said anything to anybody, you wouldn't be here. Isn't that right?"

The man shrugged. "I only do what I'm hired to do. I have no idea what you're talking about." He eased toward the front door. Brushed his hands against each other and raised them in a show of surrender. "In this case, I was hired to return the girl to her father, and I must tell you that I fully intend to do that. I have no interest in you."

Thomas shook his head. "No, I don't believe you. Monique, 375,200 base pairs. HIV vaccine. Am I right?"

She stared at him. They hadn't published that information yet. How could —

"Am I right?" he demanded.

"Yes."

"Then listen to me." Tom looked at her, then at the attacker. Tears filled his eyes. He looked desperate. "I don't know what's happening to me. I don't want to hurt anyone. I really don't, you hear me? But we have to stop this man. I mean, no matter what happens, we have to stop him. They're real, Monique. My dreams are real. You have to believe me!"

The man had taken another step toward the door. She answered to calm Tom more than to agree with him. "Yes, okay. I do. Watch him, Thomas! He's going for the jacket."

"Leave the jacket," Thomas said.

The man arched an eyebrow. He seemed to be enjoying himself.

"This is absurd," he said. "You think you can actually stop me from doing what I want? You're unarmed." He casually reached into his pocket and pulled out a switchblade. The blade snapped open. "I am not. And even if I were, you would have no chance against me."

"You promise?"

"You want me to —"

"Not you! Her. You believe me, Monique? I need you to believe me."

His conviction made her hesitate.

"This could end badly, Monique. I really, really need you to understand what's happening here."

"I believe you," she said.

The man suddenly lunged for his jacket.

Monique had never seen anyone move as

fast as Thomas did then. He didn't jump; he didn't step. He shot, like a bullet. Straight at the floor between the bed and the front door where the jacket lay folded.

He rolled once, sprang to his feet, and hit the black-clad man broadside with the heels of both hands.

Carlos had killed many men with his bare hands. He'd never, in a dozen years of the finest training, seen a man move as fast as the American. If he could get to the transmitter in the jacket, there would be no fight. He was now certain Thomas Hunter would capitulate when faced with the prospect of the French woman's terrible death.

He saw Hunter hit the floor and roll, and he knew precisely what the man intended to do. He even knew that what the man had gained by putting gravity to work in his favor might mean Hunter would reach him before he could reach the jacket. But he had to make a decision, and, all things considered, he decided to finish his attempt for the jacket. It was the only way to avoid a fight that would undoubtedly end in Thomas Hunter's death.

The fact was, he wanted Hunter alive. They needed to learn what else he knew.

The man reached him too quickly. Carlos shifted to accept Hunter's blow. The American hit him on his left arm, hard. But not hard enough to knock him from his feet.

Carlos whipped the knife in his right hand across his body. The blade sliced into flesh. The American dropped to his belly. Rolled over the jacket and came up ready. Blood seeped from cuts in both his forearms.

He flung the jacket across the room. Unfazed. He bounced on the balls of his feet twice and threw himself at the wall adjacent Carlos, feetfirst.

This time he knew the man's trajectory before he could line up his kick. He was going for the knife.

Carlos sidestepped, blocked the man's heel as it came around, and stabbed up with the knife. The blade sank into flesh.

Hunter grunted and twisted his legs against the blade, forcing it out of Carlos's hand. He landed on both feet, blade firmly planted in his right calf. He snatched it out and faced Carlos, blade ready.

The reversal was completely unexpected. Enraging. Enough — he was running out of time.

Carlos feigned to his left, ducked low, and jerked back. As expected, the move drew a quick stab with the knife. Still on his heels, he dropped back to one hand and swung his right foot up with his full strength. His shoe caught Hunter in the wrist. Broke it with a sharp crack. The knife flew across the room.

He followed his right foot with his left to the American's solar plexus.

Hunter staggered back, winded.

The phone rang.

Carlos had taken far too long. His first concern had to be the girl. She was the key to the vaccine. Another ring. The blonde? Or the front desk. Taking the American was no longer an option.

He had to finish this now.

Nausea swept through Tom's gut. The phone was ringing, and it occurred to him that it might be Kara. The ringing seemed to unnerve his attacker slightly, but he wasn't sure it mattered any longer. The man with the face scar was going to take Monique.

Both of Tom's arms were bleeding. His wrist was broken, and his right leg was going numb. The man had disarmed him without breaking a sweat. Panic began to set in.

The man suddenly broke to his left, bounded for Monique. She swung both feet at him in a valiant effort to ward him off.

"Get away from me, you —"

He swatted her feet to one side and scooped up the gun. He turned casually and pointed the weapon at Tom.

Tom's options were gone. It was now simply a matter of survival. He straightened. "You win."

The gun dipped and bucked in the man's hand. A bullet plowed through Tom's thigh. He staggered back, numbed.

"I always win," the man said.

"Thomas!" Monique stared in horror. "Thomas!"

"Lie on the bed," the man ordered.

"Don't hurt her."

"Shut up and lie on the bed."

Tom limped forward. His mind was fading already. He wanted to say something, but nothing was coming. Surprisingly, he didn't care what the man did to him now. But there was Kara, and there was Monique, and there was his mother, and they were all going to die.

And there was his father. He wanted to talk to his father.

He heard himself whimper as he fell onto the bed.

Phewt! A bullet tugged at his gut.

Phewt! A second punched into his chest.

The room faded.

Black.

Deputy Secretary of State Merton Gains ducked out from under the umbrella and slid into the Lincoln. He'd grown used to the showers since moving to Washington from Arizona. Found them refreshing, actually.

"Boy, it's really coming down," he said.

George Maloney nodded behind the wheel. "Yes it is, sir." The Irishman didn't show a hint of emotion. Never did. Gains had given up trying. He was paid to drive and paid to protect.

"Take me to the airport, George. Take me to drier parts of Earth."

"Yes sir."

Miranda had insisted on living in their Tucson home for at least the winters, but after two years, the Washington life wore thin, and she found excuses to return home even in the warmer months. Truth be told, Merton would do the same, given a choice. They were both bred in the desert, for the desert. End of story.

Rain splashed unrelentingly on the windows. Traffic was nearly stalled.

"You'll be back on Thursday, sir?"

Gains sighed. "Tucson today, California tomorrow, back on Thursday; that's right."

His cell phone vibrated in his breast pocket.

"Very well, sir. Maybe this rain will be gone by then."

Gains withdrew the phone. "I like the rain, George. Keeps things clean. Something we can always use around here, right?"

No smile. "Yes sir."

He answered the phone. "Gains here."

"Yes, Mr. Gains, I have a Bob Macklroy on the phone for you. He says it could be important."

"Put him on, Venice."

"Here you go."

At times Washington seemed like a college reunion to Gains. Amazing how many jobs had ended up in the hands of Princeton graduates since Blair had been elected president. All qualified people, of course; he couldn't complain. He'd done his own share of upping the Princeton quotient, mostly through recommendations. Bob here, for example, was not exactly a Washington insider, but he was working as the assistant secretary in the Bureau for International Narcotics and Law Enforcement Affairs office in part because he had played basketball with now Deputy Secretary of State Merton Gains.

"Hello, Bob."

"Hi, Merton. Thanks for taking the call."

"Anytime, man. Tim treating you good down there?"

Bob didn't bother answering the question directly. "He's in São Paulo for a few days. We're not sure if you're exactly the right person. This is a bit unusual, and we're not quite sure where to take this.

Tim thought the FBI might be —"

"Try me, Bob. What do you have?"

"Well . . ." Bob hesitated.

"Just tell me. And speak up a bit, it's raining hard. Sounds like a train in here."

"Okay, but it's all very strange. I'm just telling you what I know. It seemed appropriate with your involvement in the Gains Act."

Gains sat up a bit. This evasiveness wasn't like Bob. Something was up, not only in his voice but in this mention of the narrowly defeated bill Merton had introduced two years earlier when he was a senator. It was up again, with some alterations and his name still attached. The bill would impose strict restrictions on the flood of new vaccines hitting the market by demanding they pass a comprehensive battery of tests. Two years had passed since his youngest daughter, Corina, had died of autoimmune disease after mistakenly being administered a new AIDS vaccine. The FDA had approved the vaccine. Gains had successfully had it barred, but other vaccines were entering the market every month, and the casualties were mounting.

"If you don't spit it out, I'm going to send some muscle over there to force it out of you," he said. It was something he could say only to a man like Bob, the locker room cutup who'd once owned the best three-point shot in college ball. They all knew Merton Gains would go out of his way to step over an ant if it wandered onto the sidewalk.

"I'll remember to keep my door locked," Bob said. He sighed. "I got a strange call a couple of days ago from a man who called himself Thomas Hunter. He —"

"The same Thomas Hunter from the situation in Bangkok?" Gains asked. The incident had fallen in his lap earlier today. An American citizen identified as Thomas Hunter from flight records had kidnapped Monique de Raison and another unidentified woman in the lobby of the Sheraton. The French were up in arms, the Thais were demanding intervention, even the stock market had reacted. Raison Pharmaceutical wasn't exactly unknown. The timing couldn't have been worse — they'd just announced their new vaccine.

In Gains's mind, the timing was about right.

"Yes, I think it could be," Bob said.

"He called you? When?"

"A few days ago. From Denver. He said that the Raison Vaccine would mutate into a deadly virus and wipe out half the world's population. Nut-case stuff."

Not necessarily. "Okay, so we have a nut case who's managed to wing his way over to Thailand and kidnap the daughter of

357

Jacques de Raison. That much the world already knows. He say anything else?"

"Actually, yes. I didn't think about it until I saw his name today on the wires. Like you said: a nut case, right?"

"Right."

"Well, he told me that the winner of the Kentucky Derby was Joy Flyer."

"So? Wasn't the Derby three days ago?"

"Yes. But he called me before the race. He got the information from his dreams, the same place he learned that the Raison Vaccine —"

"He actually told you the name of the winner before the race?"

"That's what I'm saying. Crazy, I know."

Gains looked out the side window. Couldn't see a thing past the streams of water sliding down the glass. He'd heard of some crazy things in his time, but this was shaping up for prime bar talk.

"Did you place a bet?"

"Unfortunately, I put the call out of my mind until today, when I saw his name again. But I did some checking. His sister, Kara Hunter, won over $300,000 on the race. They were in Atlanta where they made a bit of a scene at the CDC."

Something definitely wasn't right here. "So we have two nut cases. I haven't seen her profile."

"She's a nurse. Graduated with honors.

Sharp gal, from what I can see. Not your typical nut case."

"Don't tell me you're actually thinking this kid knows something."

"I'm just saying he said he knew about Joy Flyer, and he did. And he says he knows something about this Raison Vaccine. That's all I'm saying."

"Okay, Bob. Suffice it to say that Thomas Hunter is thoroughly deluded — the street corners of America are filled with similar types, usually of the variety who carry signs and rant loudly about the end of the world. This is good. At least we have motivation. You're right, though, this needs to get to the CIA and the FBI. Have you written it up?"

"In my hand."

"Then get it out. The profilers will have a heyday with this. Fax me a copy, will you?"

"Will do."

"And do me a favor. If he calls again, ask him who's winning the NBA championship."

That got a chuckle.

Gains folded his phone and crossed his legs. And what if Thomas Hunter did know something other than who would win the Kentucky Derby? Impossible, of course, but then so was knowing who would win the Kentucky Derby.

Hunter had flown out of Atlanta. The headquarters for the CDC were in Atlanta. That would make sense. Hunter thinks a virus is about to ravage the world, he goes to the CDC, and when they grin at his preposterous claims, he goes straight to the source of the so-called virus.

Bangkok.

Interesting. A true-blue nut case. Certifiable.

Then again, how often did lunacy win you $300,000 at the horse track?

22

"Thomas."

A sweet voice. Calling his name. Like honey. *Thomas.*

"Thomas, wake up."

A woman's voice. Her hand was on his cheek. He was waking, but he wasn't sure if he was really awake yet. The hand on his cheek could be part of a dream. For a moment, he let it be a dream.

He relished that dream. This was Monique's hand on his cheek. The strongheaded French woman who'd been horrified that he might actually die. *Thomas!* she'd cried. *Thomas!*

No, no. This wasn't Monique. This was Rachelle. Yes, that was better. Rachelle was kneeling beside him, caressing his cheek with her hand. Leaning over him, whispering his name. *Thomas.* Her lips were reaching out to touch his lips. Time to wake the handsome prince.

"Thomas?"

He jerked his eyes open. Blue sky. Waterfall. Rachelle.

He gasped and sat up. He was still on the beach where he'd fallen asleep during the night. He glanced around. No animals were in sight. No Roush. Only Rachelle.

"Do you remember?" she asked.

He did remember. The lake. Diving deep. Ecstasy. It still lingered here on the sound of the waterfall.

"Yes. I'm beginning to remember," he said. "What time is it?"

"Midday. The others are preparing."

He also remembered the Crossing and Teeleh's claim that he'd crash-landed. "They're preparing for what?"

"For the Gathering tonight." She said it as though he should know this.

"Of course." He looked at the lucent waters that stretched across the lake, tempted to swim again. Could he just dive in anytime he wanted to? He pushed himself to his knees. "Actually, I don't remember everything just yet."

"What don't you remember?"

"Well . . . I don't know. If I knew, I would remember. But I think I understand the Great Romance. It's about Elyon."

Her eyes lit up. "Yes."

"It's about choosing and rescuing and winning love because that's what Elyon does."

"Yes!" she cried.

"And it's something we do because we

are like Elyon in that way."

"You're saying that you want to choose me?"

"I am?"

She arched a brow. "And now you're trying to be tricky about it by pretending that you're not. But really you're desperate for my love, and you want me to be desperate for your love."

He knew that she was exactly right. It was the first time he could admit it to himself, but hearing her say it, Tom knew that he was falling in love with this woman who knelt by him on the banks of the lake. He was meant to woo her, but she was wooing him.

She was waiting for him to say something.

"Yes," he said.

Rachelle jumped to her feet. "Come!"

He pushed himself up and brushed the sand from his seat. "What should we do?"

"We should walk through the forest," she said with a mischievous glint in her eyes. "I will help you remember."

"Remember the forest?"

They started up the slope. "I was thinking other thoughts. But that would be nice too."

She turned back and stopped. "What is that?"

He followed her eyes and saw it clearly.

A large blotch of red discolored the white sand where he'd slept.

Blood.

He blinked. His dream? The fight in the hotel flashed through his mind.

No, it couldn't be. It was only a dream. He *had* no wounds.

"I don't know," he said. "I swam through some red waters in the lake, maybe from that?"

"You never know what will happen with Elyon," she said. "Only that it will be wonderful. Come."

They left the lake. But the red stain on the sand lingered in Tom's mind. There was the possibility, however remote, that he was different from Rachelle. That he really wasn't from here. That Rachelle was falling in love with someone who wasn't what he seemed.

That Teeleh was right.

An hour later the thought was gone.

They walked and laughed, and Rachelle toyed with his mind in lovely ways that only strengthened his resolve to win her. Very slowly they began to set aside the charade and embrace something deeper.

She showed him three new combat moves Tanis had shown her, two aerial and one from a prone position, in the event one fell while fighting, she said. He managed them all, but never with the same precision she demonstrated. Once she had to catch him when he toppled off balance toward her.

She had rescued him. He found it immensely appealing.

He immediately returned the favor by fighting off a hundred phantom Shataiki, sweeping her from her feet in the process. Unlike Tanis and Palus, he did not fall. It was quite a feat, and he began to feel very good about himself.

Rachelle sauntered beside him, hands clasped behind her back, lost in thought.

"Tell me more about your dreams," she said without looking at him.

"They're nothing. Nonsense."

"Oh? That's not what Tanis thinks. I want to know more. How real are they?"

Tanis was talking about his dreams? The last thing on Earth Tom wanted to do right now was discuss his dreams. Particularly with Rachelle. But he couldn't very well lie to her. "They seem real enough. But they're the histories. A totally different reality."

"Yes, so you've said. So it's like you're really living in the histories?"

"When I'm dreaming? Yes."

"And what do you think of this place" — she motioned to the trees — "in your dreams?"

It was the worst question she could have

asked. "Actually, when I'm dreaming it's like I'm there, not here."

"But when you're there, do you remember this place?"

"Sure. It's . . . it's like a dream."

She nodded. "So I'm like a dream?"

"You're not a dream." Tom could feel himself sinking. "You're walking right beside me, and I have chosen you."

"I'm not sure I like these dreams of yours."

"And neither do I."

"You have a mother and a father in these dreams?"

"Yes."

"You have a full life, with memories and passions and all that makes us human?"

This was positively not good.

She stopped on the path when he didn't respond. "What are you doing in your dreams?"

He had to tell her at some point. She'd forced the issue now. "You really want to know?"

"Yes. I want to know everything."

Tom paced, thinking of the best way to put it so that she could understand. "I'm living in the histories, before the Great Deception, trying to stop the Raison Strain. Trust me, it's a horrible thing, Rachelle. It's so real! Like I'm really there, and all of this here is a dream! I know it's not, of course, but when I'm there, I also know *that* is real." Was this a good way to put it? Somehow he doubted there was a good way to put it.

He continued before she could ask another question. Better that he control the direction of his confession.

"And yes, I have a full history in my dreams. Memories, a family, the full textures of real life."

"That's absurd," she said. "You've created a fantasy world with as much detail as the real one. Even more because in your dreams you haven't lost your memories. You have your own history there, but here you don't. Is that it?"

"Exactly!"

"It's preposterous!"

"I can hardly stand it. It's maddening. Just before you woke me up by the lake, I was fighting a man who was intent on killing me. I think he did kill me! Three shots with a gun to the body." He tapped his chest.

"Really? A gun? Some kind of fanciful weapon, I assume. And why were you fighting this man?"

Tom spoke without thinking. "He was trying to capture Monique."

"Monique. A woman?"

"A woman who means nothing to me!" No, that wasn't completely honest. "Not in a romantic way."

"You're in love with another woman in your dreams?"

"Of course not. Not at all. Her name is Monique de Raison, and she may be the key to stopping the Raison Strain. I'm helping her because she may help me save the world, not because she's beautiful. I can't just ignore her because you don't want me dreaming about her."

Too much information.

He was sure he saw a flash in Rachelle's eyes. Jealousy obviously was a sentiment that flowed from Elyon's veins. "You talk as if your dreams are more important than reality. Do you doubt that any of this is real?" She swept her hand to indicate the forest again. "That I am real? That our romance is real?"

"Never. Only when I'm dreaming."

He had to stop before he lost her completely.

Rachelle stared at him for a long time. He decided to keep his mouth shut. It was doing him no favors. She crossed her arms and looked away.

"I don't like these dreams of yours, Thomas Hunter. I really wish that you would stop them."

"I'm sure they will stop. I don't like them either."

"You are here. With me. I watched you sleep on the shores of the lake just an hour ago. Believe me when I say you weren't fighting a man, and you weren't killed. Your body was here! If I'd pinched you, you would have woken."

"That's right. And there was no Monique. It's just a dream, I know. I'm here. With you."

Her features softened. "Maybe your dreams are nothing more than a fascinating discovery. But I'm not sure how I feel about your dreaming of another woman when I'm in your arms. Do you understand?"

"Perfectly."

Rachelle didn't seem completely satisfied. "Other than trying to save the world, what do you do in the histories?"

"Well . . . I think I'm a writer. Though not a very good one, I'm afraid."

"A storyteller! You're a storyteller. Maybe that's why you're dreaming. You've hit your head, lost your memory, and forgotten how to tell stories like you did in your own village. But your subconscious hasn't forgotten. You're making up a grand story in your dreams!"

She just could be right. In fact, more likely than not.

"Maybe. What is Tanis saying?"

"That he and you might be successful in mounting an expedition to the black forest using information from your dreams of the histories. I think it's just a storyteller's fantasy, but he's quite excited."

Alarm spread through Tom's mind. Clearly Michal's warning hadn't affected Tanis.

"He said that?"

"Yes. If I hadn't insisted on coming to the lake alone to find you when Michal told us you were here, he would have come too. He says that he has some new ideas to share with you."

Tom made a mental note to avoid the man until he sorted this out.

"I'm glad you came alone," he said.

"So am I."

"And I'll try not to dream."

"Or better, dream of me."

The gathering that night washed away any fears and doubts lingering in Tom's mind. They swept up the path to the lake, silent during the last half of the fifteen-minute trek. Tom ran onto a patch of white sand on the right side of the lake. He absently realized that the red blotch was gone.

As far as memory permitted, this was his first Gathering.

A warm mist from the waterfall already floated across the group. Many of the people were already prone on the sand, their hands outstretched toward the thundering water.

Tom fell to his knees, heart pounding with anticipation. It had been too long, far too long. A warm mist suddenly hit his face. His vision exploded with a red fireball and he gasped, sucking more of the mist into his lungs.

Elyon.

He was aware of the wetness tickling his tongue. The sweetest taste of sugar laced with a hint of cherry flooded his mouth. He swallowed. The aroma of gardenia blossoms mushroomed in his nostrils.

Ever so gently, Elyon's water engulfed him, careful not to overpower his mind. But deliberately.

The red fireball suddenly melted into a river of deep blue that flowed into the base of Tom's skull and wound its way down his spine, caressing each nerve. Intense pleasure shot down every nerve path to Tom's extremities. He dropped to his belly, body shaking in earnest.

Elyon.

The waterfall's pounding increased in intensity, and the mist fell steadily on his back as he lay prostrate. His mind reeled under the power of this Creator, who spoke with sights and colors and smells and emotions.

Then the first note fell on his ears. Flew past his ears and bit into his mind. A low note, lower than the throaty roar of a million tons of fuel thundering from a rocket's base. The rumbling tone shot up an octave, rose to a forte, and began etching a melody in Tom's skull. He could hear no words, only music. A single melody at first, but then joined by another melody, entirely unique yet in harmony with the first. The first caressed his ears; the second laughed. And a third melody joined the first two, screaming in pleasure. And then a fourth and a fifth, until Tom heard a hundred melodies streaming through his mind, each one unique, each one distinct.

All together not more than a single note from Elyon.

A note that cried, *I love you.*

Tom breathed in great gasps now. He stretched his arms out before him. His chest heaved on the warm sand. His skin tingled with each minute droplet of mist that touched him.

Elyon.

Me too! Me too! he wanted to say. *I love you too.*

He wanted to yell it. To scream it with as much passion as he felt from Elyon's water now. He opened his mouth and groaned. A dumb, stupid groan that said nothing at all, and yet it was him, talking to Elyon.

And then he formed the words screaming

in his mind. "I love you, Elyon," he breathed softly.

Immediately, a new burst of colors exploded in his mind. Gold and blue and green cascaded over his head, filling each fold of his brain with delight.

He rolled to one side. A hundred melodies swelled into a thousand — like a heavy, woven chord blasting down his spine. His nostrils flared with the pungent smell of lilac and rose and jasmine, and his eyes watered with their intensity. The mist soaked his body, and each inch of his skin buzzed with pleasure.

Tom shouted, "I love you!"

He felt as though he stood in an open doorway on the edge of a vast expanse, bursting with raw emotion that was fabricated in colors and sights and sounds and smells, blasting into his face like a gale. It was as though Elyon flowed like a bottomless ocean, but Tom could taste only a stray drop. As though he were a symphony orchestrated by a million instruments, and a single note threw him from his feet with its power.

"I love youuuu!" he cried.

He opened his eyes. Long ribbons of color streamed through the mist above the lake. Light spilled from the waterfall, lighting the entire valley so it looked as though it might be midday. The entire company lay prone as the mist washed over their bodies. Most shook visibly but made no sound that could be heard above the waterfall. Tom let his head drop back to the sand.

And then Elyon's words echoed through his mind.

I love you.
You are precious to me.
You are my very own.
Look at me again, and smile.

Tom wanted to scream. Unable to contain himself, Tom let the words flow from his mouth like a flood.

"I will look at you *always*, Elyon. I worship you. I worship the air you breathe. I worship the ground you walk on. Without you, there is nothing. Without you, I'll die a thousand deaths. Don't ever let me leave you."

The sound of a child giggling. Then the voice again.

I love you, Thomas.
Do you want to climb up the cliff?

Cliff? He saw the pearl cliffs over which the water poured.

A voice called over the lake. "Who has made us?" Tanis was on his feet, crying out this challenge.

Tom struggled to his feet. The rest were scrambling to their feet. They yelled together above the thundering falls, "Elyon! Elyon is our Creator!"

Like a display of fireworks, the colors continued to expand in his mind. He gazed about, momentarily stunned. None of the others looked his way. Their display was simple abandonment to affection, foolish in any other context, but completely genuine here.

The voice of the child suddenly echoed through his mind again.

Do you want to climb the cliff?

Tom spun toward the forest that ended at the cliff. Climb the cliff? Behind him the others started running into the lake.

Giggling again.

Do you want to play with me?

Now inexplicably drawn, Tom ran up the shore toward the cliff. If the others noticed, they showed no sign. Soon only his own panting accompanied the thundering falls.

He cut into the forest and approached the cliffs with a sense of awe. How could he possibly climb this? He considered turning back and joining the others. But he had been called here. To climb the cliffs. To play. He ran on.

He reached its base, looked up. There was no way he could climb the smooth stone wall. But if he could find a tree that grew close to the cliff, and if the tree was tall enough, he might be able to reach the top along its branches. The tree right beside him, for example. Its glowing red trunk reached to the cliff's lip a hundred meters up.

Tom swung himself up onto the first branch and began his ascent. It took him no more than a couple of minutes to reach the treetop and climb out to the cliff. He dropped from the branch to the stone surface below. To his left he could hear the thundering waterfall as it poured over the edge. He stood up and raised his eyes.

Before him, water lapped gently on a shore not more than twenty paces from the cliff's edge. Another lake. A sea, much larger than the lake. Shimmering green waters stretched to the horizon, neatly bordered by a wide swath of white sand, which edged into a towering blue-and-gold forest topped by a green canopy.

Tom stepped back and drew a deep breath. The white sandy swath bordering the emerald waters was lined with strange beasts who stood or crouched at the water's edge. The animals were like the white lions below, but these seemed to glow with pastel colors. And they lined the beach in evenly spaced increments that continued as far as he could see.

He spun to the waterfall and saw at least a hundred creatures hovering above the water cascading down the cliff, like giant dragonflies. Tom eased back toward a rock behind him. Had they seen him? He studied the creatures hovering with translucent wings in a reverent formation. What could they possibly be doing?

So this was Elyon's water. A sea that extended as far as the eye could see. Maybe farther.

"Hello."

Tom turned around. A little boy stood not five feet from him on the shore. Tom stumbled back two steps.

"Don't be afraid," the boy said, smiling. "So, you're the one who's lost?"

The small boy stood to Tom's waist. His brilliant green eyes stared wide and round beneath a crop of very blond hair. His bony shoulders held thin arms that hung loosely at his sides. He wore only a small white loincloth.

Tom swallowed. "Yes, I suppose so," he said.

"Well, I see you're quite adventurous. I believe you're the first of your kind to walk these cliffs." The boy giggled.

Incredible. For so small and frail a boy, he held himself with the confidence of someone much older. Tom guessed he must be about ten. Although he certainly didn't talk like a ten-year-old.

"Your name is Thomas?" the boy asked.

He knows my name. Is he from another village? Maybe my own? "Is this okay? I can be up here?"

"Yes. You're perfectly all right. But I don't think any of the others could get past the lake to bother climbing the cliff."

"Are you from another village?" he asked.

The boy stared at him, amused. "Do I look like I'm from another village?"

"I don't know. No, not really. Am I from another village?"

"I suppose that's the question, isn't it?"

"Then do you know who called me?"

"Yes. Elyon called you. To meet me."

There was something about the boy. Something about the way he stood with his feet barely pressing into the white sand. Something about the way his thin fingers curled gently at the end of his arms; about the way his chest rose and fell steadily and the way his wide eyes shone like two flawless emeralds. The boy blinked.

"Are you like a . . . Roush?"

"Am I like a Roush? Well, yes, in a way. But not really." The boy raised an arm to the hovering dragonfly creatures without looking their way. "They are like Roush, but you may think of me however you want now." He turned his head to the line of lionlike creatures lining the sea. "They are known as Roshuim."

Tom eyed the boy. "You . . . you're greater, aren't you? You have greater knowledge?"

"I know as much as I've seen in my time."

The boy definitely wasn't talking like a small boy. "And how long is that?" Tom asked.

The child looked at him quizzically for a moment. "How long is what?"

"How long have you lived?"

"A very long time. But far too short to even begin to experience what I will experience in my time."

The boy scratched the top of his head with one hand. He spoke again, staring out to the sea. "What is it like to come to Elyon after ignoring him for so long?"

"You know that? How do you know that?"

The boy's eyes twinkled. "Do you want to walk?"

The boy turned to the white sandy shore and walked casually without looking back. Tom glanced around and then followed him.

It was as light as day, although Tom knew it was actually night.

"I saw you looking out over the water. Do you know how great this sea is?" the boy asked.

"It looks pretty big."

"It extends forever," the boy said. "Isn't that something?"

"Forever?"

"That's pretty clever, isn't it?"

"Elyon can do that?"

"Yes."

"Well, that's . . . that's pretty clever."

The boy stopped and walked to the water's edge. Tom followed him tentatively. "Scoop up some of the water," the child said.

Tom stooped, gingerly placed his hand into the warm green water and felt its power run up his arm the moment his fingers touched its surface — like a low-voltage electric shock that hummed through his bones. He scooped the water out and watched it drain between his fingers.

"Pretty neat, huh? And there's no end to it. You could travel at many times the speed of light toward the center, and never reach it."

It seemed incredible that anything could extend forever. Space, maybe. But a body of water? "That doesn't seem possible," Tom said.

"It does when you understand who made it. It came from a single word. Elyon could open his mouth, and a hundred billion worlds like this would roll off his tongue. Maybe you underestimate him."

Tom looked away, suddenly embarrassed by his own stupidity. Did he underestimate him? How could anyone ever *not* underestimate someone so great?

The child reached up his frail hand and placed it in Tom's. "Don't feel bad," he said softly.

Tom wrapped his fingers around the small hand. The boy looked up at him with wide green eyes, and more than anything Tom had ever wanted to do, he desperately wanted to reach down and hold this child. They began walking again, hand in hand now. "Tell me," Tom asked. "There's one thing that I've been wondering about."

"Yes?"

"I've been having some dreams. I fell in the black forest and lost my memory, and ever since then I've been dreaming of the histories."

"I know."

"You do?"

"Word gets around."

"But can you tell me why I'm having these dreams? Honestly, I know this sounds ridiculous, but sometimes I wonder if my dreams are really real. Or if *this* is a dream. It would help if I knew for certain which reality was real."

"Maybe I could help with a question. Is the Creator a lamb or a lion?"

"I don't understand."

"Some would say that the Creator is a lamb. Some would say he's a lion. Some would say both. The fact is, he is neither a lamb nor a lion. These are fiction. Metaphors. Yet the Creator is both a lamb and a lion. These are both truths."

"Yes, I can see that. Metaphors."

"Neither changes the Creator," the boy said. "Only the way we think of him. Like me. Am I a boy?"

Tom felt the boy's small hand, and his heart began to melt because he knew what the boy was saying. He couldn't speak.

"A boy, a lion, a lamb. You should see me fight. You wouldn't see a boy, a lion, *or* a lamb."

Five minutes of silence passed without another word. They only walked, a man and a boy, hand in hand. But it wasn't that. Not at all.

And then Tom remembered his question about the dreams.

"What about my dreams?"

"Maybe it's the same with your dreams."

"That both are real?"

"You'll have to figure that out."

They walked on. It might have been a

cloud, not sand, that they walked on, and Thomas wasn't sure he'd know the difference. His mind was reeling. His hand was by his side, moving as he walked. In it was this boy's hand. A tremble had set into his fingers, but the boy didn't show he noticed.

Clearly he did.

"What about the black forest?" Tom asked. "I've been in it. I may have taken a drink of the water. Is that why I'm dreaming about the histories?"

"If you'd chosen Teeleh's water, everyone would know."

Yes, that made sense.

"Then maybe you can tell me something else. How is it that Elyon can allow evil to exist in the black forest? Why doesn't he just destroy the Shataiki?"

"Because evil provides his creation with a choice," the child said as though the concept was very simple indeed. "And because without it, there could be no love."

"Love?" Tom stopped.

The boy's hand slipped out of his. He turned, brow raised.

"Love is dependent on evil?" Tom asked.

"Did I say that?" A mischievous glint filled the boy's eyes. "How can there be love without a true choice? Would you suggest that man be stripped of the capacity to love?"

This was the Great Romance. To love at any cost.

The child turned back to the sea and gazed out.

"Do you know what would happen if anyone did choose Teeleh's water instead of Elyon's water?" the boy asked.

"Michal said the Shataiki would be freed. That they would bring death."

"Death. More than death. A living death. Teeleh would own them; this is the agreement. Their minds and their hearts. The smell of their death would be intolerable to Elyon. And his jealousy will exact a terrible price." The boy's green eyes flashed as though strobes had been ignited behind them. "The injustice will be against Elyon, and only blood will satisfy him. More blood than you can possibly imagine."

He said it so plainly that Tom wondered if he'd misspoken. But the boy wasn't the kind who misspoke.

"If they become Teeleh's, is there a way to win them back?" he asked.

No response.

"Anyway, I can't imagine anyone ever changing or leaving this place," Tom said.

"You don't have to leave, you know."

"Except when I dream."

"Then don't dream," the boy said.

The idea suddenly sounded like such a simple solution. If he stopped dreaming,

Bangkok would be no more!

"I can do that?"

The boy hesitated. "You could. There is a fruit you could eat that would stop your dreams."

"Just like that, no more histories?"

"Yes. But the question is, do you really want to? You'll have to decide. The choice is yours. You will always have that choice. I promise."

It was early in the morning when the boy finally led Tom back to the cliff, and after a great big bear hug, Tom descended the red tree, made his way back to the village, and quietly sneaked into bed in the house of Palus.

He might have been mistaken, but he was sure that he could hear the sound of a boy's voice singing as he drifted off to sleep.

23

"Thomas."

A sweet voice. Calling his name. Like honey. *Thomas.*

"Thomas, wake up."

A woman's voice. Her hand was on his cheek. He was waking, but he wasn't sure if he was really awake yet. The hand on his cheek could be part of a dream. For a moment he let it be a dream.

He relished that dream. This was Rachelle's hand on his cheek. The strong-headed woman who kept showing him up with her fighting moves.

"Thomas?"

His eyes snapped open. Kara. He gasped and jerked up.

"Thomas, are you okay?" Kara, face white, stood back staring at the bed. "What is this?" But Tom's eyes were on the air conditioner where rolled white sheets had been cut and Monique had been freed. She was gone.

"Thomas! Talk to me!"

"What?" He looked at her. "What's —"

The sheets were wet. Soaked in red. Blood?

Tom scrambled out of the bed. He'd been lying on sheets soaked in his blood. He grabbed his chest and belly as visions of the attacker shooting into his body flashed through his mind. Two silenced shots. *Phewt! Phewt!*

Yes, there was that, but, more important, there was the lake and the boy. He looked up at Kara.

"God is real," he said.

"What?"

"God. He's . . . wow." His head spun with the memory of the lake. He could feel a wild grin tempt his face, but his mind wasn't working in full cooperation with all of his muscles yet.

"Well, at least I dreamed that he's real," he said. "Not just real, like wow he exists, but . . . real, like you can talk to him. I mean, maybe touch him."

"Very nice," she said. "In the meantime, here, where I live, we're standing next to a bed covered in your blood!"

"I was shot," he said.

She stared at him, unbelieving. "Are you sure? Where?"

"Right here. And here." He showed her. Chest and gut. "I swear I was shot. Someone broke in; we fought; he shot me. And then he must have taken Monique."

"I called you. Was that before or after?"

"You called before. He was here when you called." Suddenly Bangkok was making more sense than the lake. "Actually, I think your call unnerved him. The point is . . ." Yes, what was the point?

"The point is what?"

"I'm not dead."

Kara looked at his stomach. Then his eyes. "I don't get it. You're saying that you were healed in your dreams?"

"It's not the first time."

"But you were shot, right? You were shot and killed. How's that possible?"

"I don't know that I was killed. I lost consciousness. But there, in my dreams, I was lying on the shores of the lake. The air was full of mist from the waterfall. Water. The water is what heals. I was probably healed before I could die."

He pulled the sheets from the bed, grabbed the mattress. Flipped it over. Kara hadn't removed her stare.

"You're dead serious."

"No, not dead."

She looked away, paced to the end of the bed. Turned back. "Do you understand the implications?"

"I don't know, do I?" He quickly untied the homemade ropes from the air conditioner. "There's a lot I'm not clear on. But one thing I am sure of is that Monique is

388

gone. The guy who took her wasn't your everyday thug."

She was still preoccupied with his healing. Tom stopped.

"Look, I'm not indestructible, if that's what you're thinking. There's no way."

"And how would you know?"

"Because I think you're right — both realities are real, at least in some ways. Evidently, if I get shot here and then fall asleep and get water poured on me there before I die, I get healed. But if I get killed here and there's no water around to heal me, I just might die."

"You're like Wolverine or somebody now? You get hit in the head or shot in the chest, and there's not a mark on you! That's incredible!"

It *was* incredible. But there was more, wasn't there? A simple bit of information that had nagged at him since he'd talked to Teeleh, that bat in the other place. The details began to buzz in his brain, and he felt the first hints of panic.

"Well, that's not all," he said. "For starters, I'm pretty sure that the guy who shot me and took Monique is the guy who's going to blackmail the world with the Raison Strain."

Tom began to pace. He'd bundled up the bloody sheets and now held them in his right hand.

"Or at least the guy works for whoever is planning this. That's not all. I'm pretty sure that the only way they even *know* the Raison Vaccine has the potential to mutate into a deadly virus is because *I* spilled the beans to someone who told them."

"That can't be. That would mean without you the mutation wouldn't happen? You're saying you're the *cause* of this thing?"

"That's exactly what I'm saying. I learn about the Raison Strain as a matter of history in my dreams, I tell someone, 'Hey, such and such is going to happen,' and they decide to make such and such actually happen. Like a self-fulfilling prophecy. If I'd kept my mouth shut and not told the State Department or the CDC, no one would even know the Raison Strain was possible."

She chewed on that for a moment. "So you've caused the very virus you're trying to stop? That's a trip."

"Where can we stash these sheets?"

"Under the bed." They stuffed the bedding under the frame.

"But if that's true," Kara said, "can't you change something now that would ruin the rest of what happens? You go back to the histories, find out that X-Y-Z happened, then return and make sure that doesn't happen."

"Maybe. Maybe not. I can't get information about the histories that easily anymore."

"What about the black forest?"

"I went to the black forest! I'm not going back again, no way!"

"What if it's a dream? And it saves us here?"

"There's more." Tom turned slowly, remembering his conversation with Teeleh. But there was something he was missing from it, he was sure. He'd gone to prove himself to Monique, and he'd done that. But he'd also learned about the antivirus.

He'd repeated the antivirus.

"What if . . ." A chill snaked down his spine. He turned back to Kara, stunned by the thought. "What if I inadvertently told them how to do it?"

"To make the virus?"

"No, they know that. Intense heat. They can figure it out. But that doesn't do anyone any good. You put the virus in the air and three weeks later, everyone's dead. Including the person who releases it. But if you have an antivirus, a cure or a vaccine to the virus, you can —"

"Control it," Kara finished. "The threat of force. Like having the only nuclear arsenal in the world."

"And I think I might have given it to them."

"How?"

"Teeleh. He tricked me. Just before he gave me the information, he cut me." He was speaking through a daze, as if to himself. "I could swear I heard myself saying it out loud."

"So then you also have it. What good is the virus to them, if you have the antivirus?"

"Do I?" He cocked his head. He couldn't remember it. "I . . . can't think of it right now."

"I'm not going to pretend to understand all of this, but we have to get out of here. The police bought my story, and I talked to Monique's father. I called because he agreed to hold the shipments. I nearly killed myself getting here unseen when you didn't pick up. I think I can get us in to see Raison, but he's pretty bent out of shape. When he finds out that Monique's gone again . . ."

She sighed.

They left the room looking lived in but not massacred.

"You what?"

The sharp nose on Jacques de Raison's angular face was red, and for good reason. He'd just lost, then found, then lost his daughter, all within eight hours.

"I didn't lose her," Tom objected. "She was taken from me. You think I would take her just to lose her?" He glanced from the dark-haired Raison to Kara and then back. He had to get the situation back in hand. Or at the very least back in mind.

"Please, if you'll have a seat, I'll try to explain."

Jacques glared at him, tall and commanding, the kind of man who had grown accustomed to getting what he wanted. He sat in a wing chair by his desk, eyes fixed on Tom.

"I'll give you five minutes. Then I call the authorities. Three governments are looking for you, Mr. Hunter. I'm quite sure they'll make quick work of you."

Tom had driven from the hotel to Raison Pharmaceutical. Kara wanted to know what had happened in the colored forest, so, with only a little encouraging, he told her. He told her about meeting Teeleh at the Crossing. About the lake. About the boy. They finally agreed that none of it proved God really did exist, but Tom was having trouble reconciling the reasoning with his experience. He changed the subject and told her about Rachelle.

The world was facing a crisis inadvertently caused by Tom, and he was off learning the fine points of romancing Rachelle. It didn't seem right, Kara had said.

Getting past the gates and in to see

Jacques de Raison required no fancy footwork on Tom's part this time. Three ambitious guards nearly took off both their heads in the courtyard before Raison Pharmaceutical's prestigious founder marched in and suggested they lower their rifles. They dipped their heads and backed off.

Jacques de Raison had ushered them into this library, with its tall bookcases and a dozen high-backed black leather chairs positioned around a long mahogany table. Now he and Kara had the prodigious task of convincing this man that his true enemy was the Raison Strain, not Thomas Hunter.

Jacques' eyes dropped to a large bloodstain on the pocket of Tom's Lucky jeans. His shirt, which had been off at the time of his shooting, had been spared the carnage.

Tom took a deep breath. "The fact of the matter is, Mr. Raison, your daughter and I were attacked. I was shot and left for dead. Monique was taken by force."

"You were left for dead," the man said. "I can see that."

Tom waved off his cynicism. "I clean up good. The man who shot me was the same person I was trying to protect your daughter from in the first place. I knew there was a potential problem. I tried to convince her of it, and when she refused, I forced her hand."

"That's utter nonsense."

"My five minutes aren't up. Just listen to me for a minute here. You may not like it, but I may be the only one who can save your daughter. Please listen."

"Please, Mr. Raison," Kara said evenly. "I told you before, this goes way beyond Thomas or Monique."

"Yes, of course; the Raison Vaccine will mutate and infect untold millions."

"No," Tom said. "Billions."

"Monique submitted the vaccine to the most ardent series of tests, I assure you."

"But not to heat," Tom said. "She told me that herself."

"The fact is, you can't substantiate any of this," Raison said. "You kidnap my daughter at gunpoint, and then you expect me to believe you did it for her own good. Forgive my suspicions, but I think it's more likely that you have her hidden away right now. At any moment I'll get a call from an accomplice demanding money."

"You're wrong. What you will get is a call demanding either information or samples of the vaccine. Test it yourself. The virus mutates under extreme heat. How long would it take to confirm that?"

It was the first thing Tom had said that seemed to sink in.

"She is my only daughter," he said. "There is nothing I love more. Do you understand this? I will do whatever it takes to bring her home safely."

"So will I," Tom said. "How long to test the vaccine?"

"You really do believe this? It's preposterous."

"Then the tests will show that I'm wrong. If I'm right, then we know we have a very big problem. How long?"

"Two weeks under normal circumstances," Raison said.

"Forget normal."

"A week. There are a number of variables. Exact temperature, length of exposure, other external elements."

"A week is too long, way too long!" Tom crossed to the long mahogany table and spun around. "If I'm right, just for the sake of argument, and they knew exactly how to initiate this mutation, how long would it take them to have a usable virus?"

"I can't answer —"

"Just pretend, Jacques. Best-case scenario, how long?"

He studied Tom. "Could be a couple of hours."

"A couple of hours. I suggest either you start taking me at my word or you start your tests, because if you're right, God help us all."

"Could take weeks. This is all impossible to believe."

The phone on Raison's desk rang.

"Then you'd better do some soul-searching, because Monique's life rests in your ability to believe."

The man stood and snatched up the phone. "Yes." He was silent for five seconds. "Who is this? Who . . ." Silence. Fear spread through the man's eyes. "How will I know . . . hello?"

The phone went limp in his hand. "They've . . . they've given me seventy-two hours to turn over all our research and all existing samples of the vaccine, or they will kill her."

Tom nodded. A lump gathered in his throat. "You'd better turn this facility into one giant testing lab. Twenty-four seven. And you're going to need a lot more than the virus. You're going to need a new antivirus."

24

The imminent threat posed to his
daughter, Monique, seemed to wilt Jacques
de Raison. Only at his urging did the
Bangkok authorities agree to delay taking
Thomas into custody. He would go, they
promised. The French and the Americans
were both breathing down their necks. But
considering the fact that another party had
evidently swooped in to take Monique, and
considering Tom's insistence that he might
be able to help, they would keep him
under house arrest in the mansion at
Raison Pharmaceutical.

Tom spent an hour with Kara, working
through their options. The most obvious
solution to the entire mess was to recall the
antivirus Teeleh had given Tom in his
dreams. But half an hour of Kara's prying
and another ten minutes of Tom beating
his head against a metaphorical wall
yielded nothing. His mind was simply
blank on the details. In the end, only one
plan made any sense to either of them.

"I need to talk to him," Tom announced

outside Raison's office.

"He is busy," the guard said.

"Did you see the tape of the man who fought your two gate guards the other day?"

The guard paused. "You're threatening me?"

"No. I was wondering if you saw it. But yes, I am that man. Please, I really need to speak to him."

The man looked Tom over. "One moment." He poked his head in the door, asked a question, then pushed the door open.

Thomas walked in. Jacques de Raison looked up from his desk, haggard and distracted.

"Any progress?" Tom asked.

"I told you a week! Seventy-two hours? There's a much simpler solution to this. If I give them what they want, they will give me Monique. We will deal with them later, through the world courts."

"Unless I'm right," Tom said. "Unless by giving them everything you have, you severely hamper any attempt to produce an antidote to the Raison Strain."

Raison slammed his fist on the desk. "There *is* no Raison Virus!"

"Monique will tell you differently when we find her. By then it will be too late."

"Then I'll give them what they want and

keep what I need to reproduce the vaccine."

"If you give them what they want, it'll slow you down. The Raison Virus will do its work in three weeks."

They faced off. Tom felt oddly resigned. There were only two things he could do now: Find Monique, who alone might be able to find a way out of the mess her vaccine would make, and prepare the world for the Raison Strain. Somehow he had to do both.

"Mr. Raison, I want you to consider something. I don't think they have any intention of releasing Monique anytime soon, even if you do meet their demands. She's too valuable to them. Alive. If I'm right —"

"If I'm right, if I'm right — how many times are you asking me to assume that you're right?"

"As many as it takes. If I'm right, the only way to get Monique back to safety is to go after her." Tom sat in one of the leather chairs facing the man. "For that we need help. And there's one way to get help."

"I have money, Mr. Hunter. If it's muscle we need —"

"No, we need more than a little muscle here. We need eyes and ears everywhere. And we need to be able to move quickly. For that we need governments. If I'm

400

right — yes, I know, there I go again — the lid is going to blow off this whole thing in the next few days. I suggest we ease the pressure now and bring in some partners."

He said it almost exactly the way he and Kara had rehearsed it. Actually, given a little space and the right training, he might make a pretty decent diplomat. Something he should take up with Tanis.

"What do you want me to do, inform the world that my vaccine is actually a deadly virus? It will kill the company. I would be better off to meet their demands."

"I'm not suggesting you tell the world any such thing. Not yet." Tom made the decision then, looking at the haggard man in front of him. "I'm suggesting you let me speak to a few key players confidentially."

"You want me to put my company's future in your hands?"

"Your company's future is already in my hands. If I'm right, there won't be a company in the future. If I'm wrong, my claims will be written off as the ravings of a maniac, and your company will be just fine. Which is why I, not you, need to make selective contact with a few leaders. A call from you, admitting that your vaccine might be quite deadly, would require them to take certain actions. Raison Pharmaceutical would be dead and buried by morning. I, on the other hand, have more latitude. I don't officially represent Raison Pharmaceutical."

The man was mulling over Tom's idea. "I'm not sure what you're asking."

"I'm asking that you let me — assist me to — make contact with the outside world. My hands are tied without you. I'm in captivity here. Let me spill the beans about the danger the Raison Strain presents to the world. It will give them reason to throw some resources behind finding Monique. Nothing like a virus to motivate the right people."

Tom knew by the look in Jacques de Raison's eyes that he was already warming to the idea. "I would have plausible deniability," Raison said.

"Yes. I'll make the calls without your official endorsement. That will insulate you even while making an appeal for help."

It was a flawless idea. He should've gone into politics.

"You're simply asking for the use of a phone? You can't just place calls to world governments and expect them to be answered."

"I want to use your personal contacts. Only those approved by you, of course. The U.S. State Department, the French government, the British. Maybe Indonesia — they have a large population nearby. The point is, we need to convince a few people with resources to take the kidnapping of your daughter as more than an industrial espionage case. We need them to consider the possibility of risk to their own national security and help us find Monique."

"And you really think I would let you do that?"

"I don't think you have a choice. This whole thing is about to hit the fan anyway. This gives us a chance. To warn the right people. To find Monique."

Jacques de Raison went one step further than lending Tom use of his contacts and a phone. He lent his secretary, Nancy.

"Tell him that if he doesn't clear a line to the secretary in the next hour, I'm going to . . ." Tom paused, considering. "Whatever. Tell him I'm going to set off a nuke or something. Don't any of these people have the foresight to even *consider* that we could be in a bit of trouble here?"

Kara watched her brother pace. They'd been at it for five hours, and the results could hardly be worse. The French were not only hopeless but, in her thinking, downright rude. She'd expected much more cooperation from Raison's home country. Evidently their current administration wasn't excited about the fact that Raison Pharmaceutical had left France in the first place. They seemed interested enough in putting on a good face in this kidnapping mess, but when it came right down to getting a politician to break his schedule for a ten-minute phone call with Tom, all interest evaporated. It was a legal matter, they said.

The British had been a little more congenial. But the bottom line was still roughly the same. The Germans, the Italians, even the Indonesian government — no one was in the mood to listen to the rantings of a crazed prophet who'd kidnapped the woman in Bangkok.

Kara walked toward her brother. The fact that it was three in the morning didn't help matters much. He was practically sleepwalking. Then again, if he was right and this was the dream, he *was* sleepwalking.

"Thomas." She rubbed his back. "You okay?"

He tried to smile. "Not really. I've gone from being terrified that there's a comet coming to being horrified that no one believes there's a comet coming."

"What do you expect? There's been a comet coming every year for two thousand years. It never lands. So now a twenty-five-year-old in jeans claims to live in his dreams, where he learns the world is about to end. He threatens to blow up the castle unless the king believes him. Why should the secretary of state break his meeting with the prince of Persia to take your call?"

"Thanks for the encouragement, sis."

"Look, I know none of this matters if no one will listen, but there is another way, you know."

He studied her face. They walked away from the desk. "You mean go back . . ."

"Well?" Kara said. "I know sleeping seems like the wrong thing here, but why not? For starters, if you don't sleep soon, you're going to fall into a coma anyway. And it's worked before, right? What if you could find out where she is?"

He shook his head. "This is different. The other stuff was a matter of histories. This is too specific. And like I said, I don't want to go back to the black forest, which is the only place I think I can get information."

He said it with so much conviction. He really did live with the constant awareness of his dreams. And he was changing.

The Thomas she knew as her brother had always been articulate, but he carried himself with a greater purpose now. He talked with more authority. Not enough to convince the French and the British, but enough to exchange a few rounds with some pretty powerful people before being sent packing, for his brazen approach to diplomacy as much as anything.

Her brother had somehow been chosen. She didn't understand how or why, and, truthfully, she wasn't ready to think it all through just yet. But she couldn't escape the growing certainty that this man who worked in the Java Hut in Denver just a few days ago was becoming someone very, very important.

"Then don't go back to the black forest. But there's a connection between your dreams and what's happening here, Thomas. Your dreams caused this, after all. There has to be a way to get more information. Go to sleep; nothing's happening here anyway."

He sighed. "You're right, I've got to sleep."

"You still can't remember the antivirus."

He shook his head. "No."

"I wish there was a way you could take me."

"Take you there? I'm not actually going anywhere, am I?"

"No. Your mind is though. Maybe there's a way to take my mind with you." She smiled. "Crazy, huh?"

"Yeah, crazy. I don't think that's possible."

"Neither is breathing in a lake," she said.

"Sir!"

Tom spun. It was Raison's secretary,

holding up a phone.

"I have the deputy secretary of the United States. Merton Gains. He's agreed to talk to you."

Deputy Secretary Merton Gains sat at the end of the conference table, listening to the others express opinions on a dozen different ways to look at yet another looming budget crisis. Paul Stanley was still out of town, but the secretary of state had never shown a reluctance to throw Gains in the mix when he was unavailable.

Half the cabinet was present, most of the notable ones excluding defense, Myers. A dozen aides. President Robert Blair sat across and down the table from Gains, leaning back as his advisers begged to differ. The subject was tax cuts again. To cut or not to cut. How hard to push. The economic fallout or gain, the political fallout or gain. Some things never changed, and the argument over taxes was one of them.

Which was only part of the reason Gains found his mind wandering. The rest of the reason was Thomas Hunter.

Fact: If his daughter hadn't died from a vaccine two years ago, he never would have spearheaded legislation to heighten scrutiny of new vaccines.

Fact: If he hadn't written the bill, his

407

friend Bob Macklroy never would have thought to call him about Thomas Hunter.

Fact: If Hunter hadn't called Bob and told him about the winner to the Kentucky Derby, Joy Flyer, Gains wouldn't have taken Hunter's call.

Fact: Hunter's prediction had been accurate.

Fact: Hunter had gone to the CDC and reported the potential outbreak. And he'd been pretty much stuffed.

Fact: Hunter had kidnapped Monique de Raison, the one person, he claimed, who could stop the virus by not shipping it in the first place.

Fact: Monique had been kidnapped again by someone else who now wanted the Raison Vaccine.

This was where the facts started fusing with Hunter's claims.

Claim: The party that took Monique did so because they, like Thomas, knew the vaccine could be turned into a deadly weapon and hoped to get what they needed through coercion.

Claim: This party also could have access to an antidote within reach.

Claim: If the world didn't get off its collective high horse, find Monique de Raison, and develop an antidote, very bad times that would make the budget crisis look like a game of dominoes were only days around the corner.

Hearing Thomas Hunter lay down the entire story, Gains couldn't help but entertain the few chills that had swept through his bones. This wasn't unlike the kinds of scenarios he'd pitched to the Senate more than once. And here it was, staring him in the face as a claim by a brazen man who was either totally deluded or who knew more than any man had any business knowing. There was something about Hunter's sincerity that tempted him to listen to more. And so he had.

Much more.

He'd even promised any help he could in the matter of Monique de Raison. What if? Just what if? Obviously old man Raison hadn't thrown Hunter out on his ear.

". . . Merton?"

Gains cleared his throat. "No, I don't think so." He glanced up. The president was looking at him with that lazy I-can-read-your-mind look. It meant nothing, but it had won him the presidency.

"Just one thing," Gains said. "I assume you all heard about the kidnapping in Bangkok yesterday. Monique de Raison, daughter of Jacques de Raison, founder of Raison Pharmaceutical."

"Don't tell me," President Blair said. "It was one of our military boys."

"No."

"My understanding is that the man originally involved was blindsided by a third party who now holds the woman," CIA Director Phil Grant said. "We're shifting some assets to lend a hand. I wasn't aware there was any new movement in the case."

"There isn't. But I've run across some information that I'll get over to your office, Phil. It seems there's a question about the stability of the Raison Vaccine, the real subject of this kidnapping. It's an airborne multipurpose vaccine that was supposed to enter the market today. Let's just say the incident in Bangkok has exposed the possibility, however slight, that the vaccine may not be stable."

"I haven't heard about this," the health secretary said. "I had the understanding the FDA was ready to approve this vaccine next week."

"No, this is new and, I might add, hearsay. Just a heads-up."

The table remained quiet.

"I'm not sure I understand, Merton," the president said. "I know you have a unique interest in vaccines, but how does this affect us?"

"This has nothing to do with the Gains Bill. It probably doesn't affect us. But if there is any truth to Hunter's claims and an unstable airborne vaccine does become a deadly virus, we could have a very significant health challenge on our hands. Just wanted to get the thought on the table." Wrong time, wrong place. You don't just stand up in a cabinet meeting, inform the leaders of the country that the sky might soon fall, and expect straight faces. Time for a bit of spin.

"Anyway, I'll get the report to each of you. It could affect health and finance at the least. Possibly homeland security. If word of this leaks, the country could react badly. People get very nervous about viruses."

There was a moment's pause.

"Seems straightforward enough," the president said. "Anyone else?"

25

Tom awoke to excited shouts outside the cottage. His confusion from the transition lasted only a moment. It was becoming customary. Every time he woke up, he had to make the switch, this time from a discussion with Deputy Secretary of State Merton Gains. They were making progress, real progress. He threw on his tunic and rushed from the house.

What greeted his eyes vanquished all thoughts of Bangkok and his success with Merton Gains.

There was a gigantic bright light suspended against the colored forest halfway up the sky. That the bright light hung in the sky wasn't so surprising — suns were known to do that. That the forest was up there as well was a different matter.

He jerked his head up and stared at the sky. Only there was no sky. The green forest was above him!

The people streamed toward the center of the village, chattering excitedly, dancing in delight as though their world suddenly going topsy-turvy was a great thing.

Tom turned, his mouth gaping, and gazed at the changed landscape. The forests rose from where they should have been and curved upward to where the sky had been. Far above him he could see meadows. And there, just to his right, at an elevation that must be over ten thousand feet, he was sure he saw a herd of horses galloping through a vertical meadow.

"It's upside down!"

"Yes, it is."

Tom whirled to find Michal squatting next to him, smiling at their new world.

"What's going on? What happened?"

"Do you like it?" the Roush asked with a childish smirk.

"I . . . I don't know what it is."

"Elyon is playing," Michal said. "He does this often, actually." Then he turned and leaped into the air after the others running for the Thrall. "Come. You will see."

Tom ran after Michal, almost tripping over a carving that someone had left in the yard. "You mean this is supposed to happen? Everything is safe?"

"Of course. Come. You will see."

It was as if the entire landscape had been painted on the inside of a gigantic sphere. The effects of gravity had been somehow reversed. Directly ahead of them, the road leading to the lake curved upward to meet it, only now the lake was slanted upward and the waterfall thundered horizontally. The only thing missing was the black forest.

The scale of things also had changed dramatically, so that the sky, which should have been many hundreds of miles above them, seemed much closer. Conversely, the other villages, which should have been visible, were not. Tom could see creatures running through the fields at impossible angles. Tens of thousands of birds dived about crazily. Half as many Roush swooped through the air as far as Tom could see, twisting and turning and flying in giant loops that reminded Tom of Gabil. It was nothing less than a circus.

They reached the Thrall and joined the others who, like Tom, stared with wide eyes at the sight before them.

It was Johan who first discovered that the atmosphere had changed as well. Changed so much, in fact, that he could stay in the air longer than usual when he jumped. Tom saw the young boy jumping, as if in slow motion.

"See, Thomas. See this?" Johan jumped again, harder this time.

He floated ten feet up and hung there.

"Thomas!" he cried. "I'm flying!"

Sure enough, Johan floated higher, about a hundred feet above the ground now, faltering slightly, screaming with laughter. Three other boys joined Johan in the air. Then the air began to fill with others who took to the air like children in their dreams.

"Tom," Michal said. Tom stood frozen by the sight. "Tom, try it."

Tom looked at the Roush with apprehension. "I can fly?"

"Of course. Elyon has changed the world for us. You'd better do it while you can because it won't last forever, you know. He is just playing. Try it."

Tom reached out instinctively and grasped the fur on Michal's head for stability. He jumped tentatively and found a lightness that surprised him. He smiled and jumped again, with more force. This time he floated several feet off the ground. The third time he leaped with all his strength, and he soared off balance into the air.

Johan buzzed by, squealing with delight. He had obviously learned how to maneuver. Tom found that he could gain momentum by shifting his body weight. There was just enough gravity to allow forward motion.

Within minutes, Tom flew with the rest of them. It wasn't long before Rachelle, Johan, and Michal joined him, and they set off to explore their new world. Chattering like children between peals of laughter, they flew to the inverted globe's highest crest and looked down on the village far below. They landed on a meadow, its flowers hanging upside down and pointing to the village now barely visible below. They walked upside down, hearts fluttering like butterflies, stepping carefully at the odd angle. Then they leaped off the grass, skimmed the trees down one side to the lake, and plunged into its jade waters.

In the warm green waters flush with light, they heard delighted laughter through the full range of the scale, from a deep, rumbling chuckle to a high, piercing giggle. And with wide-eyed glances to see if the others had also heard, they knew at the first chuckle that it was Elyon. If they were beside themselves with the staggering scope of the adventure, Elyon was beside himself at bringing it to them. And they laughed with him.

The hours fled. They played like children in an amusement park. There were no lines, and all rides were open. They flew and explored and twisted and turned, and it wasn't until after midday that the world began to reshape itself.

Within an hour it was back to normal. And Thomas remembered Bangkok.

Rachelle approached him, laughing throatily. "Now that, my dear Thomas, is what I call a fabulously good time!" She spontaneously threw her arms around his neck and squeezed him tight.

Tom was so surprised that he neglected to return the hug. Rachelle pulled back, but she didn't release him. She cocked her left leg behind her and stared into his eyes.

"Would you like to kiss me?"

"Kiss?" He could smell her sweet breath.

"I am helping you restore your memory, or have you forgotten that as well?"

"No." He swallowed.

"So then I would like to help you remember what it is like to kiss. I will have to show you, of course."

"Have you kissed anyone before? I mean, another man?"

"No. But I've seen it done. It's very clear in my mind. I'm sure I could show you exactly how it's done." Her eyes flashed. She ran a tongue over her lips. "Perhaps you should wet your lips first; they look quite dry."

He did it.

She leaned forward and touched her lips gently to his.

Tom closed his eyes. For a moment everything seemed to shut down. But in that same moment, a new world blossomed into existence.

No, not a new world. An old world.

He had done this before.

Rachelle's lips separated from his. "Trust me, dear, you're not in a dream. We'll see if that sparks your memory."

Heat spread down Tom's neck. He'd done this before. He'd kissed a woman before! He was sure of it.

He must have looked stunned, because Rachelle offered a satisfied smile. It was true, her kiss had taken his breath away, but there was more. It had brought something back.

"Tanis is coming to speak to you," she said. "He still insists that you're his apprentice in the fighting arts, but I think he's more interested in the histories." She put a finger on his lips. "Just remember, they're dreams. Don't get carried away."

Rachelle turned and stepped down the path, looking pleased and supremely confident despite her best efforts to appear nonchalant.

Tom's mind immediately chased a new thought that had presented itself while she warned him about the histories. Suppose both realities were not only real, but woven together? Like the boy had said at the upper lake, the lion and the lamb, both real. Both images of the same truth.

The same reality.

What if . . .

"Rachelle?"

She turned back. "Yes?"

If the two realities were interwoven, maybe he was meant to rescue in both. Rachelle here, Monique there. Could Rachelle lead him to Monique?

"You're staring at me," Rachelle said. "Is something wrong?"

"That was very wonderful," he said. *Very wonderful?*

She winked. "It was meant to be."

"Could I ask you a question?"

"Of course."

"If there was one place from which you would like to be rescued, where would it be?"

"That is your job. To rescue me."

He hurried forward, taken with the possibility that worked his mind. "Yes, but if there was one place. Say you were trapped and I was to rescue you. Where would that be? Please, I have to know so that I can rescue you."

"Well, I'm not exactly a storyteller. But . . ." She faced the forest and considered the question. "I would say that I would be held in a . . ." She spun toward him. "A great white cave full of bottles. Where a river and the forest meet."

"Really? Have you ever seen such a cave?"

"No. Why should I have? I am fabricating this for you, like a storyteller would."

"Is it here, in this forest, or somewhere far away?"

"Close by," she said after a moment's thought.

"And how would I find this cave?"

"By following the river, of course."

"And which direction is it from here?"

She looked at him curiously, as if objecting to his pressing for details. "That way," she said, pointing to her right. "East."

"East."

"Yes, east. I'm sure of it. The cave is a day's walk to the east."

He nodded. "Then I will rescue you."

"And when you rescue me, I should want another kiss," she said in complete seriousness.

"A kiss."

"Yes. A real kiss, not one from your silly dreams. A real kiss for a real woman who has fallen hopelessly in love with you, my dear prince."

She turned and walked down the path.

Tom walked quickly, if for no reason other than that he was thinking quickly.

Rachelle's kiss had spawned a whole new thread of possibility. It found its origin in this one thought: What if the two realities were more than just interwoven; what if they *depended* on each other?

What if what happened in Bangkok depended on what he did here? And what if what happened here depended on what happened in Bangkok? He already knew that if he was healed here, he was healed in Bangkok. And what skills he learned here, he could also use in Bangkok. But to think that the realities might *depend* on each other . . .

It was a staggering thought. Yet in so many ways it made sense. In fact, he was quite sure he'd come to the same conclusion in Bangkok. If it were another way, the boy would have said so. Elyon would have discouraged his dreams. But he hadn't. He'd left the choice up to him.

God wasn't a lamb or a lion or a boy. He was all of them if he chose to be. Or none of them. They were metaphors for the truth.

The truth. One truth. Two sides of one truth. Lion and lamb. The colored forest and Bangkok. Possible?

He still wasn't sure which reality was real, but he was that much more convinced now that *the truth* in both realities was real. And he had to be very careful to treat both as real.

Kara had said that.

Of course, this didn't mean that just because he loved Rachelle he was meant to love Monique. But it was quite possible he was meant to rescue Monique. That was why he was learning how to rescue Rachelle in this Great Romance.

It had to be. And if so, he may have just discovered *how* to rescue her. Or at least where to rescue her. He should sleep immediately, dream of Bangkok, and test this theory.

Tom stopped on the path. If he was meant to rescue Monique in the histories, then what was he supposed to do here, if this reality also depended on his dreams?

Tom stopped on the path. If Monique was real, wasn't it possible that Bill was also real? That they really had crash-landed in a spacecraft as Teeleh had insisted?

What if that was the only reality?

Maybe everything else was only a dream. He was really from Earth, being terribly affected by this strange planet. His stomach turned. The thought suddenly felt terribly compelling. It would explain everything.

He had to at least eliminate that as a possibility. The only way to know was to return to the black forest. He should at least consider —

"Thomas! Thomas Hunter, there you are!"

Tanis ran out of the forest, waving a crooked red stick in his right hand. "I have looked everywhere for you. Did you enjoy the change this morning?"

"Incredible," Tom said. "Spectacular!"

"The last time, he split the whole planet in two," Tanis said. "You may have forgotten, because it was before you lost your memory, but we could see the stars above and below. Then the fissure filled halfway with water and we dived. The dive itself lasted a full hour." Tanis chuckled and shook his head.

"That's amazing," Thomas said.

"This?" Tanis waved the stick. "You like it?"

"I meant your story's amazing — falling for an hour. What is that?"

"Well, it's something I've come up with based on something I remember from the histories. Maybe you know what it's called." He held it up proudly.

It was a stick, shaped and bent like waves with a hook on the end.

Tom shook his head. "No, I can't say that I recognize it. What does it do?"

"It's a weapon!" Tanis cried. He jabbed the air like a clumsy swordsman. "A weapon to scare off the vermin!"

"Why would that work?"

"You don't know? The Shataiki are terrified of the colored forest. This is a weapon from the colored forest. It follows that they would be terrified of it as well. We could use these weapons on our expedition."

Thomas took the device. It was a sword

of sorts from the histories. A very poor one. But the fact that it was made from the colored wood made for some interesting applications. Tom could hardly forget Teeleh's reaction to the small piece of colored wood from Johan.

Thomas swung the sword. It had an awkward feel. He looked at Tanis, saw the man was watching him with interest.

"This is called a sword. But you've forgotten to give it a sharp edge."

Tanis jumped forward. "Show me."

"Well, it needs to be flat here and sharp along this edge so that it can cut."

Tanis reached for the sword. "May I?"

Tom gave it to him. The man went to work with his hands. He was a storyteller, not a craftsman, but he had enough basic skill to quickly reshape the sword by coaxing the wood into what looked more like a sword. Tom watched, confounded by the sight. Rachelle had explained the process to him, but he'd failed miserably at all of his own attempts. Reshaping molecules with his fingers was something he would evidently have to relearn.

"There!" Tanis shoved out the sword.

Tom took it and ran his fingers along the now flat, sharp blade. Amazing. This in a matter of moments. What else could Tanis build with the proper guidance?

Tom felt a stab of caution.

"It would never work." He tossed the sword back to Tanis. "Remember, I've been in the black forest. One small sword against a million Shataiki — not a chance. Even if they are afraid of the wood."

"Agreed!" Tanis said. "It would never work." He hurled the sword into the forest. It clattered against a tree and fell to the ground.

"Now, about the histories —"

"I don't want to talk about the histories right now," Tom said.

"Your dreams are wearing you out? I understand completely. Then more training. As my apprentice, you have to apply yourself, Thomas Hunter. You're a quick study, I saw that the first time you attempted my double-back, but with the right practice you could be a master! Rachelle has taught you some new moves. Show me." He clapped twice.

"Right here?"

"Unless you'd rather do it in the village square."

Tom glanced around. They were in a small meadow. Birds chirped. A white lion watched them lazily from where it lay by a tall topaz blue tree.

"Okay." Tom took two long steps, launched himself into the air, twisted, and rolled into a forward flip. He landed squarely on his feet, back to imaginary opponent. Amazing how easy it felt.

"Bravo! Wonderful. I call that the reverse, because your opponent will never see your heel coming around on the flip. It would knock a black bat dizzy. Here, tear your tunic up the thigh to give you more freedom of movement."

Tom did so. The leather pants they often wore wouldn't present this challenge, but the tunics could be restrictive during wild kicks.

"Good. Show me another."

Tom showed him five more moves.

"Now," Tanis said, stepping forward. "Hit me!"

"I can't hit you! Why would I want to hit you?"

"Training, my apprentice. Defense. I will pretend you are a bat. You're bigger than a bat, of course, so I'll pretend you're three bats, standing on each other's shoulders. Now, you come for me and try to hit me, and I'll show you how to protect yourself."

"Sparring," Tom said.

"What?"

"It was called sparring in the histories."

"Sparring! I love it! Let's do some sparring."

They sparred for a long time, a couple of hours at least. It was the first time Thomas had been exposed to the full breadth of the fight method developed by Tanis, and it made the martial arts of his dreams feel simple by comparison.

True, all aerial maneuvers were easier here, in part, presumably, because of the atmosphere. But he suspected the moves were easier also because of the method itself. Hand-to-hand combat was far more about the mind than muscle, and Tanis had both in abundance. Not once was Thomas able to land a blow on the leader, though he got closer with each attempt.

Amazingly, Tom's stamina seemed nearly inexhaustible. He was growing stronger by the day. Recovering from his fall in the black forest.

"Enough," Thomas finally said.

Tanis lifted a finger. "Enough for the day. But you are improving with astonishing speed. I am proud to call you my apprentice. Now" — he put his hand on Tom's shoulder and turned him toward the forest — "we must talk."

The histories. The man was incorrigible.

"Tell me, what kind of weapon do you think would work against the Shataiki?"

"Tanis, have you ever confronted the Shataiki? Have you ever even stood on the banks of the river and watched them?"

"I've watched them from a distance, yes. Black bats with talons that look like they could pop a head off in short order."

"But why haven't you gone closer, if you

know they can't cross the river to harm you?"

"Where's the wisdom in that? They are tricky beasts; surely you've seen that. I would think that even to talk to them could prove fatal. They would employ all sorts of connivances to trick you into their water. Honestly, I am astounded you survived yourself."

"If you know all of this, why are you so adamant about an expedition? It would be suicide!"

"Well, I wouldn't talk to them! And you survived! Also, you know many things that might shift the balance of power. Before you came to us, I might never have seriously considered an attack, even though I wrote many stories about it. With your knowledge, we can defeat the vermin, Thomas! I know it!"

"No! We can't! They fight against the heart, not measly swords!"

"You think I don't know this? But tell me, wasn't it true that in the histories there was a device that could level the entire black forest in one moment?"

A nuclear bomb. Of course, any use of a nuclear weapon would be a landmark recorded in the histories.

"Yes. It was called a nuclear bomb. Do you know when such a device was used in the histories?"

"Not specifically," Tanis said. "Several times, if I remember. But mostly after the Great Deception. In the time of the tribulations. Are you saying that even with such a device we couldn't destroy the Shataiki?"

Tom considered this. He looked to the east where the black forest waited in darkness. What was it Michal had said? The primary difference between this reality and the histories was that here everything found an immediate expression in physical reality. You could virtually touch Elyon by entering his water. You could see evil in the Shataiki. So maybe Tanis was on to something. Maybe evil could be wiped out with the right weapons.

Tom shook his head. It sounded wrong. All wrong.

"I'm not suggesting this nuclear bomb," Tanis said. "But I'm making a point. What about a gun, as you call it? With enough guns, couldn't we hold them off at the river?"

A gun. Thomas shrugged. "A gun is only a small device. They come in bigger sizes but . . . this is ridiculous. Even if I could figure out how to make a gun, I wouldn't."

"But you could, couldn't you?"

Possible. He couldn't bring a gun here, of course. Nothing physical had ever followed him in his dreams. But knowledge . . .

"Maybe."

"Then think about it. It might be a useless idea, I must agree. But sending the lot of those beasts scrambling is a thought worth savoring. I have something else that you must see, Thomas. Come."

He steered Tom to the forest, not the least bit put off or discouraged by Tom's dismissal of his ideas.

"Now? Where?"

"Just here by the river that leads from the lake. I have an invention you must help us try."

He headed into the forest, and Tom hurried to catch him. "Who is 'us'?" Tom asked.

"Johan. He is my first recruit. We have made something that an adventuresome soul like you will appreciate. Hurry. He is to meet us there." Tanis began to run.

They broke out onto the banks of a river slightly smaller than the one at the black forest. Johan sat on a large yellow log they'd felled. He jumped to his feet and ran for Thomas.

"Thomas! First we fly, and now we float." He hugged Tom's waist. "Did you see the stick Tanis made? Where is the stick, Tanis?"

"I threw it into the forest," the elder said. "Thomas said it was a terrible idea, and I agreed. It would never work."

"Then how will we —"

"Exactly!" Tanis boomed. He stuck a finger in the air. "We won't!"

"We *won't* float our log down the river to attack the Shataiki?"

"That's what you were planning?" Tom asked. He looked at the tree and saw that they'd hollowed out half of it. He'd dreamed about one of these. It was a canoe.

"It was an idea," Tanis said. "We talked it up yesterday and we shaped this log so that it might float, but the sword was a bad idea, you said so yourself. Don't tell me you want me to fashion another, because I really am having my doubts about it now. Unless we could send a bomb down the river in this log."

They both stared at Tom with round green eyes. Innocent to the bone. But still filled with desire. The desire to create, the desire to romance, to eat, to drink, to swim in Elyon's lake.

The tension between satisfaction and desire was odd, to be sure. Dissatisfaction led to mischief as well as good.

He faced Johan. "Do you want to take this canoe onto the water?"

His eyes lit up. "Yes."

"And would you be unhappy if we didn't try?"

Johan cast a blank stare. "Unhappy?"

431

"What on earth are you talking about, man?" Tanis boomed. "You're speaking in riddles here. Is this a game of wits?" He seemed quite taken with the idea.

"No, not a game. Just my memory. A way to help my recollection of the way things are. There is happy, so there must be unhappy. There is good, so there must be evil. I was simply asking if Johan here would be unhappy if we didn't push the boat onto the water."

"Yes, there is evil, and we dispatch it regularly. And since there is happy, there must be *un*happy too. I can see what you're saying. I feel anger at the bats, of course, but unhappy? You have me tied in a knot, Thomas Hunter. Help me out."

They felt desire without dissatisfaction, Tom thought. The best of both worlds.

He, on the other hand, did feel dissatisfaction. Or at least *un*satisfaction. Perhaps because he'd been in the black forest. He hadn't taken a drink of the water, but he'd been in there, and his mind had been affected somehow.

Either that, or he wasn't from this place at all. He'd come in a spaceship.

"Just a story, Tanis," Thomas said. "Just an idea."

Tanis exchanged a glance with the boy. Then back. An idea.

"Well then, should we give it a try?"

Johan started jumping in anticipation. The invention was quite an event. Thomas ran his hand along the canoe.

"How will you steer it?"

"With the sword," Tanis said. "But I think any good stick would do."

"And how did you bring the tree down?"

"As we always do. With our hands."

"Okay, let's give it a try."

They tied a vine around its bow and then to a tree on the bank. Tom braced himself. "Are you ready?"

"Ready!" they both cried.

Together they heaved and watched the glowing yellow canoe slip out into the running water. "It works!" Tanis beamed. But almost as soon as he said it, the boat began to sink. Within a few seconds, it had disappeared under the gurgling green waters.

"It's too heavy," Tom said with a frown.

Tanis and Johan stared at the bubbles that still broke the surface. "Another story sinks," Tanis said.

Johan found this so funny that he dropped first to his knees and then to his back in uncontrolled fits of laughter. Tanis was soon joining in, and they quickly turned the laughing fits into a game of sorts: who could laugh the longest without taking a breath.

Tom tried, at their urging, and lost handsomely.

"Well, now," Tanis finally said, "what do you say we try another tomorrow?"

"I would find something else," Tom said. "I really don't think floating down to the black forest is such a great idea anyway."

"Perhaps you are right."

"Tanis?"

"Yes, what is it?"

"Rachelle told me of a fruit that makes you sleep so deeply that you don't remember your dreams."

"So deep that you don't even dream," he said. "Would you like me to find you some?"

"No. No, I need to dream. But is there also fruit that just makes you sleep?"

"And still dream?"

"Yes."

"Of course!"

"The nanka!" Johan cried. "Do you want some?"

An amazing thought. To be able to enter his dreams at will. Or to turn them off by not dreaming.

"Yes. Yes, I would like that. Maybe one of each."

26

"What?" Tom sat up on the couch.

"Sorry, you said five hours, but I fell asleep," Kara said. "It's been eight."

"What time is it?"

"Close to noon. What is it? You look like you've seen a ghost."

His head swam. "Am *I* a ghost?"

Kara ignored the question. "You found something out, didn't you? What is it?"

Tom rolled off the couch and stood. "I think I can turn off my dreams," he said.

"Completely?"

"Yes, completely. Not here. There. I can stop dreaming of this."

"And what good would that do you? This is pretty important."

"This is also a major distraction to me. I'm trying to remember my life, and instead I keep running up against this."

"So you would just fall asleep and wake up and never dream of any of this again? It would just . . . disappear?"

"Yes, I think it would."

"Well, don't you dare turn off your

435

dreams, Thomas. You don't know what would happen. What else did you learn?"

The rest of his dream came to him in a barrage of images that ended with Rachelle telling him where she would like to be rescued.

He turned to her, wide-eyed. "That's it!"

"What's it?"

"It's a map. Is Raison awake?" He ran toward the doors. "A map, Kara!" he said, turning. "We have to find a map."

"What's going on?" she demanded.

"I think she told me where to find Monique. Is Jacques awake?"

"Yes." Kara ran after him through the door. She followed him straight to the office. "Who told you?"

"Rachelle!"

"How would Rachelle know?"

"I don't know. She just made it up. Maybe she doesn't know." Tom ran past a stunned guard and threw the door open. The old man sat at his desk, dark circles prominent under his eyes. He spoke urgently into his phone.

"I think I may have it!" Tom shouted.

Raison dropped the phone into its cradle. "You know where Monique is?"

"Maybe. Yes, I think maybe I do. I need a map and someone who knows this area."

"How could you know?"

"Rachelle told me. In my dreams."

The man's face sagged noticeably. "That's very encouraging."

Tom felt his patience slip. "Well, it should be. For all I know, *you're* the dream!" He jabbed his finger at Jacques. "You ever consider that? Don't be so . . . so stuck up." He'd been better with the diplomacy last night.

"Now I'm a dream," Raison said. "Very, very encouraging. Mr. Hunter, if you think I will —"

"I don't think you will do anything. Except help me find your daughter. What if I'm right?"

"The what-ifs again."

"I know where Monique is!" he shouted.

Kara stepped forward. "I would listen to him, Mr. Raison. I don't think he's been wrong yet."

"Of course, the big sister speaks. My daughter's kidnappers-turned-saviors have spoken. The little people in their dreams have told them where my daughter is. Then let's warm up the helicopter and scoop her up, shall we?"

Tom stared, dumbfounded at Raison's arrogance. Jacques was stressed out. He needed a shock to his system.

He spun around and strode for the door. "Fine. We'll let her rot in the cell she's in."

Kara delivered one last salvo. "How dare

you mock me, you walking ox! You have no idea what a terrible mistake you're making."

They got to the door before he spoke. "I'm sorry. Wait."

"Wait?" Tom said, turning. "Now you want to sit around and wait?"

"You made your point. Tell me where you think she is."

Tom hesitated. He had the upper hand; he intended to keep it. Telling the man that Monique was in a — what was it, a great white cave full of bottles where a river and the forest meet, a day's walk to the east? Wouldn't do.

"Get me a map and someone who knows southern Thailand. And then I want Deputy Secretary Merton Gains on the line. Then I'll tell you where Monique is."

"You're making demands again? Just tell —"

"The map, Jacques! Now."

They had a large map of Thailand and the gulf countries on the conference table. Jacques insisted that he knew the region well enough, but Tom wanted a local. The bulky Thai guard who limped into the room was none other than one of Tom's security guard casualties.

Muta Wonashti was his name. Tom stretched out his hand. "Taga saan ka?"

438

Where are you from?

The man paused at Tom's use of his language. "Penang."

"Welcome to the team. Sorry about the other day."

The man seemed to straighten. He walked up to the map, limp now gone.

Jacques glared. "Satisfied?"

"Is Gains on the line?"

Nancy stepped forward with a phone. "He's waiting."

"You have no idea how embarrassing this will be if you are wrong," Jacques said. "I've expended considerable equity on you."

"Not on me, Jacques. On your daughter." Tom took the phone.

"Secretary Gains?"

"Speaking," Gains's familiar voice said. "I understand that you have some new information."

"That's correct," Tom said. "I really can't keep trying to prove myself at every turn, Mr. Gains. It's slowing us down."

There was a pause.

"You see? You still don't know whether or not to believe me. I'm not saying I blame you; it's not every day someone tells you a virus is about to wipe out the world, and they know so because they've dreamed it."

"I will remind you that I did hear you

439

out," Gains said. "And I did mention the situation to the president. In this world, that's sticking my neck out for you, son. I'm sticking my neck out for a kidnapper who's having crazy dreams."

"Which is why I'm calling. To the point: I've had a dream and in this dream, I've learned where they're keeping Monique de Raison. In front of me I have a map. I want you to begin to accept me on my terms if it turns out that I'm right about where Monique is. Fair enough?"

Gains thought about it.

"If I'm right, Mr. Secretary, and there is a virus, we'll need a few believers. I need someone on the inside."

"And that would be me."

"No one else is volunteering at the moment."

"You say you found out where they have Monique from your dreams. No other information?"

"Bona fide, 100 percent dream. Not a hint of any other intelligence."

"So if you actually find her, you think it proves that your dreams are valid and should be taken seriously," Gains said.

"It won't be the first time I'm right. I need an ally."

"Okay, son, you have a deal. Put Mr. Raison on the line."

"I don't suppose you could get me a

team of Rangers or Navy SEALs?" Tom asked.

"Not a chance. But the Thai have good people. I'm sure they'll cooperate."

"They still think I'm the kidnapper," Tom said. "Cooperation isn't exactly flowing over here."

"I'll see if I can't get them to ease up."

"Thank you, sir, you won't regret this." He handed the phone to an impatient Raison, who listened and ended the call with a polite salutation.

"Now, please tell me. I've done everything you've asked."

Tom leaned over the map. "A great white cave full of bottles a day's walk to the east where a river and the forest meet," he said. "Where is that?"

"What's that?"

Tom looked up. "That's where she is. We just have to figure out what that means."

The man's face lightened a shade. "That's your . . . that's what this is all about? A white cave full of bottles?"

"Yes, but Rachelle wouldn't know what a laboratory looked like. A white cave full of bottles has to be a laboratory, right? They took her to an underground laboratory a day's walk to the east where a river meets the forest. That's about twenty miles."

"How many kilometers?" the tracker asked.

"Roughly thirty."

"The Phan Tu River cross plain here." The squatty fighter drew his finger along a blue river line on the map. "It end here at the jungle. Thirty kilometer east. No lab. Concrete. No longer in use."

Tom stared at the man. "A concrete plant? Right there?"

"Yes."

Jacques de Raison ran both hands through his hair. "How do you know this is accurate? And how —"

"You have a helicopter, Mr. Raison," Tom said. "Is your pilot here?"

"Yes, but surely this is a matter for the authorities. You can expect —"

"I can expect that whoever attacked us in that hotel room is smarter than any team the Thai military can throw together on a moment's notice. I can expect that *they* will expect a possible rescue mission by the Thai government and are thoroughly prepared. And I can expect you would do anything, Mr. Raison, anything at all to see your daughter alive again. Am I missing something here?"

He responded momentarily. "You're right."

"Send me in with a radio and a guide, say Muta here, drop us off a few miles out, and we can at least locate her, maybe do more. At this point, we're operating on one of my dreams, not enough to bring out the U.S. Marines. But if we can get something on the ground, we have a whole new story."

The man paced, squinting and scratching at his head. "And you think you're the one to go in?"

"I know a few new tricks."

Kara raised her brow. "He does indeed."

"And I practically grew up in the jungle."

"You're under house arrest. This is just not feasible —"

Tom slapped the map. "Nothing is feasible, Mr. Raison. Nothing! Not my dreams, not the virus, not your daughter's kidnapping. We're running out of time here. If anyone can rescue your daughter, I can. Trust me. I'm *supposed* to rescue your daughter."

27

Carlos patiently led Svensson down the concrete steps. His bad leg made stairs nearly impossible. The Swiss had flown into Bangkok during the night and arrived at the old lab an hour earlier. Carlos had never seen the kind of rabid intensity that had emerged in him.

"Open it," he said at the steel door.

Carlos slid the latch and shoved the door open. The white lab gleamed under two rows of bare fluorescent bulbs. Svensson had built or converted two dozen similar labs throughout the world for an eventuality like this one. The discovery of a possible virus. If a virus presented itself in South Africa, they needed to be in South Africa. Ultimately they would return to the much larger labs and production facilities of the Alps, of course, but only when they had what they needed firmly secured and the environment it came from thoroughly analyzed.

Here, in Southeast Asia, they had six labs. Raison Pharmaceutical's move from

France to Thailand precipitated the building of this particular one. And now it was paying its dividends.

The lab was equipped with all the equipment expected of any medium-sized industrial lab, including refrigeration and heating capabilities. Monique sat in the corner, gagged with duct tape and bound to a gray chair. Carlos hadn't hurt her. Yet. But he'd talked to her at length. The fact that she refused to engage him with more than a grunt convinced him he would have to hurt her soon.

"So, this is the woman the world is screaming about," Svensson said, moving slowly over the white tile floor. He stopped three feet from Monique. "The one who's chosen not to see the light yet?"

Carlos stood with his hands clasped in front of him. He didn't answer. Wasn't expected to answer. Wouldn't have anyway. He'd done his part; now it was time for Svensson to do his part.

The Swiss's big bony hand flashed out and slapped loudly against Monique's cheek. The woman's head jerked to the side and her face flushed red, but she didn't breathe a sound.

Svensson smiled. "You've seen me. And you obviously recognize me. I believe we even met once, at the Hong Kong drug symposium two years ago. Your father and

I are practically bosom buddies, if you stretch things a bit. Do you see the problem in this?"

She didn't respond. She couldn't.

"Remove it, Carlos."

Carlos stepped forward, ripped the gray duct tape from her mouth.

"The problem is that I've committed myself to you," Svensson said. "You can now finger me. Until the time comes when I no longer care if I'm identified by you, I have to keep you under lock and key. Then, depending on how you treat me now, I will either let you live or have you killed. Does this make any sense to you?"

She drilled his face with a stare and said nothing.

"A strong woman. I may be able to use you when this is over. Soon, very soon." Svensson stroked his mustache and paced in front of her. "Do you know what happens to your Raison Vaccine when it's heated to 179.47 degrees and held at that temperature for two hours?"

Her eyes narrowed for a brief moment. Carlos didn't think she knew. In fact, *they* didn't know for sure.

"No, of course you don't," Svensson said. "You've never tested the vaccine under such adverse conditions; there'd be no need to. So let me make a suggestion: When you apply this specific heat to your miraculous drug, it mutates. You do know it's capable of mutating, because according to our internal sources, it also mutates at a lower heat, but the mutations never could sustain themselves for more than a generation or two."

Monique's eyes widened briefly. She'd just learned there was a spy in her own lab. Perhaps now she would take them seriously. Carlos was surprised that Svensson told her so much. Clearly he didn't expect her to live to tell.

"Yes, that's right, we are quite resourceful. We know about the mutations and we also know that other, much more dangerous mutations hold under more intense heat. Your Raison Vaccine becomes my Raison Strain, a highly infectious, airborne virus with a three-week incubation period." He smiled. "The whole world could have the disease before the first person showed any symptoms. Imagine the possibilities for the man who controlled the antivirus."

A tremble took Monique's face. It was the kind of response that undoubtedly had Svensson's heart pounding like a fist. He'd called her bluff, suggested an incredible possibility they'd only just pieced together themselves. And she was responding with terror.

Monique de Raison's face was screaming

her answer. And no other answer could have been better. She, too, knew all of this. Or at least suspected it with enough conviction to drain the blood from her face. She'd spent a few hours alone with Thomas Hunter, the dreamer, and she'd come away somehow convinced that her vaccine did indeed pose a real risk.

"Yes, the vaccine to the AIDS virus has 375,200 base pairs . . . isn't that what this Hunter told you? And he was right. So much information for a simpleton from America. It's too bad we don't have him as well. Unfortunately, he's dead."

Svensson turned and started to walk toward the door.

"I hope Daddy loves his daughter, Monique. I really do. We're going to do some wonderful things in the days to come, and we would like you to help us."

He limped slowly, right foot clacking on the concrete. Svensson was in his game.

Carlos pulled out the transmitter. "Don't forget the explosive in your belly," he said. "I can detonate it by pressing this button, as I've told you. But it will detonate on its own if it loses a signal past fifty meters. Think of it as your ball and chain. Don't think anyone will come for you. If they do, they will only kill you."

She closed her eyes.

Perhaps he wouldn't have to hurt her after all. Better that way.

The helicopter was a standby, an old bubble job that held four and ran on pistons. Tom and the guide dropped into a rice paddy three miles south of the concrete plant and angled for the jungle to their right. The banger lifted and banked for home. They were now dependent on the radios, Muta's nose, and Tom's tricks.

They slogged through the water to high ground, then followed the tree line at an easy jog. Both carried machetes, and Muta carried a 9-millimeter on his hip. The foliage slowed them down, forcing them to hack their way through vines and underbrush. Three miles took them a full hour.

"There!" Muta thrust his machete out at the clearing ahead. Half a dozen concrete buildings in various degrees of deterioration. An overgrown parking lot with large tufts of grass growing between the concrete slabs. A rusted conveyor nosing into thin air.

Only one building was large enough to conceal any underground work. If they had Monique there, underground, the first building on their left looked like the best bet. Although, at the moment, all bets looked pretty weak.

He'd made bold statements and fired off

thundering salvos, but standing here on the edge of the jungle, with cicadas screeching all around and the hot afternoon sun beating on his shoulders, the notion that the genesis of a worldwide virus attack lay hidden in this abandoned concrete plant struck him as ludicrous.

What if he was wrong? The question had dogged him since the helicopter had abandoned them an hour earlier. But now it went from question to haunting certainty in one giant leap. He was wrong. This was nothing more than an abandoned concrete plant.

"It is abandoned?" Muta said.

He knows it too.

"You get behind the shed," Tom said, pointing to a small structure thirty feet from the entrance to the main building. "Cover me with your gun. You can shoot that thing straight, right?"

Muta tsked in offense. "You kick so good; I shoot better. In military I shoot many gun. Nobody shoot so good as me!"

"Keep it down!" Tom whispered. "I believe you. Can you hit a man at the door from this distance?"

The man eyed the door a hundred yards off. "Too far."

Good. He was honest, then.

"Okay, you cover me. As soon as I clear the entry, you run up and follow me in."

He looked at the machete in his hand. Most of his fighting skills consisted of fist- and footwork, but what good would hand-to-hand combat do him in a place like this? True, he did have some tricks, but his main trick was falling asleep and coming back healthy. A very cool trick, to be sure, but not exactly a knockout blow in a fight.

"Ready?"

Muta released the clip from his pistol, checked it once, and slammed it home in a show of weapon-handling prowess. "You go; I follow."

Not exactly a raid by U.S. Rangers.

"Go!"

He jumped over the berm and ran low to the ground, machete extended. Muta ran behind, feet thudding on the earth.

Tom was halfway to the door when the doubts began to pile up in earnest. If the man he'd fought in the hotel room was inside this building, he'd be firing bullets. A machete might be less useful than a wet noodle. But hand-to-hand was out of the question; the man was much too skilled and powerful.

He slid to a halt, his back against the wall, the door to his left. Muta pulled up at the shed, gun extended.

Tom tried the doorknob. Unlocked. He pulled it. Braved a quick look and withdrew. The interior was dark. Vacant.

Vacant, very, very vacant. He swallowed and waved Muta forward. The man ran across the open ground, gun waving.

Tom stepped into the building.

"They're in," Carlos said, eying the monitor.

"Let them come," Svensson said. "Send a message to her father as soon as you leave. In view of his disregard for the terms we set forward, we have reduced the time for his compliance to one hour. Give him new drop-off instructions. Use the airport."

Svensson strode for the door. "Bring her to the mountain," he said. "I trust this will be the last complication."

They'd seen the pair as soon as the sensors picked them up at the perimeter. They'd even released the security bolts on the doors to let the men in. Like mice to a trap.

How Raison had found this place, Carlos couldn't begin to guess. Why he'd sent only two men, even more mysterious. Either way, Carlos was prepared. What happened to these two was inconsequential. But the lab's cover had been compromised. Svensson would be gone through the tunnels in a matter of minutes, even with his bad leg. Carlos would follow as soon as he had the vaccine.

Carlos stood. "I'll bring her within

twenty-four hours. Yes, this will be the last complication."

Svensson was gone.

Carlos took a deep breath and faced the monitor. Perhaps this was better. The mountain complex in Switzerland had a far more extensive lab. The entire operation would be launched from yet another secured facility. The six leaders who'd already agreed to participate, should Svensson succeed, had established links with the base. The complication would change —

Carlos blinked at the monitor. The lead man's face had come into full view for the first time. This was either Thomas Hunter or Thomas Hunter's twin.

But he'd killed Hunter. Impossible! Even if the man had survived a bullet to the chest, he would be in no condition to run through the jungle.

Still, there he was.

Carlos stared at the image and considered his options. He would let the mouse into his trap, yes. But should he kill him this time?

It was a decision he wouldn't rush. Time was now on his side. At least for the moment.

Vacant. Very vacant and very dark.

A flight of stairs to his right descended into blackness.

"There." He pointed the machete at the stairwell.

He ran for the stairs and descended on the fly, using the light from the gaping door above to guide his steps. A steel door at the bottom. He tried the handle. Open. The door swung in. A dark hall. Doors on either side. At the end, another door.

A thin strip of light ran like a seam beneath the far door. Tom's heart pounded. He kept his machete leveled in both hands. Two careful steps forward before remembering his backup. Muta.

He eased back, glanced up the stairs. No Muta.

"Muta?" he whispered.

No Muta. Maybe Muta had gone back to cover the front door. Maybe he'd been taken out. Maybe . . .

Tom began to panic. He breathed deliberately, shrouded in the darkness. It was a nightmare and he was the lone fugitive, panting down deserted dark hallways with the phantoms at his heels. Only his phantom had a gun, and Tom had already felt a couple of its slugs.

No way he could go back up those stairs now. Not if there was someone up there waiting.

He ran toward the door at the hall's end. Rubber soles muted his footfalls. He was passing other doors on either side.

Whoosh, whoosh, like windows into gray oblivion. Doors into terror. He ran faster. Suddenly it was a race to get into the door with the light.

He crashed into it, desperate for it to be open. It was. He burst through, blinded by light. He slammed the door shut. Shoved a bolt home and gasped for breath.

"Thomas?"

Tom spun. Monique was strapped to a chair in the corner beyond a row of white tables with bottles on them. This was the room Rachelle had wanted to be rescued from, almost exactly as he'd imagined it. But this wasn't Rachelle; this was Monique.

Her eyes were wide and her face white. "You . . . you're dead," she said. "I saw him shoot you."

Tom walked to the middle of the floor, mind reeling. She was actually here. He wasn't sure if it was an intense sense of relief or a general kind of madness that made him want to cry.

He was suddenly running again, straight for her. "You're here!" He slid behind her and ripped at the duct tape that bound her hands to the chair legs. "Rachelle told me you'd be here, in the white cave with bottles, and you're here." An uncontrolled sob was in the mix, but he recovered quickly. "This is incredible; this is absolutely incredible."

He pulled a trembling Monique to her feet, threw his arms around her, and hugged her dearly. "Thank God you're safe."

She felt stiff, but that was to be expected. The poor soul had been taken at gunpoint and —

"Thomas?" She gently pushed him away. Glanced at the door.

Tom fell back a step and followed her glance. The door was locked from this side. Monique wasn't doing backflips at his rescue, and he wondered why.

"I came to rescue you," he said. The reality of what he was doing, where he was, suddenly crashed in around him. He blinked.

"Thomas, we have a problem."

"We have to get out of here!" He grabbed her hand and pulled. Then doubled back for the machete he'd set on the ground. "Come on!"

"I can't!" She jerked her hand free.

"Of course you can! It's true, Monique, all of it. I knew about the AIDS pairs, I knew about the Raison Strain, and I knew how to find you. And I know that if we don't get out of here, we're going to have more problems than either of us can imagine."

She spoke quickly in a half whisper, hands on her belly. "He forced me to swallow an explosive device. If I go more than fifty meters from him, it will kill me. I can't leave!"

Tom looked at her stricken face, her hands trembling over her stomach. His mind went blank.

"You have to get out, Thomas. I'm sorry, I'm so sorry for not listening. You were right."

"No, it's not your fault. I kidnapped you." He stepped up to her and for a moment she was Rachelle, begging to be rescued. He almost reached out and swept her hair from her forehead.

"You have to get out now, and tell them it's all true," she said, glancing at the corner.

Tom saw the small camera and froze. Of course, they were being watched. Muta had been taken out because Monique's kidnapper had seen them coming all the way. They had let Tom walk into this trap. There would be no way out!

Monique stepped up to him and pulled him tight. Her mouth pressed by his ear. "They are listening; they are watching. Kiss my face, my ears, my hair, like we've known each other for a long time."

She didn't wait for him but immediately pressed her lips against his cheek. She was giving whoever was watching something to think about.

"They have the wrong numbers," she said, louder, but not too loudly. "Only you."

"Only . . ."

"Shh, shh," she hushed him. And then very softly. "His name is Valborg Svensson. Tell my father. They intend to use the Raison Vaccine. Tell him it mutates at 179.47 degrees after two hours. Don't forget. Take the ring carefully off my finger and get out while you can."

Tom had stopped kissing her hair. He felt the ring, pulling it off.

"Keep kissing me."

He kept kissing.

"I can't leave you here," he said.

"They will need me alive. And if they think you have more information that they need, they won't kill you."

"I'm right about the virus, then."

"You're right. I'm sorry for doubting."

He felt a strange panic grip his throat. He couldn't just leave her here! He was meant to rescue her. Somehow, in some way beyond his understanding, she was the key to this madness. She was at the heart of the Great Romance; he was sure of it.

"I'm staying. I can fight this guy. I've learned —"

"No, Thomas! You have to get out. You have to tell my father before it's too late! Go."

She gave him one last kiss, on the lips

this time. "The world needs you, Thomas! They are powerless without you. Run!"

Tom stared at her, knowing that she was right, but he couldn't leave her like this.

"Run!" she yelled.

"Monique, I can't leave —"

"Run! Run, run, run!"

Tom ran.

It happened so fast, so unexpectedly, that Carlos found himself off guard. One second he had them both trapped in the laboratory at the end of the long hall. The next Monique was suggesting that Hunter still knew something they did not. That perhaps she and Hunter had planned this together, an interesting thought.

And then Hunter was running.

The American made the hall before Carlos reacted.

He leaped over the body of the guard who'd come with Hunter, threw open the door, and sprang into the hall. Hunter hit him broadside before he had time to bring his weapon around. Then the man was past and sprinting for the stairs.

Carlos let the force of the impact spin his body toward the fleeing figure. He extended his gun, aimed at the man's back. Two choices.

Kill him now with an easy shot through the spine.

Wound him and take him alive.

The latter.

Carlos pulled the trigger. But Hunter had anticipated the shot and dodged to his left. Fast, very fast.

Carlos shifted left and fired again.

But the slug sparked against the steel door. The man was through the door and on the stairs. Carlos felt momentarily stunned. He recovered. Took after the man in a full sprint.

"Run!" the woman screamed from behind.

She stood in the doorframe of her prison.

Carlos ignored her and raced up the stairs, three at a time. Hunter was gone already? Carlos reached the door and flew through it.

The American was at the shed. Cutting behind. Carlos squeezed off a quick shot that took a chunk of concrete from the corner just above Hunter's head. He veered into the open and sprinted for the tree line.

Carlos started his pursuit, knowing the shed would offer a perfect brace for a fully exposed shot at the man. He'd taken only one step before pulling up.

If he and the woman were separated by more than fifty meters, the explosive in her belly would end her life. They needed her alive. She knew and wasn't following.

The man was stretching the distance.

Carlos could leave the transmitter, but the woman might decide to follow, find the transmitter, and escape with it. She was his ball and chain.

Carlos swore under his breath, leaned against the doorframe, and steadied his outstretched gun. The man was only twenty yards from the jungle, a bobbing blotch in the gun sight.

He squeezed off a shot. Another. Then two more in rapid succession.

Smack!

The last bullet hit the man squarely in the back of his head. Carlos saw the man thrown forward with the signature impact of the slug, saw the spray of blood. Hunter disappeared into the tall grass.

Carlos lowered the gun. Was he dead? No one could have survived such a hit. He couldn't leave to check as long as the woman was free and the transmitter was in his pocket. But Hunter was going nowhere soon.

Movement.

The grass. He was crawling?

No, he was up, there, along the trees. Running!

Carlos jerked the gun up and emptied the last clip with three more shots. Hunter vanished into the trees.

Carlos closed his eyes and settled a rage pounding in his skull. Impossible! He was sure he'd hit the man in the head.

Twice the man had eluded him after direct hits. Never again. Never!

The woman's ingenuity was quite unexpected. Admirable in fact.

He walked down the stairs and stared at Monique, who stood in the doorway, arms crossed. He very nearly put a bullet through her leg. Instead, he walked down the hall and slugged her in the gut.

Perhaps he would have to hurt her after all.

28

It happened in three segments, branded in Tom's memory, still hot from the burning. He'd been dodging a spray of bullets, sprinting for the forest, only a few steps from the first tree and sure he'd escaped. Segment one.

Then a bullet had struck his skull. It felt as though a sledgehammer had hit the back of his head. He was flying forward, headlong, parallel to the ground. Everything screamed with pain and then everything went black. Segment two.

He didn't remember landing. He was either dead or unconscious before he hit the ground. But he did remember rolling over after hitting the ground. He was panting and lying on the ground, staring at the blue sky.

He wasn't dead. He wasn't unconscious. And a quick check of his head confirmed that he wasn't even wounded. He was only winded. Segment three.

He'd scrambled for the jungle and run into the trees, chased more by thoughts of what had just happened to him than by the last few bullets.

He'd been shot in the head. He'd lost consciousness before dying. But in the moment before dying he'd awakened in the colored forest, and although he couldn't remember it, he knew he'd been healed by a fruit or the water. For all he knew, the whole journey had lasted only one second.

When he returned to the jungle, it took him two hours to reestablish contact with the base, get to the landing zone, and make the return trip in the helicopter. Time to think. Time to consider a quick trip back to the compound to get Monique out. Or retrieve Muta.

But he knew neither would be there.

A police helicopter checked the place out before his own pickup and confirmed his suspicions. Not a soul.

Even if she had still been there, he couldn't take her. He might be able to withstand the odd lethal blow, but she couldn't. He felt both indestructible and powerless, an odd mix.

Maybe he hadn't been hit. Was there blood on the grass back there? He'd been in too much of a hurry to look. It was all a bit fuzzy. Just the three segments.

Alive, dead, alive.

"You what?"

"I paid it," Jacques de Raison said.

Tom stepped into the office, dumb-struck. His dungarees were caked with mud, his shirt torn from the three-mile run back to meet the pickup, and his boots were leaving marks on Raison's floor.

"You actually gave them the vaccine?"

"They gave me one hour, Mr. Hunter. My daughter's life is on the line —"

"The whole world's on the line!"

"For me it's one daughter."

"Of course, but what about the information I radioed in?"

"The hour was up. I had to make a choice. They wanted only a sample of the vaccine and a file with a copy of our master research data left in a car two miles from the airport. Monique will be in our custody within two days. I had to do it."

Tom dug into his pocket, pulled out the ring. A gold band with a ruby perched in a four-point setting. He tossed it to Raison.

"What's this?"

"That's the ring your daughter gave me to persuade you that I was telling the truth. If you heat the vaccine to 179.47 degrees and hold that temperature for two hours, it will mutate. The man who has this information is named Valborg Svensson. He also may have the only antivirus."

Jacques de Raison's face lightened a shade. He toyed with the ring absently. "Why didn't you bring her out?"

"Are you listening to me? I understand you're distressed, but you have to pull yourself together. I found her, exactly as I said I would. If you don't buy the ring, then the fact that Svensson changed the deal on you because I found them is enough."

The man dropped heavily to his chair.

"Now they have the vaccine?" Tom ran a hand through his hair. This was the worst of all worlds. Nothing he was doing was having any real impact on the unfolding drama. Maybe there was no way to stop this matter of the histories.

Kara hurried in. "Thomas! Are you okay?"

"I'm fine. They have the vaccine. They have Monique; they have the vaccine; they know exactly how to force the mutation; they may have the antivirus."

"But the dream. It was real."

"Yes."

"Yes, Peter, I want you to change the testing parameters. Try the vaccine at 179.47 degrees and maintain the heat for two hours."

Jacques de Raison seemed to have come out of his stupor. He was on the phone with the lab. "Watch for mutations and get back to me immediately."

He dropped the phone into its cradle.

"Forgive me, Mr. Hunter. It's been a

very hard two days." All business now. "I believe you. At any rate, the tests will speak for themselves in two hours. In the meantime, I suggest we contact the authorities. I know Valborg Svensson."

"And?"

"And if it is true, if it is him . . ." Dots were being connected behind those soft blue eyes of his. "God help us," he said.

"It is him," Tom said. "Monique insisted. I want to speak to Deputy Gains immediately."

Jacques de Raison nodded. "Nancy, get the secretary on the phone."

Merton Gains sat alone at his desk and listened to Jacques de Raison for several minutes in a mild state of shock. Six hours ago, hearing Thomas Hunter lay out his test to prove himself, the idea had seemed fanciful. Now that he'd actually done it, Gains felt distinctly unnerved.

He had heard Bob Macklroy explain that Hunter had predicted the Kentucky Derby's outcome. He'd talked to Thomas and reported the possible problems with the Raison Vaccine in the cabinet meeting. He even agreed to test Hunter's dreams. But his indulgences had all seemed quite harmless until now.

Thomas Hunter had gone to sleep, learned Monique de Raison's location, gone to that location, and brought back virtual proof that the virus was in fact in the works.

"He would like to speak to you."

"Put him on," Gains said. "Thomas? How are you?"

"I'm not doing exceptionally well, sir. I hope you're going to be reasonable now, as we agreed."

"Now hold on, son. You have to slow down on me."

"Why? Svensson's obviously not slowing down."

He had a point. "Because, for starters, we don't know there actually is a virus yet. Right? Not until they run the tests."

"Then the Raison Strain will come into existence in exactly two hours. I'm giving you a head start. You have to stop Svensson!"

"We don't even know where this Valborg Svensson is!"

"Don't tell me no one could find this guy. He's not exactly unknown."

"We will find him. But we have no probable cause to —"

"I gave you probable cause! Monique told me he was planning on using the virus; what more do you need?"

Two words pounded in Merton Gains's mind. *What if?* What if, what if, what if? What if Hunter really was right and they were only days away from an unstoppable pandemic? Everyone knew that technology would eventually be used for something other than improving the human condition. The cool air spilling from the vent above his desk suddenly felt very cold. His door was closed, but he could hear the soft footfalls of someone passing by in the hall.

America was purring down the proverbial highway like a well-oiled truck. Banks were trading billions in dollars; Wall Street was noisily swapping nearly as many stocks. The president was due to make a speech on his new tax plan in two hours. And Merton Gains, deputy secretary of state, had a phone to his ear, hearing someone five thousand miles away tell him that in three weeks four billion people would be dead.

Surreal. Impossible.

But what if?

"First of all, I need you to slow down. I'm with you, okay? I said I would be with you, and I am. But you understand how the world runs. I need absolute proof if we expect anyone to listen. These are incredible claims we're dealing with. Can you at least give me that?"

"By the time I get you proof, it will be too late."

"I need you to work with me, at my pace. The first thing we need is the results of those tests."

"But you can at least find Svensson," Thomas said. "Please tell me you can find this guy. The CIA or the FBI?"

"Not in two hours, we can't. I'll get the ball rolling, but nothing happens that fast. If we have a B2 in the air circling Baghdad, we can drop a bomb in an hour, but we don't have B2s in the air or even out of the hangar. We don't even know where Baghdad is on this one; you got me?"

Hunter sighed. "Then I'll tell you what, Mr. Gains. We're toast. You hear me? And Monique . . ." His voice trailed off.

What if? What if?

Gains stood and paced, phone held tightly to his ear. "I'm not saying we can't do anything —"

"Then do *something!*"

"As soon as we hang up, I'll be on the phone with the director of the CIA, Phil Grant. I'm sure they're already all over this thing. For all we know, the Thai police already have whoever picked up the package in custody. At least the car. The kidnapping case is in full swing now, but the virus is a different matter altogether. So far, this looks like corporate espionage to everyone but you and maybe Raison."

"You don't know how slow the wheels of justice turn in Southeast Asia. And it's the virus that will bite us in the backside, not corporate espionage."

"I'll make some calls. But I need proof!"

"And in the meantime I twiddle my thumbs?"

Gains thought about that. "Do what you've been doing. You've done some pretty amazing things in the last few days. Why stop now?"

"You want me to go after Monique? Isn't this just a bit over my head now?"

"I think this is over everyone's head. You're the one with the dreams. So dream."

"Dream. Just like that? Dream."

"Dream."

The three segments — alive, dead, alive — still buzzed madly in Tom's brain. He couldn't talk about them. They terrified him.

"What did he say?" Kara asked.

"He told me to wait."

"Just wait? Doesn't he realize we don't have time to wait?"

"And he told me to dream."

Kara walked around the couch. "So he believes you."

"I don't know."

"He's at least beginning to believe that your dreams have some significance. And he's right — you have to dream. Now."

"Just" — he snapped his fingers — "like that, huh?"

"You want me to knock you out? The secretary is only half right. You don't just have to dream, you have to do the right things in your dreams. Which means doing whatever it takes to get more information on the Raison Strain."

"The black forest," he said.

"If that's what it takes."

Thomas now had two very compelling reasons to return to the black forest, one reason for each reality. The situation here had become critical — he had to accept more risk in uncovering the truth about the histories. And in the colored forest, if he recalled correctly, he was beginning to wonder if he really had crash-landed on a spacecraft.

"Maybe I can talk to Rachelle again. Find out where she wants to be rescued from again. It worked once, right?"

"It did. And what exactly does that mean? Is she somehow Monique? You're talking to Monique in your dreams?"

He sighed. "I don't have a clue. Okay. Knock me out."

Kara dug in her pocket and handed him three tablets.

29

Tom sat up. It was morning. He was in Rachelle's house.

For several long moments he sat there, frozen by a barrage of thoughts from his dream in Bangkok. The situation had gone critical — he had to uncover the truth about the Raison Strain.

True enough, unless that was all a dream.

But there was another reason, wasn't there? He had to learn the truth about Teeleh's claim that Bill and the spacecraft were real. He had to eliminate the confusing possibilities, or he would never settle into the truth.

And yesterday Tanis had shown him how he might be able to mount his own little expedition into the black forest. The colored sword. It was poison to Teeleh.

He jumped out of bed, splashed water on his face, and pulled on his clothes. After leaving Tanis and Johan yesterday, Tom had intended to eat the nanka that Johan had brought him and fall asleep. But as it turned out, he didn't need any help sleeping just yet. By the time he reached the village, it was almost time for the Gathering. He couldn't miss the Gathering.

Something strange had happened to him that evening while he was in the lake's waters. A momentary shift in his perspective. He'd imagined being shot in the head, but the vision was fleeting.

When he got back from the Gathering, they ate a feast of fruits as they had the first night. Johan sang and Rachelle danced along with Karyl and Palus told a magnificent tale.

But what was Tom's gift?

Dreaming stories, he told them. He didn't dance like Rachelle or sing like young Johan or tell stories like Palus and Tanis, but he sure could dream stories.

And so he did. He dreamed about Bangkok.

"Good morning, sleepy dreamer." Rachelle leaned against the door, backlit by the sun's rays. "What did we do in your dreams? Hmm? Did we kiss?"

Tom stared at her, caught by her beauty. The sound of women giggling drifted in from outside.

"Yes, my tulip, I believe I did dream about you."

She crossed her arms and tilted her

head. "Maybe this dreaming of yours has more possibilities than I first imagined."

In fact he *had* dreamed about Rachelle. Or at least he had dreamed of talking about his dream of Rachelle. Could he talk to her as if she were Monique?

He crossed to her and leaned against the wall. "If you were held captive and would like me to rescue you, where would —"

"We did this just yesterday," she said. "Are you forgetting again? You still haven't rescued me from the cave with the bottles."

"Well, no . . . you couldn't be rescued."

"You never tried," she said.

He stared at her for a moment, lost. Clearly it wasn't so simple.

"I think I'll go to the forest and think about how to do it," he said.

She stepped aside. "Be my guest."

The women he'd heard laughing were up the path when he stepped past her into the sunlight. They glanced back, whispering secrets.

"Okay, I'll be back."

"Don't be long," Rachelle said. "I want to hear what you've concocted. All of the delicious details."

"Okay."

"Okay."

He made it out of the village after being stopped only twice. Thankfully not by

Johan or Tanis. Even more thankfully not by Michal or Gabil. He didn't need the distraction at the moment. Or any dissuasion. He had to keep his mind on this task of his, and if Rachelle wasn't going to shed light on his dreams of Monique, he had to try the black forest before he lost his resolve.

It took him an hour to find the exact clearing where he'd met Tanis yesterday. There, twenty feet to his left, lay the sword. He wouldn't have been surprised if Tanis had returned for it himself. But he hadn't.

He picked up the sword and swung it through the air like a swashbuckler, thrusting and parrying into thin air filled with imaginary Shataiki. It felt uncommonly good. There wasn't much of a handle, but the stick fit his grip perfectly. The blade was thin enough to see through and sharp enough to cut.

He would at least test the Shataiki's reaction to this new weapon of his. What did he have to lose? Surely the beasts would have sentries posted. Within minutes of his appearance at the Crossing, the place would be covered with the bats, and he would pull out the sword and see how they reacted. If the test went especially well, he would see where it might lead.

Tom glanced at the sun. It was mid-morning. Plenty of time.

★ ★ ★

He reached the white bridge in well under an hour at a steady run. A few days ago it would have taken him longer. He was as fit as he could ever recall.

He stopped at the last line of trees and studied the Crossing. The arching bridge looked unchanged. The river still bubbled green beneath the plain white wood. The black trees on the opposite bank looked as stark as he remembered — like a papier-mâché forest created by a child, branches jutting off at ungainly angles.

The unmistakable flutter of wings drifted across the river. Sentries. Tom pulled back and dropped to one knee. For a moment the whole notion struck him as both ridiculous and absurdly dangerous. Who was he to think that he could fight off a thousand black Shataiki with a single sword?

He lifted the weapon and ran his finger along its edge. But it wasn't just any sword. If he was right, the wood alone would scatter the vermin. A surge of confidence rippled down his back.

A small stick lay at his knee, red like the sword in his hand. Not too different from what he imagined a small dagger might look like. Tom snatched it up and slipped it under his tunic at his back. Grasping the sword with both hands, he stood and stepped into the open.

He walked slowly, sword before him. Within twenty paces he reached the bridge. No sign of the bats. He paused at the foot of the bridge, then walked up the planks.

Still no sign of the Shataiki.

He reached the crest of the bridge before he saw them. A dozen, two dozen, a thousand, he couldn't tell, because they were hidden just beyond the tree line with only a few red, beady eyes to show for their presence. But they were most definitely there.

He made a slight waving motion with the sword. The bats made no move. Were they afraid? Or were they just waiting for their leader? Wafts of acidic sulfur drifted past his nostrils. They were definitely there.

"Come out, you filthy beasts," he muttered, straining to see them. Louder now, "Come out, you filthy beasts!"

The eyes didn't move. Only an occasional shift among them even told him they were alive. He took a step forward and called again. "Bring me your leader."

For a long minute there was no movement. Then motion. To his left.

Teeleh's magnificent blue wings wrapped around his golden body and dragged on the ground as he stepped into the open. Tom had forgotten just how beautiful the larger bat looked. Now, with the sun shining off his skin, the creature looked as though he had just flown down from the upper lake. At thirty paces, only his green, unblinking eyes disconcerted Tom. He would never grow accustomed to pupil-less eyes.

Teeleh refused to look directly at Tom, but aimed a stately gaze across the river. No other bats followed.

Tom swallowed, shifted the sword in his sweating palms, and brought it to his left to bear on the Shataiki leader. The creature gave Tom a fleeting glance and returned his eyes to the opposite bank. With a loud flap, he unfolded his wings to their full breadth, shrugged his shoulders, and then wrapped them around his body once again.

"So. You think with your new sword you have power over me. Is that it, human?" The beast still refused to look at him.

Tom could think of nothing smart in response.

The Shataiki finally shifted his piercing gaze to Tom. "Well? Are you going to just stand there all day? What is it you want?"

Tom cleared his throat. "I need to know more about the histories. About the Raison Strain. And then I want you to show me the ship," he said quietly.

"We have an agreement," Teeleh said. "You bring me Tanis, and I show you the ship. Is your memory still slipping? Until you can keep your agreements, you can forget about the histories as well. What does it matter anyway? They are only dreams. Your reality lies behind me, in the black forest, where we have already repaired it."

"I didn't break any agreement. You said you would trade a repaired ship for Tanis. I want to see the ship first. He is waiting to come when I call him."

The Shataiki's eyes widened. Tom knew then that the Shataiki didn't know what happened outside their miserable black forest. Teeleh was having difficulty finding a response, and Tom knew in that moment that he could beat this beast.

"You're lying," Teeleh said. "You are as deceiving as the others who've filled you full of lies."

Tom slowly stepped over the bridge toward the Shataiki. "I lie, you say. And what would this lie gain me? Surely you, the father of lies, should know that lies are spun for gain. Isn't that your chief weapon? And what do I gain by this lie?"

The Shataiki remained silent, face taut, eyes unblinking. Tom stepped off the bridge and the bat took a step backward. The stench of sulfur from the forest was almost unbearable. "Now, I think that you will show me my ship. What harm is there in that? You didn't lie to me, did you?"

The black leader considered the words. He suddenly relaxed and grinned. "Very well. I will show you. But no tricks. No more lies between us, my friend. Just co-operation. I'll help you, and you can help me."

Tom had no intention of helping this creature, and the fact that Teeleh didn't seem to understand that gave him even more courage. In the end he was just a big bat with pretty skin and green cherries for eyes.

Tom walked forward, sword extended.

On the other hand, Tom had just crossed the bridge and now stood in the black forest. Was he crazy? No, he had to continue. He had to know. If there was a ship as Teeleh claimed, the histories meant nothing. If there was no ship, he would trade information on the histories for another promise to deliver Tanis. He would never fulfill his promise, of course. This was the battle of the minds, and Tom could beat this overgrown fruit fly.

Teeleh stepped to the side and kept a respectable distance from the sword. A flock of wings took noisy flight when he reached the tree line. Tom glanced back at the colored trees one last time before stepping into the dark forest.

30

The moment Tom stepped into the black forest, Teeleh took to the trees with a mighty *swoosh*. Tom gripped the red sword with renewed intensity. No fruit, no green, nothing but black. Like walking through a burned-out forest at night.

He stopped. "Which way?"

Teeleh looked down from a tree just ahead. The bat looked too large for the spindly branch he clung to. His beady eyes stared at Tom, a cross between wonder and disbelief. Or was Tom simply projecting his own disbelief that he was actually heading in willfully?

Teeleh swept into the air and flew on without responding. He wanted Tom to follow.

Tom followed. His heart hammered steadily. He knew he didn't belong here, but still he kept pushing one foot in front of the other.

Clicking and fluttering all around him. No voices. Only the sound of endless wings beating the air and countless claws grabbing at branches as the bats moved from tree to tree.

The air was cool. It was dark down here on the forest floor. Without leaves to block the sun, he would've thought . . .

Tom looked up. The trees did have a canopy — a hundred thousand black bats directly above, peering down with red eyes. Wordless. Flapping, clicking. They formed a giant black umbrella that followed him deeper and deeper into the forest.

Light from a clearing dawned ahead, and Tom picked up his pace, drawn by the prospect of getting out from under the living canopy.

Coming into the forest was a mistake. He knew that now. He didn't care if there was a spaceship ahead; the shroud of evil hovering above him would never allow him to escape alive. He would catch his breath in this clearing and return to the Crossing. Maybe he could negotiate with —

Tom stopped. Sunlight reflected off a shiny metal surface across the bare meadow. A ship?

His heart bolted.

A spaceship.

Tom stumbled forward three steps.

He knew it! He was a pilot from Earth. He had gone through a wormhole or something and crash-landed on this distant planet trapped in time. Here there was good and there was evil, and the two hadn't mixed. But he was different because he was from Earth.

Tom sprinted toward the spaceship. A dark flock of Shataiki flew in circles above the meadow, whooping and sneering in shrill pitches. The craft sat on its belly, majestic. He remembered this. It was a space shuttle with broad wings. The white shell looked shiny and new. There was a flag on its tail, Stars and Stripes. United States. Big blue letters on the side read *Discovery III.*

Tom reached the ship just as the drove of Shataiki settled on trees above the craft. He glanced their way and, seeing no change in their behavior, ran his hand along the smooth metal of the fuselage. No tears, no patches. Restored.

Tom rounded the craft and pulled the release latch. With a hiss that startled him, the door swung slowly up. The hydraulics still worked. He shoved the sword through the opening and clambered in after it.

The sword glowed in the darkness, giving off just enough light for Tom to see his old cockpit. He couldn't remember any of it, but apparently it, too, had been completely repaired. He stood and walked to the main control panel, using the sword to light his way. The master power switch rested in the *off* position. Surely there could be no power after such a long time. Then again, whoever repaired this craft surely knew mechanics as well as they knew upholstery.

Tom held his breath, reached down, and flipped the red toggle. Immediately the air filled with a hum. Lights blinked on all around him. He wiped at the sweat gathered above his eyes and gazed at the lighted instruments before him. He stroked the leather captain's chair and smiled in the cabin's artificial light. But the smile immediately faded. He had no clue what to do with this magnificent craft.

Bill. He needed Bill. *Please let Bill be alive.*

Tom flipped the switch back off, returned to the door, and lowered himself through the hatch.

If the Shataiki had killed Bill . . .

He shoved the sword into the ground and turned to close the hatch. He grabbed the door with both hands and pulled down against the hydraulic pressure.

Wings fluttered behind him. He released the door and whirled around just in time to see Teeleh descending on the sword still stuck in the earth. His heart leaped into his throat. How could the bat touch the sword? It was like poison, Tanis had said!

But even as he thought it, he realized that the sword had changed. It no longer glowed with the red luster it had just seconds ago. The Shataiki ripped the useless stick out of the ground with a snarl.

"Now you are mine, you fool! Seize him."

Every last nerve in Tom's body froze at the words. A dozen shrieking Shataiki streaked out of the trees and descended on him before he could convince his muscles to move.

The ship! He could get into the ship!

Tom spun around. There was no ship.

THERE WAS NO SHIP!

Michal's words strung through his mind. *He is the deceiver.*

A scream wrenched itself from his chest, the kind of full-throated scream that shreds vocal cords. Talons bit into his flesh. He gasped, swallowing the scream.

The small stick at his back! He had to reach it.

Tom grasped at his back, but the world tipped and he landed on the ground, hard. He tried to strike out. Furry bodies suffocated him. He had to get the colored wood from his waist, but the bats were in his face, digging at his flesh. He instinctively brought his knees up in a fetal position and buried his face in his arms.

"Bring him to the forest!"

A single talon swiped at his back and cut to his spine. Tom arched his back and groaned. They lashed twine around his neck and feet, and he was powerless to fight against it. Then they began to pull, dragging him a few inches at a time along the ground, wheezing and groaning against his weight.

"Use this, you imbeciles," he heard a Shataiki screech. Bitter, high-pitched arguing. "This way . . ."

"No, you fool . . ."

"Hurry . . ."

"Let go, or I'll cut your hand off!"

"Out of my way . . ."

He was being dragged slowly along the forest floor. They'd tied a tow-rope to his bindings, and no fewer than a hundred black bats were successfully pulling him along the ground.

Sharp objects cut into his back. He moaned and felt the world spin around him. The last thing he saw was the clearing beyond his feet.

The one without a spaceship.

Tom awoke to the violent, stinging drag of a taloned claw across his face.

"Wake up!" a distant voice screamed at him. "Wake up! You think you can just sleep through this? Wake up!"

He pried his eyes open and saw a fire dancing at his feet. Where was he? He struggled to raise his head. A clawed fist beat down on his cheek, snapping his head to one side. He began to slip away.

Another loud slap on his right cheek brought him back. "Wake, you useless slab of meat!" Teeleh's voice.

Tom opened his eyes and saw that he'd been strapped to an upright device by his wrists and his ankles. Scores of the hairy creatures danced about a huge fire roughly thirty feet away. Thousands of beady eyes dotted the dark forest.

He lifted his eyes slowly. Maybe hundreds of thousands. Teeleh stood on a platform to his right.

A Shataiki swooped in from his perch, screeching with delight. "He's awake! He's awake! Can I —"

With a throaty snarl, a huge black beast whirled and swatted the smaller Shataiki from the air. The bat fell to the ground with a thud. Others quickly pounced on him and dragged his twitching body into the shadows.

A hush fell over the gathering. Fire crackled. Shataiki wheezed. A sea of red eyes hovered over him. But it was the image of the large bat, drilling him with glowing red eyes, that struck terror in Tom's heart.

This was Teeleh.

He'd changed. His skin was pitch-black and cracked, oozing a clear fluid. His wings were flaking, shedding long swaths of fur. Lips peeled back to reveal crusted, yellow fangs. A fly slowly crawled over one of his eyes — red now — but the beast didn't appear to notice.

Tom rolled his head from left to right. The device on which they had hung him creaked with his movement. He was bound to a crude wooden beam planted upright with a similar beam fixed perpendicular. A cross. They had bound him to the cross with twine. Streaks of blood ran from a dozen gashes on his chest.

He slowly turned farther to his right. The beast's red eyes bulged larger than he remembered. If his hands had been free, he could have reached out and clawed the morbid balls from the fiend's face. As it was, he could only stare into Teeleh's torrid eyes and fight his own terror.

"Welcome to the land of the living," Teeleh said. His once musical voice sounded low and guttural, as if he was speaking past a throat full of phlegm. "Or should I say, the land of the dead. We make no real distinction here, you know." The assembled Shataiki hissed with a laughter that sent chills down Tom's spine.

"Silence!" the leader thundered.

The laughter ceased. The large beast's vocal range was incredible. He could switch from a high-pitched squeal to a deep-throated growl effortlessly.

The huge Shataiki turned back to Tom, leaned forward, and opened his mouth. His breath was moist and smelled like a septic tank. Tom tried to recoil. He managed a flinch.

Teeleh extended a claw to his face. "You have no idea how delighted I am that you came back to us, Thomas." He began to delicately stroke Tom's face with the tip of his talon.

"It would have been such a disappointment if you had stayed away." He spoke in a soft, purring voice now. A sick smile pulled his lips back to reveal yellow fangs. Bits of fruit flesh were lodged between his teeth.

"I have always loved you hairless animals, you know. Such beautiful creatures." He ran the back of his furred claw down Tom's cheek. "Such soft skin, such tender lips. Such . . ."

"Master, we have him," another Shataiki suddenly blurted, staggering from the trees.

The leader's eyes flashed at being interrupted. But then his expression changed to one of amusement and he spoke without turning to face the new Shataiki.

"Bring him in," he commanded. And then to Tom, "I have prepared a special treat for you, Thomas. I think you will like it."

The throng looked on as a dozen Shataiki dragged another cross into the clearing. A creature had been fixed to the beams. They managed to erect the cross and drop it into a fresh hole not ten feet from Tom.

A man.

The man's naked body sagged, battered almost beyond recognition. Wide swaths of flesh had been stripped from his torso.

Tom groaned at the sight.

"Lovely, isn't it?" the beast sneered. He giggled in delight. "You do remember this one, don't you?"

Bill.

But wasn't Bill just a figment of his imagination? He was right here, bleeding in front of him. Real.

"I know what you're thinking," Teeleh said. "You're thinking that the spaceship isn't real and so Bill isn't real. But you're wrong on both counts."

Bill's bloodstained body moved ever so slowly on the cross. The poor soul's hands had been nailed to the horizontal member of the wooden cross, not tied as Thomas's had been. A large spike also jutted from a deep wound in his feet. His eyes had swollen shut, leaving only thin lines. His upper lip had been split open. A tangled mat of red hair fell to the man's shoulder. Tom closed his eyes and trembled with horror.

Teeleh laughed. "You like it? He's alive, waiting for you to rescue him." At that the throng roared with laughter. Tom kept his eyes closed. A fresh wave of nausea washed through his stomach.

Teeleh let the laughter continue for a few short moments. "Enough!"

Once again to Tom, with a mocking tone: "Now, here is your means of escape, Thomas. You really do have to escape, because unless you do, you'll never be able to bring me Tanisssss."

Tanis?

Without removing his eyes from Tom, Teeleh motioned to the darkness. A lone Shataiki hopped toward the platform, dragging Tom's sword. He lifted it up to the leader and promptly disappeared into the trees. Teeleh took the dark sword and twirled it in the air.

"And to think that you thought you could defeat me with one measly sword. You see, it's useless. Nothing can withstand my power."

A snicker ran through the audience of Shataiki. Teeleh took a step closer to Tom, eyes glaring. "I told you, this is my kingdom, not his. Here, if you don't take up the sword, you lose its power. You're a fool to think you can defeat me on my own land."

The Shataiki suddenly swung the sword

broadside at Tom's midsection. With a thump, the hard wood struck his bare flesh. He heaved in pain. The night grew fuzzy for a moment and he thought he might pass out.

"Now we will see how bright you are, you stupid sap." Teeleh shoved the sword out toward Bill. "Take this sword and kill this slab of flesh. Kill him, and I will release you. Otherwise, I will let you both hang here for a very long time."

The night turned deathly silent.

Kill Bill?

Bill wasn't real, Michal said.

But Bill was real.

Or was he just a figment?

Or was it a test? If he killed Bill, he would be obeying Teeleh by killing another man who in fact could be real. He would be following the wish of Teeleh, regardless of whether Bill was real.

On the other hand, if he *refused* to kill Bill because he believed Bill to be alive, then he was also following the word of Teeleh, who, contrary to Michal, claimed that Bill was real.

No matter what he did, Teeleh would claim a victory.

On the other hand, who cared what Teeleh claimed? Tom had to survive.

He lowered his head and struggled for a decent breath. He could seem to get enough air into his lungs only when he pushed up and gave his chest muscles room to function.

"What are you waiting for, you fool? You think this miserable soul deserves to live? Look at him!"

Tom wasn't sure he had the strength to raise his head again. Another blow to his midsection changed his mind.

"Look at him!" the Shataiki snarled.

Tom raised his head. Even if Bill were real, he wouldn't feel the sword in his current condition. Death would put him out of his misery. How had they managed to keep the poor soul alive this long? He shuddered.

"This human has rejected what you have accepted," Teeleh said in an authoritative voice. "He has greedily indulged in the pleasure of his own flesh by drinking the water. He has already been sentenced to death. You would do him a significant favor by finishing him off."

There was no way out. If Tom didn't kill this poor soul, they would both die. He closed his eyes, took another pull of air, and groaned.

"What was that, a yes?"

"Yes."

The hushed mob of Shataiki erupted in a frenzy of excited whispers and hisses.

"A wise choice," Teeleh said softly. "Pull

him down! Let the human show us what he's made of."

A dozen black bats immediately flew to the cross and began to pick at the twine that held Thomas. His right hand came free first and he slumped forward at an odd angle that almost pulled his left shoulder out of joint. His feet fell free next, and for an unbearable moment he hung only by his left arm. The rope tore loose and he crashed to the ground.

The Shataiki began singing in odd, twisted voices that pierced eerily into the night — grossly absent of melody, yet heavy with meaning.

"Kill . . . kill . . . kill . . ."

The leader leaped off the platform and stood to one side. The fire seemed to burn brighter as the throng pressed in closer.

Tom pushed himself up to a kneeling position. He faced the cross on which Bill hung.

Teeleh spread his wings to their full breadth. The volume of the Shataiki's song slowly grew, drumming deep into Tom's mind.

"Now, my son. Show me your submission by taking the sword with which you came to kill me, and kill this man instead." With that, the Shataiki shoved the sword deep into the earth at Tom's knees.

The freakish pounding of voices behind

the leader continued, and in that moment Tom doubted very much they would set him free without horrific consequences. Coming into the forest had been a terrible —

Tom suddenly flinched.

"What?" Teeleh demanded.

The stick at his back. The dagger! Had they taken it? No, they hadn't even seen it. It was under his tunic. It had been in contact with his flesh the whole time.

"Take the sword!" Teeleh thundered.

Tom felt a surge of energy spread through his bones. He gripped the blackened sword with his hands and used it as a crutch to drag himself to his feet.

The chanting grew louder. Its pitch rose higher.

Tom's head swam, and without the sword to steady himself he might have collapsed. He leaned on the black stick and waited for his legs to steady. Teeleh stood still, no more than three paces to his right, wings now wrapped around his shoulders in stately fashion. Tom gripped the sword with both hands and pulled it free from the ground.

He looked up at the body that hung on the cross, close enough to touch. He slowly raised the sword in his right fist.

The chanting rose to a roar, and the leader grinned wickedly.

Still shaking on his feet, Tom slipped his left hand behind his back and under his tunic.

There. It was still there! He gripped the dagger with his fingers and jerked it into the open.

The effect was immediate. A hundred thousand Shataiki fell mute, as if somewhere in the back, behind the stage, some little idiot bat had tripped over a cord and pulled the plug.

Tom stared at the glowing red dagger in disbelief. He swung to Teeleh, holding the knife out before him.

The large black Shataiki's face was frozen in the firelight. Teeleh took a step back from the blade. Tom waved the knife a few inches and watched in amazement as the beast leaped back in fear. He felt the corners of his mouth edge up. Adrenaline poured new strength into his muscles.

He staggered to the edge of the clearing. Bats scattered, screeching.

Bill. He couldn't leave Bill.

Tom spun around. But there was no Bill. Of course there was no Bill. Just as there was no spaceship.

Tom looked at Teeleh. "You see what Elyon can do with only one *human?*" he asked quietly. "One human and one small blade of wood, and you're nothing but a sack of leather."

The leader's face twisted in rage. He thrust a wing forward. "Attack him!" he screamed. A single Shataiki with inordinate courage streaked from a low branch toward Tom. A dozen others followed.

Tom's heart froze. Maybe he had spoken too early. He shifted the dagger toward the first onrushing bat and stiffened for the impact.

But the shrieking bat's extended talons, followed by the rest of its body, fell limp the instant the glow from the extended dagger touched its skin. Its momentum carried the bat hurtling into the ground, where it crumpled in a heap of dead fur.

Two other bats made the same journey before the rest broke off the attack, shrieking in defeat. Tom shifted his shaking limbs. He looked back toward Teeleh, who stood trembling.

"Never!" he shouted. "Not now, not ever. You will never win."

With that, Tom turned from the throng and staggered into the forest, dagger held high.

The bats kept their distance, but it sounded like every last one of them was following. Flapping, clicking, and now shrieking.

He still had to find the Crossing. How far had they carried him after attacking him at the clearing? It had been roughly midday, and then night when he came to on the cross. Now it was moving toward morning.

He hadn't dreamed while unconscious. Or if he had, he couldn't remember what he'd dreamed. Strange. What was happening in Bangkok? Maybe nothing. Maybe there was no Bangkok, just as there was no spaceship and no Bill. Maybe that's why he wasn't dreaming anymore.

It was the rising sun that saved him. A very soft glow in the east. Tom pulled up in a clearing. If that was east, then the river was directly ahead, north.

A black canopy moved against the dim sky.

"Get away!" Tom shouted, waving the dagger.

Shrieks echoed and the canopy lifted from the trees. Then settled again. Somewhere out there Teeleh watched.

Watched and waited.

He hit the river an hour later. No Crossing. The question was: Right or left? His back and chest burned with deep cuts. If he couldn't find the Crossing soon, he would just jump into the river and swim across. Could he do that?

Tom turned east and jogged along the river. The bats followed in the trees. On the other side of the river, the colored forest glowed like a rainbow.

Tom was seriously considering a dive into the river when he caught the glint of white directly ahead.

He pulled up, panting. There, arching lazily over the bubbling green waters, a white bridge stretched from the dark, harsh ground on which he stood to a lush landscape, bursting with color and life.

The Crossing.

He swallowed at the sight and surged forward on wobbly legs. He had made it.

He had actually made it! Twice now he'd talked to Teeleh and survived. The big, ugly bat wasn't all that powerful after all. It was simply a matter of knowing how to defeat him. Knowledge was the key. You know what to do, and you —

Tom stopped midstride.

There, near the bridge on the opposite shore, silhouetted by the lucent forest, stood the unmistakable figure of a human.

Tanis!

The man stared at Tom, frozen like a statue. In his hands he held a red sword like Tom's. A sword?

A rush filled the air. Teeleh settled to the ground, directly opposite Tanis. He was no longer the black creature, but the beautiful bat, glowing blue and gold. A chill swept down Tom's spine.

The Shataiki folded his wings and

opened his mouth wide. At first nothing happened. And then he began to make a noise.

The sound that issued past Teeleh's trembling pink tongue was unlike any Tom had ever heard. It was not speech. It was song. A song with long, low, terrifying notes that seemed to crackle in heavy vibration, slamming into Tom's chest.

It was as though the beast had harbored the song for a thousand years, perfecting each tone, each word. Saving it for this day.

Words came with the song now.

"Firstborn," the leader sang out, spreading his wings. In his right wing he carried a fruit. "My friend, come in peace."

The song reverberated through the air. A lovely song. A song of peace and love and joy and fruit so delicious that no person could possibly resist.

And Tom knew that he must, at all costs.

Tanis watched Teeleh with bulging eyes.

Tom found his voice. He began to yell, to scream at Tanis. But Teeleh only sang louder, drowning him out.

There were two melodies, spun as one, twisted and entwined into a single song. On one strand, beauty. Breathtaking life. On the other, terror. Endless death.

He looked at Tanis. The expression of

delight plastered on the man's face told Tom that Tanis could not hear the other notes. The twisted ones. He heard only the lovely song. The pure tones of song that rivaled those spun by Johan, or those sung by —

And then he recognized one of the melodies. It was from the lake! A song from Elyon!

Tom struggled to his feet as the song's meaning became clear. He forced air through his lungs. "Run, Tanis!" Tom screamed across the river. "Run!"

Tanis stood transfixed by the large Shataiki.

"Tanis, run!" Tom bellowed.

He reached the Crossing and staggered up its arch. His vision swam from exhaustion and pain, but he forced his feet on. Behind him, Teeleh's song continued to fill the air.

"Get out of here!" Tom gasped. He crashed into Tanis. Knocked him from his feet. The sword spun into the river.

"Have you lost your mind?"

The man stammered something and scrambled to his feet.

"Run! Just run!" Tom propelled Tanis into the forest.

Behind them Teeleh's voice rang out a new chorus. "I have powers beyond your imagination, Tanisssss!"

And then the sounds from the Crossing fell away.

They reached the clearing in which Tom had first been healed, fifty paces from the river, and Tom knew that he could not manage another step. His world tipped crazily, and he collapsed on the grass. For a moment he was vaguely aware of Tanis kneeling over him with a fruit in his hands.

Then he was aware of nothing but the distant beating of his heart.

31

Tom sagged on the couch, looking peaceful and sad at the same time, Kara thought. But behind his closed eyes, only God knew what was really happening. He'd been sleeping two hours, but if she was right, two hours could be two days in the colored forest, assuming he didn't sleep there.

Amazing. If only there was a way for him to bring Rachelle back with him. Or for her to go with Tom.

The bustle of security and secretaries and white-coated lab technicians had eased for the moment, leaving them alone in the large room they were coming to think of as their situation room.

Six hours had passed since Raison had ordered the tests. And still no answer. No definitive answer, anyway. There'd been a ruckus just after Tom had fallen asleep, when Peter had barged into the situation room, mumbling incoherently. Peter turned on his heels and hurried into Raison's office, white smock flying behind.

But when Kara ran in, Raison insisted

the results weren't conclusive. Even mixed. They had to be sure. Absolutely positive. Another test.

She glanced at her watch. If she didn't wake him soon, he wouldn't sleep well tonight, when he might very well need to. She shook him gently.

"Thomas?"

He bolted up. "Tanis!"

Tom's eyes jerked about the room. He yelled the name of the firstborn from the colored forest. "Tanis!"

"You're in Bangkok, Thomas," Kara said.

He looked at her, closed his eyes, and dropped his head. "Man. Man, oh man, that was bad."

"What happened?"

He shook his head. "I'm not sure. I went into the black forest."

"And? Did you learn anything?"

"There's no ship. He's black! Teeleh is —" He swallowed.

Kara rubbed his back. "Easy. It's okay. You're here now."

He quickly reoriented himself.

"Did you learn anything about the Raison Strain?"

"No . . . he wouldn't tell me. I . . ." Tom gripped his head, and she saw that his hands were trembling. "Crazy. It was crazy, Kara."

505

She put her arm around him and pulled him close. "You're okay, Thomas. Easy."

He looked up. "Did anything happen?"

"Nothing positive. They're still testing."

Tom sighed and sat back into the couch. Kara stood and paced the carpet, thinking. "You sure you're okay? I've never seen you wake this upset."

"I'm fine," he said, but he wasn't fine.

"Maybe we should bring in a psychologist," Kara said. "Maybe there's more of a connection to your dreams than we're understanding. Or maybe there's a way to control them more. Give you suggestions while you're sleeping or something."

"No. The last thing I want is a shrink crawling around in this crazy mind of mine. The fact is, they have the Raison Strain by now, and I know Teeleh will never tell me what we need to know. It's hopeless."

"And is it hopeless there as well?"

"Where?"

"In the colored forest?"

He stood abruptly, gaze lost. He walked to the window and peered out.

He's fried to the bone.

"I don't know," Tom said. He faced her. "If I don't get back, it might be! Something's happening to Tanis. If he crosses . . ." Tom hurried over to her. "I have to get back, Kara. You have to help me get back!"

"You just woke up! We need you here. And you're asleep there right now, right?"

"I'm unconscious there," he said.

"You'll wake when you wake. It doesn't matter how long you're awake here. The times don't correlate, remember? For all you know, someone could be kneeling over you right now, waking you. You can't control that. What you can control is how long you stay awake here. We need you to be awake now. We need your mind here. The results from the tests will be coming down any minute."

He thought about it and then nodded. They sat on the couch, side by side.

"You're sure that you can't get any more information from the black forest?"

"I'm sure."

"And Rachelle wasn't helpful?"

"No."

"Then what do we have left?"

He frowned in thought. "Monique. I think there's something about Monique. We need to find her. Maybe there's something else I can do in the colored forest to find her."

"I think you're right; she's the key."

"I had her, Kara. She was right there in my arms. I could have thrown her over my shoulders and made it. At the very least, I should have stayed."

"You had Monique in your arms?"

"She kissed me; that was her distraction while she told me about Svensson and the virus. But that's not the point."

"Maybe it is the point," Kara said. "You obviously have a thing for her, and you hardly know her."

"That's ridiculous."

"Maybe not. Any other time, maybe. But right now it makes sense." She stood from the couch. "All this talk of rescuing Rachelle, while at the same time Monique is in desperate need of exactly that. And maybe the connection is even stronger. Maybe you're right. Maybe you *have* to rescue Monique. Maybe it's not a matter of stopping Svensson, but rescuing Monique. Maybe your dreams are telling you that. Why else are you falling in love with her?"

He started to object but thought better of it.

"I mean, from everything I've heard, stopping someone from spreading a virus is almost impossible anyway. Fine, let the authorities do that."

"Great, and Tom goes after Monique. No need for professionals, CIA, Rangers, SWAT teams. No fear, Tom is here."

"You managed pretty well this morning," Kara said.

He turned back to the window, hands on hips. "I can't do this anymore."

"Yes, you can," Kara said. "And for all we know, it's just starting. Maybe you need a few new skills."

He didn't answer.

"I'm serious, Tom. Look at you. You don't die; you don't fight like any man I've seen. You —"

"Trust me, that guy could break my neck with one kick. Fact is, he *did* kill me. Twice."

"You don't sound very dead to me. Listening to you on the phone, you're sounding anything *but* dead these days. You're even turning into a bit of a romantic. Stop being so stubborn about this. I'm just supporting you."

He took a deep breath. "I'm just Tom, Kara. I didn't ask for this. I don't want to do this. I'm tired, and I feel like a wet rag." He suddenly looked like he was on the verge of tears.

Kara walked up to him and put an arm around his waist. He lowered his head on her shoulder.

"I'm sorry, Tom. I don't know what else to say. Other than I love you. You're right, you're just Tom. But I have a feeling Tom is a much bigger person than anyone, including myself, can possibly guess. I think we've all just seen the beginning."

The door flew open to their right. Jacques de Raison stepped in, face blank.

"So?" Tom said. "You have it?"

"Monique's right. You're right. The vaccine mutates at 179.47 degrees. As far as we can tell, the resulting virus is extremely contagious and very probably quite lethal."

"What a surprise," Thomas said.

Valborg Svensson wore a soft smirk that refused to budge from his face. In his right hand he held a sealed vial of yellow fluid that diffused the glare of an overhead spotlight. His left hand rested on his lap, quivering slightly. He squeezed his fingers together.

"Who would ever have guessed?" he said. "History changed because of a few drops of such an innocuous-looking yellow liquid and one man who had the stomach to use it."

Eight technicians milled in the lab below, talking, stealing furtive glances up at the window behind which he sat. Mathews, Sestanovich, Burton, Myles . . . the list went on. Some of the world's most accomplished and, as of late, highest-paid virologists. They had sold their souls for his cause. All in the name of science, of course. With a little misdirection from him. They were simply developing lethal viruses for the sake of antiviruses. How many of them truly believed what they were doing was so innocuous, Svensson didn't care.

The fact was, they all took his money. More important, they all understood the price of compromising confidentiality.

"Bring her up," he said.

Carlos left without a word.

How many billions had he invested in this venture? Too many to count offhand. They meticulously explored the most advanced science, and yet, in the end, it came down to a vaccine and a bit of luck.

Svensson knew the history of biowarfare well enough to recite in his sleep.

1346: Tartars send soldiers infected with the plague over the wall in the siege of Caffa on the Black Sea.

1422: Attacking forces launch decaying cadavers over castle walls in Bohemia.

American Revolution: British forces expose civilians to smallpox in Quebec and Boston. The Boston attempt fails; the one in Quebec ravages the Continental Army.

World War I: Germans target livestock being shipped into Allied countries. Overall impact on war: negligible.

World War II: Unit 731 of the Imperial Japanese Army directs biowarfare on a massive scale against China. As many as ten thousand die in Manchuria in 1936. In 1940, bags of plague-infected fleas are dropped over the cities of Ningbo and Quzhou. By the end of the war, the Americans and the Soviets have developed significant bioweapons programs.

Cold War: Both the United States and the Soviet Union bioweapons programs reach new heights, exploring the use of hundreds of bacteria, viruses, and biological toxins. In 1972, more than one hundred nations sign the Biological and Toxin Weapons Convention, banning production of biological weapons. There is no enforcement. In 1989, Vladimir Pasechnik defects to Britain and tells of the Soviets' genetically altered superplague, an antibiotic-resistant inhalation anthrax. The Soviet program employs thousands of specialists, many who scatter when the Soviet Union crumbles. Some of these specialists take up residence in Iraq. Others take up residence in the Swiss Alps, under the thumb of Valborg Svensson.

Dawn of the twenty-first century: The first truly successful use of any biological weapon is unleashed. The Raison Strain redefines modern power structures.

The last wasn't yet a matter of history, of course. But the vial in Svensson's hand said it would be soon. In reality, biological weapons were still in their infancy, unlike nuclear weapons. Anyone who understood this also understood that whoever won the unspoken race to perfect the right bioweapon would wield more power than any man who had ever preceded him. Period.

The door opened and Carlos marched a disheveled Monique de Raison forward.

"Sit," Svensson said.

She sat with a little encouragement from Carlos.

"Do you know what would happen if I dropped this vial?" Svensson asked. He didn't expect an answer. "Nothing for three weeks, if your friend is right. And I will say that our people think he very well may be. He was right about the virus, why not about the incubation period?"

Still no reaction. She believed this much already.

"If you only knew the trouble we've accepted over numerous years to be in this position today. Monoclonal antibody research, gene probes, combinatorial chemistry, genetic engineering — we've scoured every corner of Earth for the right breakthrough."

Her eyes remained on the vial.

"And today I have that breakthrough. The Raison Strain — it has a nice ring to it, don't you think? What I need now is the antivirus, or an antidote. There are two ways I can proceed with this task. One: I can have my people work on the numbers we already have. They will eventually develop precisely what I need. Or, two: I can persuade you to develop what I need. You know more about these genes than anyone

513

alive. Either way, I will have an antivirus. But I rather prefer a quick solution to one that drags out for days or weeks or months, don't you?"

"You honestly think I would lift a finger to help you with any part of this . . . this insanity?" She had the look of someone who was seriously considering an assault. If her hands weren't bound, she might have tried. Her spirit was entirely noble.

"You already have," he said. "You've created the vaccine, and you've provided more research than I could have hoped for. Now it's time to help us with the cure. A cure doesn't interest you, Monique?"

"Without the antivirus, you have nothing."

"Not true," Svensson said. "I have the virus. And I will use it. Either way."

"Then throw it on the floor now," she said evenly. "We'll die together."

He smiled. "Don't tempt me. But I won't, because I know that you will help us. If nothing else, the fact that this virus now exists will force your hand. Every day that passes without a way to protect the world's population against this disease is a day closer to your torment."

"You think my father isn't already working on an antivirus?"

"But how long will it take him? Months, best case. I, on the other hand, have some idea where to begin. I'm confident we can do it in a week. With your help, of course."

"No."

"No?"

"No."

She would change her mind within twenty-four hours.

"I'll give you twelve hours to change your mind on your own. Then I will change it for you."

She didn't react.

"No more word, Carlos?"

"None."

The first call from the authorities had come two hours ago. A courtesy call from his own government, requesting an interview of the highest priority. It meant that they suspected him already. Fascinating. It was Thomas Hunter, of course. The dreamer. Carlos had said he'd killed the man in the hotel room, but the media said differently. Carlos either had lied deliberately or, more likely, had been bested by this man. It was something he would keep in mind.

The authorities didn't have enough for a search warrant. He'd granted them their interview, but not for two more days. By then it wouldn't matter.

"Everything is ready?"

"Yes."

"Then I will handle the next move. I want you to eliminate the American."

He watched Carlos. Not a flinch, just a steady gaze. "I shot the American twice. You're saying that he's not dead?"

The woman glanced up at Carlos. She, too, knew something.

"He's alive enough to be in the news. He's also the source of the antivirus. I want him dead at all costs."

Monique turned to him. "Are you aware that your right-hand man is lying to you? One of the men who came for me outside Bangkok was Thomas Hunter. Carlos knows that. Why is he hiding this from you?"

"Thomas Hunter?" Carlos looked at the woman with some surprise. "I don't think that's possible. He may not be dead, but he has two bullets in his chest. And he's a civilian, not a solider."

Her accusation was meant to sow distrust. Smart. But he had far more reason to distrust her than Carlos.

The man from Cyprus faced him. "I will leave immediately. Thomas Hunter will be dead within forty-eight hours. On this you have my word."

Svensson looked back into the lab. The technicians were huddled over three different work stations now, assessing the information Carlos had reported from

Thomas Hunter, this string of numbers.

Svensson now faced two very significant risks. One, that his operation would be found out. Unlikely, considering all their meticulous planning, but a risk nonetheless. Timing was now critical.

The second significant risk was that neither his people nor Monique could develop an antivirus in time. He was willing to accept that risk. His name was now out there; sooner or later they would know the truth. If he didn't succeed now, he would either spend the rest of his life in a prison or die. The latter was more appealing.

"I will be contacting the others in a few hours. Meet us at the control facility as soon as you've eliminated Hunter. Take her."

Tom stared at the monitor that displayed what the electron microscope had uncovered. The Raison Strain. He tried to imagine how a sea of these tiny viruses could possibly hurt a flea, much less slaughter a few billion people. They looked like an Apollo lunar-lander, a miniature pod on legs that had landed its host cell.

"That's the Raison Strain?"

"That's the Raison Strain," Peter said. "Looks harmless, doesn't it?"

"Looks like a tiny machine. So the mutation is sustained even when the temperatures come down?"

"Unfortunately, yes. It's terribly unusual, you know. No regulation or protocol even suggests testing vaccines at such a high temperature. No one could have possibly guessed that mutation was even possible at such a temperature."

Tom straightened. Jacques de Raison stood by Kara and a half-dozen other technicians in white coats.

"And how can you tell what the virus will do?"

Peter looked at Raison, who nodded. "Show him."

Peter led them to another computer monitor. "We're basing the conclusions on a simulation. Two years ago this would have taken a month, but thanks to new models that we've developed in conjunction with DARPA, we're down to a few hours." He tapped several keys and brought the screen to life.

"We feed the genetic signature of the virus into the model — in this case human — and then let the computer simulate the effect of infection. We can squeeze two months into two hours."

"Put it on the big screen, Peter," Raison said.

The image popped up on an overhead screen.

"Hold on . . . there."

A single cell appeared.

"That's a normal cell taken from a human liver. Lodged on its outer membrane you can see the Raison Strain, introduced through the blood supply —"

"I don't see it."

"It's very small, one of the reasons it fares so well as an airborne agent." Peter stepped up and pointed to the left side of the cell with a wand. "This small growth here. That's the Raison Strain."

"That's the deadly beast?" Tom said. "Hard to believe."

"That's it on day one, before lysogeny —"

"Could you explain it in layman's terms? Pretend I'm a fifth grader."

Peter smiled awkwardly.

"Okay. Viruses aren't cells. They don't grow or multiply like cells do. They consist basically of a shell that harbors a little bit of DNA. You know what DNA is, right?"

"Blueprint for life and all that."

"Good enough. Well, that shell we call a virus is able to attach to a cell wall and squirt its viral DNA inside. Think of it as a nasty little bug. The squirted DNA makes its way into the DNA of the host cell, in this case a liver cell, so that the host cell will be forced to make more viral shells as well as pieces of identical viral DNA. Follow?"

"This little bug can do all that? You'd

think it has a mind of its own."

"That and more. Viruses are assembled; they do not grow. They take over the host and turn it into a factory for more viral shells, which repeat the process."

"Like the collective Borg in *Star Trek*," Thomas said.

"In many ways, yes. Like the Borg. The way they kill the cell is by making so many shells that the cell literally explodes. This is called lysogeny."

"Somehow I missed all this in biology."

Peter continued. "Some viruses linger and wait until the host is under stress before constructing themselves. That's called latency. In this case our virus is a very slow starter, but after two weeks it becomes very aggressive, and its exponential growth overtakes the body in a matter of days. Watch."

Peter returned to the keyboard and punched in a command. Slowly the image on the screen began to change. The virus injected the host cell like a scorpion. The liver cell started to change and then hemorrhaged.

"Lysogeny," Thomas said.

"Exactly."

The view expanded, and thousands of similar cells went through the same process.

"A human body infected by this virus

will literally eat itself up from the inside out."

He hit another key. They watched in silence as the same simulation was shown on a human heart. The organ began to break apart as its countless cells hemorrhaged.

"Quite deadly," Peter said.

"How long?" Tom asked.

"Based on this simulation, the virus will require under three weeks to build enough momentum to affect organ functionality." He shrugged. "It is then a matter of days, depending on the subject."

Tom faced Raison. "I take it we are now in agreement?"

"Yes. Clearly."

"And you've informed the CDC?"

"We're in the process now. But you must understand, Mr. Hunter: This is a scenario, not a crisis. Outside this laboratory, the Raison Strain doesn't even exist. It would never occur in nature."

"I realize that. But I have it on pretty good authority that someone is going to go around nature. It may be too late, but on the off chance it's not, we have to mobilize as if it is a crisis. We need to stop Svensson, and we need an antivirus within a couple of weeks."

"That's impossible," Raison said.

"So I keep hearing," Tom muttered. He turned to Peter. "You can't create an antivirus with all this computing power?"

"I'm afraid it's an entirely different matter. Two months, best case, but not three weeks."

Tom caught Kara's stare. She had that look. This would be up to him. But he didn't want it to be up to him.

"If we had Monique," Peter said, "we might have a chance. She engineers certain particulars into all of her vaccines to protect them against theft or foul play. It's essentially a backdoor switch that's triggered by the introduction of another uniquely engineered virus, which renders the vaccine impotent. If her engineering survived the mutation, her unique virus could also kill Svensson's lethal strain."

"So she may have the key?"

"Maybe. Assuming the mutation didn't destroy her back door."

The room went silent.

"You don't have this switch of hers? She keeps this where, in her head? That seems stupid."

"Until a vaccine is approved by the international community, she keeps the key to herself. It's her way of making sure no one, including employees, steals or tampers with the technology."

"And she keeps no records."

"It's not a complicated matter if you know which genes to manipulate," Peter said. "If there are records, no one here knows where they would be. Either way, it's a long shot. The switch may have mutated along with the vaccine."

"Naturally, we will search," Jacques de Raison said. "But as you can see, we must find my daughter."

"Agreed," Tom said. "We should also wake up the world."

Tom left the meeting exhausted and, worse, powerless. He was still under house arrest for kidnapping. He made a dozen phone calls but was quickly reminded of why he came to Bangkok in the first place. News of this sort wasn't received well from a source as unlikely as him. Especially now that he was quite famous for kidnapping Monique.

Fortunately Raison Pharmaceutical commanded far more respect.

Reports of the potential mutation of the Raison Vaccine hit all the appropriate teletypes and computer screens throughout the massive bureaucracy of health services.

It did not send the world scrambling for answers.

It was not a crisis.

It was hardly even a problem.

It was only a possible scenario in one of the models held by Raison Pharmaceutical.

Tom collapsed into bed at nine that night, weary to the bone but frazzled by the knowledge that the probability of this particular scenario was 100 percent.

It took him a full hour to fall asleep.

32

Tanis sat alone on the hill overlooking the village. The events of the morning still buzzed about in his mind. For the first time in his life, he'd actually seen the creature from the black forest, and the experience had been astounding. Exhilarating. Most surprising had been the song. This stunning creature was not the terrible black beast of his vivid imagination and stories.

He had saved Thomas. That was justification enough for his visit to the black forest. So then, it was a good thing he'd gone.

Tanis had stayed with Thomas for a short time before leaving. Oddly, he had no desire to be with the man when he awoke.

He'd returned and spent some time in the village. Rachelle had asked him if he'd run into Thomas, and he'd told her that he had, and that Thomas was sleeping.

He'd wandered around the village feeling very much in place and at peace. By midday, however, he felt as though he must go somewhere by himself to consider the events continuing to nag his mind. And so he had come here, to this hill overlooking the entire valley.

Tanis had gone to fetch the sword he'd thrown in the woods yesterday and found it missing. And not only that, but Thomas was also missing. He wasn't sure why he'd concluded that Thomas had taken the sword to the Crossing — perhaps because this very thought was on his own mind — but after searching high and low for the man, he decided to make another sword and go in search at the Crossing.

What interested him most was the fact that Thomas had come from the black forest and lived to tell of it. Not just once, but twice.

The creature . . . now the creature had been something else altogether. He'd never imagined Teeleh as he appeared. Indeed, he hadn't imagined that such a beautiful being could have existed in the black forest at all. Admittedly, he looked rather unique with those green eyes and golden fur. But the song . . .

Oh, what a song!

The fact of the matter was that Tanis wanted very much to meet this creature again. He had no desire to cross into the black forest and drink the water, of course. That would mean death. Worse yet, it was forbidden. But to meet the black creature at the river — that had not been forbidden.

And Thomas had done it.

Tanis glanced at the sun. He had been sitting on the hill, turning the events over in his mind, for over an hour now. If he were to leave now, he could reach the black forest and return without being missed again.

He stood shakily to his feet. The eagerness he felt was odd enough to cause a slight confusion. He couldn't remember ever feeling such strange turmoil. For a moment he thought he should just return to the village and forget the creature at the black forest completely. But he quickly decided against it. After all, he wanted very much to understand this terrible enemy of his. Not to mention the song. To understand one's enemy is to have power over him.

Yes, Tanis wanted this very much, and there was no reason not to do what he so greatly desired. Unless, of course, it went against the will of Elyon. But Elyon had not prohibited meeting new creatures, regardless of where they lived. Even across the river.

With one last look to the valley floor, Tanis turned his back and struck out for the black forest.

Tom woke with a start. The sweet smell of grass filled his nostrils. He'd dreamed again. Bangkok. They were running ragged in Bangkok because they'd finally accepted the virus at face value. The Raison Strain now existed, if only in laboratories. He had to find Monique, but he had no idea how. And here —

He jerked up. *Tanis?*

He scrambled to his feet and looked around. "Tanis!"

The rush of the river drifted from the east. It was midafternoon. Tanis must have left him near the Crossing and returned to the village.

It took him an hour to reach the valley, fifteen minutes of that retracing his way north after missing the path that led to the village. He had to reach Tanis and explain himself. If ever the man was capable of confusion, it would be now. And the fact that Tanis had made himself another sword after their discussion only yesterday didn't bode well for the man.

He was bitten with the bug. His curiosity was turning. His desire was outpacing his satisfaction. He'd gone to the Crossing because he was tired of not knowing.

Well, now he knew, all right. The only question was, How much knowledge would suffice? And for how long?

Of course, Tom had gone across as well. But he was different; there could no longer be any question about that. He hadn't taken any water, but according to Teeleh, he'd eaten the fruit before losing his memory, and he'd managed to survive. It was like a vaccine, perhaps.

No, that couldn't be right. Still, Tom was quite sure that he was different from Tanis. Maybe the people from his village far away had more liberties. But that made even less sense. Maybe he *was* from Bangkok. He might be from Bangkok when he was dreaming, but in reality he was from here. This was his home, and his dreams of Bangkok were wreaking havoc here.

He should eat the rhambutan fruit and rid himself of these silly dreams. They were meddling with a tenuous balance. If not for him, Tanis wouldn't have gone to the black forest today.

"Thomas!"

A Roush swept in from his right.

"Michal!"

The Roush hit the ground hard, bounced once, and flapped furiously to keep from crashing.

"Michal?"

"Oh, dear, dear! Oh, my goodness!"

"What's wrong?"

"It's Tanis. I think he is headed for the black forest."

"Tanis? The black forest?" Impossible! He'd just been to the black forest a few hours ago!

"He was headed straight for it when I left to find you. And he was running. How is that for being sure?" Michal hopped about nervously as though he had stepped on a hot coal.

"For the sake of Elyon, why didn't you stop him?"

"Why didn't I stop *you?* It's not my place; that's why! He's mad! You're both mad, I tell you. Just plain mad. Sometimes I wonder what the point was. You humans are just too unpredictable."

Tom tried to think clearly. "Just because he's running in that direction doesn't mean he's going to enter the black forest."

Michal's eyes flashed. "We don't have time to discuss this! Even if we go now, you could be too late. Please. Do you know what this could mean?"

"He can't be that stupid," Tom said. He meant to reassure Michal, but he didn't even believe himself.

Neither did Michal. "Please, we must go now."

The Roush ran along the grass, flapping madly. Then he was in the air. Tom sprinted to catch him.

An image of the boy at the upper lake filled his mind. That had been two days ago. What had come over them? He suddenly felt suffocated with panic.

"Elyon!" he breathed.

But Elyon had grown completely silent.
"Michal!" he yelled.

The Roush was preoccupied with his own thoughts. Tom quickened his pace. There was no way he could let Tanis do anything even remotely so unreasonable as talk to Teeleh.

Not while he was alive.

The scene that greeted Tanis when he broke onto the banks of the river stopped him cold.

As far as he could see in either direction, black creatures with red eyes crowded the trees along the edge of the black forest like a dense, shifting black cloud. There had to be a million of them. Maybe many more.

His first thought was that Thomas had been right — there were far too many to easily dispatch with a few well-placed kicks.

His second was to run.

Tanis jumped back under the cover of the trees. He had never heard that so many other creatures shared their world. He held his breath and peered around a tree at the wondrous sight.

And then he saw the beautiful creature standing on the white bridge. The one he had seen at sunrise! The beast wore a bright yellow cloak and a wreath fashioned with white flowers around his head. He gnawed on a large fruit, the likes of which Tanis had never seen, and stared directly at him with glowing, green eyes.

Silence. All but the river was deathly silent. It was as if they had expected him. What a lovely creature Teeleh was.

He caught himself. These were the Shataiki. Vermin. They were meant to be beaten, not coddled. But, as the histories had so eloquently recorded, to defeat your enemy you must know him. He would speak to the big beautiful one only. And he would pretend to be a friend. In this way he would outwit the creature by learning his weaknesses, then return one day and be rid of him.

And he would do it holding the colored wood.

He grabbed a small green stick about the length of his arm and stepped out onto the bank.

"Greetings," he called. "I am Tanis. By what name are you called?"

He knew, of course, but Tanis didn't want to tip his hand. The beast tossed the half-eaten fruit behind him and rubbed the juice from his mouth with a hairy blue wing. He smiled with crooked yellow teeth. "I am Teeleh," he said. "We have waited for you, my friend."

Tanis glanced back at the colored forest. Well, then. Here was the creature he had come to meet. Tanis felt an uncommon flutter in his heart and stepped out to meet Teeleh, the leader of the Shataiki.

He stopped at the foot of the bridge and studied the creature. Of course! This was trickery! How could the leader of the Shataiki be different from his legions?

"You're not what I expected," he said.

"No? And what did you expect?"

"I had heard that you were quite clever. How clever is it to pretend you're different than you really are when you know you'll be found out?"

Teeleh chuckled. "You like that, don't you?"

"I like what? Exposing you for what you are? Are you afraid to show me who you really are?"

"You like being clever," Teeleh said. "It's why you've come here. To be clever. To learn more. More knowledge. The truth."

"Then show me the truth."

"I intend to."

Teeleh's eyes turned first, from green to red. Then his wings and body, slowly to gray, then black. All the while his smile held true. Talons extended from his feet and dug into the wood. It was a shocking transformation, and Tanis gripped the colored stick tighter.

"Is that better?" The bat's voice had

changed to a low, guttural growl.

"No. It's much worse. You're the most hideous creature I could ever have imagined."

"Ah, but I possess more knowledge and truth than you could ever have imagined as well. Would you like to hear?"

The invitation sounded suspect, but Tanis couldn't think of an appropriate way to decline. How could he reject the truth?

Teeleh's snout suddenly gaped wide, so that Tanis could see the back of his mouth, where his pink tongue disappeared into a dark throat. A low, rumbling note rolled out, followed immediately by a high, piercing one that seemed to reach into him and touch his spine. Teeleh's song ravaged him with its strange chorus of terrible beauty. Powerful and conquering and intoxicating at once. Tanis felt an overwhelming compulsion to rush up the bridge, but he held firm.

Teeleh closed his mouth. The notes echoed, then fell silent. The bats in the forest peered at him without a stir. Tanis felt a little disorientated by all these new sensations.

"This is new to you?" Teeleh asked.

Tanis shifted the makeshift sword to his left hand. "Yes."

"And do you know why it's new?"

It was a good question. A trick? No, just a question.

"Are you afraid of me?" Teeleh asked. "You know that I can't cross the bridge, yet you stand at the bottom in fear."

"Why would I be afraid of what can't harm me?"

No, that's not entirely true. He can hurt me. I must be very careful.

"Then walk closer. You want to know more about me so that you can destroy me. So walk closer and see me clearly."

How did the beast know this?

"Because I know far more than you do, my friend. And I can tell you how to know what I know. Come closer. You're safe. You have the wood in your hand."

Teeleh could have guessed his thoughts; they weren't so unique. At any rate, he should show this beast that he was not afraid. What kind of warrior quivered at the bottom of the bridge? He walked up the white planks and stopped ten feet from Teeleh.

"You are braver than most," the bat said, eying his colored sword.

"And I am not as dense as you think I am," Tanis said. "I know that even now you're trying your trickery."

"If I use this . . . trickery and persuade you by it, wouldn't that mean I am smarter than you?"

Tanis considered the logic. "Perhaps."

"Then trickery is a form of knowledge. And knowledge is a form of truth. And you want more of it; otherwise, as I said, you wouldn't be here. So if by using trickery I persuade you to accept my knowledge, it can only be because I am smarter than you. I have more truth."

It was confounding, this logic of his.

"The reason my song is new to you, Tanis, is because Elyon doesn't want you to hear it. And why? Because it will give you the same knowledge that I have. It will give you too much power. Power comes with the truth; you already know that."

"Yes. But I won't have you talking about Elyon like this." Tanis jabbed his stick forward. "I should stick you through now and be done with this."

"Go ahead. Try it."

"I might, but I'm not here for battle. I'm here to learn the truth."

"Well, then. I can show it to you." Teeleh pulled a yellow fruit from behind his back. "There is in this fruit some knowledge. Power. Enough power to make all the creatures behind me cringe. Wouldn't you like that? One word from you, and they will squeal in pain. Because they will know you have the truth, and with that truth comes great power. Here, try it."

"No, I can't eat your fruit."

"Then you don't want the truth?"

"Yes, but —"

"Is it forbidden to eat this fruit?"

"No."

"Of course not. If there was harm in eating this fruit, Elyon would have forbidden it! But there is no harm, so it is not forbidden. There is only knowledge and power. Take it."

Tanis glanced back at the colored forest. What the bat said was true. There was no harm in eating the fruit. There was no evil in it. It wasn't forbidden.

"Just one bite," Teeleh said. "If you find that what I've said isn't true, then leave. But you owe it to yourself to at least try it. Hmm? Don't you think?" The large beast made no effort to hide his talons, which tapped impatiently on the wood bridge.

Tanis looked past the large black bat and hesitated. "Well, you know I won't drink any of your water."

"Heavens no! Just the fruit. A gift of truth from me to you."

Tanis held the colored stick firmly and stepped forward to take the fruit.

"Keep the wood to your side, if you don't mind," Teeleh said. "It is the color of deception, and it doesn't sit well with my truth."

Tanis stopped. "See, I already have the

power. Why do I need yours?"

"Go ahead, wave it at my subjects and see how much power you have."

Tanis glanced at the throngs behind Teeleh. He motioned at them with the sword, but none so much as flinched.

"You see? How can you compare your power to mine, unless you first know? Know your enemy. Know his fruit. Taste what Elyon himself has invited you to taste by *not* forbidding it. Just keep your stick at your side so that it doesn't touch me."

Tanis now wanted very much to try this mysterious yellow fruit in Teeleh's claw. He lowered the sword to his side, ready to use it at a moment's notice, stepped forward, and took the fruit. It felt daring, but he was a warrior, and to defeat this enemy he had to employ his own trickery.

He stepped back, just out of Teeleh's reach, and bit into the fruit. Immediately his world swam in stunning color. Power surged through his blood, and his mind felt numb.

"Do you feel the power?"

"It's . . . it's quite strong," Tanis said. He took another bite.

"Now, raise your hand and command my legions."

Tanis looked at the black bats that lined the trees. "Now?"

"Yes. Use your new power."

Tanis lifted an unsteady hand. Without a single word, the Shataiki began to shriek and turn away. The sound made him cringe. Terror swept through their ranks. This with a single outstretched arm.

"You see? Lower your arm before you destroy my army."

Tanis lowered his arm.

"Can I take this fruit with me?"

"No. Please hand it back."

Tanis did so, though somewhat reluctantly. The Shataiki continued their ruckus.

"Not to worry, my friend. I have another fruit. More truth. More power. This one will open your mind to the forbidden truth. That is the truth only the wise ones possess. You can't command armies with power alone. You must have the mind to lead. This fruit will show it to you."

Tanis knew he should leave, but there was no law forbidding even this.

"It's the same fruit your friend Thomas ate," Teeleh said.

Tanis looked up, shocked. "Thomas ate your fruit?"

"Of course. It's why he's so wise. And he knows the histories because he drank my water. Thomas has the knowledge."

The revelation made Tanis dizzy. That was how Thomas knew the histories. He reached out his hand.

"No, for this fruit you must put your sword on the railing here, on my side of the bridge. I can't touch it, of course. But you must hold this fruit with both hands."

The bat's reasoning sounded very strange, but then Tanis's mind wasn't entirely clear. As long as the sword was right there where he could grab it if needed, what harm would there be in setting it down? If anything, it put a greater barrier between him and the bat.

Tanis stepped forward and set the stick on the railing. Then he reached both hands for the fruit in Teeleh's outstretched claw.

When they broke from the forest, Tanis already stood before the horrid beast, like a dumb sheep bleating to its butcher. Tom skidded to a halt. Michal landed on a branch to his right.

"Michal!" Tom rasped.

"We're too late!" the Roush said. "Too late!"

"He's still talking!"

"Tanis will decide."

"What?"

Tom turned back to the scene before him. Tom stood frozen by the moment. He could barely hear his friend's voice above the shrieking bats.

"This is the fruit that Thomas ate?" Tanis took the fruit from the grinning black beast with both hands.

Tom released the tree he had gripped with white knuckles and leaped forward. *No, Tanis! Don't be such an utter fool. Throw it back at him!*

He wanted to yell it, but his throat was frozen.

"It is indeed, my friend," Teeleh said. "Thomas is a very wise man indeed."

Half the Shataiki lining the trees now noticed him. They flew into a fit, pointing in panic, shrieks now earsplitting.

Tom raced across the bank toward the arching bridge. "Tanis!"

But Tanis didn't turn. Had he already eaten?

Tanis took one step backward, and Tom was sure that he was about to fling the fruit back at the beast and leave him standing on the bridge's crest. The man paused and said something too softly for Tom to hear above the bats. He stared at the fruit in his hands.

"Tanis!" Tom cried, rushing onto the bridge.

Tanis calmly brought the fruit to his mouth and bit deeply.

The throng of bats in the trees behind Teeleh suddenly fell silent. The wind whistled quietly and the river below murmured, but otherwise a terrible stillness swallowed the bridge.

"Tanis!"

Tanis whirled around. A stream of juice glistened on his chin. The fruit's yellow flesh was lodged in his gaping mouth.

"Thomas. You've come!"

He closed his lips over the piece between his teeth and held the bitten fruit out toward Tom. "Is this the same fruit you ate, Thomas? I must say, it is very good indeed."

Tom slid to a halt halfway up the arch. "Don't be a fool, Tanis! It's not too late. Drop it and come back." He shook as he spoke. "Now! Drop it now!"

"Oh, it is you," the beast behind Tanis sneered. "I thought I heard a voice. Don't worry, Tanis, my friend. He would like to be the only one to eat my fruit, but you know too much now, don't you? Has he told you about his spaceship?"

Tanis swiveled his head from Tom to the beast and back again, as though unsure of what he was expected to do.

"Tanis, don't listen to him. Get ahold of yourself!"

Tanis's eyes seemed to float in their sockets. The fruit was taking its toll on the man.

"Thomas? What spaceship?" Tanis asked.

"He's afraid to tell you the truth," Teeleh snarled. "He drank the water!"

"It's a lie!" Tom said. "Do *not* cross the

bridge. Drop the fruit."

Tanis wasn't listening. Yellow juice from the fruit trickled down his cheek, staining his tunic. He turned back to the beast and took another bite.

"Very powerful," he said. "With this kind of power, I could defeat even you."

"Yesssss." The hideous bat grinned. "And we have something you cannot possibly imagine."

He withdrew a leather pouch.

"Here, drink this. It will open your eyes to new worlds."

Tanis looked at the bat, then at the pouch. Then he reached one hand for the pouch.

Teeleh turned, and in doing so he bumped into something Tom hadn't seen before. A stick resting on the railing. A dark stick that had lost its color. The wood slid off the railing and fell into the river.

Tom whirled around. Michal was watching in silence. "Elyon!" Tom screamed. Surely he would do something. He loved Tanis desperately. "Elyon!"

Nothing.

He spun back to the bridge. What was happening was happening because of him. In spite of him. He felt as powerless and as terrified as he could ever remember feeling.

Teeleh walked slowly, ever so slowly, favoring his right leg. Down the bridge to the opposite bank. "More knowledge than you can handle," he said. "Isn't that so, my friends?" he bellowed to the throngs lining the forest.

"Yesss . . . yessss," rasped a sea of voices.

"Then bid our friend drink," he cried out, stepping onto the opposite bank. "Bid him drink!"

"Drink, drink, drink, drink," the Shataiki chanted slowly, in one throbbing, seductive tone. A song.

Tom felt the hair on his neck stand on end. Tanis looked back at him, eyes glazed over, a grin twisting his face. He released a nervous chuckle.

Tom's mind began to swim in panic. Tanis was falling for it!

In final desperation, he lunged up the arch toward the intoxicated man. "Tanis, don't. Don't do it!" he cried over the bewitched song. "You have no idea what you're doing!"

Tanis turned back to the chanting throng and took a step toward the opposite shore.

Images of Rachelle and little Johan flashed before Tom's eyes. This was not going to happen, not if he could help it.

He leaped forward, gripped the railing with his left arm, and flung his other arm around the man's waist. Planting his feet hard, he jerked Tanis back, nearly pulling him from his feet.

With a snarl Tanis swung around and planted a kick on his chest. Tom flew back and sat hard on the deck.

"No, Thomas! You are not the only one who can have this knowledge! Who are you to tell me what I must do?"

"It's a lie, Tanis! I didn't drink!"

"You're lying! You're dreaming of the histories. No one has ever dreamed of the histories."

"Because I fell!"

A brief look of confusion crossed the firstborn's face. He turned away with a tear in his eye, lifted the pouch to his lips, and poured the water into his mouth.

Then he walked over the bridge and stepped onto the parched earth beyond.

What happened next was a sight Tom would never forget as long as he lived. The moment Tanis set foot on the ground next to the large black bat, a dozen smaller Shataiki stalked out to greet him. Tom scrambled to his feet just as Tanis extended a hand in greeting to the nearest Shataiki. But instead of taking his hand, the Shataiki suddenly leaped from the ground and slashed angrily at the extended hand with his talons.

For a moment, time seemed to cease.

The pouch dropped from Tanis's hand. His half-eaten fruit tumbled lazily to the ground. Tanis lowered his eyes to his hand just as the white walls of a deep gash began to fill with blood.

And then the first effects of his new world fell on the elder like a vicious, bloodthirsty beast.

Tanis screamed with pain.

Teeleh faced the black forest, standing tall and stately.

"Take him!" he said.

The groups of Shataiki who had greeted Tanis dived for him. Tanis threw his hands up in defense, but in his state of shock it was hopeless. Fangs punctured his neck and his spine; a wicked claw sliced at his face, severing most of it in one terrible swipe. Then Tanis disappeared in a mess of flailing black fur.

Teeleh raised his wings in victory and beckoned the waiting throngs that still clung to the trees. "Now!" he thundered above the sounds of the attack on Tanis. "Now! Did I not tell you?" He lifted his chin and howled in a voice so loud and so terrifying that it seemed to rip the sky itself open.

"Our time has come!"

A ground-shaking roar erupted from the horde of beasts. Above the cheer Tom heard the leader's throaty, guttural roar. "Destroy the land. Take what is ours!"

Teeleh swept his wings toward the colored forest.

★ ★ ★

Tom watched, frozen by horror, as a massive black wall of bats took flight. The wall ran as far as he could see in either direction and seemed to move in slow motion for its sheer size. A dark shadow crept across the ground. It moved over the black forest, then up the bridge toward Thomas. The white wood cracked and turned gray along the forward edge of the shadow. The pungent odor of sulfur swarmed him.

Tom whirled and ran just ahead of the shadow. He leaped off the bridge and hit the grass in a full sprint. Michal was gone!

"Michal!" he screamed.

He dared a quick glance back at the trees that marked the edge of the colored forest. The grass behind him was turning to black ash along the leading edge of the shadow, as if a long line of fire had been set ablaze beneath the earth and was incinerating the green life above it.

But he knew the death didn't come from below. It came from the black bats above. And what would happen to his flesh when the shadow overtook him?

He screamed and pumped his legs in a blind panic, knowing full well that panic would only slow him down. "Elyon!"

Elyon wasn't responding.

The shadow from the wall of black bats above reached him when he tore into the clearing just beyond the riverbank. He tensed in anticipation of the searing pain of burning flesh.

The burned grass under his feet crackled. The colored light from the trees on either side winked out, and the green canopy began crumbling in heaps of black ash. The air turned thick and difficult to breathe.

But his flesh didn't burn.

The shadow moved on, just ahead of him. His strength began to fade.

The wall of bats was moving toward the village. No! It would reach them long before Tom could sound any warning.

The animals and birds howled and shrieked in aimless circles of confusion.

Here in the shadow was death. Ahead, before the shadow, there was still life. The life of the colored forest. The life that allowed Tanis to execute incredible maneuvers in the air with superhuman strength. The life that had fed Tom's own strength over the previous days.

One last wedge of hope lodged stubbornly in Tom's mind. If only he could catch the shadow. Pass back into the life ahead of it. If only he could summon the last reserves of his strength from any fruit on the trees, from any life in the land.

If he could just stay ahead of the bats.

The fruit was falling from the charred

trees and thudding to the ground like a slow hail. Tom veered to his left, dipped down and grabbed a piece of fruit, and bit off a chunk of flesh. He swallowed without chewing.

Immediately, strength returned.

Clenching his hands around the fruit, he tore forward. Juice seeped around his knuckles. He shoved another bite in his mouth and swallowed and ran.

Slowly, very slowly, he gained ground on the shadow. Why the bats didn't swoop down and chew him to pieces, he didn't know. Perhaps in their eagerness to reach the village they ignored this one human below.

He sucked down two more chunks of fruit and chased the shadow for ten minutes in a full sprint before catching it. But now his panic had left him. The moment he passed in front of the canopy of bats, his strength surged.

He snatched a piece of unspoiled fruit and ripped off a huge bite.

Sweet, sweet release. Tom shivered and sobbed. And he ran.

With a strength beyond himself, he ran, gaining on the shadow, on the approaching throng shrieking high above him. First fifty yards, then a hundred, then two hundred. Soon they were a massive black cloud well behind him.

From a hill he could see their approach with stunning clarity. From this vantage point he saw what was happening in a new light. The black forest was encroaching on the green in a long, endless line that blocked the sun and burned the land to a crisp.

He raced on, vision blurred with tears, screaming in rage.

The sky above the valley was empty when Tom broke from the forest. It was, in fact, the only sign that there was anything at all askew. At any other time at least a dozen Roush would be floating in lazy circles above the village, or tumbling along the grass with the children. Now there wasn't a single one to be seen. No Michal, no Gabil.

Below, the villagers went about peacefully, ignorantly. Children scampered between the huts, laughing in delight; mothers cuddled their young as they sang softly and stepped lightly in dance; fathers retold their tales of great exploits — all unaware of the approaching throng that would soon tear into them.

Tom tore down the hill. "Oh, Elyon," he pleaded. "Please, I beg you, give me a way."

He ran into the village screaming at the top of his lungs. "Shataiki! They're coming! Everyone grab something to defend yourselves!"

Johan and Rachelle skipped toward him with smiles on their faces, waving eagerly. "Thomas," Rachelle called. "There you are."

"Rachelle!" Tom rushed up to her. "Quick, you have to protect yourself." He glanced up the hill and saw the wall of bats above the crest. Thousands of the black creatures suddenly broke rank and poured into the valley.

It was too late. There was no way they could defend themselves. These weren't the ghosts with phantom claws that they had learned how to combat with fancy aerial kicks. Like Tanis, they would be pummeled by the bloodthirsty beasts.

Tom whirled around and grabbed both of their hands. "Come with me!" he demanded, sprinting down the path. "Hurry!"

"Look!" Johan yelled. He'd seen the coming Shataiki. Tom glanced over and saw the boy's wide eyes looking back at the beasts now descending on the village.

"The Thrall!" he cried. "The Thrall. Run!"

Rachelle sprinted by his side, face white. "Elyon!" she cried. "Elyon, save us!"

"Run!" Tom yelled.

Johan kept wanting to turn around,

forcing Tom to repeatedly jerk him back down the path. "Faster! We have to get into the Thrall!"

Tom urged them up the stairs, two at a time. Behind them, screams filled the village. "Don't look back! Go, go, go!" He shoved them roughly through the doors and spun back.

No fewer than ten thousand of the beasts dived into the village, claws extended. The screams from the villagers were overwhelmed by a high-pitched shrieking from thousands of open Shataiki throats. Talons swiped like sickles; fangs gnashed ravenously in anticipation of meat.

To his right, a Shataiki descended on a young boy fleeing down the street. He fell to the ground, smothered by a dozen bats, who sank their talons into his soft flesh. The boy's screams became one with the Shataiki's shrieks.

Not ten paces from the boy, a woman flailed her arms wildly at two beasts who had attached themselves to her head and gnawed madly at her skull. The woman whirled about, screaming, and despite the blood covering her face, Tom recognized her. Karyl.

Tom groaned in shock. All around the village, the helpless fell easy prey to the bloodthirsty Shataiki.

And still they came. The sky was now

black with a hundred thousand of the creatures, streaming over the hills into the valley. He knew it was this way in every village.

Tom slammed the large doors shut, gasping. He threw the large bolt and turned to Rachelle and Johan, who stood on the green floor, holding each other's hands innocently.

"What's happening?" Rachelle asked in a trembling voice, her wide green eyes fixed on Tom. "We have to fight back!"

Tom ran across the floor and shut the rear doors that led to an outer entrance.

"Are these the only two entrances?" he demanded.

"What is —"

"Tell me!"

"Yes!"

No Shataiki could get into the Thrall without breaking down the doors. He turned back.

"Listen to me." He paused to catch his wind. "I know this is going to sound strange, and you may not know what I'm talking about, but we've been attacked."

"Attacked?" quipped Johan. "Really attacked?"

"Yes, really attacked," he said. "The Shataiki have left the black forest."

"That's . . . that's not possible!" Rachelle said.

"Yes, it is. Possible and real."

Tom walked over to the front doors and tested them. He could barely hear the sounds of the attack beyond the walls of the Thrall. Rachelle and Johan remained still, hand in hand, at the center of the jade floor where they had danced a thousand dances. They had no way to understand what was really happening outside. They had no idea how dramatically the colorful world they had known so well just a few moments ago had forever changed.

Tom walked up to them and put his arms on their shoulders. And then the adrenaline that had rushed him through the forest and into this great hall evaporated. The full realization of the devastation racking the land beyond the Thrall's heavy wooden doors descended upon him like ten tons of mortar. He hung his head and tried to remain strong.

Rachelle placed a hand on his hair and stroked it slowly. "It is all right, Thomas," she said. "Don't cry like this. Everything will be just fine. The Gathering is in a short time."

Like a flood, despair swept through Tom's chest. They were doomed. He strained to maintain a semblance of control. How could Tanis have been deceived so easily? What a fool he'd been to even *listen* to the black beast! To even go near the black forest.

"Please, don't cry," Johan said. "Please, don't cry, Thomas. Rachelle is right. Everything will be fine."

An agonizing half-hour crept by. Rachelle and Johan tried to ask him questions about their plight. "Where are the others? What will we do now? How long will we stay here? Where do these black creatures live?"

Each time, Tom shrugged them off as he paced about the great room. The jade hall would become their coffin. If he did answer Rachelle or Johan, it was with a nondescript putoff. How could he explain this betrayal to them? He couldn't. They would have to discover it themselves. For now, their only objective was to survive.

At first the Shataiki attacks on the outer Thrall came in waves, and at one point it sounded as though every last one of the dirty beasts had descended on the dome, beating and scratching furiously to gain entrance. But they could not.

An hour must have passed before Tom noticed the change. They had sat in silence for a good ten minutes without an attack.

He stood shakily to his feet and crossed the floor to the front doors. Silence. The bats either had left or waited quietly on the roof outside, waiting to attack the moment the doors opened.

Tom faced Rachelle and Johan, who still, after all this time, stood in the center of the green floor. It was time to tell them.

"Tanis drank the water," he said simply.

They stiffened, mouths gaping. Together they dropped their heads, obviously unfamiliar with the new emotions of sorrow washing through them. They knew what this meant, of course. Not specifically, but in general they knew something very bad had happened. It was the first time anything bad had happened to either one of them.

Silently their shoulders began to shake, gently at first, but then with greater force until they could stand it no longer, and they threw their arms around each other and sobbed.

The sting of tears returned to Tom's eyes. How could such a tragedy have happened at all? For a long time they clung to each other and cried.

"What will we do? What will we do?" Rachelle asked a dozen times. "Can't we go to the lake?"

"I don't know," Tom responded quietly. "I think everything's changed, Rachelle."

Johan looked at Tom with a tear-streaked face. "But why did Tanis do that when Elyon told us not to?"

"I don't know, Johan," Tom said, taking the boy's hand. "Don't worry. Earth may have changed, but Elyon will never change. We just have to find him."

Rachelle tilted her head back and raised her hands, palms up. "Elyon!" she cried. "Elyon, can you hear us?" Tom looked on hopelessly. "Elyon, where are you?" Rachelle cried again.

She dropped her hands and looked despondently at Tom and Johan. "It's different," she said.

He nodded. "Everything is different now." He glanced up at the green-domed roof. *Except for the Thrall.* "We will wait until morning and then, if it seems safe, we will try to find Elyon."

33

The night had been pure agony for Tom. He'd awakened screaming, soaked in a cold sweat, at two in the morning. He couldn't go back to sleep, and he couldn't bring himself to tell Kara about the nightmare. He could scarcely comprehend what it all meant himself. The images of the black wall of bats spreading over the land and then tearing into the village hung on him like a sopping, heavy cloak.

The early morning hours had been torture, relieved only in part by the onset of a new distraction.

"Do we have Internet access?" he asked Kara at six.

"Yes. Why?"

"I need a distraction. Who knows, maybe a little crash course in survival may help me out in the land of bats."

She looked at him, taken aback.

"What?" he asked.

"I thought we were more interested in how that reality can save this world than how to build weapons to blow away a few black bats for Tanis."

If only she knew. He couldn't bring himself to tell her, not yet. She would never understand how utterly real it all felt.

"I need a distraction," he said.

"So do I," she said.

They spent the next three hours browsing subjects on Yahoo! that Tom thought might come in handy. Maybe Tanis had been onto something with this idea of his to build weapons. If they were right, the only things that were transferable between the realities were skills and knowledge. He couldn't take a gun back with him, but he could take back the knowledge of *how* to build a gun, couldn't he?

"What good is a plan to build a gun if you don't have metal to build it with?" Kara asked. "Will the wood there sustain an explosion?"

"I don't know."

He doubted there was any more wood that could be reshaped. Or anyone who could reshape it. He clicked off the weapons page and searched for the basics. Finding ore and building a forge. Swords. Poisons. Survival skills. Combat strategy. Battle tactics.

But in the end he came to the horrible conclusion that no matter what he did, the situation in the colored — or was it all black now? — forest was ultimately hopeless.

Things were hardly better here. They had proof that the Raison Vaccine could mutate into one very bad virus, and no one seemed to want to make sure it didn't. True, in less than a day he'd been dropped in by helicopter with Muta, found Monique, barely escaped with his scalp in one piece, and finally confirmed the reality of the Raison Strain, but Tom still felt like nothing was happening. If Merton Gains was working his promised magic, he was doing it way too slowly.

Jacques de Raison entered the room mid-morning, and Tom spoke before the Frenchman could explain his presence.

"I feel like an animal trapped in a cage," Tom said. "I walk around like an idiot under this house arrest while they sit around and talk about what to do."

"They've lifted the house arrest," Raison said. "At my request."

Tom faced the haggard-looking pharmaceutical giant. "They have? When?"

"An hour ago."

"Now you tell me?"

The man said nothing.

"I need a cell phone," Tom said. "And I need a few phone numbers. Can you do that?"

"I think that can be arranged."

"Our car is still here?"

"Yes. In the parking lot."

"Can you have it brought around? Kara, you ready to leave?"

"Nothing to get ready. Where to?"

"Anywhere but here. No offense, Jacques, but I can't just sit around here. I'm free to go, right?"

"Yes, but we're still looking for my daughter. What if we need you? Secretary Gains could call at any minute."

"That's why I need a cell phone."

Their feet clacked along the Sheraton lobby's tile floor. Tom pressed the cell phone to his ear patiently, scanning the room. Hundreds of people loitered in the grand atrium, completely clueless that the young American named Thomas Hunter and the pretty blonde at his elbow were bargaining for the fate of the world.

Patricia Smiley came back on the line for the fourth time in the last half-hour. He was driving her rabid, but he didn't care.

"It's Tom Hunter again," he said. "Please, please tell me he's not in a meeting or on the phone."

"I'm sorry, Mr. Hunter, I told you before, he's on the phone."

"Can I be frank? You don't sound sorry, Patricia. Did you tell him I was on the phone? He's waiting for my call. Did I tell you I was in Bangkok? Put him on; I'm dying over here!"

"Raising your voice won't —" Her voice went mute. She was talking to someone in the office. "I'll put you through now, Mr. Hunter."

Click.

"Hello?" Had she hung up on him? "Don't you dare hang up on me, you —"

"Thomas?"

Merton Gains.

"Oh. I'm sorry, sir. I was just on the phone with . . ." He stalled.

"Never mind that. I'm sorry I haven't been able to get through sooner, but I've been clearing my schedule. How you looking for ten o'clock tonight?"

Tom stopped.

"What?" Kara asked at his elbow.

"Ten o'clock for what?"

"For me. My flight leaves in an hour. I'll have the director of the CIA with me. We still have some calls to make, but we think we can get Australian Intelligence, Scotland Yard, and the Spanish there as well. Ten, fifteen people. It's not exactly a summit, but it's a start."

"For what? Why?"

The phone hissed.

"For you, boy. I want you to have everything ready, you understand? Everything. You tell them the whole thing, from start to finish. I'll have Jacques de Raison there to present their findings on the virus. I'll

562

have a CDC representative on the plane to hear those findings. The president has given me discretion on this, so I'm running with it. From this point forward, we treat this as a real threat. With any luck, we'll have the ears of a few other countries by day's end. Trust me, we'll need them. I don't have a lot of believers here at home."

"You want me to present this at the meeting?"

"I want you to tell them what you told me. Explaining dreams isn't something that comes naturally to me."

"I can do that." Tom wasn't sure if he really could, but they were way beyond such insignificant considerations. "And someone is locating Svensson, right? He has to be stopped."

"We're working on that. But we're dealing with international laws here. And Svensson is a powerful man. You don't just drop the hammer on him without evidence."

"I have evidence!"

"Not in their minds, you don't. He's agreed to an interview tomorrow. Don't worry; we have a ground team paying him a visit in a few hours. They'll set up surveillance. He's not going anywhere."

"That could be too late."

"For crying out loud, Thomas! You want fast; this *is* fast! I have to catch a flight. I'll instruct my secretary to patch your calls through. You're at the Sheraton, right?"

"Right."

"Ten o'clock at the Sheraton. I'll have a conference room reserved." Merton Gains paused. "Have you . . . learned anything else?"

The nightmare swept through Tom's mind. The Fall. A sense of impending dread settled in his gut like a lead brick. "No."

"Fine."

"Okay."

He hung up.

"What was that?" Kara asked. "He's coming?"

"He's coming. With an entourage. Ten o'clock."

"That's twelve hours. What happens in the next twelve hours? You're briefing them, right? So we need more information."

Tom suddenly felt faint. Sick. He settled into a chair in the open dining room and stared out at the lobby.

"Thomas?" Kara slid into a chair opposite him. "What is it?"

He massaged his temples. "We have a problem, Kara."

"Why do you say that? They're finally starting to listen."

"No, not with them. With me. With

whatever's happening to me."

"Your dreams?"

"The colored forest has come apart at the seams," he said.

"What . . . what do you mean?"

"The colored forest. It's not colored anymore. The bats have broken past the river and attacked —" Tom broke off.

She stared at him as if he'd lost his mind. "That's . . . is that possible?"

"It happened."

"What does that mean?"

"I don't know." He hit his hand on the table. The plates clattered. A couple seated two tables away looked over.

Again, not as loud. "I don't know; that's the problem. As far as I know, I won't even go back. And if I do go back, I have no idea what the land will be like."

"It's that bad?"

"You can't imagine."

"This explains your sudden interest in weapons."

"I guess."

"Then you have to sleep! You can't meet with all those people without knowing what's going on over there. Our whole case hinges on this . . . these dreams of yours. You're saying it's over? We have to get you to sleep!"

"I'm not going to *tell* them what's going on over there!" he said. "That's for us,

Kara. It's bad enough talking about what I learned in my dreams, but there's no way I can give them any specifics. They'll lock me up!"

"But you still have to know. For yourself."

They sat quietly for a moment. She was right — he had to find out if he could go back. They had twelve hours.

"Tell me what happened," Kara said quietly. "I want to know everything."

Tom nodded. It had been a while since he'd told her everything. "It'll take a while."

"We have time."

Twelve hours had come and gone, and Svensson hadn't forced Monique to change her mind as promised. But one look at his face when he opened the door to her white-walled cell, and Monique suspected that was about to change.

They'd moved her during the night. Why or where she had no idea. What she did know was that the plan unfolding about her had been the subject of immense planning and foresight. She'd picked up enough between the lines to conclude that much.

Virologists had speculated for years that one day a bioweapon would change history. In anticipation of that day, Valborg

Svensson had laid exhaustive plans. His stumbling upon the Raison Virus might have been a fluke, but what he would now do with it was anything but. Actually, he hadn't stumbled upon it at all. He'd invested in a vast network of informants so that at the first sign of the right virus, he could pounce on it. In effect, he had many thousands of scientists working for him.

This man standing tall in the doorway to her white room was a brilliant man, Monique thought. And perhaps completely insane.

"Hello, Monique. I trust we've treated you well. My apologies for any discomfort, but that will change now. The worst is behind you, I promise. Unless, of course, you refuse to cooperate, but that is beyond my control."

"I have no intention of cooperating," she said.

"Yes, well, that's because you don't know yet."

She didn't indulge him with the obvious question.

"Would you like to know?"

She still didn't. He chuckled. "You have a strong backbone; I like that. What you don't know is that in exactly fourteen hours, we — yes, we; I'm certainly not alone in this, not even close, although I would like to think I play a significant role — are going to release the Raison Strain in twelve primary countries."

Monique's vision swam. What was he saying? Surely he wasn't planning to . . .

"Yes, exactly. With or without an antivirus, the clock starts ticking in fourteen hours." He grinned wide. "Astonishing, isn't it?"

"You can't do that . . ."

"That's what some of the others argued. But we prevailed. It's the only way. The fate of the world is now in my hands, dear Monique. And yours, of course."

"The virus could wipe out the earth's population!"

"That's the point. The threat has to be real. Only an antivirus can save humanity. I trust you would like to help us create that antivirus. We have a very good start already, I must say. We may not even need you. But your name is on the virus. It seems appropriate that it also be on the cure, don't you think?"

34

The first thing Tom realized was that he was back. He was waking up in the Thrall with Rachelle and Johan curled by his feet. He'd dreamed of Bangkok and was getting ready to enter a meeting with some people who were finally willing to consider the Raison Strain.

They'd spent the evening huddled together on the Thrall's floor. The night seemed colder than usual. Depression hung in the room like a thick fog. Rachelle had even tried to dance once, but she just couldn't find the right rhythm. She gave up and sat back down, head in her hands. They soon grew silent and finally drifted off to sleep.

Sometime in the middle of the night, they were awakened by a scratching on the roof, but the sound passed within a few minutes and they managed to return to sleep.

Tom was the first to wake. Morning rays lit the translucent dome. He quietly stood, walked to the large doors, and pressed his ear against the glowing wood. If anything alive was waiting beyond the doors, it made no sound. Satisfied, he hurried across the room to a side door that Rachelle said led to storage. He opened it and descended a short flight of steps to a small storage room.

A clear jar containing about a dozen pieces of fruit sat against the far wall. Some bread. Good. He closed the door and returned upstairs.

Rachelle and Johan still slept, and Tom decided to leave them to their sleep as long as he could. He walked over to the main doors and put an ear to the wood again.

He listened for a full minute this time. Nothing.

He eased the bolt open and cracked the door, half expecting to hear a sudden flurry of black wings. Instead, he heard only the slight creak of the hinges. The morning air remained absolutely still. He pushed the door farther open and cautiously peered around. He squinted in the bright light and quickly scanned the village for Shataiki.

But there were none. He held his breath and stepped out into putrid morning air.

The village was deserted. Not a soul, living or dead, occupied the once lively streets. There were no dead bodies as he had expected. Only patches of blood that had soaked the ground. Nor were there

Shataiki perched on the rooftops, waiting for him to leave the safety of the Thrall. He twisted to look at the Thrall's roof, thinking of the scratching during the night. Still no bats.

But where were the people?

Apparently even the animals had been chased from the valley. The buildings no longer glowed. The entire village looked as though it had been covered by a great settling of gray ash.

"What happened?" Rachelle and Johan stood dumbstruck.

"It went dark inside," Johan said, staring past Tom with wide eyes.

He was right; the wood inside had lost its glow as well. It must have been somehow affected by the air he had let in when he opened the door. He turned back to the scene before him.

Tom felt nauseated. Scared. His pulse beat steady and hard. Had evil entered him somehow, or was it just out here in this physical form? And what about the others?

"It's all changed!" Rachelle cried. She grabbed Tom's arm with a firm, trembling grip. Frightened? She'd known caution before. But fear? So she, too, felt the effects of the transformation even without being torn to shreds.

"What . . . what happened to the land?" Johan asked.

The meadows surrounding the village were now black. But the starkest change in the land was the forest at the meadow's edge. The trees were all charred, as though an immense fire had ravaged the land.

Black.

For a long time they stood still, frozen by the scene before them. Tom looked to his left where the path snaked over scorched earth toward the lake. He placed his arms around Johan and Rachelle.

"We should go to the lake."

Rachelle looked at him. "Can't we eat first? I'm starving."

Her eyes. They weren't green.

He lowered his arm and swallowed. The emerald windows to her soul were now grayish white. As though she'd contracted an advanced case of cataracts.

It took every ounce of his composure not to jump. He stepped back cautiously. Her face had lost its shine and her skin had dried. Tiny lines were etched over her arms.

And Johan — it was the same with him!

Tom turned around and looked at his own arm. Dry. No pain, just bone dry. The nausea in his gut swelled.

"Eat? Don't you want to go to the lake first?"

He waited for a response, afraid to face them. Afraid to look into their eyes. Afraid to ask whether his eyes were also gray saucers.

They weren't responding. See, they were afraid too. They'd seen his eyes and were stunned to dumbness. They stood on the steps of the Thrall, ashamed and silent. Tom certainly felt —

He heard a loud smacking sound and spun around, fearing bats. But it wasn't bats. It was Rachelle and Johan. They'd descended the steps and were stuffing some fruit he hadn't seen into their mouths.

Whose fruit? Everything else here appeared to be dead.

Teeleh's.

"Wait!" He took the steps in long leaps, rushed over to Rachelle, and ripped the fruit from her mouth.

She whirled around and struck him, her hand flexed firm and her fingers curved to form a claw. "Leave me!" she snarled, spewing juice.

Tom staggered in shock. He touched his cheek and brought his hand away bloody. Rachelle snatched up another fruit and shoved it into her mouth.

He shifted his gaze to Johan, who ignored them totally. Like a ravenous dog intent on a meal, he greedily chewed the flesh of a fruit.

Tom backed to the steps. This couldn't

be happening. Not to Johan, of all people. Johan was the innocent child who just yesterday had walked around the village in a daze, lost in thoughts about diving into Elyon's bosom. And now this?

And Rachelle. His dearest Rachelle. Beautiful Rachelle, who could spend countless hours dancing in the arms of her beloved Creator. How could she have so easily turned into this snarling, desperate animal with dead eyes and flaking skin?

A flurry of wings startled Tom. He spun his head to the blackened entrance of the Thrall. Michal sat perched on the railing.

"Michal!"

Tom bounded up the steps. "Thank goodness! Thank goodness, Michal! I . . ." Tears blurred his vision. "It's terrible! It's . . ." He turned to Rachelle and Johan, who were making quick work of the fruit scattered below.

"Look at them!" he blurted out, flinging an arm in their direction. "What's happening?" Even as he said it, he felt a sudden desire to cool his own throat with the fruit.

Michal stared ahead, regarding the scene serenely. "They are embracing evil," he said quietly.

Tom felt himself begin to calm. The fruit looked exactly like any fruit they'd eaten at a table set by Karyl. Intoxicating, sweet.

He shivered with growing desperation. "They've gone mad," he said in a low voice.

"Perceptive. They're in shock. It won't always be this bad."

"Shock?" Tom heard himself say it, but his eyes were on the last piece of fruit, which both Rachelle and Johan were heading for.

"Shock of the most severe nature," Michal said. "You've tasted the fruit before. Its effect isn't so shocking to you, but don't think you're any different from them."

Johan reached the fruit first, but his taller sister quickly towered over him. She put one hand on her hip and shoved the other at the fruit. "It's mine!" she screamed. "You have no right to take what is mine. Give it to me!"

"No!" Johan screamed, his eyes bulging from a beet-red face. "I found it. I'll eat it!" Rachelle leaped on her younger brother with nails extended.

"They're going to kill each other," Tom said. It occurred to him that he was actually less horrified than amused. The realization frightened him.

"With their bare hands? I doubt it. Just keep them away from anything that can be used as a weapon." The Roush looked at them with a blank stare. "And get them to the lake as soon as you can."

Rachelle and Johan separated and circled each other warily. From the corner of his eyes, Tom saw a small black cloud approaching. But he kept his eyes on the fruit in Johan's fist. He really should run down there and take the fruit away himself. They'd eaten more than enough. Right?

Tom cast a side glance at Michal. The Roush had his eyes on the sky. "Remember, Thomas. The lake." He leaped into the air and swept away.

"Michal?" Tom glanced at the sky that had interested the Roush.

The black cloud swept in over blackened trees. Shataiki!

"Rachelle!" he screamed. These black beasts terrified him more now than they had in the black forest.

"Rachelle!" He bounded down the stairs and seized first Rachelle and then Johan by their arms, nearly jerking them from their feet. He glanced at the skyline, surprised at how close the Shataiki had come. Their shrieks of delight echoed through the valley.

Rachelle and Johan had seen, too, and they ran willingly. But their strength was gone, and Tom had to practically drag them up the stairs into the Thrall. Even with Rachelle finally pulling free and stumbling up the steps on her own, they just managed to flop into the dark Thrall and shove the doors closed when the first Shataiki slammed into the heavy wood. Then they came, shrieking and beating, one after another.

Tom scrambled back, saw the door was secure, and dropped to his seat, panting. Rachelle and Johan lay unmoving to his right. He had no idea how to follow Michal's last request. It would be hard enough to sneak undetected to the lake by himself. With Rachelle and Johan in their present catatonic state, it would be impossible.

Neither of them stirred in the Thrall's dim light. The once brilliant green floor was now a dark slab of cold wood. The tall pillars now towered like black ghosts in the shadows. Only the weak light filtering in through the still-translucent dome allowed Tom to see at all.

He rolled over and pushed himself to his feet. The Shataiki still slammed unnervingly against the door, but the period between hits began to lengthen. He doubted they could find a way to break into the building. But it wasn't the Shataiki he feared most at the moment. No, it was the two humans at his feet who sent shivers up his spine. And himself. What was happening to them?

The fruit in the storage room. Tom

scrambled to his feet and pounded down the steps. Had the air destroyed that fruit as well? Actually, now that he thought about it, the fruit in the forest had dropped to the ground as he ran by, but it hadn't turned black. Not right away.

He slammed into the door and pulled up. This door had been closed before they'd opened the main Thrall doors. If he opened it, would the air that now filled the Thrall destroy the fruit?

He would have to take that chance. He threw the door open, stepped in, and slammed it behind him. The jar stood against the far wall. He bounded over, grabbed one fruit out, and immediately stuffed rags in the top. He had no clue if this would work, but nothing else came to mind.

Tom lifted the one red fruit up and blew out a lungful of air.

Bad air, he thought. *Too late.*

The fruit didn't wilt in his hand. How long would it last?

He shoved the fruit into his mouth and bit deep. The juice ran over his tongue, his chin. It slipped down his throat.

The relief was instantaneous. Gentle spasms ran through his stomach. Tom dropped to his knees and tore into the sweet flesh.

He'd eaten half the fruit before remembering Rachelle and Johan. He grabbed an orange fruit from the jar, stuffed the rag back into its neck, and tore up the stairs.

Rachelle and Johan still lay like limp rags.

He slid to his knees and rolled Rachelle onto her back. He placed the fruit directly over her lips and squeezed. The skin of the orange fruit split. A trickle of juice ran down his finger and spilled onto her parched lips. Her mouth filled with the liquid and she moaned. Her neck arched as the nectar worked into her throat. In a long, slow exhale, she pushed air from her lungs and opened her eyes.

Eying the fruit in Tom's hand with a glint of desperation, she reached up, snatched the fruit, and began devouring. Tom chuckled and pressed his half-eaten fruit into Johan's mouth. The moment the young boy's eyes flickered open, he grabbed the fruit and bit deeply. Without speaking they ravenously consumed flesh, seeds, and juice.

If Tom wasn't mistaken, some color had returned to their skin, and the cuts they had sustained during their argument were not as red. The fruit still had its power.

"How do you guys feel?" he asked, glancing from one to the other. They both stared at him with dull eyes. Neither spoke.

"Please, I need you with me here. How do you feel?"

"Fine," Johan said. Rachelle still did not respond.

"We have more, maybe a dozen or so."

Still no response. He had to get them to the lake. And to do that he had to keep himself sane.

"I'll be right back," he said. He left them cross-legged on the floor and returned to the basement, where he ate another whole fruit, a delicious white nectar he thought was called a sursak.

Eleven left. At least they weren't spoiling as quickly as he'd feared. If Rachelle and Johan showed any further signs of deterioration, he would give them more, but there was no guarantee they would find any more. They couldn't waste a single one.

The next few hours crept by with scarcely a word among them. The attacks at the door had stopped completely. Tom tried his patience with futile attempts to lure them into discussing possible courses of action now that they had found a temporary haven from the Shataiki. But only Johan engaged him, and then in a way that made Tom wish he hadn't.

"Tanis was right," Johan bit off. "We should have launched a preemptive expedition to destroy them."

"Has it occurred to you that that's what

he was doing? But it obviously didn't work, did it?"

"What do you know? He would have called *me* to go with him if he was going to battle. He promised me I could lead an attack! And I would have too!"

"You don't know what you're saying, Johan."

"I wish we would have followed Tanis. Look where you got us!"

Tom didn't want to think where this line of reasoning would lead the boy. He turned away and broke off the conversation.

Two hours into the unbearable silence, Tom noticed the change in Rachelle and Johan. The gray pallor was returning to their skin. They grew more restless with each passing hour, scratching at their skin until it bled. In another hour, tiny flaking scales covered their bodies, and Johan had rubbed his left arm raw. Tom gave them each another fruit. Another one for him. They were now down to eight. At this rate, they wouldn't last the day.

"Okay, we're going to try to make it to the lake."

He grabbed both by their tunics and helped them to their feet. They hung their heads and shuffled to the back entrance without protesting. But there didn't seem to be a drop of eagerness in them. Why so reluctant to return to the Elyon they once were so desperate for?

"Now, when we get outside, I don't want any fighting or anything stupid. You hear? It doesn't sound like there are any black bats out there, but we don't want to attract any, so keep quiet."

"You don't have to be so demanding," Rachelle said. "It's not like we're dying or anything."

It was the first full sentence she had spoken for hours, and it surprised Tom. "That's what you think? The fact is, you're already dead." She frowned but didn't argue.

Tom pressed his ear against the door. No signs of Shataiki. He eased the door open, still heard nothing, and stepped out.

They stood on the threshold and looked over the empty village for the second time that day. The bats had left.

"Okay, let's go."

They walked through the village and over the hill in silence. An eerie sense of death hung in the air as they walked past the tall trees looming black and bare against the sky. The bubbling sound of running water was gone. A muddy trench now ran close to the path where the river from the lake had flowed. Had they waited too long? It had been only a few hours since Michal urged him to go to the lake.

Lions and horses no longer lined the road. Blackened flowers drooped to the ground, giving the appearance that a slight wind might shatter their stems and send them crumbling to join the burned grass on the ground. No fruit. None at all that Tom could see. Had the Shataiki taken it?

Tom stayed to the rear of Rachelle and Johan, carrying the jar of fruit under one arm and a black stick he had picked up in the other hand. His sword, he thought wryly. He expected a patrol of beasts to swoop down from the sky and attack them at any moment, but the overcast sky hung quietly over the charred canopy. With one eye on the heavens and the other on the incredible changes about him, Tom herded Rachelle and Johan up the path.

It wasn't until they approached the corner just before the lake that Johan finally broke the silence. "I don't want to go, Tom. I'm afraid of the lake. What if we drown in it?"

"Drown in it? Since when have you drowned in any lake? That's the most ridiculous thing I've heard."

They continued hesitantly around the next bend. The view that greeted them stopped all three in their tracks.

Only a thread of water dribbled over the cliff into a small grayish pond below. The lake had been reduced to a small pool of water. Large white sandy beaches dropped a hundred feet before meeting the pool. No animals of any kind were in sight. Not a single green leaf remained on the dark circle of trees now edging the dwindling pool.

"Dear God. Oh, dear God. Elyon." Tom took a step forward and stopped.

"Has he left?" Rachelle asked, looking around.

"Who?" Tom asked absently.

She motioned to the lake.

"Look." Johan had fixed his eyes on the lip of the cliff.

There, on the high rock ledge, stood a single lion, gazing out over the land.

Tom's heart bolted. A Roshuim? One of the lionlike creatures from the upper lake? And what of the upper lake? What of the boy?

The magnificent beast was suddenly joined by another. And then a third, then ten, and then a hundred white lions, filing into a long line along the crest of the dried falls.

Tom turned to the others and saw their eyes peeled wide.

The beasts at the head of the falls were shifting uneasily now. The line split in two.

The boy stepped into the gap, and Tom thought his heart stopped beating at first sight of the boy's head. The lions crumpled to their knees and pressed their muzzles flat on the stone surface. And then the boy's small body filled the position reserved for him at the cliff's crest. The boy stood barefooted on the rock, dressed only in a loincloth.

For a few moments, Tom forgot to breathe.

The entire line of beasts bowed their heads in homage to the boy. The child slowly turned and gazed over the land below him. His tiny slumped shoulders rose and fell slowly. A lump rose in Tom's throat.

And then the boy's face twisted with sorrow. He raised his head, opened his mouth, and cried to the sky.

The long line of beasts dropped flat to their bellies, like a string of dominoes, sending an echo of thumps over the cliff. A chorus of bays ran down the line.

The air filled with the boy's wail. His song. A long, sustained note that poured grief into the canyon like molten lead.

Tom dropped to his knees and began gasping for air. He'd heard a similar sound before, in the lake's bowels, when Elyon's heart was breaking in red waters.

The boy sank to his knees.

Tears sprang into Tom's eyes, blurring the image of the gathered beasts. He closed his eyes and let the sobs come. He couldn't take this. The boy had to stop.

But the boy didn't stop. The cry ran on and on with unrelenting sorrow.

The wail fell to a whimper — a hopeless little sound that squeaked from a paralyzed throat. And then it dwindled into silence.

Tom lifted his head. The beasts on the cliff fell silent but remained prone. The boy's chest heaved now, in long, slow gasps through his nostrils. And then, just as Tom began to wonder whether the show of sorrow was over, the small boy's eyes flashed open. He stood to his feet and took a step forward.

The boy threw his fists into the air and let loose a high-pitched shriek that shattered the still morning air. Like the wail of a man forced to watch his children's execution, with a red face and bulging eyes, screaming in rage. But all from the mouth of the small boy standing high on the cliff.

Tom trembled in agony and threw himself forward on the sand. The shriek took the form of a song and howled through the valley in long, dreadful tones. Tom clutched his ears, afraid his head might burst. Still the boy pushed his song into the air with a voice that Tom thought filled the entire planet.

And then, suddenly, the boy fell silent, leaving only the echoes of his voice to drift through the air.

For a moment, Tom could not move. He slowly pushed himself up to his elbows and lifted his head. He ran a forearm across his eyes to clear his vision. The child stood still for a few moments, staring ahead as though dazed, and then turned and disappeared. The beasts clamored to their feet and backed away from the cliff until only a deserted gray ledge ran along the horizon. Silence filled the valley once again.

The boy was gone.

Tom scrambled to his feet, panicked. No. No, it couldn't be! Without looking at the others, he sprinted down the white bank and into the dwindling water.

The intoxication was immediate. Tom plunged his head under the water and gulped deeply. He stood up, threw his head back, and raised two fists in the air. "Elyon!" he yelled to the overcast sky.

Johan ran only a step ahead of Rachelle, down the bank and facefirst into the water. Now numb with pleasure, Tom watched the two dunk their heads under the surface like desperately thirsty animals. The contrast between the terror that consumed the land and this remnant of Elyon's potent power, left as a gift for them, was staggering. He flopped facedown into the pool.

But there was a difference, wasn't there? Elyon?

Silence.

He stood up. The water seemed to be lower.

Rachelle and then Johan stood from the water. A healthy glow had returned to their skin, but they looked down, confused.

"What's happening?" Rachelle asked.

The pond was sinking into the sand. Draining. Tom splashed water on his face. He drank more of it. "Drink it! Drink it!"

They lowered their heads and drank.

But the level fell fast. It was soon at their knees. Then their ankles.

"So, now you know," a voice said behind Tom.

Michal stood on the bank. "I'm afraid I have to go, my friends. I may not see you for a while." His eyes were bloodshot, and he looked very sad.

Tom splashed out of the pond. "Is this it? Is this the last of the water? You can't go!"

Michal shifted away and stared at the cliff. "You're not in a position to be demanding."

"We'll die out here!"

"You're already dead," Michal said.

The last of the water seeped into the sand.

Michal took a deep breath. "Go back to the Crossing. Walk through the black forest due east from the bridge. You'll come to a desert. Enter the desert and keep walking. If you survive that long, you may eventually find refuge."

"Through the black forest again? How can there be refuge in the black forest? The whole place is swarming with the bats!"

"Was swarming. The other villages are much larger than this one. The bats have gone for them. But you'll have your hands full enough. You have the fruit. Use it."

"The whole planet is like this?" Rachelle asked.

"What did you expect?"

Michal hopped twice, as if to take off. "And don't drink the water. It's been poisoned."

"Don't drink any of it? We have to drink."

"If it's the color of Elyon, you may drink it." He hopped again, readying for flight. "But you won't be seeing any of that soon."

He took off.

"Wait!" Tom yelled. "What about the rest? Where are the rest?"

But the Roush either didn't hear or didn't want to answer.

They left the charred valley and ran for the Crossing.

Tom stopped them within the first mile and insisted they all spread ash over their bodies — the bats might mistake them for something other than humans. They picked their way through the landscape like gray ghosts. The ground was littered with fallen trees, and their unprotected feet were easily cut by the sharp wood, slowing them to a walk at times. But they pressed forward, keeping a careful eye to the skies as they went.

There were still a few pieces of fruit here and there that hadn't dried up, and what juice remained still held its healing power. They used the juice on their feet when the cuts became unbearable. And when the shriveled fruit became scarce, they began using the fruit from the jar. They were soon down to six pieces.

"We'll each take two," Tom decided. "But use them sparingly. I have the feeling this is the last we'll see."

Slowly and silently they made their way toward the Crossing. It was midmorning before they saw the first Shataiki formation, flying high overhead, at least a thousand strong. The Shataiki were headed toward the black forest and flapped on. They either did not see the party of three or were fooled by the ash.

An hour later they reached the Crossing. The old grayed bridge arched over a small stream of brown water. The rest of the riverbed was cracked dry.

Johan ran to the bank. "It looks okay."

"Don't drink it!"

"We're going to die of thirst out here!" he said. "Who says we have to listen to the bat?"

The bat? Michal.

"Then eat some fruit. Michal said not to drink the water, and I for one will follow his advice. Let's go!"

Johan frowned at the water then reluctantly joined them on the bridge.

The far bank showed a dark stain where the Shataiki had torn Tanis to shreds, but otherwise there was nothing peculiar about the black forest. It looked just like the ground they had already traversed.

"Come on," Tom urged after a moment. He swallowed a lump in his throat and led them over the bridge and into the black forest.

They slowly made their way through the forest, stopping every hundred meters or so to wipe more juice on the soles of their feet.

"Use it sparingly," Tom insisted. "Leave enough to eat." He hated to think what would happen when they ran out.

Shataiki sat perched in the limbs above, squealing and fighting over petty matters. Only the more curious looked down at the trio passing beneath them. *It must be the ash,* Tom thought. Deceptive enough to confuse the mindless, deceptive creatures.

They had picked their way through the forest for what seemed a very long time when they came to a clearing.

"The desert!" Rachelle said.

Tom glanced around. "Where?"

"There!" She pointed directly ahead.

Black trees bordered the far side of the clearing. And beyond a fifty-foot swath of trees, glimpses of white sand. The prospect of getting out of the forest was enough to make Tom's pulse scream in anticipation.

"That's my girl. Come on!" He stepped forward.

"So I'm still your girl?"

Tom turned back. She wore a sly smirk. "Of course. Aren't you?"

"I don't know, Thomas. Am I?"

She lifted her chin and walked past him. She was. At least he hoped she was. Although it occurred to him that the Great Romance had been blackened like everything else in this cursed land.

He shoved the thoughts from his mind and trudged after her. Their need for survival was greater than any romance. He quickly passed her and led the way. He might not be the man he was, but he could at least put on a front of protection. Famed warrior, Tom Hunter. He grunted in disgust.

They had reached the field's midpoint when the first black Shataiki dived from the sky and settled to the ground ahead of them. Tom looked at the bat. *Keep moving. Just keep moving.*

He adjusted his course, but the bat hopped over to block his passage.

"You think you can pass me so easily?" the Shataiki sneered. "Not so easy now, eh?"

Johan jumped forward and put up his fists as if to take the bat on. Tom lifted a hand to the boy without removing his eyes from the Shataiki. "Back off, Johan."

"Back off, Johan," the bat mimicked. Its pupil-less red eyes glared. "Are you too weak for me, Johan?" The bat raised one of its talons. "I could cut you open right here! How does that feel? Welcome to our new world." The Shataiki cackled with delight and bit deeply into a fruit it had withdrawn from behind.

"Want some?" he taunted and then laughed again as though this had been a hilarious assault.

Tom took a step in the direction of the bat. The Shataiki immediately flared his wings and snarled. "Stay!" A flock of Shataiki had now gathered in the sky and circled above them, taunting. "You tell him," one with a raspy voice taunted.

"You tell him," another mimicked.

And the first Shataiki did. "You stay put!" it yelled now, even though Tom hadn't moved.

Tom reached into his pocket and squeezed his last fruit so that the juice from the flesh seeped out between his fingers.

He turned calmly around and faced Rachelle and Johan. "Use your fruit," he whispered. "When I say, run."

"Face me when I talk to you, you —"

It was as far as the Shataiki got. Tom flung the dripping fruit at the Shataiki. "Run!" he yelled.

The fruit landed squarely in the Shataiki's face. Burning flesh hissed loudly. The beast screamed and swatted at his face. A strong stench of sulfur filled the air as Tom rushed by, followed by Johan then Rachelle.

"It's a green fruit!" a bat cried from among those that circled the scene. "They have the green fruit! They're not dead. Kill them!"

Tom tore through the field. No less than twenty Shataiki dived toward them from behind.

"Use your fruit! Rachelle!"

She spun and hurled her fruit at the swarm. They scattered like flies. Rachelle flew by him. Then Johan. But the bats had reorganized and were coming again. Johan clutched their last fruit between his fingers. They shouldn't have thrown the fruits.

"Wait, Johan! Don't throw it." They ran

into the trees. "Give me your fruit."

Johan ran on, desperate to reach the white sand.

"Drop it!"

The fruit fell from his fingers. Tom scooped it up and whirled around. A hundred or more of the bats had materialized from nowhere. They saw the fruit in his hand and passed him. Straight for Johan.

"Back!" Tom screamed. He raced for the boy, reached him, and shoved the fruit into the face of the first bat to reach them.

The Shataiki shrieked and fell to the ground.

And then they were through the trees and running on white sand.

"Stay together!" Tom panted. "Stay close."

They ran a hundred yards before Tom glanced back and then stopped. "Hold up."

Rachelle and Johan stopped. Doubled over, heaving for breath.

The bats flew in circles over the black forest, screeching their protests. But they weren't following.

They weren't flying into the desert.

Johan jumped into the air and let out a whoop. Tom swung his fist at the circling bats. "Ha!"

"Ha!" Rachelle yelled, flinging sand at the forest. She laughed and stumbled over to Tom. "I knew it!" Her laughter was throaty and full of confidence, and Tom laughed with her.

She straightened and walked up to him wearing a tempting smile. "So," she said, drawing a finger over his cheek. "You're still my fearless fighter after all."

"Did you ever doubt?"

She hesitated. He saw that her skin was drying out again.

"For a moment," she said. She leaned forward and kissed him on the forehead. "Only for a moment."

Rachelle turned and left him standing with two thoughts. The first was that she was a beautifully mischievous woman.

The second was that her breath smelled a bit like sulfur.

"Rachelle?"

"Yes, dear warrior?"

He took a big bite out of their last fruit and tossed her the rest. "Have some fruit. Give the rest to Johan."

She caught it with one hand, winked at him, and bit down hard. "So, which way?"

He pointed into the desert.

The last of their exuberance vacated them at midday, when the sun stood directly overhead.

They navigated by the ball of fire in the sky. Deeper into the desert. East, as

596

Michal had said. But with each step the sand seemed to grow hotter and the sun's descent into the western sky slower. The flats quickly gave way to gentle dunes, which would have been manageable with the right shoes and at least a little water. But these small hills of sand soon led to huge mountains that ran east to west so that they were forced to crawl up one side and stagger down the other. And there was not a drop of water. Not even poisoned water.

By midafternoon, Tom's strength began to fail him. In his cautiousness, he'd had much less fruit since leaving the lake than either of them, and he guessed that it was beginning to show.

"We're walking in circles!" Rachelle said, stopping at the top of a dune. "We're not getting anywhere."

Tom kept walking. "Don't stop."

"I will stop! This is madness! We'll never make it!"

"I want to go back," Johan said.

"To what? To the bats? Keep going."

"You're marching us to our deaths!" he yelled.

Tom whirled around. "Walk!"

They stared at him, stunned by his outburst.

"We can't stop," Tom said. "Michal said to walk east." He pointed at the sun. "Not north, not south, not west. East!"

"Then we should take a break," Rachelle said.

"We don't have *time* for a break!"

He marched down the hill, knowing they had no choice but to follow. They did follow. But slowly. So as not to be too obvious, he slowed and let them catch up.

The first hallucinations began toying with his mind ten minutes later. He saw trees that he knew weren't trees. He saw pools of water that weren't the least bit wet. He saw rocks where there were no rocks.

He saw Bangkok. And in Bangkok he saw Monique, trapped in a dark dungeon.

Still he plodded on. Their throats were raw, their skin was parched, and their feet were blistering, but they had no choice. Michal had said to walk east, and so they would walk east.

He began to mumble incoherently in another half-hour. He wasn't sure what he was saying and tried not to say anything at all, but he could hear himself over a hot wind that blew in their faces.

Finally, when he knew that he would collapse with even one more step, he stopped.

"Now we will rest," he said and collapsed to his seat.

Johan plopped down on his right, and Rachelle eased to her seat on his left.

"Yes, of course, now we have time for a rest," Rachelle said. "Half an hour ago it would have killed us because Michal said to walk east. But now that you're babbling like a fool, now that our mighty warrior has deemed it perfectly logical, we will take a rest."

He didn't bother to respond. He was too exhausted to argue. It was a wonder she still had the energy to pick a fight.

They sat in silence on the tall dune for several minutes. Tom finally braved a glance over at Rachelle. She sat hugging her knees, staring at the horizon, jaw firm. The wind whipped her long hair behind her. She refused to look at him.

If he had it in him, he might tell her to stop acting like a child.

Ahead the dunes rose and fell without the slightest hint of change. Michal had told them to come to the desert because he knew the Shataiki wouldn't leave their trees. But why had he insisted they go deeper into the desert? Was it possible that the Roush was sending them to their deaths?

"You're already dead," he'd said. Maybe not in the way Tom had first assumed. Maybe "dead" as in, *I know you'll follow my direction because you have no other choice. You'll walk into the desert and die as you deserve to die. So really, you're already dead.*

Dead man walking.

"You're still dreaming about Monique."

The hallucinations were back. Monique was calling to him. Kara was telling him —

"I heard you speak her name. At a time like this, she's on your mind?"

No, not Monique. Rachelle. He faced her. "What?"

Her eyes flashed. "I want to know why you're mumbling her name."

So. He'd mumbled about the woman from his dreams — her name, maybe more — and Rachelle had heard him. She was jealous. This was insane! They were facing their deaths, and Rachelle was drawing strength from a ridiculous jealousy of a woman who didn't even exist!

Tom turned away. "Monique de Raison, my dear Rachelle, doesn't exist. She's a figment of my imagination. My dreams." Not the best way to put it, actually. He emphasized his first point. "She doesn't exist, and you know it. And arguing about her definitely won't help us survive this blasted desert."

He stood to his feet and marched down the hill. "Let's move!" he ordered, but he felt sick. He had no right to dismiss her jealousy so flippantly. Just this morning he'd stared at her and Johan fighting over the fruit, horrified by their disregard for each other, yet he was no different, as

Michal had pointed out.

Johan was the last to stand. Tom had already reached the next crest when he looked back and saw the boy facing the way they'd come.

"Johan!"

The boy turned slowly, looked back one last time, and headed down the dune after them.

"He wants to go back," Rachelle said, walking past him. "I'm not sure I blame him."

They walked another two hours in forlorn silence, taking breaks every ten or fifteen minutes for Rachelle's and Johan's benefit now as much as his own. The wind died down and the heat became oppressive.

Every time Tom felt the onset of hallucinations, he stopped them. He might not be much of a leader any longer, but he was leading the way by default. He had to keep his mind as clear as possible under the circumstances.

They walked with the dread knowledge that they were walking to their deaths. Slowly, painfully now, the mountainous dunes fell behind them, one by one. The only change was the gradual appearance of boulders. But no one even mentioned them. If boulders didn't hold water, they didn't care about boulders.

The valley they were in when the sun

dipped below the horizon was maybe a hundred yards wide. A cropping of boulders rose from the valley floor.

"We'll stop here for the night," Tom said. He nodded at the boulders. "The rocks will block any wind."

No one argued. Tom collapsed by the rocks and set his head back in the sand as the setting sun cast a rich red glow across the desert floor. He closed his eyes.

The sky was black when he opened them again. Whether it was complete exhaustion or the unbearable silence that kept him from sleep, he wasn't sure. Johan had rolled into a ball and lay under the rocks. Rachelle lay twenty feet away, staring at the sky. He could see the moonlight's reflection in her glassy eyes.

Awake.

It was an absurd situation. They were as likely going to die out here as live, and the only woman he could ever remember loving was lying twenty feet away either fuming or biting her tongue, or hating him, he didn't know which.

But he did know that he missed her terribly.

He pushed himself to his feet, walked over to her, and lay down beside her.

"Are you awake?" he whispered.

"Yes."

It was the first word she'd spoken since

telling him that Johan wanted to go back, and it was amazing how glad he was to hear it.

"Are you mad at me?"

"No."

"I'm sorry," he said. "I shouldn't have yelled at you."

"I guess it's been a day to yell," she said.

"I guess."

They lay quietly. Her hand lay in the sand, and he reached over and touched it. She took his thumb.

"I want you to make me a promise," she said.

"Okay, anything you want."

"I want you to promise not to dream about Monique ever again."

"Please —"

"I don't care what she is or isn't," Rachelle said. "Just promise me."

"Okay."

"Promise?"

"I promise."

"Forget the histories; they don't mean a thing anymore anyway. Everything's changed."

"You're right. Forget dreams about Bangkok. They seem silly now."

"They are silly," she said, then she rolled over and pushed herself to one elbow. The moonlight played on her eyes. A beautiful gray.

She leaned over and gently kissed him on the lips. "Dream of me," she said. She settled on her side and curled up to sleep.

I will, Tom thought. *I will dream only about Rachelle.* Tom closed his eyes feeling more content than he'd felt since trudging into this terrible desert. He fell asleep and he dreamed.

He dreamed about Bangkok.

35

The conference room boasted a finely finished cherry-wood table large enough to seat the fourteen people in attendance with room to spare. A lavish display of tropical fruits, European cheeses, cold roast beef, and several kinds of bread had been set as a centerpiece. They sat in wine-colored leather chairs, looking important and undoubtedly feeling the same.

Thomas, on the other hand, neither looked nor felt much more than what he actually was: a twenty-five-year-old wannabe novelist who'd been swallowed by his dreams.

Still, he had their attention. And in contrast to the events in his dreams, he felt quite good. Fourteen sets of eyes were fixed on him seated at the head of the table. For these next few minutes, he was as good as omniscient to them. And then they might decide to lock him up. The Thai authorities had gone out of their way to make it clear that regardless of the circumstances, he, Thomas Hunter, had committed a federal offense by kidnapping Monique de Raison. What they should do about it was unclear, but they couldn't just ignore it.

He looked at Kara on his immediate right and returned her quick smile.

He winked but didn't feel nearly as confident as he tried to look. If there were any skills he needed now, they were diplomatic ones. Kara had suggested he try to find a way to cultivate those in the green forest, as he had his fighting skills. Clearly, that was no longer an option.

Lately, the reality of the desert seemed more real to him than this world here. What would happen if he died of heat exhaustion in the desert night? Would he slump over here, dead?

Deputy Secretary Merton Gains sat to Tom's left. Very few back in Washington knew that he'd left earlier in the day for this most unusual meeting. Then again, very few were aware the news that had punctuated the wires over the last forty-eight hours had anything to do with more than a crazed American who'd kidnapped Raison Pharmaceutical's chief virologist on the eve of the Raison Vaccine's long-awaited debut. Most assumed Thomas Hunter was either cause-driven or money-driven. The question being asked on most news channels was, Who put him up to it?

Gains's square jaw was in need of a shave. A young face betrayed by gray hair. Opposite him sat Phil Grant, the taller of the two dignitaries from the States. Long chin, long nose with glasses riding the end. The other American was Theresa Sumner from the CDC, a straightforward woman who'd already apologized for his treatment in Atlanta. Beside her, a Brit from Interpol, Tony Gibbons.

On the right, a delegate from the Australian intelligence service, two high-ranking Thai officials, and their assistants. On the left, Louis Dutêtre, a pompous, thin-faced man with sagging black eyebrows from French intelligence whom Phil Grant seemed to know quite well. Beside him, a delegate from Spain, and then Jacques de Raison and two of his scientists.

All here, all for him. He'd gone from being thrown out of the CDC in Atlanta to hosting a summit of world leaders in Bangkok within the span of just over a week.

Gains had explained his reason for calling the meeting and expressed his confidence in Tom's information. Tom had laid out his case as succinctly and clearly as he could without blowing them away with details from his dreams. Jacques de Raison had shown the simulation and presented his evidence on the Raison Strain. A string of questions and comments had eaten away nearly an hour.

"You're saying that Valborg Svensson, whom some of us know quite well by the way, is not a world-renowned pharmaceutical magnate after all, but a villain?" the Frenchman asked. "Some man hidden deep in the mountains of Switzerland, wringing his hands in anticipation of destroying the world with the invincible virus?"

A gentle chuckle supported several smiles on either side of the table.

"Thank you for the color, Louis," the CIA director said. "But I don't think the deputy secretary and I would have made the trip if we thought it was quite that simple. True, we can't verify any of Mr. Hunter's assertions about Svensson, but we do have a rather unusual string of events to consider here. Not the least of which is the fact that the Raison Strain appears to be real, as we've all seen with our own eyes tonight."

"Not exactly," the CDC representative said. Theresa. "We have some tests that reportedly show mutations, granted. But we don't have true behavioral data on the virus. Only simulations. We don't know exactly how it affects humans in human environments. For all we know, the virus can't survive in a complex, live, human host. No offense, but simulations like this are only, what, 70 percent?"

"Theoretically, 75," Peter said. "But I'd put it higher."

"Of course you would. It's your simulation. In reality you've injected mice?"

"Mice and chimps."

"Mice and chimps. The virus seems comfortable in these hosts, but we don't have any symptoms yet. Am I right? They've survived a couple of days and have grown, but we have a long way to go to know their true effect."

"True," the Raison employee said. "But —"

"Excuse me, could you restate your name?" Gains said.

"Striet, Peter Striet. Everything we see about this virus gives us the chills. True, the testing is only a day old, but we've seen enough viruses to make some pretty educated guesses, with or without the simulations."

"We need to know how long it will live in a human host," Theresa said.

"Are you volunteering?"

More chuckles.

She didn't think it was funny. "No, I'm recommending caution. The initial outbreak of MILTS infected only five thousand and killed roughly one thousand. Not exactly an epidemic of staggering proportions. But the fear it spread dealt a massive economic blow to Asia. An estimated five million people in the tourism industry alone lost their jobs. Do you have any idea what kind of panic would ensue if word about a planet-killing virus hit the Drudge Report? Life as we know it would stop. Wall Street would close. No one would risk going to work. Don't tell me: You've bought a boatload of duct tape stock?"

"I'm sorry?"

"Six billion people would tape themselves into their homes with duct tape. You'd get rich. Meanwhile, millions of elderly and disadvantaged would die from neglect at home."

"Overstated, perhaps, but I think she makes an excellent point," the Frenchman said. Several others threw in their agreement. "I agreed to come precisely because I understand the explosive nature of what is being so loosely suggested."

That would be him doing the loose suggesting, Tom realized. Kara's jaw flexed. For a moment he thought she was going to tell the Frenchman something. Not this time. This was different, wasn't it? The real deal. Not exactly a college debate.

The Frenchman pressed his point. "This could easily be nothing more than Chicken Little crying that the sky is falling. There is the issue of irresponsibility to be considered."

"I resent that remark," Gains said. "On more than one occasion, Tom has proved me wrong. His predictions have been nothing short of astounding. To take his statements lightly could prove to be a terrible mistake."

"And so could taking his statements seriously," Theresa said. "Let's say there is a virus. Fine. When that virus presents itself, we deal with it. Not when it becomes a widespread problem, mind you, but when it first rears its ugly little head. When we have even a single case. But let's not suggest it's a problem until we have absolute certainty that it is. Like I said, fear and panic could be much larger problems than any virus."

"Agreed," the Spanish delegate said. "It is only prudent." The man's collar was too tight, and half his neck folded over his shirt. "Until we have a solution, there is no benefit in terrifying the world with the problem. Especially if there is even the slightest chance that there may not be a problem."

"Precisely," the Frenchman said. "We have a virus. We're working on a way to deal with that virus. We have no real indication that the virus will be used maliciously. I don't see the need for panic."

"He has my daughter," Raison said. "Or does that no longer concern you?"

"I can assure you that we'll do everything we can to find your daughter," Gains said. He glared at Louis Dutêtre. "We've had a team on the ground at Svensson's laboratories for several hours."

"We should get a report at any time," Phil Grant said. "Our deepest sympathies, Mr. Raison. We'll find her."

"Yes, of course," Dutêtre said. "But as of yet, we don't know that Svensson had anything to do with this understandably tragic kidnapping. We have hearsay from Mr. Hunter. Furthermore, even if Svensson is somehow connected to her disappearance, we have no reason to believe the kidnapping in any way predicts a malicious use of a virus — a virus we haven't proved to be lethal, I might add. You're making a leap of faith, gentlemen. Something I'm not prepared to do."

"The fact of the matter is, we have a virus, deadly or not," Gains said. "The fact of the matter is, Tom told me there would be a virus before any physical evidence surfaced. That was enough to get me on a plane. Granted, this isn't something we want to leak, but neither can we ignore it. I'm not suggesting we start barring the doors, but I am suggesting we give contingencies some thought."

"Of course!" Dutêtre continued. "But I might suggest that your boy is the real problem here. Not some virus. It occurs to me that Raison Pharmaceutical is now in the toilet, regardless of how this plays out. I wonder what Thomas Hunter is being paid to kidnap and fabricate all of these tales."

Heavy silence descended on the room as if someone had dropped a thousand pounds of smothering flour on everyone. Gains looked stunned. Phil Grant just stared at the smiling Frenchman.

"Thomas Hunter is here at my request," Gains said. "We did not invite —"

"No," Tom said. He held his hand out to Gains. "It's okay, Mr. Secretary. Let me address his concern."

Tom pushed his chair back and stood. He put a finger on his chin and paced to the right, then back to the left. The air seemed to have been sucked out of the room. He had something to say, of course. Something pointed and intelligent.

But suddenly it occurred to him that what he thought was intelligent might very well sound like nonsense to the Frenchman. And yet, in his silence, stalking in front of them at this very moment, he had complete if momentary power. The realization extended his silence at least another five seconds.

He could trade power too.

"How long have you been working in the intelligence community, Mr. Dutêtre?" Tom asked. He shoved a hand into his pocket. His khaki cargo pants weren't exactly the going dress in this room, but he shoved the thought from his mind.

"Fifteen years," Dutêtre said.

"Good. Fifteen years, and you get invited to a gig like this. Do you know how long I've been at this game, Mr. Dutêtre?"

"Never, from what I can gather."

"Close. Your intelligence is off. Just over one week, Mr. Dutêtre. And yet I was also invited to this gig. You have to ask yourself how I managed to get the deputy secretary of state and the director of the CIA to cross the ocean to meet with me. What is it that I said? What do I really know? Why are these men and women gathered here in Bangkok at my request?"

Now the room was more than silent. It felt vacant.

"In a word, Mr. Dutêtre, it is extraordinary," Tom said. He put the tips of his fingers on the table and leaned forward. "Something very extraordinary has occurred to compel this meeting. And now you're sounding very plain and boring to me. So I've decided to do something that I've done a number of times already.

Something extraordinary. Would you like that, Mr. Dutêtre?"

The Frenchman glanced at Phil Grant. "What is this, a pony show?"

"Would you like to see me float into the air? Maybe if I did that you'd be convinced?"

Someone made a sound that sounded like a half chuckle.

"Okay, I will float for you. Not like you might expect, hovering in mid-air, but what I'm going to do will be no less extraordinary. Just because you don't understand it doesn't change that fact. Are you ready?"

No comment.

"Let me set this up. The fact is, I knew who would win the Kentucky Derby, I knew that the Raison Vaccine would mutate, and I knew exactly under what circumstances it would mutate. Mr. Raison, what's the probability that you, much less I, could do that?"

"Impossible," the man said.

"Theresa, you must have a good working knowledge of these matters. What would you say the probability would be?"

She just stared at him.

"Exactly. There *are* no probabilities, because it's impossible. So for all practical purposes, I already have floated for you. Now I'm saying I can float again, and you have the audacity to call me a fraud."

The Frenchman was smiling, but it wasn't a pleasant smile. "So you remember exactly how the virus mutates, and you think you may have given some information about the antivirus to this Carlos character, but you forget how to formulate it yourself?"

"Yes. Unfortunately."

"How convenient."

"Listen to me carefully," Tom said. "Here comes my floating trick. The Raison Strain is a highly contagious and extremely lethal airborne virus that will infect most of the world's population within the next three weeks unless we find a way to stop it. Delaying one day could make the difference between life and death for millions. We will learn of its release within seven days, when the community of nations, perhaps through the United Nations, receives notice to hand over sovereignty and all nuclear weapons in exchange for an antivirus. This is the course history is now on."

Louis Dutêtre leaned back in his chair and tapped a pencil on his knuckles. "And what you would like to do is bring on World War III before it's here. Monsters aren't conquered by heroes on white horses in this world, Mr. Hunter. Your virus may kill us all, but believing in your virus *will* kill us all."

"Then either way, we're all dead," Tom said. "You can accept that?"

Gains lifted a hand to stall the exchange. "I think you see his point, Tom. There are complications. It may not be black and white. We can't run around yelling virus. Frankly, we don't have a virus yet, at least not one that we know will be used or even could be used. What do you propose?"

Tom pulled his chair out and sat. "I propose we take Svensson out before he can release the virus."

"That's impossible," the CIA director said. "He has rights. We're moving, but we can't just drop a bomb on his head. Doesn't work that way."

"Assuming you're right about Svensson," Gains said, "he would need a vaccine or an antivirus to trade, right? So that gives us some time."

"Nothing says he has to wait until he has the antivirus before releasing the virus. As long as he's confident he can produce an antivirus within a couple of weeks, he could release the virus and call our bluff, claiming to have the antivirus. Right now the race is to stop Svensson before he can do any damage. Once he does his damage, our only hope will ride with an antivirus and a vaccine."

"And how long would that take?" Gains asked, turning to Raison.

"Without Monique? Months. With her?" He shrugged. "Maybe sooner. Weeks." He didn't mention the possible reversal of her genetic signature, as Peter had explained to Tom yesterday.

"Which is another reason why we have to go after Svensson and determine if he has Monique," Tom said. "The world just may depend on Monique in the coming weeks."

"And what suggestion do you have short of taking out Svensson?" Gains asked Tom.

"At this point? None. We should have taken out Svensson twenty-four hours ago. If we had, this would all be over now. But then what do I know? I'm just a wannabe novelist in cargo pants."

"That's right, Mr. Hunter, you are," the Frenchman said. "Keep that in mind. You're firing live bullets. I won't have you galloping around the world shooting your six-guns. I for one would like to pour a little water down your barrels."

Grant's phone chirped, and he turned to answer it quietly.

"I would like to consider some contingency planning in the event we do end up with a problem," Gains said. "What are your thoughts on containment, Mr. Raison?"

"It depends on how a virus would break

out. But if Svensson is behind any of this, he will know how to eliminate any containment possibilities. That's the primary difference between natural occurrences of a virus and forced occurrences as in bioweapons. He could get the virus into a hundred major cities within a week."

"Yes, but if —"

"Excuse me, Merton." Grant snapped his cell shut. "This may all be moot. Our people have just finished a sweep of Svensson's facilities in the Swiss Alps. They found nothing."

Tom sat up. "What do you mean, nothing? That's not —"

"I mean, no sign of anything unusual."

"Was Svensson there?"

"No. But we spoke to his employees at some length. He's due back in two days for an interview with the Swiss Intelligence, which we will also attend. He's been at a meeting with suppliers in South America. We confirmed the meeting. There's no evidence that he's had anything to do with a kidnapping or any massive conspiracy to release a virus."

Silence engulfed them.

"Well, that's good news, I would say," Gains said.

"That's not news at all," Tom said. "So he's not at his main lab. He could be anywhere. Wherever he is, he has both

Monique and the Raison Strain. I'm telling you, you have to find him now!"

Gains put his hand out. "We will, Tom. One step at a time. This is encouraging; let's not pour water over it just yet."

With those words Tom knew that he had lost them all. Except Kara. Merton Gains was as much of an advocate as he could expect. If Gains was expressing caution, the game was over.

Tom stood. "I really don't think you need me to discuss contingencies. I've told you what I know. I'll repeat it one more time for those of you who are slow tonight. History is about to take a plunge down a nasty course. You'll all know that soon, when unthinkable demands come from a man named Valborg Svensson, although I doubt he's working alone. For all I know, one of you works for him."

That kept them in a state of mild shock.

"Good night. If for some inexplicable reason you need me, I'll be in my room, 913, hopefully sleeping. Heaven knows someone has to do something."

Kara stood and lifted her chin evenly. They walked out side by side, brother and sister.

Exhaustion swamped Tom the moment the conference room door thumped shut behind him. He stopped and gazed down the empty hall, dazed. He'd been running through this madness for over a week without a break, and his body was starting to feel like it was filled with lead.

"Well, I guess you told them," Kara said quietly.

"I have to get some rest. I feel like I'm going to drop."

She slipped her arm through his and guided him down the hall. "I'm putting you to bed, and I'm not letting anyone wake you until you've caught up on your sleep. That's final."

He didn't argue. There was nothing he could do at the moment anyway. There might not be anything more he could do. Ever.

"Don't worry, Thomas. I think you said what needed saying. They'll have a change of attitude soon enough. Right?"

"Maybe. I hope not."

She understood. The only thing that would change their attitudes would be an actual outbreak of the Raison Strain, and nobody could hope for that.

"I'm proud of you," she said.

"I'm proud of you," he said.

"For what? I'm not doing anything! You're the hero here."

"Hero?" He scoffed. "Without you I would probably be in some fighting ring downtown trying to prove myself."

"You have a point," she said.

They entered the elevator and rode up alone.

"Since you seem agreeable to my suggestions, do you mind if I make another one?" Kara asked.

"Sure. I'm not sure if my tired mind is up to understanding anything more at the moment."

"It's something I've been thinking about." She paused. "If the virus is released, I don't see how anyone can physically stop it. At least not in twenty-one days."

He nodded. "And?"

"Especially if it's already a matter of history, as you've learned in the green forest, which is where all this is coming from, right?"

"Right."

"But why you? Why did this information just happen to be dumped in your lap? Why are you flipping between these realities?"

"Because I'm connected somehow."

"Because you're the only one who can ultimately make a difference. You started it. The virus exists because of you. Maybe only you can stop it."

The elevator stopped on the ninth floor and they headed for their suite.

"If that's true," he said, "then God help us all because, believe me, I don't have a clue what to do. Except sleep. Even then, we've been abandoned. Three days ago my entire understanding of God was flipped on its end, at least in my dreams. Now it's been flipped again."

"Then sleep."

"Sleep. Dream."

"Dream," she said. "But not just dream. I mean *really* dream."

He led her into the room. "You're forgetting something."

"What?"

"The green forest is gone. The world's changed." He sighed and plopped into a chair by the table. "I'm in a desert, half dead. No water, no fruit, no Roush. I get shot now, and I really do die. If anything, the information will have to flow the other way to keep me alive there." He cocked his head. "Now there's an idea."

"You don't know that. I'm not saying you should go out and get shot and see what happens, mind you. But there's a reason why you're there. In that world. And there's a reason you're here."

"So what exactly are you suggesting?"

She dropped her purse on the bed and faced him. "That you go on an all-out search for something in that reality that will help us here. Take your time. There's no correlation between time there and time here, right?"

"As soon as I fall asleep there, I'm here."

"Then find a way not to be here every time you sleep. Spend a few days in that reality, a week, a month, however much time you need. Find something. Learn new skills. Whoever you become there, you will be here, right? So become somebody."

"I am somebody."

"You are, and I love you the way you are. But for the sake of this world, become someone more. Someone who can save this world. Go to sleep, dream, and come back a new man."

He looked at his sister. So full of optimism. But she didn't understand the extent of the devastation in the other reality.

"I have to get some sleep," he said, walking toward his room.

"Dream, Thomas. Dream long. Dream big."

"I will."

36

Tom's mind flooded with images of a young boy standing innocently at the center of a brightly colored room, chin raised to the ceiling, eyes wide, mouth gaping.

Johan. And his skin was as smooth as a pool of chocolate milk. His deep-throated song suddenly thundered in the room, startling Tom.

He rolled over in his sleep.

For a moment the night lay quiet. Then the boy began to sing again. Quietly this time, with closed eyes and raised hands. The sweet refrains drifted to the heavens like birdsong. They ascended the scale and began to distort.

Distort? No. Johan always spun a flawless song to the last note. But the sound climbed the scale and grew to more of a wail than a song. Johan was wailing.

Tom's eyes sprang open. The morning's soft light flooded his vision. His ears filled with the sound of a child singing in broken tones.

He pushed himself to an elbow, gazed

about, and rested his eyes on the boulder twenty paces from where he and Rachelle lay. There, facing the forest they had left behind, sitting cross-legged on the boulder with his back turned to them, Johan lifted his chin in song. A weak, halting song to be sure. Strained and off key. But a song nonetheless.

Rachelle raised to a sitting position next to him and stared at her brother. Her skin was dry and flaking. As was his own. Tom swallowed and turned back to Johan, who wailed with his arms spread wide.

"Elyon, help us," he sang. "Elyon, help us."

Tom stood up. Johan's whole body trembled as he struggled for notes. The boy sounded as though he might be crying. Crying under the waning power of his own notes, or perhaps because he could not sing as he once did.

Beside Tom, Rachelle rose slowly to her feet without removing her eyes from the scene. Tears wet her parched cheeks. Tom felt his chest constrict. Johan raised his small fists in the air and wailed with greater intensity — a heartbreaking rendering of sorrow and yearning and anger and pleading for love.

For long minutes they stood facing Johan, who lamented for all who would hear. Grieving for all who would take the time to listen to the cries of an abandoned, tortured child slowly dying far from home. But who could possibly hear such a song in this desert?

If only Michal or Gabil would come and tell them what to do. If only he could speak one more time, just one last time, to the boy from the upper lake.

If only he could close his eyes and open them again to the sight of a boy standing on the rise of sand to their left. Like the boy standing there now. Like —

Tom froze.

The boy stood there, on the rise beside the boulders, staring directly at Johan. The boy from the upper lake!

As though conducted by an unseen hand, both Johan and Rachelle ceased their sobbing. The boy took three small steps toward the boulder and stopped. His arms hung limply by his sides. His eyes were wide and green. Brilliant, breathtaking green.

The boy's delicate lips parted slightly, as if he were about to speak, but he just stood, staring. A loose curl of hair hung between the boy's eyes, lifting gently in the morning breeze.

The two boys gazed directly at each other, as if held by an invisible bond. Johan's eyes were as round as saucers, and his face was wet from tears. To Tom's

627

right, Rachelle took a single step toward Johan and stopped.

And then the little boy opened his mouth.

A pure, sweet tone, crystal-clear in the morning stillness, pierced Tom's ears and stabbed at his heart like a razor-tipped arrow. He caught his breath at the very first note. Images of a world far removed flooded his mind. Memories of an emerald resin floor, of a thundering waterfall, of a lake. The notes tumbled into a melody.

Tom dropped to his knees and began to cry again.

The child took a step toward Johan, closed his eyes, and lifted his chin. His song drifted through the air, dancing on their heads like a teasing angel. Rachelle sat hard.

The boy opened his arms, expanded his chest, and let loose a deep, rumbling tone that shook the ground. Then the boy formed his first lyrics, encased in notes rumbling gently over the dunes.

I love you.
I love you, I love you, I love you.

Tom closed his eyes and let his body shake under the power of the words. The tune rose through the octave, piercing the still air with full-bodied chords.

I made you,
and I love the way I made you.

The song reached into Tom's heart and amplified the resonance of each chord a thousandfold so that he thought his heart might explode.

And then, with an earsplitting tone, like a concert of a hundred thousand pipe organs blowing the same chord, the air shattered with one final note and fell silent.

Tom lifted his head slowly. The boy still gazed at Johan, who had slipped down from the boulder and stood with both arms stretched out toward the boy.

Their first steps seemed tentative, taken almost simultaneously toward each other. The two boys suddenly broke free from the ground and raced toward each other with wide arms.

They collided there on the desert floor, two small boys about the same height, like two long-lost twins reunited. They all heard the slap of bare chest against bare flesh followed by grunts as the boys tumbled to the sand, giggling hysterically.

Rachelle began to laugh out loud. She clapped excitedly, and although Tom assumed she'd never met the young boy, she knew his name. "Elyon!" She said the name like an ecstatic child. "Elyon!" She wept and laughed as she clapped.

The boys sprang to their feet and chased each other around the boulder, tagging each other in play, still giggling like schoolchildren passing a secret.

And then the boy turned toward Tom.

Still kneeling, Tom saw the boy run directly for him. His eyes flashed like emeralds, a twisted grin lifted his cheeks. The boy sprinted right up to Tom, slid to a stop, put an arm around his neck, and placed his soft, warm cheek against Tom's. His hot breath brushed Tom's ear. "I love you," the boy whispered.

A roaring tornado rushed through his mind. Forceful winds blasted against his heart with pure, raw, unrefined love. He heard a feeble grunt fall from his mouth.

Then the boy was on to Rachelle. He repeated the embrace and Rachelle shook with sobs. The boy turned and sprinted from the camp. He stopped a dozen paces to the east and twirled around, eyes sparkling mischievously.

"Follow me," he said, then turned back to the dune and ran up its slope.

Johan raced past Tom and Rachelle, panting.

Tom struggled to his feet, eyes fixed on the boy now cresting the dune. He tugged Rachelle to her feet. They followed the boy like that — Johan leading, Tom and Rachelle running behind.

No one spoke as they ran through the barren desert. Thomas's mind was still numb from the boy's touch. Sweat soon drenched Tom's clothes. His breathing came in gasps as he clambered up the sandy dunes, following this little boy who ran as though he owned this sandbox. *But I'd follow him anywhere. I'd follow him over a cliff, believing that after leaping I'd be able to fly. I'd follow him into the sea, knowing I could breathe underwater.* It was the boy's song. It was his song, his eyes, his tender feet, the way his breath had rushed through Tom's ears.

They ran on in silence, keeping their eyes fixed on the boy's naked back, glistening with sweat. He loped steadily into the desert — slowing up the face of sandy slopes and then bounding down the other side. Not fast enough to lose them, not slow enough to allow them any rest.

The sun stood high when Tom staggered over a crest marked by the boy's footprints. He pulled himself up not ten feet from where Johan had stopped. The boy stood just ahead of Johan. Tom followed their gaze.

What he saw took his breath away.

Below them, in the middle of this desolate white desert, lay a huge valley. And in this valley grew a vast green forest.

Tom stared, mouth hanging open

dumbly. It had to be several miles across, maybe more. Maybe twenty miles. But in the far distance where the trees ended, the valley floor rose in a mountain of sand. The desert continued. The forest wasn't colored. Green. Only green. Like the forests in his dreams of Bangkok.

"Look!" Rachelle extended her arm. Her pointing finger quivered. Then Tom saw it.

A lake.

To the east, several miles inside the forest, the sun glinted off a small lake.

The boy whooped, thrust his fists into the air, and tore down the sandy slope. He tumbled once and came to his feet, flying fast.

Johan ran after him, whooping in kind. Then Tom and Rachelle, together. Whooping.

It took them twenty minutes to reach the edge of the forest, where they slid to a stop. The trees stood tall, like sentinels intent on keeping the sand from encroaching. Brown bark. Large, leafy branches. A flock of red-and-blue parrots took flight and squawked overhead.

"Birds!" Johan cried.

The boy looked back at them from the forest's edge. Then, without a word, he stepped between two trees and ran in.

Tom ran after him. "Come on!"

They came, running behind.

The canopy rose overhead, shading the sun. They passed between the same two trees the boy had slipped through.

"Come on, hurry!"

The sound of their feet brushing through sand changed to a soft crunch when they hit the first undergrowth.

Tom strained for glimpses of the boy's back between the trees. There, and there. He raced on, hardly aware of the forest now. Behind him, Rachelle and Johan had the easier task of following him.

Tom glanced up at the canopy. It all looked vaguely familiar. For a moment it seemed as if he were rushing into the jungles of Thailand. To rescue Monique.

The boy never ran out of sight for more than a few seconds. Deeper into the jungle they ran. Straight for the lake. There were birds on almost every tree it seemed. Monkeys and possums. They passed through a meadow with a grove of smaller trees heavy with a red fruit. Not the same kind of fruit they'd eaten in the colored forest, but very similar.

Tom snatched up a fallen apple and tasted it on the run. Sweet. Delicious. But no power. He grabbed another and tossed it back to Rachelle. "It's good!"

A pack of dogs barked from the other end of the meadow. Wolves? Tom picked up his pace. "Hurry!"

They hurried. Through tall trees squawking with birds, past large bushes bursting with berries, over a small creek sparkling with water, through another brightly flowered meadow and past a startled stampede of horses.

Rachelle and Johan were as frightened as the horses. Tom was not.

And then, as suddenly as they had entered the forest, they were out. On the lip of a small valley.

A gentle slope descended to the shores of a glistening green lake. A thin blanket of haze drifted lazily above sections of the glassy surface. Trees, heavy with fruit, lined its shore. Colors of every imaginable hue splattered the trees.

Wild horses grazed on the high green grass of the valley floor. A bubbling creek meandered into the lake from the base of the cliff to their right, and then back out, down the valley.

The boy walked back to them, grinning. He wasn't breathing hard like they were. Only a light sweat broke his brow.

"Do you like it?" he asked.

They were too stunned to respond.

"I thought you would," he said. "I want you to take care of this forest for me."

"What do you mean?" Tom asked. "Are you going?"

The boy tilted his head slightly. "Don't

worry, Thomas. I'll come back. Just don't forget about me."

"I could never forget!"

"Most of them already have. The world could get very bad very quickly. It will be easier to spill blood than water. But" — he pointed to the lake — "if you bathe in the water once a day, you'll keep the disease away. Never allow blood to defile the water."

Then the boy gave them a list of six simple rules to follow.

"The others lived?" Rachelle asked. "Where . . . where are they?"

The boy eyed her softly. "Most are lost, but there are others like you who will find one of seven forests like this one." He smiled mischievously. "Don't worry, I have an idea. My ideas are usually pretty good, don't you think?"

"Yes. Yes, definitely good."

"When you think it can't get any worse, there will be a way. In one incredible blow we will destroy the heart of evil." He walked up to Rachelle, took her hand, and kissed it. "Just remember me."

He walked to Johan and looked into his eyes. For a moment Tom thought he saw a dark look cross Elyon's eyes. He leaned forward and kissed Johan on the forehead.

Then he came to Tom and kissed his hand.

"Could you tell me one thing?" Tom asked quietly. "I dreamed of Bangkok again last night. Is it real? Am I supposed to rescue Monique?"

"Am I a lion or a lamb? Or am I a boy? You decide, Thomas. You are very special to me. Please . . . please don't forget me. Don't ever, ever forget me. I have a lot riding on you." He winked.

Then he turned around, ran down the bank, planted his foot on a rock, and launched himself into a swan dive. His body hung in the air above the lake for a moment, and then broke the surface with barely a ripple before disappearing.

He has a lot riding on me. The idea terrified him.

Johan was the first to move. He plummeted down the shore and into the lake with Tom and Rachelle hard on his heels. They dived in together, one, two, three splashes that almost sounded as one.

The water wasn't cold. It wasn't warm. It was clean and pure and crystalline clear, so that Tom could immediately see the rocks on the bottom.

This lake had a bottom.

And apart from the wonderfully clean feeling it gave him, the water didn't shake his body or tingle against his skin as in the other lake. He knew immediately that he couldn't breathe it.

But he did drink it. And he did laugh and cry and splash around like a child in a backyard pool. And the water did change them.

Almost immediately their skin returned to normal, and their eyes . . .

A soft green replaced the gray in their eyes.

For a while.

"We will build our home here," Tom said, looking around at the clearing. "It's only a stone's throw from the lake, and there's plenty of sunshine. Our first order of business will be to build a shelter."

"No, I don't think so," Rachelle said.

He looked at her, taken aback by her tone.

"Our first order of business will be to deal with Monique," she said.

"Come on, Rachelle."

"I want you to tell me everything. All of your dreams."

He spread his arms. "But they're nothing. They're just dreams!"

"Is that why you asked the boy about them just an hour ago? Is that why you mumble her name in your sleep? Even last night after you promised me you wouldn't, you whispered her name as if she is the sweetest fruit in the land! I want to know it all."

"Maybe we should bathe again."

"After you tell me. If you hadn't noticed, there is you and there is me in the land now. One man and one woman. Or is it one man and two women? Have you chosen me, or not?"

"I did choose you. That's why you're here. Did I pull another woman into the Thrall to protect? No, I pulled you because I chose you, and we will marry immediately. And I want to tell you about Monique anyway." He walked over to the boulders and sat. These dreams would be his ruin. "Where's Johan?"

"He's gone exploring. Tell me about your dreams."

Tom looked back into the forest. "You let him go? What if he gets lost? I'm worried about him. We have to keep our eyes on him."

"Don't change the subject. I want to hear everything."

So Tom told her. She sat beside him on the rock at the center of the clearing, and he told her almost everything he could remember dreaming, leaving only a few parts sketchy.

He told her about being shot at in Denver and about flying to Bangkok and about kidnapping Monique and about the Raison Strain. Then he told her about the entire world constructed in his dreams, or at least as much of it as he could remember, because when he wasn't dreaming it seemed distant and vague.

"Do you know what this sounds like to me?" Rachelle said when he'd finished.

"No, what?"

"It sounds like you're imagining something similar to what happened to us, here. I told you where I would like to be rescued, and so you dreamed of exactly such a place to rescue another woman. And here the black forest has threatened to destroy us and now does, and so you dream of a blackness that will destroy another world. A plague. Bangkok is a figment of your dreams that reflects what's happening in your real life."

"Maybe I can stop the virus where I failed to stop Tanis."

"No, you're not going to stop it."

"Why not?"

"First of all, it's a dream! Listen to you. Even now you're talking of making a difference in a world that doesn't even exist! It's no wonder Michal refused to fuel your dreams with more information from the histories."

Rachelle stood and crossed her arms. "Second, if you're right, the only way to stop it is to find this Monique woman you seem to have grown somewhat attached to. I won't have it."

"Please, I hardly know her. It's not romantic. She's a figment of my imagination; you said so yourself."

"I won't have you dreaming of a beautiful woman named Monique while I'm suckling your child," Rachelle said.

That stopped him cold.

"So you really do want to bear children?"

"Do you have a better idea?" She paused. "I don't see another man around. And I do love you, Thomas, even if you do dream of another woman."

"And I love you, Rachelle." He reached for her hand and kissed it. "I would never dream of another woman. Ever."

"Unfortunately it seems as though it's beyond your control. If we only had the rhambutan fruit, I would feed it to you every night so that you would never dream again."

Tom stood.

"What?"

"The boy . . ."

"Yes? What about the boy?"

"He told me at the upper lake that I would always have the choice not to dream."

She searched his face. "And yet you dreamed last night. Was that your choice?"

"No, but what if there *is* rhambutan fruit?"

"The fruits aren't the same anymore."

"But maybe he left this one. How else would I not dream? He made me a promise."

Her eyes lit up. She scanned the edge of the forest.

"Okay, let's bathe."

They spent several hours searching for rhambutan fruit and, while they were at it, material they could use to build a shelter in the clearing.

By midday their hope of finding any rhambutan in this forest had faded, but then so had Tom's urgency to find it, although he didn't share this with Rachelle. The dreams seemed distant and abstract in the face of their new surroundings. The whole notion that he was dreaming of another woman of whom Rachelle should be jealous seemed absurd.

He watched her walk ahead of him through the forest, and he knew without the smallest shred of doubt that he could never love any woman as he loved her. She had the spirit of an eagle and the heart of a mother. He even liked the way she argued with him, full of mettle.

He loved the way she walked. The way her hair fell over her shoulders. The way her lips moved when she talked. She was beautiful, even with dry skin and gray eyes, though when she first stepped from the pool with smooth skin and green eyes, laughing in the sunlight, she was breathtaking.

The idea that she had anything to fear from a dream was absurd. He suggested that she keep looking while he turned his attention to the shelter they had to build. He had some ideas on how to build one. He might even know how to make metal.

And what ideas are those, she wanted to know.

Something from my dreams, he'd made the mistake of saying.

Maybe the rhambutan was a good idea after all.

Johan had finally returned from his scouting trip and helped Tom with the first lean-to, constructed out of saplings and leaves. Tom knew how it should look, and he knew how to make it.

"How did you know to tie those vines like that?" Johan asked when they'd finished the roof. "I've never seen anything like it."

"This," Tom said, rubbing the knots lovingly, "is how they do it in the jungles of the Philippines. We'll strap palm leaves to these —"

"Where's the Philippines?" Johan asked.

"The Philippines? Nowhere, really. Just something I made up."

And it was true, he thought. But with

less conviction now.

Rachelle strode into camp about the time Tom was thinking they should go looking for her.

"How are my men? My, that is a handy-looking thing you have there." She studied the lean-to. "What on earth is it?"

"This is our first home." Tom beamed.

"Is it? It looks more like one wall." She walked around it. "Or a falling roof."

"No, no, this is more than a wall," Tom said. "It's the entire structure. It's perfect! You don't like it?"

"Functional enough, I suppose. For a night or two, until you can build me bedrooms and a kitchen with running water."

Tom wasn't sure how to respond. He rather liked the open feel of the place. She was right, of course. They would eventually have to build a house, and he had some ideas of how to do that as well. But he thought the lean-to was quite smart.

She looked at him and winked. "I think it's very clever," she said. "Something a great warrior would build." Then she brought her hand from behind her back and tossed him something. "Catch."

He caught it with one hand.

It was a rhambutan.

"You found it?"

She smiled. "Eat it."

"Now?"

"Yes, of course now."

He bit into the flesh. The nectar tasted like a cross between a banana and an orange but tart. Like a banana-orange-lemon.

"All of it," she said.

"I need all of it for it to work?" he asked with the one bite stuffed in his cheek.

"No. But I want you to eat all of it."

He ate all of it.

Rachelle watched Thomas sleep. His chest rose and fell steadily to the sound of deep breathing. A slight gray pallor covered his body, and she knew that if she could see his eyes they would be dull, like her own. But none of this concerned her. The lake would wash them both clean as soon as they bathed.

What did concern her were these dreams of his. Dreams of the histories and dreams of this woman named Monique. She told herself it was more about the histories. After all, an argument could be made that a preoccupation with the histories had gotten Tanis into trouble. But her concern was as much about the woman.

Jealousy had been an element of the Great Romance, and she made no attempt to temper it now. Thomas was her man, and she had no intention of sharing him with anyone, dream woman or not.

If Thomas was right, eating Teeleh's

fruit in the black forest before he'd lost his memory had started his dreams in the first place. Now she desperately prayed that what remained of Elyon's fruit would wash his mind clean of them.

"Thomas." She leaned over and kissed his lips. "Wake up, my dear."

He moaned and rolled over. A pleasant smile crossed his face. Deep sleep? Or Monique? But he'd slept like a baby and not once mumbled her name.

Rachelle couldn't extend her patience. She'd been awake for an hour already, waiting for him to wake.

She slapped his side and stood. "Wake up! Time to bathe."

He sat up with a start. "What?"

"Time to bathe."

"It's late. I've been sleeping this whole time?"

"Like a rock," she said.

He rubbed his eyes, stood up, and marched out to the fire. "Today I will begin building your house," he announced.

"Wonderful." She watched his face. "Did you dream?"

"Dream?" He seemed to be searching his memory.

"Yes, did you dream?"

"I don't know. Did I?"

"Only you would know."

"No. The fruit must have worked. That's

why I slept so well."

"You can't remember anything? No phantom trips to Bangkok? No rescuing the beautiful Monique?"

"The last thing I dreamed about was falling asleep in Bangkok after the meeting. That was two nights ago." He spread his hands and grinned purposefully. "No dreams."

She knew he was telling the truth. The fruit did as the boy had promised. "Good," she said. "Then it works. You will eat this fruit every day."

"Forever?"

"It's also very healthy and makes a man fertile," she said. "Yes, forever."

So Thomas ate the rhambutan fruit every day and not once did he dream of Bangkok. Or of anything.

Weeks passed, then months, then years, then fifteen years, and not once did Thomas dream of Bangkok. Or of anything.

He became a mighty warrior who defended the seven forests against the desert Hoards who marched against them. But not once did he dream. Not of Bangkok, not of anything.

Perhaps Rachelle was right. Maybe he would never dream again. Maybe he would eat the rhambutan fruit every day forever and never again dream of Bangkok.

Or of anything.

37

Valborg Svensson stood at the head of the table and eyed the gathered dignitaries. All from governments that had been coaxed for three years with promises of power. Until now, none of them knew enough to damage him significantly. And if they did know more than they should, they hadn't damaged him, so the point was moot. There were seven, but they needed only one country from which to build their power base. All seven would be useful, but they needed the keys to one of their kingdoms as a backup. If they only knew.

Carlos was in Bangkok now, only hours away from eliminating Hunter once and for all. Armand Fortier was making the necessary arrangements with the Russians and the Chinese. And he, Valborg Svensson, was dropping the bomb that would make everything possible. So to speak.

He extracted his pointer and tapped off the cities on the wall map to his left. "The Raison Strain has already entered the air space of London, Paris, Moscow, Beijing,

New Delhi, Cape Town, Bangkok, Sydney, New York, Washington, D.C., Atlanta, and Los Angeles. These are the first twelve. Within eight hours, we will have twenty-four entry points."

"Enter the air space — as in . . ."

"As in the virus is airborne. Delivered by couriers over twenty-four commercial aircraft, spreading as we speak. It's highly contagious, more so than any virus we've seen. Fascinating little beast. Most require some kind of assistance to get around. A cough, fluid, touch, high humidity at least. But this pathogen seems to do quite well in adverse environmental conditions. A single virus shell is enough to infect any adult."

"You've already done it?"

"Naturally. By our most conservative models, three million people will be carriers by day's end. Ninety million within two days. Four billion within one week."

They sat dumbfounded. Not a single one truly comprehended what he'd just said. Not that he blamed them. The reality was staggering. Too significant to digest in one sitting.

"The virus is gone? There's no way to stop it?"

"Gone? Yes, I suppose it is gone," Svensson said. "And no, there's no way to stop it."

They were all jumping into the mix now.

"And who will be infected?"

"Everyone. Myself, for example. And you. All of us are infected." He pointed to a small vial on the counter. "We were infected within minutes of stepping into this room."

Silence. The yellow liquid sat undisturbed.

Their objections came in a barrage of angry protests. "You have a vaccine; we should be inoculated at once! What kind of sick joke is this?"

"A very sick joke," Svensson said. "There is no vaccine."

"Then what, an antivirus?" the man demanded. "I demand to know what you're doing here!"

"You know what we're doing. Unfortunately, we don't have the antivirus quite yet either. But not to worry, we will very soon. We have less than three weeks to perfect one, but I'm confident we'll have it by the end of the week. Maybe sooner."

They looked at him like a ring of rats frozen by a wedge of cheese.

"And if not?"

"If not, then we will all share the same fate with the rest of the world."

"Which is what?"

"We aren't precisely sure. An ugly death, we're quite sure of that. But no one has yet died from the Raison Strain, so we can't be sure about the exact nature of that death."

"Why?" To a man they were incredulous. "This was *not* what we discussed."

"Yes, it was. You just weren't listening very well. We have a list of instructions for each of your countries. We trust you will comply in the most expeditious fashion. For obvious reasons. And I really wouldn't think about trying to undermine our plans in any way. The only hope for an antivirus rests with me. If I am inhibited, the world will simply die."

The gentleman from Switzerland, Bruce Swanson, shoved his seat back and stood, face red. "This is not what I understood! How dare you proceed without consulting —"

Svensson slipped a pistol out from under his jacket and shot the man in the forehead at ten paces. The man stared at him, his new third eye leaking red, and then he toppled backward, hit his head on the wall, and crumpled to the floor.

Svensson lowered the pistol. "There is no way to stop the virus," he said. "We can only control it now. That was the point from the beginning. Dissension will only hinder that objective. Any argument?"

They did not argue.

"Good." He set the gun on the table. "As we speak, the governments of these affected countries are being notified of our demands. These governments won't react immediately, of course. This is preferred. Panic is not our friend. Not yet. We don't need people staying home for fear of catching the disease. By the time they realize the true nature of our threat, containment will be out of the question. It virtually is already."

He took a deep breath. The power of this moment, standing over seven men — six living — was alone worth the price he'd paid. And it was only the very beginning. He'd resisted a smile, but now he smiled for them all.

"It's a wonderful day, my friends. You find yourselves on the right side of history. You will see. The die has been cast."

Markous had been guaranteed two things for this assignment: his life and a million dollars cash. Both he valued enough to cut off his own leg if needed. The cash he had already received. His life was still in their hands. He doubted neither their will nor their ability to take his life or give it.

He stood in the bathroom stall and flicked the small vial with his fingernail. Hard to believe that the yellow liquid could do what they insisted it would do. Unnerved by a few drops of amber fluid.

He held his breath and pulled the rubber cork out of the vial's neck. Now only air separated him — his nose and his eyes and his skin — from the virus. Had he been infected already? No, how could he be?

He exhaled the air from his lungs, held his breath at the bottom, and then slowly inhaled, imagining invisible spores streaming into his nostrils. If it were scented, like a perfume, he would notice. But the objective was not to notice.

So then, he was now infected.

Markous impulsively splashed some of the fluid on his jacket, his hands, rubbed his face. Like a cologne. He tested it with his tongue. Tasteless. He drank a little and swished it around his mouth. Swallowed.

Markous stepped from the men's room. Travelers crowded Bangkok International Airport despite the early hour. He looked both ways, straightening his tie. Rarely did he mix with women at nightclubs or other common social institutions, despite his handsome Mediterranean features. But at the moment, spreading a little love seemed appropriate.

He saw what he was looking for and walked toward a gathering of four blue-suited flight attendants talking by a phone bank.

"Excuse me." All four women looked at him. Their luggage tags read "Air France." He smiled gently and zeroed in on a tall brunette. "I was just walking by, and I couldn't help but notice you. Do you mind?"

They exchanged glances. The brunette lifted an eyebrow self-consciously.

"Could you please tell me your name?" Markous asked. She wasn't wearing a nametag.

"Linda."

He stepped closer. His hands were still moist with the liquid. He imagined the millions of cells swimming in his mouth.

"Come here, Linda. I would like to tell you a secret." He leaned forward. At first she hesitated, but when two of the others chuckled, she spread her hands. "What?"

"Closer," he said. "I won't bite, I promise."

Her face was red, but she complied by leaning a few inches.

Markous stepped into her and kissed her full on the mouth. He immediately pulled back and raised both hands. "Forgive me. You are so beautiful, I simply had to kiss you."

The shock registered on her face. "You . . . what do you think you're doing?"

Markous grabbed the hand of the woman next to the brunette. He coughed. "Please, I'm terribly sorry." He backed out quickly, dipping with apology. Then he was gone, leaving four stunned women in his wake.

He walked by the airport's first-aid station, where a mother was asking a nurse for something while her two blond-headed children played tag about the waiting bench. An older man with bushy gray brows watched him take his still-moist jacket off and hang it on the coatrack. With any luck, the man would report the jacket and security would confiscate it. Before he took five paces, the mother, her two children, the nurse, and the old man were infected.

How many more he infected before leaving the airport, he would never know. Perhaps a hundred, though none with such tenderness as his first. He stopped in a morning market on his way through the city and worked his way down the crowded aisles. How many here, he couldn't guess. At least several hundred. For good measure, he tossed the shirt he'd soaked into the Mae Nam Chao Phraya River, which wound its way lazily through the city center.

Enough. By end of day, Bangkok would be crawling with the virus.

Job done.

Carlos parked his car in the Sheraton's underground parking structure at eight o'clock and rode the elevator to the lobby. The morning crowd was already bustling. He crossed to the main elevators, waited for an empty car, and stepped in. Ninth floor.

The meeting with Deputy Secretary Gains and the gathered intelligence officers had gone late last night, and his latest intelligence had it that Hunter was still in his room. Asleep. The source was impeccable.

In fact, the source had actually been *at* the meeting.

If they only knew to what extent Svensson had gone to execute this plan. The only caveat was Hunter. A man who learned from his dreams. A man none of them could possibly control. A man Carlos had killed twice already.

This time he would stay dead.

The elevator bell rang and Carlos slipped down the hall, tried and found the room next to Hunter's, which was open as arranged.

There were two critical elements in any operation. One, power; and two, intelligence. He'd engaged Hunter once, and despite the man's surprising skill, he'd handled him easily enough. But he'd underestimated the man's endurance. Hunter had somehow managed to survive.

This time there would be no opportunity for a fight. Superior intelligence would prove the victor.

Carlos approached the door that adjoined the suite next door to this one. He withdrew a Luger and screwed a silencer into its barrel.

Superior intelligence. For example, he knew that at this very moment this door was unlocked. The inside man had made sure of that. Past this door, one door on the left, was the door to Thomas Hunter's room. Hunter had been sleeping in the room for seven hours now. He would never even know he'd been shot.

All of this Carlos knew without the slightest doubt. If anything changed — if his sister, who slept in the suite's other bedroom, woke, or if Hunter himself woke — the video operator would simply page him, and the receiver on Carlos's belt would vibrate.

Intelligence.

Carlos opened both doors separating the suites and walked to the room on his left. Cartridge chambered. All was silent. He reached for the doorknob.

A phone rang. Not the main house phone — the one in the sister's room on his right. Immediately his pager vibrated. He ignored the pager and paused to listen.

The phone beside Kara's bed rang once. She opened her eyes and stared at the ceiling. Where was she?

Bangkok. She and Thomas had attended a meeting the night before with deputy secretary of state Merton Gains because the Swiss, Valborg Svensson, had kidnapped Monique de Raison for one reason only: to develop the antivirus to the virus he would unleash on the world. At least that was what Thomas had tried to persuade them of. They hadn't exactly run to him and kissed his feet.

The phone rang again.

She sat up. Thomas was hopefully still asleep in the suite's other bedroom. Had he dreamed? Was he still dreaming? She'd suggested he dream a very long time and become someone new, an absurd suggestion on the face of it, but then so was this whole alternate-world thing he was living through. The spread of evil in one world, the threat of a virus in the other one.

The phone was ringing. She'd taken the phone in Tom's room off the hook last night. He wouldn't hear it.

She grabbed the receiver. "Hello?"

"This is Merton Gains. Kara?"

She switched the phone to her right ear. "Yes. Good morning, Mr. Secretary."

"I'm sorry to wake you, but it seems that we have a situation on our hands."

"No, no, it's okay. What time is it?" *What time is it?* She was speaking to the deputy secretary of state, and she was demanding he tell her what time it was?

"Just past eight in the morning local,"

Gains said. His voice sounded strained. "The State Department received a fax from a party claiming to be Valborg Svensson."

A chill washed down Kara's spine. This was what Thomas had predicted! Not so soon, but —

"He's claiming that the Raison Strain has been released in twelve cities including Washington, D.C., New York, Los Angeles, and Atlanta," Gains said, voice now very thin.

"What?" Kara swung her legs off the bed. "When?"

"Six hours ago. He claims that the number will be twenty-four by the end of the day."

"Twenty-four! That's impossible! They did it without the antivirus! Thomas was right. Has any of this been verified?"

"No. No, but we're working on it, believe me. Where is Thomas?"

She glanced at the door. "As far as I know, he's sleeping next door."

"How long has he been sleeping?"

"About eight hours, I think."

"Well, I don't have to say it, but it looks like he may have been right."

She stood. "I realize that. You realize that this could have been prevented —"

"You may be right." He wasn't the one who'd doubted Thomas. She had no right to accuse him. What was she thinking? He was the deputy secretary of state for the United States of America, for heaven's sake!

"If this new information turns out to be right, your brother may be a very important person to us."

"He may be or he may not be. It could be too late now."

"Can I talk to him?"

She hesitated. Of course they could talk to Thomas. They were powerful men who could talk to anyone they wanted to. But they'd taken too long to talk to him already.

"I'll wake him," she said.

"Thank you. I have some calls to make. Bring him down in half an hour. Will that be enough time?"

"Yes."

The line clicked off.

Kara got halfway to the bedroom door and stopped. Half an hour, the secretary had said. *Bring him down in half an hour.* If she woke Thomas now, he'd demand to go down immediately. Besides, he'd hardly slept a decent stretch in over a week. And if he was dreaming, which she had no reason to doubt, then every minute of sleep — for that matter, every second — could be the equivalent of hours or days or even weeks in his dream world. A lot could happen. Answers could come.

Six hours ago, Svensson had released the virus. It was a mind-bending thought. She should wake her brother now, not later.

Right after she used the toilet.

Carlos had heard enough. He hadn't anticipated hearing their reaction like this, but he found it quite satisfying.

He twisted the knob. Cracked the door. The sound of breathing.

He readied his gun and slipped in.

Thomas Hunter lay on his back, sleeping in a tangle of sheets, naked except for boxer shorts. Sweat soaked the sheets. Sweat and blood. Blood? So much blood, smeared over the sheets, some dried and some still wet.

The man had bled in his sleep? *Was* bleeding in his sleep. Dead?

Carlos stepped closer. No. Hunter's chest rose and fell steadily. There were scars on his chest and abdomen that Carlos couldn't remember, but nothing to suggest the slugs Carlos was sure he'd put into this man in the last week.

He brought the gun to Hunter's temple and tightened his finger on the trigger.

He couldn't resist a final whisper. "Good-bye, Mr. Hunter."

660

38

Rachelle was wrong.

Thomas did not eat the fruit forever.

He only ate it for fifteen years. Not once in those fifteen years did he dream, but then, in the worst of times, when they didn't think it could possibly get any worse, just as the boy had foretold, Thomas dreamed again.

And when he did, he dreamed that a gun was hovering by his left temple. Three words whispered menacingly in his ear: "Good-bye, Mr. Hunter."

About The Author

Ted Dekker is known for novels that combine adrenaline-laced stories packed with unexpected plot twists, unforgettable characters, and incredible confrontations between good and evil. He is the best-selling author of *THR3E*, *Blink*, *Heaven's Wager*, *When Heaven Weeps*, and *Thunder of Heaven* and the co-author of *Blessed Child* and *A Man Called Blessed*. Raised in the jungles of Indonesia, Ted now lives with his wife and children in the mountains of Colorado.

Visit Teddekker.com

The employees of Thorndike Press hope you have enjoyed this Large Print book. All our Thorndike and Wheeler Large Print titles are designed for easy reading, and all our books are made to last. Other Thorndike Press Large Print books are available at your library, through selected bookstores, or directly from us.

For information about titles, please call:

(800) 223-1244

or visit our Web site at:

www.gale.com/thorndike
www.gale.com/wheeler

To share your comments, please write:

Publisher
Thorndike Press
295 Kennedy Memorial Drive
Waterville, ME   04901